S.D. #3254

A Saskatchewan Potpourri

Mary McConville Stensrud

Saskatchewan is from the Cree words:
"Kishiski" meaning rapid and "djiwan" meaning current.
The derivation is more clearly seen if you drop the "Ki" at the beginning and use close sounds rather than the letters as the two words become one.

Self published by author.

Printed by ABBOTT'S PRINTING, Yakima, Washington.

First Edition

Library of Congress Catalog Card Number 96-091396
Printed in the United States of America
by Abbott's Printing
Yakima, Washington

Quimper S.D. #3254—A Saskatchewan Potpourri
Mary McConville Stensrud

Previous book by Mary Stensrud
Mount St. Helens Ash Potpourri — Yakima's Story

ISBN 0-2039-0455-4

Cover photo courtesy of Wilma McCoy Adams.
Back cover picture courtesy of Steve Noble.

Dedicated to Quimper's homesteaders who, against grave hardships, not only made a good life for themselves, but passed on to their children high moral standards which in turn are now the legacy of succeeding generations.

Josiah Coppersmith was arrested for attempting to extort funds from innocent people by exhibiting a device he says will convey human voice over wires.

For 18 years Henry Ford refused to make any changes, no matter how obvious the need, to his Model T (or Tin Lizzie, its affectionate name by common folk). For example, the door on the driver's side of the touring car didn't open, necessitating a neat vault to get into the driver's seat.

So called "one horse towns" (but why would you have 3 drays, 2 livery barns and a harness shop for one horse?) sprang up like mushrooms all along branch lines of the Canadian Pacific and Canadian National Railways as their networks, in the teens and twenties, spread throughout the prairies. Most were almost carbon copies of each other. In addition to all the businesses and residences, there would always be two or more churches.

Row 4: Alma Bjore, Minnie McConville, Dorothy Claydon, Kate McCullough, Jack Bender, Maude McConville, Louis Bjore, Marie Klein, Walter McConville, Connie Claydon, Freida Bender, Mina Klein. Row 3: Arnold Bjore, Mary Donald, Alice Bjore, Bessie Donald, Gertrude Klein, Anna Klein, Bob McConville, Albert Bender, Andy McConville. Row 2: Hilda McConville, Jim McConville, Mary McConville, Evelyn McConville, Alice McConville, Ethel McConville, Isabelle McConville, Gordon Donald, Jessie McKenzie, Manuel Bender. Front row: Allan Claydon, Jim Cross, Jim McKenzie, Walter Cross, Fred Bender.

LOCATING QUIMPER

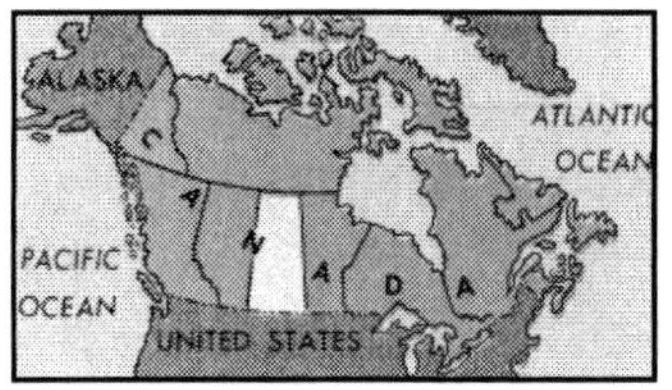

Saskatchewan becomes a province, 1905.

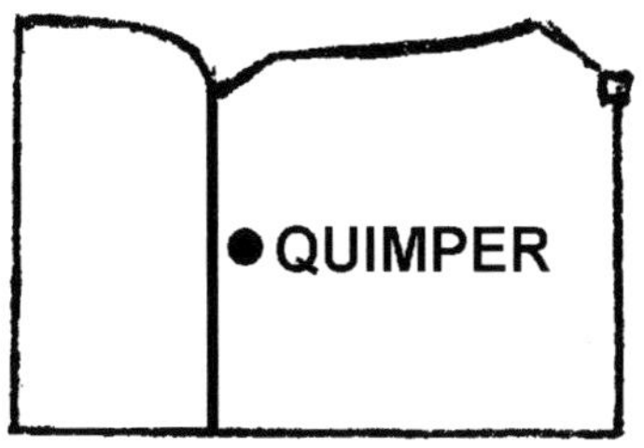

Pinpointing Quimper in relationship to Regions 1 and 2.

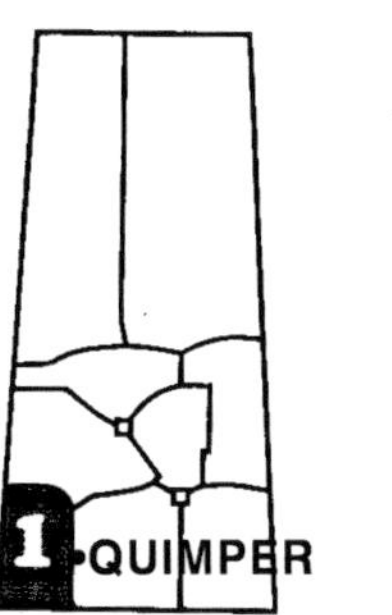

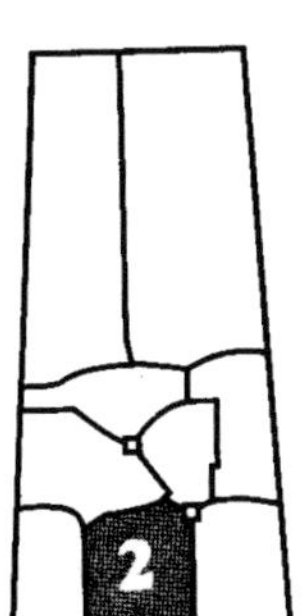

These regional divisions of the province were made very recently by Saskatchewan Tourism.
1 = HorseShoe Region
2 = Great Trails Getaway Region

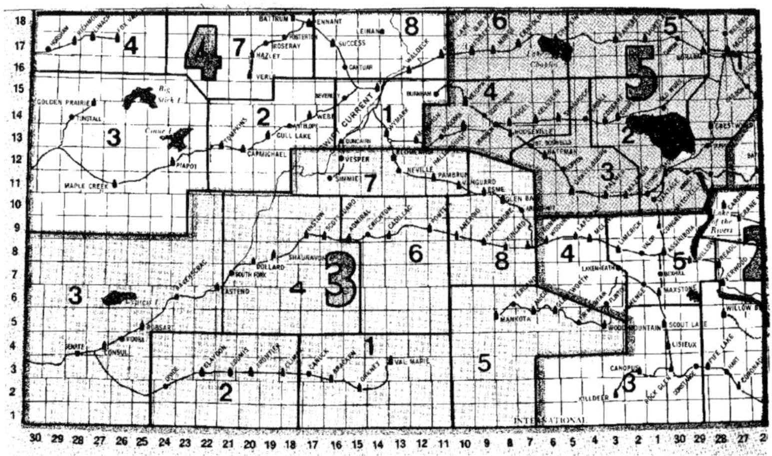

This is the lower southwest portion of a Wheat Pool map on which it is very easy to locate small towns in the area. It corresponds roughly to regions one and part of two in the small maps above.

AREA CODES AND TIME ZONES MAP

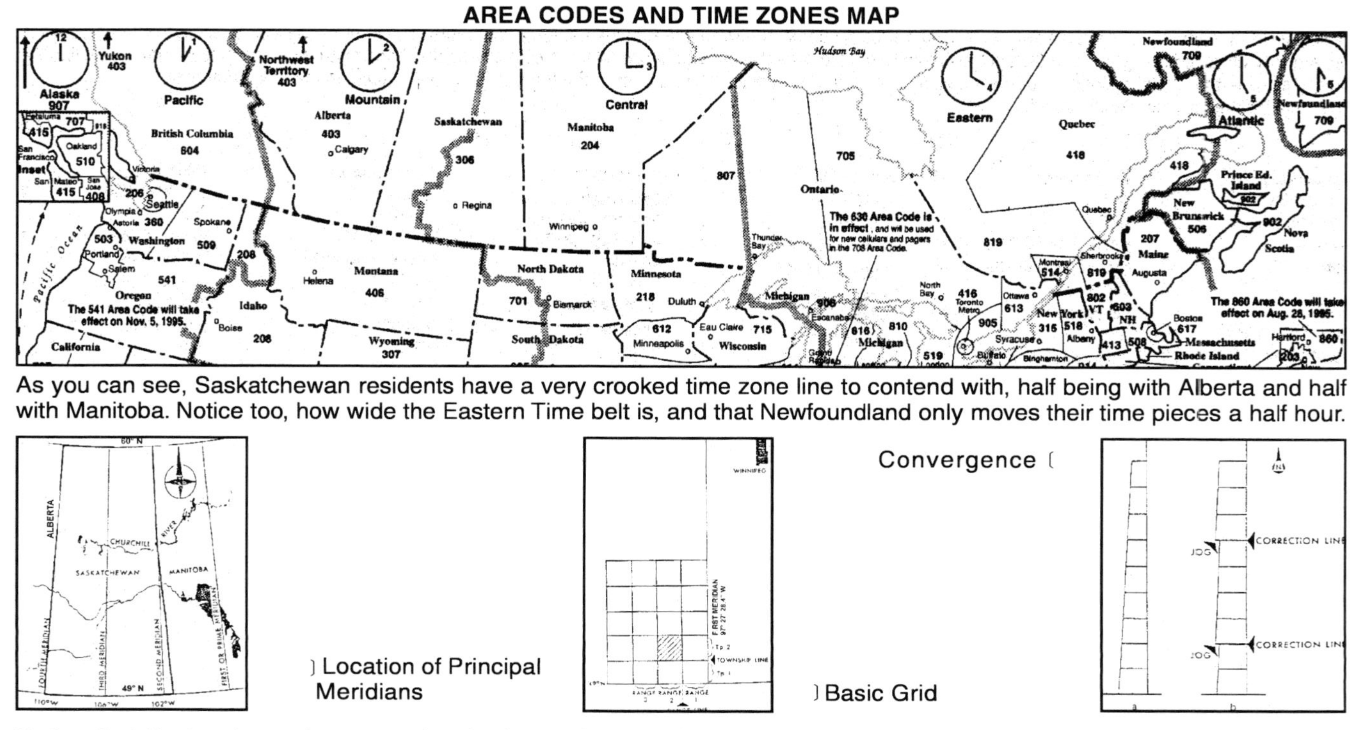

As you can see, Saskatchewan residents have a very crooked time zone line to contend with, half being with Alberta and half with Manitoba. Notice too, how wide the Eastern Time belt is, and that Newfoundland only moves their time pieces a half hour.

Location of Principal Meridians

Basic Grid

Convergence

Notice that Saskatchewan's eastern border is *not* the meridian. It could not be ascertained how Saskatchewan got this skinny triangle of extra land.

Foreword

Mary McConville-Stensrud has a fondness for the places that have been her homes as well as for the events that she and her husband, George, have shared with their relatives, friends and acquaintances.

She has gathered the great events, along with interesting details, to recreate literary images of those events, people, places and times.

The May, 1980 eruption of Mount St. Helens, just 80 miles upwind of the Stensrud's Yakima, Washington home, deposited tons of volcanic ash on a people and place that had never before known the emotional impact of a darkness of midnight at noon.

While professional journalists gave extensive attention to the phenomenon, Stensrud saw something special in the human drama among those shoveling ash off roofs and sidewalks, wearing makeshift cloth filters over their faces, phoning elderly relatives and friends, and staring wide-eyed through windshields while gingerly maneuvering automobiles to and from the grocery store.

She felt that what she saw should be shared with the world. She wrote a book and named it Ash Potpourri. She calls it her "ash book".

Following the publication of her "ash book", thoughts of volcanic ash took the author's recollections back some years to reading about the Delmar McLean family's home in Saskatchewan with its admired seventeen-inch walls of materials from prehistoric volcanic ash deposits.

Recollections of other Saskatchewan persons and events fell into place. They were gathered and edited until another book, **Quimper Saskatchewan Potpourri**, was published.

Now, climb aboard the author's special time-and-tour bus to return by way of a trail of retired calendar pages leading to the early years of this century in the southwestern locales of Saskatchewan, Canada. She steers us to the town of Ponteix as well as to Aneroid, her birthplace. Included on the itinerary are the school districts of Royer, Erinlea, Pinto River, Hulbert, Westerleigh, and Atoimah, which surround her own Quimper.

As you go from place to place, the author has many comments. She recalls her first day of school, tagging along with her older brother and picking crocuses along the way to present to the teacher.

Daily living in this part of the province included party-line telephones by which those who were lonely for the sound of human voices could listen in on the conversations of others. It was known as "rubbering".

The chapter, "Quimper Vignettes," presents thought-provoking items, such as the single-plowed strip from a settler's home to the schoolhouse that kept his children from getting lost along the way. Other sketches include the two ways to take an egg from a laying hen, **The Canadian Hymnal**, and her homemade birchbark Christmas cards.

The content of **Quimper Saskatchewan Potpourri** reflects the endearment that the author holds for many of the places, persons and events that have given meaning to her life.

— Don Ide

A Glenvern Reunion?

It's 4:30 a.m.! An attack of insomnia will last through the next hour or more — all because of a thinking jag — triggered I believe, by reading through the lists of performers on seven of those old Glenvern flyers from back in the 30's. As I came to realize how many of us are still active in both body and mind, the idea of a Glenvern reunion began to take shape. I even chose a possible date — the weekend of August 17, 18, a year from now in 1997.

We could pattern it after those very successful Diamond Jubilee celebrations of 1980 as well as some of the smaller specialized family or school reunions many of us have attended in recent years. We would have lots of things to contribute to a remembrance table and those of us who have played for dances and sing-a-longs have no doubt, oodles (yes, that word is in Webster's) of sheet music and tapes. I even have some tapes of the "Swift Current Old Time Fiddlers" and some square dance ones with the calls right on them, as well as many other types. Of course, live music would be best, but perhaps it would be easier to use some of the "canned" as well.

If some of us are now past the stage of independent travel, perhaps with arrangements being made far enough ahead, our children or grandchildren could lend a hand in getting us there — and they would also get a taste of *those days* and *their roots.*

If you are now dreaming with me, how about posting this dream on the fridge and in the car so you'll see it each day — advice in a book I've just read, "Dreams, Plans and Goals," by Ken Gaub.

Table of Contents

Introduction

Seeking the opinion of a younger person, a baby boomer that is, I asked **Jill Andreotti** if she would read my near-the-end proofs. She consented and set about doing this with both enthusiasm and curiosity. In only a minute or so, she looked up and said, “What is sod?” I knew at that moment that this book had a purpose other than just to satisfy nostalgia for we older folks. Younger folks needed a glimpse into the era of our youth. I hope it accomplishes both goals.

Previous to this moment, even over the period of more than a year, I had written a number of introductions, each one leaving me feeling dissatisfied and frustrated. I desperately needed that gem of inspiration. It was one more example of many experiences I’ve had, first with my ash book and now with my Quimper book — of something or someone coming on the scene and falling into place at some opportune moment — even a last minute available slot in time or space. It is also another illustration of a method of learning, seldom consciously applied perhaps — that of putting a work to soak for awhile when one reaches a plateau or faces a brick wall which is stymieing one’s efforts. In a strange sort of way this may open a door to that next successful step ahead. This same quirk of the mind may also be the solution to finding something, or trying to remember a certain fact that has been eluding one for days on end — even longer sometimes! I always smile at that facetious prayer “Please give me patience, Lord — right now.”

Nevertheless, before attempting to put my own words on paper, I invariably read a lot of examples in others’ books, so just last night I was doing this, and again I was led to read just the right one — **Stuart McLean’s** introduction to his book “Welcome Home — Travels in Smalltown Canada.” I had found this book in the Calgary airport bookstore. My eye had been caught by the title and then by the town chosen for Chapter one, **Maple Creek**, Saskatchewan. It seemed clear, after all my “example” reading, that I had very few, if any, rules to follow on content, length or style. So with this sort of *liberty*, coupled with the *patience* and *soaking* I’ve already spoken of, I was finally ready to get at my own book’s introduction. However, just before sitting down to do just this, I was rummaging around and came across two things that had been “soaking” for some time — the book “Chronicle of a Pioneer Prairie Family” by **L.H. Neatby** — a small paperback that had been pushed far back in on the shelf and was barely visible. It is the story of a well-to-do English family who came to homestead in Saskatchewan in 1906. My other find was a poem by my cousin, **Walter**. Though it is a Christmas one, most of it can well apply to most any day of the year. Therefore, it will serve very nicely for a conclusion to this introduction. It was gratifying to realize that many specifics in both these sources — the book and the poem — had been woven into my book.

Note: I usually remember how, when and where I got a certain book, but this Chronicle one baffles me. Therefore if it is *yours*, please tell me so I can return it with my apologies for negligence and forgetfulness.

Merry Christmas, 1994

"It's such a long wait," wails the youngster,
    "The Day takes forever to come."
"The years go so fast," sighs the oldster
    "but we're both still around, aren't we, Mum?"

As each of us readies for Christmas
    we try, in a meaningful way,
to figure the uppers and downers
    we've gone through since *last* Christmas day.

Despite our complaining, the good times
    have outweighed the bad ones by far
and most of us, deep down, are thankful
    for who, what, and where we all are.

We feel for the millions whose life styles
    are much less secure than our own
because of political problems,
    displacement, and powers overthrown.

We wonder, if *we* were in *their* shoes,
    devoid of direction or hope,
deprived of resources and loved ones
    and frantic with fear — could we cope?

We sense their predicament clearly
    but shove care and guilt to one side
for, even at Christmas, world newscasts
    have numbed us and toughened our hide.

Dear God, give us grace to recover
    our former goodwill, our concern,
benevolent service, and kindness
    before *we* are stricken in turn!

— Walter T. McConville

A Last Minute Laugh

Kathy just handed me what is to be the last proof. As she did so, she looked at me seriously and said "Guess what? I've found something that will need taking care of." I thought "Oh no — not a serious mistake at this late stage!" Then she smiled and opened it up to show me a *whole blank page*.

You see, it has become somewhat of a joke that I just can't let a space go to waste — a trait I attribute to having lived through the Depression — a compulsion to use *everthing* up — even blank spaces!

Kathy has also had to put up with my tiny handwriting, another hangover from Depression days, as I would try to crowd the greatest number of words into the smallest amount of space.

So now I'm happily scribbling away some last minute thoughts for this windfall space — a bit of philosophy, news of some new invention project, cause or organization or whatever. (I can still take advantage of the fact that this book is a *potpourri* afterall.)

Finally I'm settling on what I think is an original thought — after listening to a radio program just now, which triggered this idea. Most of us know what Mom and Pop stores are (or should I use the past tense, seeing as most of these wonderful little businesses have been squeezed out of existence by the huge conglomerates of today?). The program was about MOPS — an acronym for "Moms of Pre-schoolers" — an organization now in operation internationally. I thought, "This is all fine and good, but what about a companion one — POPS for "Pops of Pre-schoolers"? After all, we are pushing hard these days to get more fathers in on the job of raising children. Wouldn't such a project be a good one for the men's group "The Promise Keepers" to take up?

So now I've used up my unexpected blank page and can rest easy!

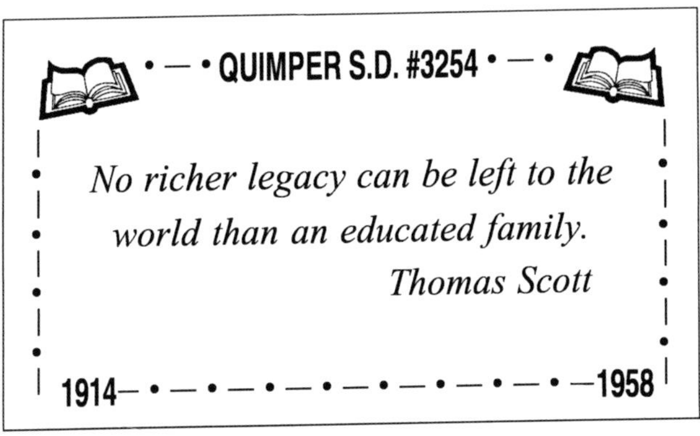

QUIMPER S.D. #3254
No richer legacy can be left to the world than an educated family.
Thomas Scott
1914—1958

Teach children how to live and they will remember it all their lives. — Prov. 22:6

1 — Quimper in Two Locations

NOTE: Some fiction is woven into this account and the mini-dramas. For instance, that either Mr. Boulter or Miss Buss played the organ or that Mary's memory is quite this accurate!

The Author's First Day of School

Records show that five year olds often began school in April — a sort of orientation in today's vernacular. The following is the author's recollections of her first day of school, tagging along with her year-and-a-half older big brother.

It is a lovely bright spring day as they set off across the field for Quimper School. She is very happy and full of anticipation and curiosity. Her brother, Robert (she calls him "Rob"), has told her some of what to expect, but she's anxious to find out for herself what school is all about.

"Come on, Rob. It's time to go isn't it? I can hardly wait. Goodbye Mommy and Daddy."

They have hardly left the house when they spy some crocuses —

those beautiful pale blue-mauve fuzzy-petalled wild flowers with that perfume no prairie person can ever forget. Crocuses pop into view just as the snow is disappearing.

"Oh, Rob, look. There are some crocuses. Let's pick some and take them to Teacher."

They pick a few and skip along aways, lifting the flowers for a sniff every little while. But they haven't gone far when she says, "Oh, I hear a meadowlark. There it is over there. Let's see if we can find its nest."

In a minute or so they have found that little bowl-shaped nest scooped out of the sod, lined with grass and almost hidden by a tuft of grass. The meadowlark is one of the most beautiful distinctively-colored song birds of the prairies with its yellow throat and breast, black collar, striped head and speckled plumage. Though their songs are similar, there are slight differences in their tunes as any bird lover soon can detect. It is one of the few birds that walk rather than hop or run.

As they walk away from the nest, Mary says "Listen, Rob. I can sing its song." She does a credible job and then says, "I wonder how long it will be till the eggs hatch. Let's come by this nest every day to see, eh? I like to see those little birds which have such big mouths that are always wide open. I know their mommy and daddy feeds them insects so I hope they find lots of mosquitoes for them. Let's keep close track of when they look big enough to fly. Maybe we'll be lucky enough to see them get up in the air. I sure hope a hawk doesn't get them."

As they arrive, they happily greet the other children, for they all know each other well. After all, their families have visited many times and they've been in Sunday School together. Just then the teacher comes to the door and rings his big bell. All the pupils quickly line up in a double line in front of the steps and he says, "Good morning children. What a nice day it is! Ready! Mark time. Left, right, left, right, forward march."

They all march in and stand beside their desks with the little beginners sticking close by bigger brothers and sisters until the teacher points them to the small empty desks awaiting their new occupants. The teacher chooses one of the older children for the flag salute. Then they sing "O Canada" with the teacher playing the pump organ. At its conclusion, he says "Take your seats now."

(In the winter the flag salute is indoors, but when the weather is warm, they have this ceremony outdoors as a rule. Then the flag would be unfolded, hooked on the rope and hoisted to fly atop the schoolhouse.

Mary is thinking how happy she is to have her new scribbler with the picture of the little puppies on the front (she had lots of pictures to choose from at the store in town), and she likes the nice sharp point her daddy has put on her pencil with his jack knife. She watched him carefully as he did this, wondering if she would be able to do it herself someday. Just then **Mr. Boulter** hands each of the beginners their new green-colored Canadian readers. They have never been opened before. What a thrill to be the first to do this! Mary is thinking, "I'm going to ask daddy to help me make a cover for my reader. I want to keep it nice and clean." (We made these brown paper covers for all our hardbacks.)

Just then one of the bigger pupils hands each beginner three little boxes, a brown one filled with tiny pieces of cardboard with words printed on them; a grey one full of little colored pegs and a green one with plasticene in it. Her teacher says "Put the box full of word pieces into your desk. In a few days I will be showing you how to use them. With the pegs, you can make a picture on the top of your desk right now."

Mary happily lays out the pegs for a house and trees. After the teacher's "Well done, Mary" the pegs are scooted back into the box, the lid put on and it, too, goes into her desk.

This is hardly finished when another bigger child lets each one choose a picture sewing card. Mary is quickly engrossed in putting that little shoe-lace-type cord in and out of the holes thinking, "This is fun. I hope we get one to do every day." After completing them and showing the teacher, they are told, "Now undo your sewing so the cards are ready for others tomorrow."

Mary enjoys all the other activities of the day, including a bit of time to play with her plasticene, and at closing time is thinking "Oh, I can hardly wait to tell Mommy and Daddy what I did today. I sure like school and my teacher, too. I'm glad he liked the crocuses we gave him."

All the way home she is talking about school to her brother who is having trouble feeling any of her excitement and joy. As a very shy child, his first days at school had not been ones he liked to remember. He had in fact, played hooky his second day, staying in the field, but within sight of the school and heading home when he saw the kids leaving. Needless to say, this did not happen again! Neverthcless, his whole first year of school was not like the happy experience of his sister.

Quimper Was Unique

Yes — that is *the word* which pops into mind simultaneously with *Quimper,* the spot which I called home from birth till the day I married. Even the *setting* for the original planning of our school district was unique — the only sod school house in Saskatchewan.

C.S. Lewis, that famous English theologian and writer, has some words of advice regarding errors that turn up in print, laying responsibility on those who find them to do what they can to prevent them being passed on. Little did I think as I read those words that this advice would come home to roost so soon. In one book, **Indianola** was said to be Saskatchewan's *only sod school house*. Then in another book, along with another picture, was the statement that **Winona** was the *only known sod schoolhouse* and built in 1907. Their teacher, **Miss G. McGill**, is in the foreground of the picture. (It did not give the nearby town so it may be up to some reader of *my book* to determine which is right.)

And though the name Quimper and the municipality in which it was located are both of *French* origin, there wasn't a French name on either the school board or the roster of Quimper's first pupils.

Then came our phone service in the early 20's. The west half of the district was on the **Ponteix** line, the east half on **Aneroid's**, so that to call a neighbor only half a mile away cost 15 cents. This set-up led to a unique way of dodging these long distance charges — just use the school kids as messenger "go-betweens" for the two halves. It was never quite clear to me why *I* was *our* homes' note carrier rather than my older brother. Perhaps my parents thought that giving me this responsibility might help to cure my frustrating forgetfulness. It didn't!

Our district was also divided by both language and religion. In the west half there were more *French speaking Roman Catholics* while the east half had more *English speaking Protestants.* Some of us in the middle, like the McConvilles, did business and got our mail in *Ponteix*, but went to *Aneroid* for church and social events. One family didn't fit either of these predominant patterns — a Roman Catholic family from *Holland.*

A unique twist of fate was instrumental in saving the lives of this family. They had been booked to sail on the **Titanic**, but due to overbooking, they had been asked to take a smaller slower boat. The Titanic passed them on the high seas and they did not know, till docking in **Halifax,** that it was by then on the ocean floor and had taken many lives with it.

If French speaking children entered Quimper as beginners, as did the Dumonts, they knew no English, but it was not long before they fit in just fine. In contrast, the **Lalliers**, who came first in the higher grades, could speak English very well. Apparently the teaching of it at the convent had greatly improved from the 20's. But we did not learn French, sad to say. In high school we took French, but it was mostly book learning rather than conversational. I do not remember any ill feelings over our language differences — only the gales of laughter when I was riding home from school with the **Lalliers** in the buggy (they had another mile to go after dropping me off.) We would leave school vowing *not* to say a *word* of *English.* This ploy didn't work either but we sure had a lot of fun.

Now how did we get the name **Quimper** you may ask? Well, both the name itself and how we got it were unique. Quimper is the *only* town in the world by that name and how our school got this name was in odd fashion also. **Father Royer**, one of the founders of **Notre Dame**, (later to be Ponteix), had come from **Quimper, France** and apparently this name was a suggestion on file with the Department of Education, for some newly organizing district. (Six years later a district to the north of ours was organized and named Royer).

When the five name suggestions for our school were listed in order of preference, Quimper was at the head of the list. Everyone, French and English alike, probably thought it the best name we could have. It was short, easy to spell and *unique.* But research on this name brought even more strange facts to light. It really is a *Spanish* name, for, though Quimper is in France, it is in an area which, in the early days of exploration, was more akin to an area of **Spain** called **Catalonia** than it was to the rest of France. Even today the people in this northwest peninsula of France speak Spanish.

Many of you know my love of folk dancing — and in one of my magazines I spied a **Port Townsend, Washington** address and phone for their group which meets in *Quimper Hall.* The lady I got in touch with, **Betty Phouts**, did some research for me, telling me that their town had quite a number of places with the name Quimper — an inn, a credit union, a grange, a bookstore, and a number of other establishments. In history books for that area she found that an early Spanish explorer, **Captain Manuel Quimper,** had sailed up the northwest coast of the **United States** and this was how some places in their vicinity came to be named after him. I learned from **Jim Cross** that **Victoria, B.C.** in the **Oak Bay** section, has a street named after him, also.

A friend of minc in **Yakima**, **Pat Wright**, knew of Quimper's fame for its pottery and glassware, and she gave me a page from an old 70's catalogue, adding that prices are probably higher now. A friend of hers has a set of Quimper glassware, so at these prices and higher, she has a very valuable collection.

Quimper Pottery was made in Finistere, France, after 1900.
Most of the pieces found today were made during the twentieth century.
A Quimper factory has worked in France since the eighteenth century.

Quimper, Bell, With Lady, Signed 16.50
Quimper, Bowl, Mixing, Yellow, Orange, Blue, Stripes, Man, 11-5/8 In. Diameter . 28.00
Quimper, Bowl, Pink, Woman, Flowers, Handles, Signed, Pair 11.00
Quimper, Coffeepot, Signed H. Quimper, Girl & Floral Decor, 7 in. High 35.00
Quimper, Creamer, Peasant Boy, Signed, 4-1/4 in. Tall 12.50
Quimper, Cup, Saucer, Eggcup, Porringer, & Plate, Man's, Marked HB, France ... 30.00
Quimper, Cup, Saucer, Porringer, & Plate, Women's, Marked HB, France 30.00
Quimper, Knife Rest, French Faience, Man & Woman, Pair 36.00
Quimper, Matchbox Holder .... *Illus* 22.50
Quimper, Plate, Peasant Lady, Flowers, 6-3/4 in. Pair 15.00
Quimper, Plate, Peasant Scene, Men, Women, 8-1/2 in. Diameter 10.00
Quimper, Plate, Sailboats, Fish Border, Artist J. Louchard, 9-1/4 in. 6.50
Quimper, Vase, Floral Design, Tub Shape, Green, Blue, Yellow, Black Rim, Signed7.00

But in the final analysis, it is *not* all these *facts* unearthed by research that make Quimper unique. It is the *people* who settled there, made it their home, set the standards for bringing up their children, worked hard under some gruelling circumstances, but learned how to enjoy life, too. I welcome the opportunity to tell some of their stories and to show in a small way how their lives fit into that era — the now vanished days of the rural schools.

Quimper's Forerunner

About five miles from where Quimper School would be built, there once stood a sod schoolhouse.

On June 14, 1993 a plaque was unveiled commemorating this school, **Indianola #2704.** Four former students were honored **Calra Provencal, Annie Pain, Hobart Brooks** and **Alf Corbin**, all now in their late nineties.

Though sod was the material at hand, and was used by most *settlers* for their *first houses,* it took some persuading to convince a skep-

The Indianola Sod Schoolhouse at Aneroid, Sask., built in 1911. On roof two Douglas children, Tom Boyce, Earl Igo. On ground L. to R.: Harry Douglas, Dick Lloyd, George Corbin.

tical Department of Education that it *would do* for a *school.* **George Corbin**, an apprenticed builder from England, had swayed those at an organizational meeting into believing it *could* be done, but the task of getting the department to agree fell to **Dick Lloyd.**

The first letter of reply might have disheartened lesser folks. This was the word from Regina: "Your proposition is too weird to consider. A building of brick, logs, stones or boards, yes, but who ever heard of a sod schoolhouse?" More letters went back and forth until finally the committee had a meeting in *Swift Current* with the *Deputy Minister of Education.* After long hours, they received his very reluctant permission. Their dream of twenty-one pupils sitting at desks in a sod schoolhouse with the Union Jack fluttering above was soon to be a reality. School opened Tuesday, April 4, 1911. It operated only until the railway came to Aneroid in 1913, but it served its purpose well. It was comfortably warm in winter and cool in summer. However, *rain outside* meant *rain inside* accompanied by garter snakes who often decided that the *schoolroom* was a *better* place to be than *inside* those thick sod walls!

As with any other rural school on the prairies, Indianola was the centre of community events, dances, concerts, political meetings, church services, etc. Dad told us that he sang at concerts there and I have twice visited with **Annie Pain**, in the Ponteix Manor to hear first- hand other stories about this unique school. (Annie, remember, was at the plaque unveiling in 1993.)

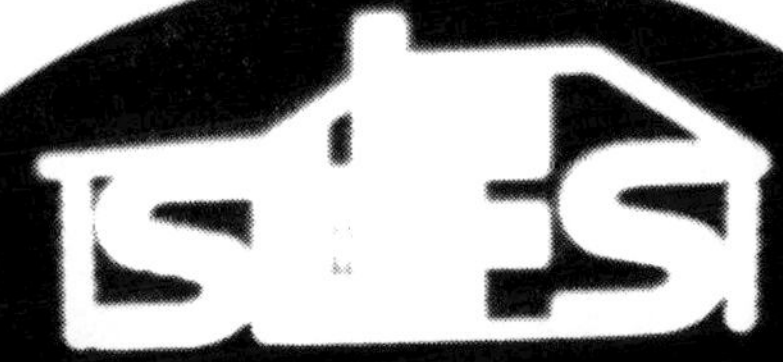

INDIANOLA SCHOOL DISTRICT NO. 2704

THE ONLY SOD SCHOOL HOUSE IN WESTERN SASKATCHEWAN. OFFICIALLY FOUNDED IN 1910, THE SCHOOL WAS LOCATED ON THE SE 1/4-6-9-10-WS. IT WAS NAMED INDIANOLA BY SOME OF THE SETTLERS FROM INDIANOLA, IOWA.

SCHOOL OPENED ON TUESDAY, APRIL 4, 1911, WITH TEACHER MISS IDA BLIESNER AND 20 PUPILS. THE SCHOOL CLOSED IN 1913 AND THE STUDENTS WERE TRANSPORTED TO ANEROID. THE LAST TEACHER WAS LAURA BLAIR.

SCHOOL HOUSE SITE IS LOCATED ONE MILE SOUTH OF THIS MARKER.

ERECTED 1989 BY THE ANEROID COMMUNITY

"Gathering, preserving and sharing the history and folklore of Saskatchewan"

Getting Organized — A Mini Drama

For this playlet I have woven together fact and fiction, but sticking closely to what *could have been.* Facts have come from John Charyk's book "The Little White Schoolhouse", the Aneroid and Ponteix history books, copies of materials from Saskatchewan's educational archives and best of all perhaps, first hand recollections of Quimperites.

Getting Organized — Scene I

Place: The Indianola schoolhouse.

Time: Friday, Dec. 19, 1913, 2:00 a.m.

Characters: Settlers of Indianola School District and those wanting a new district.

Circumstances: Because of the raging blizzard outside, the decision has been made *not* to go home till daylight. Mothers are tending little ones. Some babies are awake to nurse. Others are asleep on the wide window ledges or on the teacher's desk. Toddlers have dropped off to sleep in whatever spot they found to lie down and are covered with coats. Older girls and some mothers are cleaning up after the late supper of sandwiches, cakes and coffee. Older boys are stoking the pot-bellied stove or standing around trying to act grown up.

Herb McCoy: Our Charlie is eight already so he needs to be in school. How many pupils do we have to have?

George Corbin: eight, ages five to sixteen. The Department of Education gives out a book upon request which gives all the steps in turn for what must be done. (George had been on the Indianola organizing committee.) Your first job is to get a committee of three. All must live in the district to be organized.

Walter Lord: Well, how about a meeting soon to do this? What about at your place, Jack?

Jack McKenzie: Sure, that's fine, but my place isn't very big. How many do you suppose will come?

W.R. McKenzie: It's hard to say, but I think we'd get a pretty good idea if we made a list of the families who have children they want to get into school.

Albert Dunnell: (He was reeve of the municipality.) I can get a map of the municipality showing the location of all the settlers. On it we could show our proposed boundaries.

George Corbin: Along with the forms and information from the department, you get a map showing the boundaries of schools already existing in the vicinity. They want a district to be as nearly square as possible, and not to exceed five miles length or breadth and there must be at least four ratepayers. We must avoid having children hindered from attending by such things as lakes, impassable streams or other barriers and a road allowance must be at the centre.

Jim Innes: Well, we may have a problem or two there with our *alkali flat dead centre* and there's those *coulees* on the south end. The **Westerleigh District** is already organized on the west, but we're clear north and east if we work fast enough.

Albert Dunnell: I've talked to one or two in Westerleigh and they tell me we must file this petition in good form with *all* information *in full* even including the *quarter sections* that would be within the boundaries. Also, it requires the signature of a member of the committee, and a notary public or a justice of the peace.

Herb McCoy: How do we go about choosing a name?

George Corbin: Oh, I forgot to tell you. When the petition goes in, it must have four or five of your name suggestions.

Sam McConville: I think we'd better get that committee named right away. It sounds as if they'll have some work to do.

Ed Shaddock: Jack, how soon can you have us?

Jack McK: Well, I guess as soon as everyone wants to come. It would probably be good to set a time tonight while we're all here. How about next Tuesday at 1:00?

Bert Cross: Sounds fine to me. Is there anyone not here who needs to be notified?

Frank Morin: That's right, Bert. We must not leave anybody out. Besides, we need everyone involved to get this project underway. Let's each take it upon ourselves to tell anyone not here tonight. But it's not as important to have everyone at this meeting to select the committee as it will be when *voting* day arrives. Am I right?

Ed Shaddock: Yes, I'm sure you're right. We're getting pretty close to Christmas, too, but we shouldn't let that delay us.

Jack McKenzie: We'll look for you all next Tuesday then. That's the 23rd.

Scene II

Time and Place: 1:00 p.m., Dec. 23, 1913 at Jack McKenzie's.

Jack McKenzie: Glad you could all make it. It's good our blizzard let up. I think we were wise to wait till daylight last Friday night before heading home. Well, we don't want to take more time than necessary with our chit-chat as I know you want to get home. I told Maggie not to bother with tea for us as she's busy getting some baking done for Christmas. I guess our only business is to get our committee of three named and voted on. Bill (W.R. on the records), how about you taking the minutes?

W.R. McKenzie: Fine. Just get me a piece of paper and a pen, please. I suppose these notes should go into a minutes book. I'll provide one for the next meeting.

Ed Shaddock: I nominate Albert Dunnell.

H.C. Edwards: I second your nomination.

Frank Fountain: I nominate Herb McCoy.

James Innes: I second that.

Frank Morin: I nominate Jim McCullough.

Bert Cross: I second your nomination, Frank.

Jack McKenzie: Are all of you willing to serve on this committee?

All: Yes.

Jack: All in favor of these three men being our committee, raise your right hand. (*All* do.)

Jack: There being none against, I declare you are elected by acclamation. Albert, seeing as you were the first nominated, I guess you take over the meeting now.

Albert Dunnell: Yes. Thank you. Jack, I have that map from the office I spoke of the other night. I guess we can draw on it our proposed boundaries for the district and the site we choose for the school. We will have to indicate why we can't build at the centre. Could we have a short discussion on alternatives?

Ed Shaddock: It seems to me a half mile to the north would be best. It may sound selfish but right now anyway, there are more families in the north half than the south. Also, it would be a little nearer to town, so we would have less distance to haul supplies for the building. (Pause. There is no more discussion.)

Albert Dunnell: Hearing no further discussion, let's vote. All in favour of locating the site one half mile north of true centre say Aye. Opposed. Nay. The Ayes have it. Bill, will you call a meeting please as soon as you receive the department's approval of what we have proposed today? Oh, there is one more item of business — our suggestions for a name. Bill, will you please write these down and then we will list them in the order of preference.

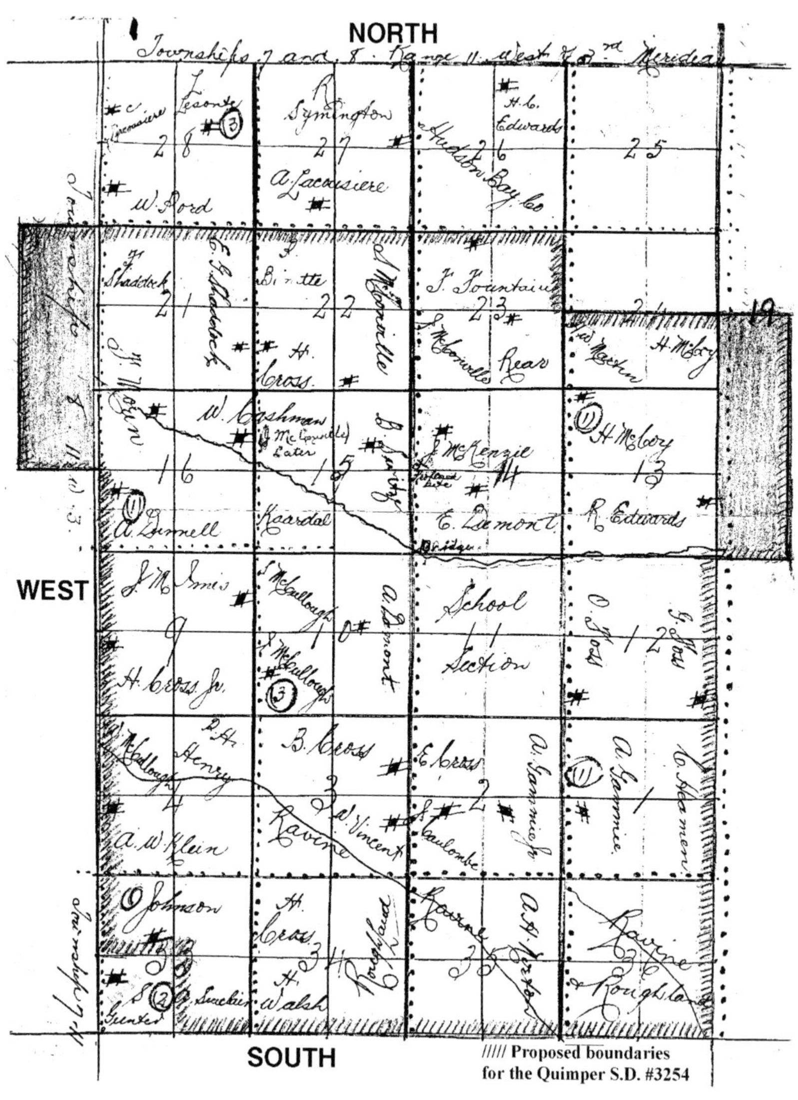

This map is the work of the committee, Dec. 23, 1913 circa. Area marked ////// plus shaded areas indicate the proposed and later accepted boundaries of the Quimper School District #3254. The site chosen, a half mile north of true centre was not approved till sometime later.

Note: A letter dated Jan. 19, 1914, showed this list to be as follows: (1) Quimper; (2) McKenzie; (3) Wallace; (4) Grand Valley; (5) Innes. No records have turned up apparently, so we don't know *whose* suggestions these were or their *reasons* for them, but that letter corrected what I'd often heard, that names with "Cross" in it had been suggested.

Another factor also favoured choosing the name Quimper. We already had a post office with this name which had been located at Wallard but recently had been moved north about ten miles to my Uncle Sam's place.

For that all-important first school meeting following notice that the Department of Education had approved their proposal, there were some very strict rules. *Notices* were to be posted in widely-separated places in the district at least *fourteen* days prior to the date of the meeting. *One* person was to announce their posting and was to keep track of time and place of such postings, and on each was to be recorded the lands to be included in the district. The meeting was to begin at *one o'clock sharp*. Ratepayers present were to elect a chairman and secretary, with the chairman signing a declaration as soon as elected and, immediately following, all others who desired to vote or take an active part in the meeting, signed also. *Unqualified* signers would be *fined* ten dollars, but *late-comer eligible individuals could* sign. After all signatures were made and witnessed to by both chairman and secretary, the chairman announced, "The poll will be open for one hour." As each one came forward, he was asked (1) What is your name?; (2) Do you vote for or against the formation of the proposed School District? At conclusion of the voting, he announced, "It is passed — 14 for and 1 against. (Why, one wonders, was there this one negative vote?) This document along with all others required by the department were then mailed. It was dated Jan. 1, 1914 and signed by A. Dunnell, H. McCoy and James McCullough along with a second signature of A. Dunnell who had posted the notices. On Jan. 6, 1914, the *municipality* gave its approval.

When the letter of approval from the Department of Education came, apparently all was in order for the next step — with the possible exception of Section 46 of the School Act. They hadn't yet, it seemed, given final permission to build at *any site* other than the *centre*. Eventually, all authorities did give their approval. Not long afterward — April 30, 1914 — the *land ownership statement* came. It would be used for tax assessment. Of the 38401 total acreage, the Hudson Bay Company owned 480. On June 27, 1914, a list of expected expenditures in applying for a

debenture totalling $2000 was put on file. Here it is:

School site 2 acres	$50
School House and Stable	1460
Fencing and School Grounds	55
Grass Seed	5
Supplies for School House	187
"Waterbury" Heating and Ventilating System	150
Extras	93
Total	$2000

(Note: There was a terrible blizzard on January 11, 1917. At the Congress School north of Admiral, five little girls and their teacher attempted to go to the outdoor toilet, but with no fence around the yard, they were soon hopelessly lost. The teacher and one girl finally reached safety, though badly frostbitten, but four litle girls were found two days later frozen to death. After this tragedy it became mandatory to have a school yard fenced.)

Other items the $187.00 would have to cover: desks, teacher's desk and chair, big bell, tap bell, wall brackets and coal oil lamps, globe, chalk and brushes, broom, dust pan and dust bane, pencil sharpener, ink powder, pail, wash basin and soap, foolscap, colored paper and big dictionary. Also, the Department of Education mandated that $25.00 be spent each year on books for the school library.

On July 13, 1914, they got their loan.

Some records from here on are missing or not clear so I was unable to find the *date* the school actually opened, or the *listing* of the pupils' names. In fact, there is confusion of just *who* was the first teacher. In one place it stated a **Mr. Davis** had been hired in 1914, but **Miss Buss** is listed for 1915 and **Jas. E. Davis** for 1916 and 1917.

In any case, they must have been working against time and weather as they didn't get *started* to build until sometime during the last half of July. Then again, maybe they, and those who were selling them materials, were so *sure* of the loan going through that they had been advanced some money. So, guesstimating as they say now, my little playlet about the first day of operations for Quimper #3254 will be *Tuesday, Sept. 2, 1914*.

It seems there was no requirement to send in an annual report prior to 1917, so this listing of the first pupils, year of birth and age upon starting school is based on the Aneroid and Ponteix History books

The water cooler that eventually replaced the pail and dipper in most rural schools. It was always emptied after school. Forgetting even once in winter time could spell disaster as tem—peratures went below freezing overnight.

The Waterbury jacket stove, common in most schools which didn't have a basement. It also provided good air ventilation.

and the recollections of those I got in touch with by letter or phone.

Year of Birth	Name	Age
1904	Mary Kelman	10
1904	Minnie Gammie	10
1906	Charlie McCoy	8
1906	Doug McCullough	8
1907	Alex Kelman	7
1909	Eddie McCullough	5
1909	Winnefred Taylor	5
1909	Margaret Symington	5

If this is correct, it would appear they just got in under the wire — 8 pupils between ages 5 and 16. Lena McCullough was 14 and she may have come. If she did, she would surely have been a big help to the teacher being the oldest by four years.

The First Day — A Mini Drama

There didn't seem to be any particular guidelines as to how a teacher was to begin with a group of pupils of various ages and aca-

GOVERNMENT OF THE PROVINCE OF SASKATCHEWAN.

DEPARTMENT OF EDUCATION.

Regina, Sask. March 19, 1914

Sir: —

I have the honour to inform you that an order has this day been issued, erecting the Quimper School District No. 3254 of Saskatchewan. Notice of the formation of the district will appear in the next issue of the Gazette, a copy of which will be sent to you when published. Upon receiving the Gazette, the notice should be carefully checked and in case of any error, the Department should be notified at once.

As the trustee elected for the longest term, it is your duty to call a meeting of the trustees as provided by Section 38 of The School Act. At this meeting one of the trustees should be selected to act as chairman of the School Board. A secretary and a treasurer or a secretary-treasurer should also be appointed.

To enable your board to proceed with the issue of debentures, a full set of forms required is being forwarded to your address under separate cover.

I beg to further call your attention to the provisions of Section 46 of The School Act. You will note by referring thereto that unless the site selected by your board is at the centre of the district it will be necessary to secure the approval of the Minister of Education or the municipal council as the case may be of any other site.

Any further information you may require at any time will be furnished upon application.

Your obedient servant,

Deputy Minister.

W.R. McKenzie, Esq.,
Quimper, Sask.

(Re-typeset from original to save space.)

demic backgrounds. Some could probably read and write and do a little arithmetic due to some teaching at home by parents or older brothers and sisters. Some may have attended school before the family moved here. So it was up to Miss Ruth Buss to assess the situation quickly and use all the ingenuity she could muster.

Scene: Inside Quimper School with everything new.

Time: Tuesday, Sept. 2, 1914, 9:00 a.m.

Miss Buss has just rung the bell; the children have entered in haphazard fashion and are waiting for word on just what to do.

Miss Buss: (in her white blouse and long dark skirt) Good morning children. Welcome to Quimper School #3254. (When the provinces of Alberta and Saskatchewan were formed, Alberta decided to go on with their previous numbering, but Saskatchewan began at number one — thus our 3254 meant there were 3253 other schools prior to ours.)

I see you all have a lunch pail. Just put it there along the back wall. We do not have any place to keep food cold, so be sure to bring only foods that are fine at room temperature. I see quite a few look-alike pails, Swift's Lard or Roger's Syrup, so tomorrow please have your name on your own pail. Also, we do not have a well. How many of you have a jar of water in your pail? (No hands go up.) Well, don't worry. McKenzie's is only about a quarter of a mile and we have a pail, so I'll send a couple of boys over for some in a little while. They will dump it into that water cooler there and whenever you want a drink, just put your hand up and ask permission. The same goes for having to go to the toilet. We all want some privacy for this, so that is why there are those wooden screens in front of the doors and of course, you'll see one is for boys and one for girls. You don't need to *say* anything to ask permission to go to the toilet, just put up your hand with either one or two fingers and I will know what you man. (The kids don't dare ask, but will soon hear from those in-the-know about this odd custom.) But please, get a drink or go to the toilet mostly at noon and recess time. We want as few interruptions as possible during school time.

Please take a seat now. I want you to call me **Miss Buss**, but if you forget it at first, "Please Teacher" will do for a few days. (Gets the register out.) This long book is called the school register. In it I will now write all your names along with your ages, birthdays and how far you live from school. So now, one at a time, I want you to stand by your desk and tell me these things about yourself. Please speak loud enough and clearly so I don't have to ask you to repeat it. This wastes time. Alright, Mary. Let's start with you. (The younger ones gain confidence from hearing the older oncs go first.) We won't ask for your middle names. (When this is done she says,) Tomorrow when I take roll, as I call your name you will answer "Here". If you're late or absent, I have to put that down too in this record book. I hope you will all come regularly and be on time.

How many of you have heard of germs? (A couple of hands go up so Miss Buss says "Yes, Minnie, what are they?)

Minnie: Teeny, tiny bugs so small we can't see them, but they can make you sick.

Miss Buss: That is right and we may not even know we have them, yet they'll still get from one to another. How can this happen? (A hand goes up.) Yes Charlie?

Charlie: By coughing or sneezing probably.

Miss Buss: You are right, so to prevent them getting passed around, we must each have our own handkerchief and cover our nose and mouth if we cough or sneeze. Let's all try to remember this. In fact, it's a good idea never to share *any* personal things like combs, brushes, and so on. We need our own drinking cups, too. So when you go home today, please ask your mother for one that you can bring and leave at school. I will put your names under those hooks by the water fountain and I want you to always hang your cup in the right place. I see all of you brought a scribbler and a pencil with you today. That's good. Right now please put your name on it. You will know yours without this, I'm sure, for I see there are different pictures on them. Did you have the chance to pick out the one you wanted in town? *You* may know your own scribblers by the pictures but I wouldn't remember which is which so your names on them will help me when you hand in some work for me to check. Soon I would like you to have at least *three* scribblers each — one for arithmetic, one for spelling and the third for other things. If any of you little ones don't know how to print your name, raise your hand and one of the older ones can help you. To the two who offer their assistance she nods and says "Thank you, Mary and Charlie."

Miss Buss: Oh I see some of you don't have your pencil sharpened while others do. I'm sure some daddies were busy last night with their jack knives. But I know you'll all enjoy using that pencil sharpener there (points). If your pencil isn't sharpened yet, just walk over there to sharpen it. But, let's not use it more than we have to. Pencils cost money and we must not waste them. Some of you have a rubber, too, I see (this was before they were called erasers). That's fine. I would like all of you to have one of your own. You older boys and girls will be using a pen soon, so you'll need a double one. One end erases pencil the other ink. Pencil rubs out much easier than ink, to be sure, but we do the best we can. After all, your scribbler won't look very good with holes in the pages, will it? You'll need a blotter, too. However, you don't need to buy ink. We will have that at school for you. Also we have quite a number of little things to keep track of so it will be a good idea to have a box to keep them in. If you don't have a regular pencil box, a cigar or chocolate box works very well.

Most of you can tell time and I see some of you glancing at the clock. Yes, we have a regular time for recesses, noon hour and going home. Did you see the little bell on my desk? This is how I will use it. When it is recess time — and that is right now in fact — I'll tap the bell once which means your books are to be off the top of your desk and put inside and then, you are to sit up straight. The next tap means to stand beside your desk facing the front. The third tap means to turn and face the back of the room. Then I will say "Dismissed. Now you are free to go and play outside until I ring the big bell in fifteen minutes. O.K. are you ready?

(They are dismissed with this procedure. When they are back in their desks...)

Miss Buss: I know you sat in any desk when we started school this morning, but now we will move into desks that fit us better. After this you will always go to that desk when you come in. Tomorrow we will open school in a different way. The flag should always be flying when school is on unless the weather is too bad, so when I ring the bell tomorrow, we will all gather near the flag rope and pulley. We'll learn how to unfold the flag, hook it on and pull it up to the top. Then just before we go home, we will take it down, fold it up correctly and put it in the cupboard ready for the next day. After the flag is up we'll march in a line into school. Then you will stand by your desks at attention and we'll sing, "O Canada," our national anthem. Before going home at 3:30 we will sing "God Save the King". It is good we have an organ. I will play it when we sing now, but if any of you can play, that would be better. Please take your seats now and we will have some schoolwork. Right now I can't put you in the right grades because I don't know how much each of you knows about reading, writing, arithmetic, spelling and other things, so for awhile we will work without grades. In fact, I have here a big book called a curriculum which is made specially for an ungraded school. It has suggestions on what I'm to teach until you are all in the right classes.

From the many suggestions in it, I have chosen just one for today. You all know something about paper, don't you? But it is also true that all of us can learn a lot more about it — where it comes from, how it is made, its many uses and so on. So right now I want each of you, starting with the youngest to tell me one thing you know about paper. As you take your turn, don't repeat what someone else has said and please speak loud enough so I don't have to ask you to say it again. (After this is done . . .)

Miss Buss: Now let's take about ten minutes to put some of what we've said into our scribblers. You older ones who can write, put down two or three sentences or a paragraph. Those of you who cannot write yet, but are seven or older, please stand there in a row facing the front and I will write a little on the blackboard for you. Then in the time you have, copy what you can into your scribblers. But for you little five year olds, even that is too hard, so you will try to print the word "paper" in your scribbler. I will help you learn to hold your pencil the right way and guide your hand to print this word. Then we'll put your name under it and you will have something to take home to show daddy and mommy one thing you did today.

Miss Buss: It's time for lunch. (She taps her bell, waits while they clear their desk tops, and says. . .) It is such a nice day, you may eat your lunch anywhere you wish except you must stay within the school yard. Perhaps you'd like to sit in your buggy with someone else. That would be nice. (She taps her bell twice more and says "Dismissed".)

Though it was terribly tempting to peek at the back of our scribblers for these tables, we were expected to memorize most of them — especially those we would use frequently. There were numerous drills of all kinds for adding, take away (we didn't call it subtraction), multipling, and dividing.

ADDITION TABLE.

…and …re 2	2 and 1 are 3	3 and 1 are 4	4 and 1 are 5	5 and 1 are 6	6 and 1 are 7	7 and 1 are 8	8 and 1 are 9	9 and 1 are 10	10 and 1 are 11	11 and 1 are 12	12 and 1 are 13
- 3	2 - 4	2 - 5	2 - 6	2 - 7	2 - 8	2 - 9	2 - 10	2 - 11	2 - 12	2 - 13	2 - 14
- 4	3 - 5	3 - 6	3 - 7	3 - 8	3 - 9	3 - 10	3 - 11	3 - 12	3 - 13	3 - 14	3 - 15
- 5	4 - 6	4 - 7	4 - 8	4 - 9	4 - 10	4 - 11	4 - 12	4 - 13	4 - 14	4 - 15	4 - 16
- 6	5 - 7	5 - 8	5 - 9	5 - 10	5 - 11	5 - 12	5 - 13	5 - 14	5 - 15	5 - 16	5 - 17
- 7	6 - 8	6 - 9	6 - 10	6 - 11	6 - 12	6 - 13	6 - 14	6 - 15	6 - 16	6 - 17	6 - 18
- 8	7 - 9	7 - 10	7 - 11	7 - 12	7 - 13	7 - 14	7 - 15	7 - 16	7 - 17	7 - 18	7 - 19
- 9	8 - 10	8 - 11	8 - 12	8 - 13	8 - 14	8 - 15	8 - 16	8 - 17	8 - 18	8 - 19	8 - 20
- 10	9 - 11	9 - 12	9 - 13	9 - 14	9 - 15	9 - 16	9 - 17	9 - 18	9 - 19	9 - 20	9 - 21
- 11	10 - 12	10 - 13	10 - 14	10 - 15	10 - 16	10 - 17	10 - 18	10 - 19	10 - 20	10 - 21	10 - 22
- 12	11 - 13	11 - 14	11 - 15	11 - 16	11 - 17	11 - 18	11 - 19	11 - 20	11 - 21	11 - 22	11 - 23
- 13	12 - 14	12 - 15	12 - 16	[illegible] 17	12 - 18	12 - 19	12 - 20	12 - 21	12 - 22	12 - 23	12 - 24

…STRACTION.—By reversing the above Table Subtraction is learnt, thus: instead of saying 1 and 1 are 2, say 1 from 2 and 1 remains; 1 from 3 and 2 remains.

MULTIPLICATION TABLE.

…imes …are 2	3 times 1 are 3	4 times 1 are 4	5 times 1 are 5	6 times 1 are 6	7 times 1 are 7	8 times 1 are 8	9 times 1 are 9	10 times 1 are 10	11 times 1 are 11	12 times 1 are 12
- 4	2 - 6	2 - 8	2 - 10	2 - 12	2 - 14	2 - 16	2 - 18	2 - 20	2 - 22	2 - 24
- 6	3 - 9	3 - 12	3 - 15	3 - 18	3 - 21	3 - 24	3 - 27	3 - 30	3 - 33	3 - 36
- 8	4 - 12	4 - 16	4 - 20	4 - 24	4 - 28	4 - 32	4 - 36	4 - 40	4 - 44	4 - 48
- 10	5 - 15	5 - 20	5 - 25	5 - 30	5 - 35	5 - 40	5 - 45	5 - 50	5 - 55	5 - 60
- 12	6 - 18	6 - 24	6 - 30	6 - 36	6 - 42	6 - 48	6 - 54	6 - 60	6 - 66	6 - 72
- 14	7 - 21	7 - 28	7 - 35	7 - 42	7 - 49	7 - 56	7 - 63	7 - 70	7 - 77	7 - 84
- 16	8 - 24	8 - 32	8 - 40	8 - 48	8 - 56	8 - 64	8 - 72	8 - 80	8 - 88	8 - 96
- 18	9 - 27	9 - 36	9 - 45	9 - 54	9 - 63	9 - 72	9 - 81	9 - 90	9 - 99	9 - 108
- 20	10 - 30	10 - 40	10 - 50	10 - 60	10 - 70	10 - 80	10 - 90	10 - 100	10 - 110	10 - 120
- 22	11 - 33	11 - 44	11 - 55	11 - 66	11 - 77	11 - 88	11 - 99	11 - 110	11 - 121	11 - 132
- 24	12 - 36	12 - 48	12 - 60	12 - 72	12 - 84	12 - 96	12 - 108	12 - 120	12 - 132	12 - 144

…IVISION.—To apply this Table to Division reverse it, thus: instead of saying 3 times 1 are 3, say 3's in 3 are 1, or go once; 3's in 6 are 2, or go twice.

ARITHMETICAL TABLES.

Numeration.

…its 1
…s 12
…ndreds 123
…ousands 1,234
…s of Thousands 12,345
…f Thousands 123,456
…lions 1,234,567
…f Millions 12,345,678
…f Millions 123,456,789
…he number represented …he last line is read: One …ndred and twenty-three …lion, four hundred and …-six thousand, seven …ndred and eighty-nine.

Numerals.

…ABIC.	ROMAN.
…	I.
…	II.
…	III.
…	IV.
…	V.
…	VI.
…	VII.
…	VIII.
…	IX.
…	X.
…	XX.
…	L.
…	C.
…	D.
…	M.

…bic, or Solid Measure.

… Inches......1 Solid Foot
… Feet ....1 Solid Yard
… Feet ...1 Ton Shipping
… Feet......1 Cord Wood

Paper.

…heets.............1 Quire
…uires... ....1 Ream

Long Measure.

12 Lines............1 Inch
4 Inches.............1 Hand
12 Inches.........1 Foot
3 Feet ....1 Yard
6 Feet ....1 Fathom
5½ Yards......1 Rod or Pole
40 Rods..........1 Furlong
8 Furlongs ....1 Mile
3 Miles ....1 League
69¼ Miles ....1 Degree
1760 yds. or 5280 ft. ...1 Mile
6075·81 ft....1 Nautical Mile

Avoirdupois Weight.

16 Drams ....1 Ounce
16 Ounces.... .....1 Pound
14 Pounds............1 Stone
25 Pounds 1 Quarter, Can.
28 Pounds..1 Quarter, Eng.
4 Quarters ..1 Hundredw't
20 Hundredw't ..... }
2000 lbs., Can. ...... } 1 Ton
2240 lbs., Eng........ }

Troy Weight.

24 Grains ....1 Pennyw't
20 Pennyw'ts........1 Ounce
12 Ounces ....1 Pound

Apothecaries' Weight.

20 Grains...........1 Scruple
3 Scruples...........1 Dram
8 Drams ....1 Ounce
12 Ounces ....1 Pound

Cloth Measure.

2¼ Inches ....1 Nail
4 Nails ....1 Quarter
3 Quarters....1 Flemish Ell
4 Quarters...........1 Yard
5 Quarters ....1 English Ell
6 Quarters......1 French Ell
37 Inches ......1 Scotch Ell

Time Measure.

60 Seconds ....1 Minute
60 Minutes ....1 Hour
24 Hours ....1 Day
7 Days ....1 Week
4 Weeks ....1 Month
12 Months, or 365¼ Days } ... 1 Year
100 Years..........1 Century

Arithmetical Signs.

+ Plus, sign of Addition.
− Minus, sign of Subtract'n.
× Sign of Multiplication.
÷ Sign of Division.
= Sign of Equality.
: :: : Signs of Proportion.
√ Sign of the Square Root.
° Degree, ′ Minute.
″ Second, ∴ Therefore.

Square or Land Measure.

144 Sq. Inches....1 Sq. Foot
9 Sq. Feet .. ...1 Sq. Yard
30¼ Yards......1 Square Rod
40 Poles..............1 Rood
4 Roods ....1 Acre
640 Acres ....1 Sq. Mile

Days in the Month.

30 days hath September,
April, June and November;
February has 28 alone.
And all the rest have 31;
But Leap Year coming once in four,
February then has one day more.

Land Survey Measure.

7·92 Inches ....1 Link
100 Links ....1 Chain
1 Chain...............66 Feet
10 Sq. Chains ....1 Acre

Dry Measure.

2 Pints..............1 Quart
4 Quarts ....1 Gallon
2 Gallons ....1 Peck
4 Pecks ....1 Bushel
36 Bushels ......1 Chaldron

Measure of Capacity.

4 Gills ....1 Pint
2 Pints ....1 Quart
4 Quarts ....1 Gallon
9 Gallons.............1 Firkin
36 Gallons..........1 Barrel
63 Gallons ......1 Hogshead

English Money Table.

4 Farthings ....1 Penny
12 Pence ....1 Shilling
20 Shillings ....1 Pound

A Florin is 2s. ....45c.
A Half Crown is 2s. 6d. ..60c.
A Sovereign is 20s. $4.86

Aliquot Parts of a Pound.

s.	d.		£
10	0	is	1 half.
6	8	..	1 third.
5	0	..	1 fourth.
4	0	..	1 fifth.
3	4	..	1 sixth.
2	6	..	1 eighth.
2	0	..	1 tenth.
1	8	..	1 twelfth.
1	3	..	1 sixteenth.

Of a Shilling.

d.	s.	d.	s.
6	is 1-half.	2	is 1-6th.
4	.. 1-third.	1½	.. 1-8th.
3	.. 1-fourth.	1	.. 1-12th.

Of a Ton.

cwt.	Ton.	cwt.	Ton.
10	is 1-half.	2½	is 1-8th.
5	.. 1-4th.	2	.. 1-10th.
4	.. 1-5th.	1	.. 1-20th.

(After an hour for lunch, the bell has been rung and all are in their seats once again.)

Miss Buss: This afternoon we are going to spend more of our time singing, reading, drawing pictures and learning a little more of what school is all about. I hope all of you will like coming to school. We will also be talking about some things you can do at home tonight to get ready for tomorrow. Everyday right after lunch I will be reading to you. If you have some books at home you would like me to read to the class, please with your parent's permission, bring them to school to share. Today I will begin a story from one of my own books. When I am finished you can draw a picture to show that you listened carefully. You will need some drawing paper so we'll get some out of the cupboard there.

Do any of you know someone who is blind? I'm going to read the story of Helen Keller in her own words. This is called an autobiography. She wasn't only blind but deaf, too. How could she be taught anything? You will learn in her story how a wonderful teacher was able to reach this little girl in her desperation and loneliness.

After giving them about 10 minutes for their pictures, she will take another 5-10 minutes to talk about each one. Then she will say "Now we'll do something different. I'm sure you all know some rhymes don't you? How about nursery rhymes? Let's hear some of the ones you know." After a few of these she says, "Some little rhymes are made to teach us something. Did you know that? Right now we are going to learn three such ones. Tomorrow I'm going to see if you remember them. The first we'll learn will teach us how to remember the number of days in each month. Let's just say together the months of the year. OK, that's fine. Now here is the way the rhyme goes:

Thirty days hath September
    April, June and November.
All the rest have thirty-one,
    February alone has twenty-eight
Except leap year coming once in four
    February then has one day more.

Our next rhyme is about the directions. It's easy enough to remember them, but did you know that if you put them together in the right order they will spell a word? Does anyone know this word?" Pauses, but none speak up, so she hints this way "It is often part of a newspapers' name." Oh, say two or three almost in unison. "It's News."

<u>Miss Buss</u>: Right! Now here's our little rhyme: All of you stand and do what it says:

Sunrise, face east, hands by your side
South to your right
North to your left
West behind you not in sight.

Our last little rhyme is about that clock (points) and about you (points to all).

There's a neat little clock
In the schoolroom it stands
And it points to the time
With its two little hands.
And may we like the clock
Keep our face clean and bright
With hands ever ready
To do what is right.

<u>Miss Buss</u>: We know it's been a long day for you little ones. Even if you fell asleep for a little while, don't worry. It won't be long until you'll be able to stay awake during school time. Right now let's play a little game that gives you a chance to walk around the room a bit. It's called "I Spy".

Alex volunteers "I know how to play it."

<u>Miss Buss</u>: That's fine. How about you being "It"? Do you think you can tell the others how to play it?

<u>Alex</u>: I'll try.

They play it two or three times through and then are asked to sit in their desks again to hear a few end-of-the-day instructions.

<u>Miss Buss</u>: Oh, I should tell you that our study about paper will go on for a few days and along the way we'll be learning about *what* things people write with and about printing, too. We'll be looking up different countries on a map of the world so history and geography will both be part of our lessons. Those of you who have encyclopedias, an atlas and even a dictionary at home, will find all sorts of information in them to share in class. And some of you may know how to fold paper certain ways to make hats, boats, ornaments and so on. We want you to teach the rest of us someday how to do these things. I have a little booklet (holds it up) here called "The Romance of Paper". It is small, but it has lots of interesting things in it. Maybe we'll learn so much that we can put together a little skit — do you know what that is — yes a

short play. If it turns out well enough, perhaps we could make it part of a little program for your parents. Well, I see by the clock it's time to clear off our desks and get ready to go home. Let's go outside in orderly fashion and stand near the flag rope. (Miss Buss had put the flag up that morning.) When the flag is down, unhooked and folded, they all stand at attention and sing "God Save the King".

Miss Buss: Good-bye children. I'll see you tomorrow.

All: Good-bye Miss Buss.

God, Man and Mice

An event which took place at the first quarter mark in Quimper's forty-four year history really shook community spirit. This was the moving and remodelling of the school in 1925-26. After searching in vain for details about this, I came to see it all as a *blessing* instead of a real *frustration*. The story in essence is this: When the population centre of the district moved south, there was a clamor to have the school nearer to them. It seemed only fair, as those in the north had had it located in their favour for many years. In spite of much dissension, the school *was moved* a mile south and remodelled with a full basement and inside toilets. They also built swings and see-saws.

Did I see God's hand in this? *Records* which may have been kept, did He keep from surfacing? Did He touch hearts on both sides enabling them to really *see* the others' point of view as they contemplated the effects of their quarrelling on their children? And did *mice* lend a hand helping to heal the wounds by doing a thorough job of eating up the evidence? It all made me think of a couple of lines from a song in **South Pacific**. "You have to be taught to hate before you're six or seven or eight." I can't speak for others, but I don't remember any ill feelings among us school kids over this event — perhaps because we were so elated over our full basement, indoor toilets, the swings and teeter-totters and other improvements.

Gleanings from Annual Reports

As I searched through these old records I was struck with the truth of a wise old saying, "Every question that is answered spawns two more for which you search in vain for answers." For example, I was unable to track down *any* information on the *qualifications* required to be an inspector or even what salary they might have received. It was interesting to note that, though the teacher was told to expect a *half day visit each term* from him, (no woman had this job apparently), some years he never got to Quimper at all! I wondered, if behind the scenes, he *did visit* when there had been a special request by the board for him to do so or if, on the other hand, he *didn't visit* because he knew from a previous visit that things were going along just fine without him showing up?

When I was teaching, the anticipation of that knock on the door kept me constantly alert, yet somehow when he did come, introduced himself and said, “Just go on with what you're doing,” I didn't go to pieces. I was able, it seems, to convince myself that he was there to lend me a helping hand and to answer some of my questions and I wasn't nervous. In at least three ways I had prepared for the moment. First, I had my time table posted in a conspicuous place as stressed at Normal School (I couldn’t find a single teacher who saved one of these to copy for this book). Second, my register was always up to date. Third, I had all the kids primed to greet him with a friendly “Good Morning” or “Good Afternoon” (he always came first thing in the morning or afternoon). After a shorter first period than usual, he would have you dismiss them all for recess and interview you alone, asking how things were going, where he might help you and giving some suggestions on ways to improve. Following his visit, one stewed for a couple of weeks wondering if his all important report would be good or bad as it could perhaps make or break your career. At last, one day the secretary would show up with the report in hand. Again you did a little shaking in your boots. Thank goodness I *made it* each time! There was no duplicate copy for the teacher. If you wanted one, you asked if you might keep it a day or so and you copied it by hand. After your first year of teaching, it helped when applying for a second school, to be able to quote from a good report.

It was odd that up to 1938-39 there wasn't even a *blank* on the form for *his signature*. In 1940-41 his title was changed to *Superintendent*.

In later years the form provided a blank for visitor's signatures. One was **Everett Baker**, the Saskatchewan Wheat Pool Head and along with him came two women, **Mrs. F. Smith** and **Mrs. R. Blake**, but in the “Reason” spot, there was nothing!

Even more puzzling was an *illegible* signature but the *reason was plain* — a *Helping Teacher*. One might be tempted to ask just what kind of a job this person would do in helping to teach the children to *write well* — a subject that had high priority in those days.

In the mid 50's there was the first and only visit of a Public Health

Nurse and no reason was given. Again, one is tempted to read between the lines.

I was troubled by the inconsistencies in the filling out of those yearly reports. Although some were done very well, others were so poorly done, I wondered how the department tolerated the laxity, for I remember very distinctly, that when I was teaching and the inspector arrived, almost immediately he asked to see my register, and I might have had a heart attack on the spot if it hadn't been up to snuff!

Enrollments — 1914-1958

As nearly as could be determined, the school opened at or very near the required number of 8 students and ended with very few, only 13.

One year, just six prior to closing, there were only nine enrolled. Within only three years of the school's opening, there were 25, but it was during the 30's that the school was bursting at the seams as it attempted to accommodate not only all the *public* school pupils, but also all the *high* school students on correspondence courses. When I was in Grade Eleven, they had run out of desks, so I had my own little table and chair right behind a door!

For many years the **McConville** name dominated the rolls as fifteen of them from three different families came up through the grades. As the last of this "clan" as someone called us, graduated, the name **Dumonceaux** took its place with fourteen from one family.

Teacher Qualifications

It was very sad to note the deterioration of the quality of teachers in the latter years until, only a year prior to the school's closing, one person with *no certificate* or *experience* was hired and therefore could not claim the official title of *teacher*. It had become practically impossible to get a qualified teacher because of the low pay and other depressing aspects of the job. During and after the war, community life had gone downhill into near oblivion. Rural residents now went to town for church services, dances, sports events, political meetings and so on. The buildings, equipment, and the whole general tenor of the school was in a downward spiral, accelerating with each passing year. The inevitability of Quimper's eventual closing and becoming part of a large consolidated district was disheartening to all who remembered so well its hey-day and the community it served. The writing was on the wall.

The author (on right), and three friends, Betty (Sutherland) Teeter (room mate on left), and new friends, Victoria and Gertie. We were attending Saksatoon University winter school in 1940 taking one of two required steps toward securing a Permanent First Class Certificate.

The other requirement was a summer school course. The Department of Education would have preferred that I take this in Saskatchewan, but finally let me take it in Victoria, B.C.I did get to take classes in two of my favourite subjects, art and music, but was disappointed in my grade in folk dancing. I bit off a little more than I could chew as I really was just a beginner.

PROVINCE OF BRITISH COLUMBIA
SUMMER SCHOOL OF EDUCATION
GRADE REPORT

Attach in Record Book. Session. S. S. 1941.

Classification of Student.	Number of Course.	NAME OF COURSE	Units of Credit.	Grades.
1st I.	10	Educational Psychology	1¼	A
	56	Mod. Art for the Middle & Upper Grades.	1¼	A
	175	Adv. Folk & Chr. Dancing	1¼	B

Report of McConville, Mary, Ponteix, Sask. Date: Aug. 11/41

Clerk: M;R.

SYSTEM OF GRADES: A, honour; B, C, intermediate; D, low pass; E, failure; F, failure, repeat course; W, withdrawn; S, satisfactory; I, incomplete.

2M-840-6506

PROVINCE OF SASKATCHEWAN

DEPARTMENT OF EDUCATION

Interim First Class Certificate

It is Hereby Certified that Mary McConville, having complied with the conditions respecting academic qualification and professional training as prescribed by the Department of Education of the Province of Saskatchewan for First Class Teachers has been awarded an Interim First Class Certificate valid until the thirty-first day of December, 1941.

Dated at Regina this twenty-seventh day of June, 1938.

Registered No. 522-38.

Countersigned

Registrar

Minister of Education

Above, Interim First Class Certificate. Below, Permanent First Class Certificate. Notice how much fancier the Interim is than the Permanent. Seems backward.

PROVINCE OF SASKATCHEWAN

DEPARTMENT OF EDUCATION

Permanent First Class Certificate

It is Hereby Certified that Mary McConville, having complied with the conditions respecting academic qualification, professional training and successful experience as prescribed by the Department of Education of the Province of Saskatchewan for First Class Teachers, has been awarded a Permanent First Class Certificate valid during the pleasure of the Minister.

Dated at Regina this sixteenth day of July, 1942.

Registered No. 265-42

Countersigned

Registrar

Minister of Education

Curriculums

One can hardly tell about schools without covering, at least in general, curriculums — the basic teaching manual. **The Saskatchewan Archives** sent me partial copies for the years 1914, 1931, 1941 and 1984. Though the 1914 one was before my time, I saw few fundamental changes between its contents and what I was being taught in my Quimper school years. However, this was not true for 1941 as there had been an almost across-the-board textbook change in 1938-39, my first year of teaching. When I got married in 1945 and moved to the States, I no longer had direct connections to Saskatchewan's school system. However, as I looked at the 1984 portion I did have, I saw many resemblances to what our own children and grandchildren were learning in school in Yakima. But it wasn't the changes in *content* that struck me nearly as much as the newer philosophies of education and the changes which came into schools with the advent of new technologies, particularly in such fields as copying — all the way from carbon copies and hectograph to color copies; from black and white snapshots to space and underwater videos; from the one big clock on the schoolroom wall to almost every child having their own digital watch; from no machine of any kind in a schoolroom to a computer in almost every room; lastly, from button shoes in 1914 (but lace-ups for our school days, rather than buttons) to today's velcro. (Good riddance, parents, big brothers and sisters and sometimes teachers, too, might say to that ever recurring frequent plea, "Please, can you get this knot out of my shoelace?")

However, in all years, in all kinds of schools and with all curriculums, *one* thing remains constant and crucial in a child's education — what kind of *teachers* do they have over that span of years from their entrance into school to their graduation from high school? What I read just the other day is still true — if society permits an educational system to operate as it should — then "A good teacher will inspire pupils and help them to reach the goals they set for themselves."

Salaries and Certificates

There was not always a direct relationship between salaries and certificates. The economy, the labor market and other factors were often higher regulating factors. For example, records show that *my first teacher* in *1923* was getting the *same* salary with the *same* Permanent First Class Certificate as I was getting during my last six months

(Continued on page 35)

Above, Mary Kelman, Winnie Taylor, Eva Gorrill, Doug McCullough, Alex Kelman, Ed McCullough, Phoebe McConville, Margaret Symington, Maude McConville, Stan Taylor, Donnie Symington, Cliff Taylor, circa 1915. Notice flag rope.

Patriotism and allegiance to Great Britain always fostered.

Four Quimper ponies, circa 1924 (judging by the big hair ribbon style). Picture courtesy of Alice Bjore Collins.

Quimper, as most rural schools of the day, had a Junior Red Cross Society and were proud of the banner they made. Circa 1925.

Quimper pupils — 1927. Notice the broken window. Playing baseball in the basement, the author batted the ball through a window, this one? Families represented here: Kleins, Bjores, Claydons, Benders, McKenzies, Donalds, Goffinets, McConvilles (3), McCoys, Gammies.

Bottom, right: Quimper pupils — 1938. Teacher: Ruth Bush. Pupils: back row: Roland Dumont, Jim McConville, Bob McConville, Jim Cross, Walter Cross; 2nd row: Dennis Shaddock, Jim McKenzie (face obscured); 3rd row: Helen Gammie, Jessie McKenzie, Alma Bjore, Isabelle McConville, Evelyn McConville, Allan Claydon; 4th row: Jim Gammie, Mary McKenzie, Nellie McConville, Olive McConville, Hilda McConville, Ken Donald; 5th row: Audrey Claydon, Maggie McKenzie, Theodora Claydon, Dorothy Gammie, Gladys Gammie, Aileen McCoy, Marion Cross; 6th row: Raymond Bjore, Willard McCoy, Fernand Dumont, Roderick McKenzie.

Quimper's Grade VIII class — 1929. They would take their department examinations at another school. Pupils: Louis Bjore, Willie Bender, Alice Bjore, Miena Klein, Mary Donald, Andy McConville.

1995. Four former students of Quimper school: Mary (McConville) Stensrud, Karen (McConville) Atherton (daughter of Robert McConville), Nellie (McConville) Schmidt, and Arnold Bjore. The actual school sat, as Arnold said, "Where you see that little mound over there."

1955. Concert productions barely kept alive — few pupils, no music and community support and enthusiasm at low ebb.

A sorry sight. The old Quimper School as it looks now (1996), far from its home site.

Photo courtesy of Mrs. Carl Belza.

My steps along the way to becoming a teacher.

Top, left to right: Quimper School in first locaton; Quimper School, 1939, in second location (picture courtesy Bill Busch); Center: Moose Jaw Normal School where most from southwest Saskatchewan took their training — one year at this time. I attended in 1937-38; Bottom: Mac Coleman is also a writer. Four of his books are listed in Bibliography for Chapter 7 on Play.

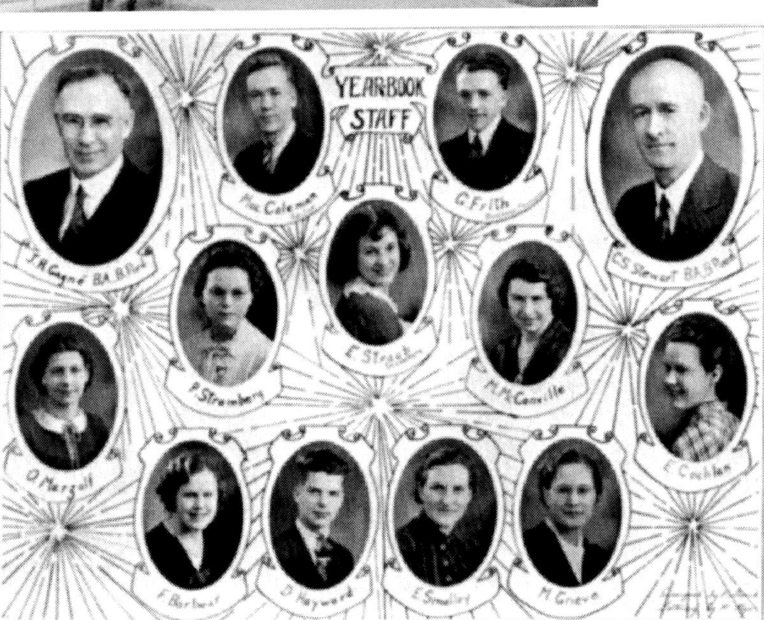

Room B put on H.M.S. Pinafore by Gilbert and Sullivan in which I had the part of Little Buttercup. This was one of the most challenging things I did at Normal School. My disguise let me be "another person."

of teaching in *1945*. Some teachers hired near the time of school closings, with perhaps neither training nor experience, were finding that an offer of *six* times as much as I got in my first year, was still too little to entice them to a rural school.

A few details on salaries during Depression-Dust-Bowl years may prove interesting for young people of today and will surely revive memories for those of us now in our 70's, 80's or even 90's.

In August of 1938 I was hired at the annual rate of $400.00, but my district could not pay even this amount, so I was on relief (welfare) at the same time getting a monthly check for $7.56 plus a bag of flour — both of which were immediately turned over to my landlord (the lady of the house had died so hired girls were working there). My board and room was $15.00 a month, so I owed the difference. At Christmas I got my first check — $50. Out of it and a similar one in June, I left owing nothing, but the *rest of my salary* was in *IOU's*. These were all eventually paid off with a little interest by either the government or the school district.

Even at this, salaries were beginning to edge upwards when I started to teach and there were more than enough teachers seeking positions. If you didn't have experience, you might not get a job at all. You hoped that your other qualifications would do the trick. For my second year of teaching, I learned that I was chosen over another because of my hand writing. Also, it was a big boost to one's chances if they could play the piano. (How often in so many ways have we Jim McConvilles been thankful for the gift of lessons from Dad and Mom!)

To illustrate just how crucial *experience* was, there was a father — a little better off, I guess, than most at that time — who actually *paid a school board* to *hire* his daughter so that the following year she could put on her application that she had *experience*.

Discipline and Punishments

A school with no discipline is a disaster. Those who want to learn can't, and those cutting-up have acquired terrible personal power. Because it was thought that a man teacher might get a school gone out of control back into shape better than a woman, some schools advertised for a *male-only applicant*. Others didn't specify the gender, but did put "good disciplinarian wanted." I *very carefully* avoided answering such ads so — would one say — fate stepped in when I came to a school that had had *just that in their ad*? The school I *had* applied for had just hired their teacher, so they passed on all left-over applications to their neighboring school. When I got the phone call and agreed to come, I had no inkling of this being one of the qualifications they hoped I would have. But it didn't prove to be as bad as I would have expected had I seen the ad. And this was the school where I met the man who became my husband!

Nevertheless, I found having to keep good discipline one of the most stressful aspects of teaching. I knew it *had* to be done so I *did it* and inspectors spoke well of me in this regard. But it was still too hard on me and one fall I didn't even apply for a school as I took time to contemplate just whether or not to even stay in a teaching career. The school I did go to the following term proved to be the one I liked the best of all in a number of ways, so that my faith in my ability to teach well was built up, and some close friendships from those days are a treasured part of my life today.

Though there was the advice at Normal School and again from the secretary who greeted you at your school, not to be reluctant to use the strap, *there* that *ugly* thing greeted me every time I opened that drawer in my desk. I never used it but came perilously close a time or two when facing a situation where, as they say, "You use it or lose it." In most cases, if respect is gained when first on the job, other milder forms of punishment will suffice — standing in the corner, writing something a hundred times on the blackboard at noon or recess, or keeping them in at recess or after school.

At one school some of the children were fond of *playing* school *at* school on cold winter days. I would be at my desk eating my lunch and in their eyes, paying no attention at all to their play-acting. Talk about seeing yourself as others see you! But it was good too to see that they liked their teacher.

A School Scene, Friday Jan. 6, 1933

At the beginning of this chapter I tried to take you back in time to a warm September day in Quimper School in 1914. Can you now move your imaginations ahead to a winter day in February 1933? Same schoolroom — another excellent teacher and many of the same family names on the roll. But there are *many differences* too — a crowded classroom — high school students in the big desks studying with their correspondence courses — priscilla curtains at the windows and house plants on the window sills — a hot air register on the wall with a furnace in the basement — a gas lamp hanging from the ceiling instead of coal oil lamps in wall brackets — a piano instead of a pump organ — fountain pens instead of straight pens — a blizzard outside instead of sunshine. The teacher and students are dressed in similar fashion to what we were wearing later in the 50's or even nowadays. A set of **Compton's Pictured Encyclopedias** is on hand which we could go to whenever we wished. (Our teacher, Miss Rogers, had brought them with her.) Lastly, though we were deep into the Depression, there was no sign of dejection in our schoolroom — just an everyday-looking rural school atmosphere. If a younger one needed help, an older one already finished with their own assignment might be asked to lend a hand. Because it was now February, the old Christmas-design chalk border was being rubbed off and two or three pupils who liked doing this sort of thing, were busy putting on a new one, which might have been homemade. While two held each end of the stencil in place, another would pat it with brushes loaded with chalk dust to make the dust go through the pin prick holes. This put the outline on the blackboard. Matching up the ends as they went, the design would finally stretch along the whole top. As they proceeded, there could be quite a few following up with colored chalk, until it wasn't long before this *job* — or was it mostly fun — was completed. All were happy with themselves and knew it would please others too - especially perhaps the parents who would soon see it when they all came to the dance that Friday night.

At recesses and noon the *furnace room* was the boys' domain — after they had taken care of the horses. Girls may have been *drivers* or had ridden to school , but the boys gallantly took care of their horses during the day. Because the teenaged girls wanted to look their best at the dance, their cloakroom was turned into a *beauty parlor* for recesses and noons on Thursdays and Fridays. Some girls had become "unlicensed" hair dressers, while others made "appointments" to get their hair done. *Done* meant getting it waved with hairset made of the slimy goop you got when you boiled and strained flax seed. Some could comb out their own hair when it was dry while others had a second "appointment" for this.

There was lingering euphoria and talk about the Christmas concert, always the highlight of the year in just about every rural district. Each school could, I'm sure, fill a book with *their own* concert stories, but many of the best of these were compiled into a beautiful coffee-table book by John Charyk, titled, "The Biggest Day of the Year". (His other books you will find listed in the mini bibliography at the end of this chapter.) Quimper gets a nod in some of his books including this one on Christmas concerts.

It was good during these Depression years to have the Lallier girls in our school. The other French-speaking families in our district — Dumonts and Goffinets, had always sent their children to Quimper and the Klein children, who were Catholic, attended the convent part time, but were with us most of the time. The Lallier family had, on the other hand, always attended convent school in Ponteix, so strange as it seems, until they came to Quimper, we would not have known them had we met them on the street! How sad to be neighbors geographically, but strangers otherwise!

Some Move Back East

This family moved down east to Quebec in 1938 and we didn't see any of them again for many, many years. We did keep in touch though, through letters, pictures and phone calls.

When my sister, **Nellie,** and I were attending a folk dance festival in Windsor, Ontario in 1987 and visiting old Quimper friends, how delighted we were when three of the Lallier sisters and their brother, Joe, drove many, many miles from **Black Lake**, **Quebec** to **Cobourg**, **Ontario** for an all too brief visit when we all met in **Mildred Cross's** home. (You will see Mildred in a number of Quimper pictures as she was very active in our community before they too, the Earl Cross family, moved back to Ontario, as did a third Quimper family, the Donalds.)

Normal School in Moose Jaw

At this time, in the 30's, there were really few choices for girls who wanted a career — teaching, nursing and business was about it. Well, by quick elimination of the last two, that left *teaching*. In 1937 our family as most others, was about as hard up for cash as possible, but dad had one last resort — cashing in a life insurance policy. By working for my board and room, it would be possible to go.

I was barely started when who should I meet on a street in **Moose Jaw** but **Mr. Lallier**. He couldn't speak much English and I've already told you of my limited French, so we surely looked a bit odd trying to converse that day. Later, I checked with **Geraldine** as to what we had each understood from the other. Yes, the family was about to move back east to Quebec, she confirmed, and her dad got it right that I was going to Normal School.

This year, my first away from home, had some real high spots but

The author off to work — her first year of teaching, 1938. The aviator hat may not be much for looks, but was wonderful for warmth!

Phoebe as a nurse in a play, but in real life she did a lot of nursing, too.

A secretary in the making. Nellie ready to go to class. Regina, 1945.

also some of my lowest. A fellow classmate, **Mac Coleman** has written a series of four books. Once Upon (1) a Childhood; (2) A Little Town — (Vanguard); (3) The World and Me; (4) Toronto, the third being the one telling of his Normal School Days and his first years of teaching. I related so well to many things he spoke of, though of course, there were great differences, too — the most obvious perhaps being that he had much more self-confidence than I, and he rented a room and batched it while I worked for my room and board. We were both in **Gilbert** and **Sullivan**'s H.M.S. Pinafore, so he calls me "Little Buttercup" in his autograph. This happy performance followed on the heels of one of my most devastating experiences. Because I was so nervous, I tested *lowest* in our room on ability in *music*. And in working for board and room, I had both highs and lows. *One high* — the privilege of practicing piano accompaniment for a professional singer — *one low* working for a lady with a grating personality.

Romances

Even having both certificate and teaching job in hand, it was possible, maybe even, probable, to have some ulterior motives lurking in the back corners of the mind — "Maybe I'll find my life's mate in this new phase of my life in this spot where everything and everyone is new to me."

In turn, those who are native to this spot are casting glances towards the new teacher. Quimper, as did most districts, produced a few such romances. I can only speak for a limited part of the forty-four years Quimper operated as a school, the years from 1923 through 1945. Couples who found each other in these years were (not in chronological order):

Bill Busch and Ethel McConville
Ed McCullough and Madge Rogers
Alex Kelman and Ruth Bush
Bill McCullough and Lottie Fitzgerlad
Aylmer Boulter and Emma Daniels
Nellie Foss and Garfield Gorrill (through this couple was already married when she became a teacher at Quimper).

But other Quimper young folks did not have to make connections with strangers. Some found their sweethearts either in a fellow classmate or in a nearby district where they often had known one another from childhood, through family visiting or inter-community events. In this category we have these couples:

Robert McConville and Alma Bjore
Dennis Shaddock and Lorraine Perkins
Mary Kelman and Howard Broley
Lena McCullough and Curly Gunter
Alice Bjore and Micky Collins
Gerald Robins and Alice McConville
Evelyn McConville and Clarence Fox
Hilda McConville and Jim Hardement
Minnie McConville and Kelso Walls
Mary Donald and Frank Adshead
Gladys Gammie and Claude Baragar
Charlie McCoy and Nellie McBlain
Wilma McCoy and Eldon Adams
Phoebe McConville and Wellington Simpson
Isabelle McConville and Stan Cadel
Andrea Gammie and Robbie McBlain
Walter Cross and Ruby Baragar
Marion Cross and Clifford Simpson

The Teachers and Pupils of Quimper 1914-1958

Code: "F" = These pupils attended the first day in 1914.

Code: "L" = These names were on the last annual report.

QUIMPER PUPILS: Alphabetically by letter of last names only and minus middle names and nicknames. Spellings may vary according to different records, for instance, the Klein family anglicized some first

Bjore, Louis
Bjore, Alice
Bjore, Alma
Bjore, Arnold
Bjore, Raymond
Burns, Violet
Barnard, Arnold
Barnard, George
Bender, William
Bender, Freda
Bender, Jack
Bender, Albert
Bender, Manuel
Bender, Fred
Beliveau, Gerald
Beliveau, Norman
Beliveau, Giles
Cross, Walter
Cross, Marion
Cross, Jim
Cross, Allison
Claydon, Tom
Claydon, Connie
Claydon, Dorothy
Claydon, Allan
Cyrenne, Lorraine (L)
Cyrenne, Gilles (L)
Chalman, Lana
Cross, Ruth
Cross, William
Cross, Millicent (L)
Cross, David (L)
Cross, Nora (L)
Claydon, Betty (L)
Claydon, Richard (L)
Claydon, Jack or (John)
Claydon, Theo
Claydon, Audrey
Claydon, Joseph
Donald, Mary
Donald, Bessie
Donald, Gordon
Donald, Kenneth
Donald, Keith
Dumont, Maurice
Dumont, Camille
Dumont, Madeleine
Dumont, Roland
Dumont, Fernand
Dumont, George
Dumont, Theophile
Dumonceaux, Mildred
Dumonceaux, Paul
Dumonceaux, Albert
Dumonceaux, Helen
Dumonceaux, Peter
Dumonceaux, Agnes
Dumonceaux, Sylvia
Dumonceaux, Maurice
Dumonceaux, Gilbert (L)
Dumonceaux, Hector (L)
Dumonceaux, Marie
Dumonceaux, Marcel
Dumonceaux, Edna

Dumonceaux, Arthur
Gorrill, Harold
Gorrill, Eva
Gorrill, Jervis
Gorrill, Russel
Gammie, Minnie (F)
Gammie, Helen
Gammie, Gladys
Gammie, Dorothy
Gammie, Jimmy
Goffinet, John
Goffinet, Joseph
Goffinet, Marguerite (L)
Goffinet, Paul
Goffinet, Rose (L)
Gammie, Elvina
Gammie, Andrea
Hobbins, Marie
Innes, Bruce
Jacaobsen, Kathleen
Kelman, Mary (F)
Kelman, Alex (F)
Klein, Nellie
Klein, Catherine
Klein, Marie
Klein, Miena
Klein, Trouda
Klein, Anna
Lasante, Leo
Lasante, Arno
Lasante, Peter
Lemaire, Paul
Lallier, Ernestine
Lallier, Julienne
Lallier, Geraldine
Lallier, Therese
Lallier, Cecile
Lallier, Joseph
McCullough, Lena
McCullough, James
McCullough, Doug (F)
McCullough, Eddie (F)
McCullough, Kate
McConville, Phoebe
McConville, Maude
McConville, Andy
McConville, Alice
McConville, Evelyn
McConville, Hilda
McConville, Walter
McConville, Minnie
McConville, Ethel
McConville, Jim
McConville, Isabelle
McConville, Olive
McConville, Robert
McConville, Mary
McConville, Nellie
McConville, Karen (L)
McCoy, Charlie (F)
McCoy, Wilma
McCoy, Terence
McCoy, Marilyn (L)
McCoy, Willard
McCoy, Aileen
McCullough, Lena
McCullough, Eddie
McCullough, Kit
McKean, Russel
McKenzie, William
McKenzie, Jessie
McKenzie, Mary
McKenzie, James
McKenzie, Maggie
McKenzie, Bill
McKenzie, Norman
McKenzie, Ronald
McKenzie, Roderick
Morin, Suzanne
Robins, Kenneth
Robins, Jean
Robinson, Albert
Symington, Margaret (F)
Symington, Don
Shaddock, Dennis
Schafer, Leonard
Schafer, Florence
Simpson, Jimmie
Taylor, Winnefred (F)
Taylor, Clifford
Taylor, Stan
Total: 155

Quimper Teachers

Established March 19, 1914

Year	Teacher(s)
1914-1915	No Teacher Listed
1915-1916	Buss, Ruth
	Davis, Jas. E.
1916-1917	Davis, Jas. E.
	Foss, Agnes
1917-1918	Foss, Gertrude
	Foss, Agnes
1918-1919	Foss, Agnes
	Jewitt, Mary Alma
1919-1920	Fitzgerald, Lottie
1920-1921	Fitzgerald, Lottie
1921-1922	Beauchene, Victoria
1922-1923	Pollock, Elwood
1923-924	Boulter, Aylmer
1924-1925	Boulter, Aylmer
1926-1927	Armstrong, Annie
1927-1928	Armstrong, Annie
	Wynne-Jones, Margaret
1928-1929	Wynne-Jones, Margaret
	Searles, Marion
	Ellis, Ruth
1919-1930	Searles, Marion
	Ellis, Mrs. Esther
	Thompson, Jennie L.
1930-1931	Thompson, Jennie L.
1931-1932	Rogers, Margaret
1932-1933	Rogers, Margaret
1933-1934	Rogers, Margaret
	Miller, Kenneth M.
1934-1935	Miller, Robert K.
1935-1936	Miller, Robert K.
1936-1937	Bush, Jeanette Ruth
1937-1938	Bush, Jeanette Ruth
1938-1939	Bush, Jeanette Ruth
1939-1940	Wiggins, May
1940-1941	Child, Georgie
	Kelman, Mrs. J.R.
	Busch, William John
1941-1942	Busch, William John
1942-1943	Busch, William John
	Zaremba, Mrs. Adelina
1943-1944	Zaremba, Mrs. Adelina
	Gorrill, Mrs. Nellie
1944-1945	Gorrill, Mrs. Nellie
1945-1946	Gorrill, Mrs. Nellie
	Corbin, Wayne A.
1946-1947	Claydon, Theodore
1947-1948	Woolger, Theodore
1948-1949	Sloman, Elsie
1949-1950	McCoy, W.B.
	Blake, Clare H.
1950-1951	Watson, Audrey
1951-1952	McCarthy, Ceona
1952-1953	Woolger, Theodore
1953-1954	Woolger, Theodore
1954-1955	Woolger, Theodore
1955-1956	Mahon, Frances
1956-1957	Nostbakken, Geraldine
1957-1958	Sincennes, Noella
	Hanlon, Patricia
1958	(Fall) Closed Students went to either Aneroid or Ponteix

names later on — e.g. Meina — Mina.

The Doors Close

The doors of Quimper School closed for the last time in the fall of 1958, its few remaining pupils divided between Ponteix and Aneroid. After twenty one years, **Charlie McCoy** no longer had his job of secretary. An era had ended with a whimper, not a shout. The school building itself would be moved and function as a school for another year or two down near **Val Marie** in the **Wood River District**. The barn would be in use again less than a mile away at the **Walter Cross** farm. (His grandparents had been Quimper's very first settlers.)

1995 saw the location of the Quimper School marked, finally,

(Continued on page 44)

Family Farm Heritage Award

presented to

ROBERT J McCONVILLE

to honour the heritage of your family farm of which SW¼ 23-8-11 W3M has been continuously operated by members of the family since 1910

Presented in celebration of Saskatchewan's 75th Anniversary Year 1980

Hon. Gordon MacMurchy
Minister of Agriculture

Hon. Ed Tchorzewski
Minister-in-charge of
Celebrate Saskatchewan

When Saskatchewan was celebrating its Diamond Jubilee in 1980 the government gave a Heritage Plaque to all families who were still on the original homestead. In Quimper there were five who qualified — Robert McConville, Joe Goffinet, Allan Claydon, Dennis Shaddock, and Bill McKenzie.

"Kissing gophers." As a young couple views the destruction of these prolific little rodents: <u>**She**</u>: But what cute little animals! Do we really *have* to kill them? <u>**He**</u>: Well, if we don't, there will be very little of our crop left, so let's get this poison out before it gets too hot.

Erma Froyman in the Erinlea district in 1919 won first prize for sending in the most gopher tails. When Mr. Donald was reeve, his kids got the stinky job of counting such tails before they were burned.

July 1987. An excellent picture of our farm 9 miles southeast of Ponteix, Saskatchewan.

with a newly erected marble plaque. It is hoped that seeing it will remind following generations of what went on in *that spot* so long ago — not only the education of its many pupils during forty-four years, but of wonderful community events which took place there — church services, Sunday school, whist drives, concerts, political meetings, young peoples' meetings, and last but not least, the forming of friendships that are on-going to this day.

The Neighborly Man — By Edgar Guest

Some are eager to be famous, some are striving to be great,
Some are toiling to be leaders of their nation or their state,
And in every man's ambition, if we only understood,
There is much that's fine and splendid; every hope is mostly good.
So I cling unto the notion that contented I will be
If the men upon life's pathway find a needed friend in me.

I rather like to putter around the walks and yards of life,
To spray at night the roses that are burned and browned with strife;
To eat a frugal dinner, but always to have a chair
For the unexpected stranger that my simple meal would share.
I don't care to be a traveler, I would rather be the one
Sitting calmly by the roadside helping weary travelers on.

I'd like to be a neighbor in the good old-fashioned way,
Finding much to do for others, but not over much to say.
I like to read the papers, but I do not yearn to see
What the journal of the morning has been moved to say of me;
In the silences and shadows I would live my life and die
And depend for fond remembrance on some grateful passers-by.

I guess I wasn't fashioned for the brilliant things of earth,
Wasn't gifted much with talent or designed for special worth,
But was just sent here to putter with life's little odds and ends
And keep a simple corner where the stirring highway bends,
And if folks should chance to linger, worn and weary through the day
To do some needed service and to cheer them on their way.

From **A Heap O'Livin'**, ©1916.

Bibliography

Canadian Readers, First through Fifth
The Little White Schoolhouse, © 1968, John Charyk
The Pulse of the Community, © 1970, John Charyk
Those Bittersweet School Days, © 1977, John Charyk
Syrup Pails and Gopher Tails, © 1983, John Charyk
The Biggest Day of the Year, © 1985, John Charyk
When the School Horse Was King, © 1983, John Charyk
The Prairie World, ©1969, David Costello
NOTE: I also have some school texts used in the 30's and 40's — History, Geography and Hygiene.

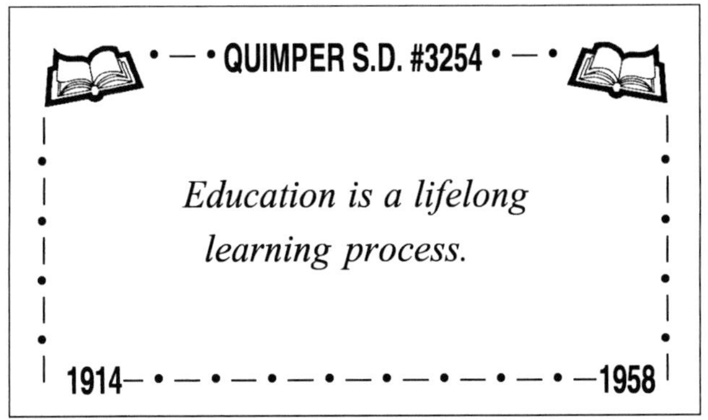

There is a right time and a right way to do everything but we know so little. — Eccl. 8:6

2 — The Western World Prior to 1914

A Changed Attitude

Have you changed as I have? In my youth I very frequently voiced my dislike of history. To me it seemed mostly just memorizing the dates of battles, wars, and treaties; learning who was head of state here and there or tracking the routes of those explorers searching for the Northwest Passage. Of course my thinking has matured over the years, but it was the giant eruption of **Mount St. Helens** in 1980 which sent me and countless others scurrying to history books. At first my interest was centered on *volcanoes* but inevitably I was led down many other pathways: the *migration of peoples* — why, how and where; *how people lived* in different environments; and even the *reasons* for *those conflicts* I had been memorizing the dates of so long ago. Many museums and a few trips have also enlarged my interest in the past. And how can one study history without making *connections* with geography, politics, languages, religions, industries, and, in fact, every facet of life?

However, for my purpose in this book, I will try to pass on to you just enough of the results of my many engrossing hours of research to provide a glimpse of where **Quimper** fits into the picture. Perhaps this can be likened to finding the very last — the tiniest of tiny pieces to complete a giant jigsaw of North America.

A map made around 1545. Ancestors of Quimperites were all in Europe, mostly serfs no doubt, under the feudal system, not yet knowing of the huge land mass in which their descendants would be living some day.

Prehistoric Times

To most Quimperites, volcanoes are seldom a topic of conversation, I would guess. After all, not even *one* is in sight and the effects of those which erupt far away have minimal, if any, discernible effects on their lives.

However, when some *volcanic ash* did come their way in *May of 1980*, and most everyone got some first hand news about **Mount St. Helens** from friends and relatives who were directly affected by its eruption, they quickly came to the realization that even volcanoes far off in the **Cascade Range** *could indeed* impact lives at great distances, even those in Quimper.

After all, their fertile soil is in great measure due to volcanic action in prehistoric times, along with glaciers and ice ages alternating with eras of tropical climate. And seeing the recovery of the devastated area around Mount St. Helens illustrates the process of how natural forces gave the prairies its *grass,* or *wool* as it was sometimes called. In the tall grass areas, before the land came under cultivation, it could even hide a man.

Delmar McLean's House

To bring into focus but one close connection between a volcanic ashfall and a prairie home, you can read in the **Simmie History Book** about **Delmar McLean's** ash house. He had found on his farm a pit of clay-like material which was actually volcanic ash. Solid chunks of it he used as bricks for his house, while the softer deposits he mixed with straw and water to use as mortar. However, with a big dam being built not far away, his house was in imminent danger of being flooded as waters were backing up to form a lake. So the family, working against time, knocked the house down, loaded it on a truck and moved it to **Swift Current**, setting it up again there, but with the walls only half their previous thickness of seventeen inches. The cost was estimated at approximately *half* of one built of *lumber*, and proved to be very cool in summer and warm in winter. (I wonder how many other prairie folk had this building material at hand but failed to recognize it.) This ingenious man figured out a number of other uses for ash also. Mixed with water he used it as a floor covering which, when his wife painted it and topped it with sponge work in two or three colors, completely disguised the divisions between the floor boards. Ash also served as a marvelous hand cleaner. (Was the "Skat" we used as kids made with ash also, do you suppose?) And because he mixed it into the hen's feed, they laid hard-shelled eggs. It also proved to be good for certain repair jobs, being used just as we would use many of today's commercial fillers

So how would you draw a buffalo from a word description given to you by some 16th century explorer?

The first fur traders had headquarters on the St. Lawrence River. Later, with the establishment of the Hudson's Bay Company, the whole of western Canada east of the Rockies was involved.

This map illustrates very graphically Canada's wealth of trees. The grass area in contrast is very small, but its soil is it's wealth. How wonderful it seemed to prairie homesteaders not to have to precede their first plantings with the back-breaking job of clearing the land of trees! Notice the treed area on the prairies in the Cypress Hills. The park belt receives 14 to 19 inches of precipitation, the plains area 11 to 15 inches. Northwest winds prevail in sunny weather, southeast winds give promise of rain or snow.

and cleaners. He even found it satisfactory for cleaning teeth. (My dentist told me that they import sterile, graded volcanic ash from Italy for this purpose.) None of these uses, of course, begin to approach its value as an *ingredient in fertile soil.* So let us be grateful that in those years so very long ago, our Creator placed some volcanoes *over there,* had them *erupt* from time to time, set up a wind of just the right direction and at sufficient velocity to send ash in **Quimper's** direction, so that, over time, after it was incorporated into the soil, it would help make that soil so fertile that Saskatchewan farmers would be able to grow some of the best wheat in the world.

Coal and Oil

When the West was running on raw horse power, there was little need for these wonderful energy sources of *coal* and *oil* far below the good hunting, ranching or agricultural land. Oh, people knew they were superior to wood and candles for heat and light, but the *real need* for coal only became crucial when the iron horses on railroads and steamboats on the rivers were so numerous as to require huge quantities for their boilers. Factories, too, required enormous amounts. The need for oil and its main bi-product, gas, came into even clearer focus when those huge airliners began to dominate the skies. (Have you read how many gallons their tanks hold?) How fortunate were **Alberta** and **Saskatchewan** when geologists discovered they had unbelievably large deposits of oil! There have been laws and lawsuits over *who* owns what is *on top*, the land, or what is *underneath,* the minerals. In the eastern half of Saskatchewan the homesteaders *had mineral rights* on their property, but by the time the western half of the province was settled, the government had wised up, as they say today, and mineral rights no longer went with the land. During the Depression, however, most eastern Saskatchewan farmers sold their rights for a bit of ready cash, little thinking that in a few years oil would be found on their land. Now those "rooster heads" are bobbing everywhere. (I wonder about those continuous flames we see at some oil well sites. It seems so very wasteful to our untrained eyes.)

Lake Agassiz

Though we read of **Lake Agassiz** in our school texts, and *lived* on the very land which for long years in prehistoric times was under water, it is still very difficult to realize that this enormously large lake covered millions of square miles as it stretched from **Alberta** to

Manitoba. Only recently did I learn that it was an ice sheet blocking the flow of rivers into Hudson's Bay that caused the lake to form, and that when the ice melted back sufficiently to allow the rivers to flow again in their previous courses, that Lake Agassiz drained into Hudson Bay once more. (How well I remember all those tiny seashells on our alkali flat!) When travelling down the lane at the Shulstad farm in northern Minnesota (Delia is my sister-in-law) it is very clear that the rolling hills and woods to the east are beyond the lake escarpment, while the flat black-soil area to the west was once covered with the waters of Lake Agassiz.

Now all that remains of this huge ancient body of water are **Lake Winnepeg** and two smaller lakes nearby. In an old geography text I learned something else about the waters in this valley. When the ice pack was in place, the Red River ran *south* to the Mississippi, but after it melted, the river *reversed* direction, once again letting the water drain into Hudson's Bay.

Cypress Hills

Before we leave this section on prehistoric times, it is necessary to tell of **Cypress Hills** — one of the most unique and beautiful areas of our province, though we share about a quarter of its 1000 sq. mile area with Alberta. Here you will find flora and fauna found nowhere else because, at 4,516 feet altitude, it is the highest point in Saskatchewan. This caused the ice cap to split and go on either side. But when we were at Cypress Hills a few years ago, it was a *fragrance* rather than a *scene* that really caught our attention. It was that of a flower dear to all prairie folks, the wild rose. The bush on which these flowers are found in the wild is a straggly sort, but here we were beside a large, compact, symmetrically-shaped rose bush in full bloom, so strongly emitting *that perfume*, we stood for awhile in pure ecstasy. We had never seen wild roses on such a bush so we wonder if our gratitude is due some horticulturist who has done an outstanding feat of plant breeding in order to give us such a delightful experience.

Connecting the Old and New Worlds

The Europeans called these two huge continents the *New* World, a term the Indians object to as it is *their Old* World! Caucasians glibly say they *discovered* it while its natives say they *weren't discovered*, they knew *who* they were and *where* they were and didn't need to be *discovered*! Nevertheless, we will speak in white man's terms for this book. The discovery of the New World was, as we all know, a serendipity. Explorers were *not* looking for a new land. They had *set sail for the west* hoping to get to *the East* with its spices and other treasures — those things they had been enjoying for many years. However, these luxuries were now in danger of being cut off by the Turks, who were marauding the land trade routes. Some scientists were by this time fully convinced that the world *was round* and likewise some learned seamen, two of whom were **Columbus** and **Cabot**.

But almost four hundred years prior to their expeditions, other Europeans had not only *set foot* on the North American continent, but had even established a *settlement* in the area they named **Vinland**, later to be called New England. The Ericsson family — the father's nickname **Eric the Red,** from his red hair, and his oldest son, **Leif the Lucky** and two other brothers — were **Vikings** whose home was in **Iceland**. But Eric the Red, though a quick, strong, skillful sailor and a good farmer, had a hot temper, and in a quarrel had killed a man, and for punishment had been banished from the country. Many years prior to this, a Viking had been blown off course by a storm and had reached an *unknown* land. This tale had been told at firesides for many years so now, without a country, he decided to see if he could find this land again. He did. In fact, he decided to settle there, but first he would try to persuade friends back home to join him. He had called this land **Greenland** because he said "There's nothing like a fair name to bring settlers." Sometime later, after they had their settlement established, others got lost in a thick fog and came to a *different* land, one with trees. Years later, his son Leif, now grown-up and himself an able seaman, decided to find once more, this land of trees. He was joined by thirty-five other bold sailors. They were off and travelling south. By their descriptions, it is believed they found **Labrador** and **Newfoundland** before finally landing farther south, where they found luscious grapes. They wintered here in this pleasant spot building log huts, catching salmon in the river and living quite comfortably. The following year they took a cargo of lumber back to Greenland. On a subsequent trip, a younger brother, **Thorwald**, encountered Indians at Vinland. They fought and Thorwald was killed. Ten years elapsed before a second settlement took place here. But, again, they quarrelled with the Indians and this time gave up the venture for good.

All the explorers who came later, starting with **Columbus**, were obsessed with the quest for the *Northwest Passage.* To them this huge land mass, at first thought to *be the East* — thus the erroneous name of

Indians for the natives — was just one big barrier which just *had* to have *some* way *around* it, *over* it, or *through* it. They had tunnel vision, seeming not to comprehend that the riches they *were* finding — the cod fish, the lumber, the fertile land, and the fur bearing animals, would far exceed the value of what they were so desperately in search of — the spices, perfumes, silks and other luxury goods of **The East**. Loyalty to their native country was often not as strong as to some sovereign who would provide money for their expeditions. For example, **Columbus** and **Cabot** were both born in **Genoa**, Italy, but Columbus claimed land for **Spain** and Cabot (his Italian name **Giovani Caboto**) claimed land for **England**. When the fur trade became the all encompassing business in the New World, the land itself seemed secondary to the fur bearing animals roaming upon it. It was interesting to read again — this time with my positive, curious attitude — about these explorers, the rivalry between the **Hudson's Bay Company** and the **Nor'Westers**, and just *how names* were chosen for the *rivers* they discovered and the *trading posts* they established. The first forts or posts on the **St. Lawrence** were followed by those on **Hudson Bay**, finally, in leapfrog fashion, by inland ones on all the main rivers — even as far west as the Columbia. (I thought of giving thumbnail sketches of these explorers, but realized that those of you who wished to review this facet of history could easily hunt up their stories for yourselves. If you would like to have a little humor injected into your search, get the book "Charlie Farquharson's Histry of Canada" by **Don Harron.** [Yes, he misses the "O" on purpose.] His brand of humor is delightful. However, just for easy reference, here are last-name-only explorers: (1) **Cabot**; (2) **Cartier**; (3) **Cook**; (4) **Champlain**; (5) **Hudson**; (6) **Radisson**; (7) **Groseillers**; (8) **LaSalle**; (9) **La Verendrye**; (10) **Mackenzie**; (11) **Hearne**; (12) **Kelsey;** (13) **Thompson.**)

Indians

But all these explorers, fur traders and other white men are Johnny-come-lately folks to the Indians who trod this terrain for thousands of years before. About six main tribes roamed Canada's northern plains — **Sioux, Ojibway, Cree, Gros Ventre, Blackfeet and Assiniboine**. Until the surveying of the 49th parallel, **Indian Territory** was the *whole western plain.* In 1830 the United States instigated one of the saddest chapters in the nation's history, moving all Indians *east* of the Mississippi to *west* of it, to an area that eventually became the state of Okla-

(Continued on page 55)

INDIAN TREATIES (1871-1921)

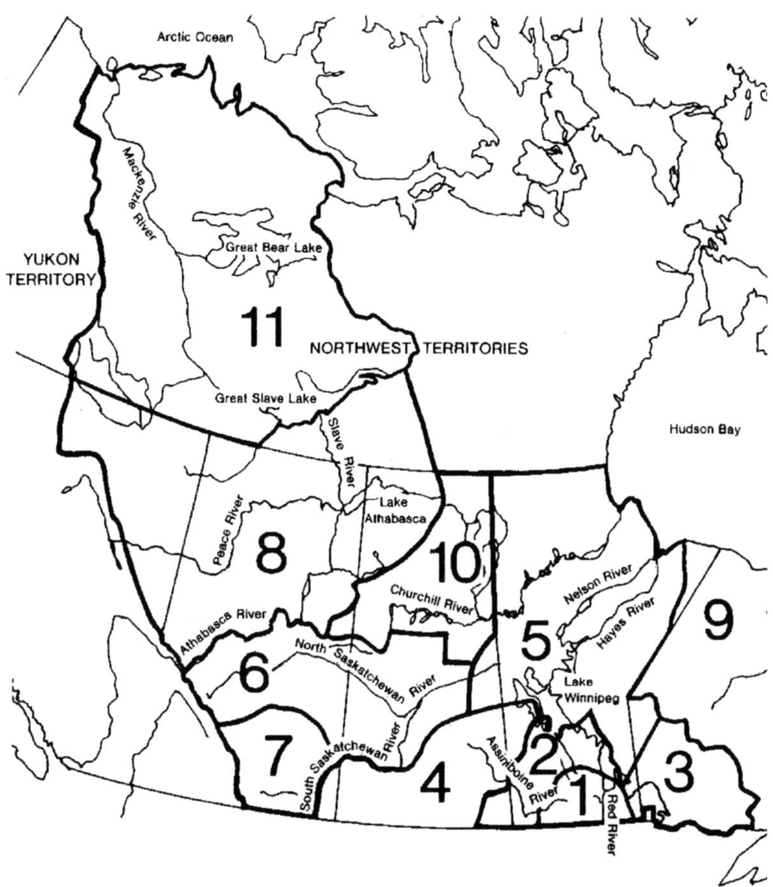

Treaty No. 1, 1871: Ojibwa and Swampy Cree in southern Manitoba

Treaty No. 2, 1871: Ojibwa in southern and southwestern Manitoba, and in southeastern Saskatchewan

Treaty No. 3, 1873: Ojibwa in northwestern Ontario and southeastern Manitoba

Treaty No. 4, 1874: Cree and Ojibwa, mostly in southern Saskatchewan

Treaty No. 5, 1875: Swampy Cree and Ojibwa, mainly in northern Manitoba

Treaty No. 6, 1876: Plains Cree and Wood Cree in central Saskatchewan and central Alberta

Treaty No. 7, 1877: Blackfeet, Blood, Piegan, Sarcee, and Stoney in southern Alberta

Treaty No. 8, 1899: Cree, Beaver, and Chipewyan in northern Alberta, northeastern British Columbia, and south of Great Slave Lake

Treaty No. 9, 1905: Ojibwa and Cree in that part of Ontario whose rivers drain down to Hudson Bay

Treaty No. 10, 1906: Chipewyan and Cree, mostly in northeastern Saskatchewan

Treaty No. 11, 1921: Slave, Dogrib, Loucheux, Hare, and Kutchin in lands drained by the Mackenzie River

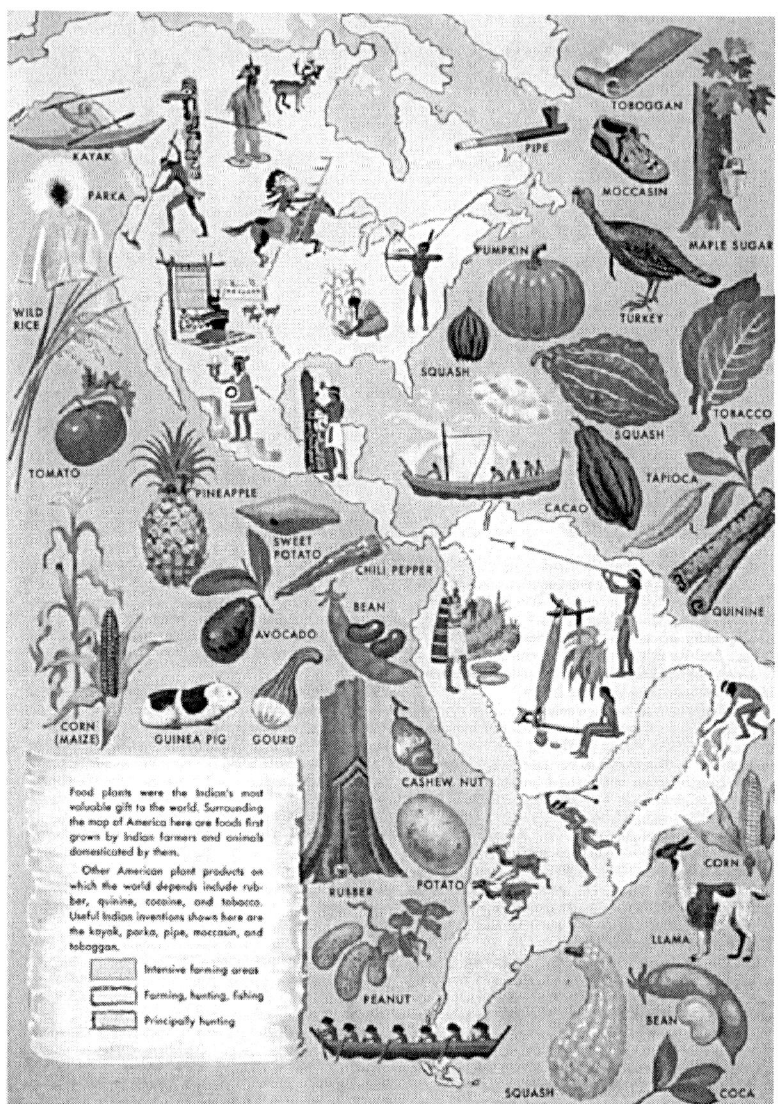

THE AMERICAN INDIAN AND HIS GIFTS TO THE WORLD

Here the Indian's gifts to the world surround a map of the Americas. Sketches on the map indicate Indian ways of life, or cultures, in various regions. In North America are hunters, and women gardening and weaving; in Middle America, an Aztec priest and a Mayan sculptor. In South America are an Inca official in the Andes; a blowgun hunter, a woman squeezing manioc, and a farmer burning underbrush, in the tropical north; and a guanaco hunter and fishermen in a canoe, in the south.

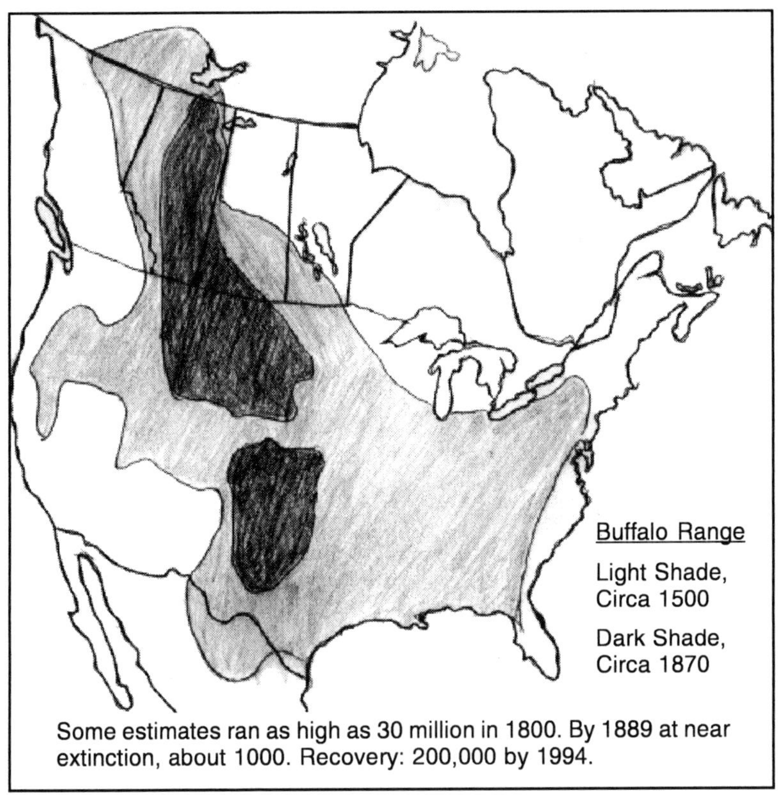

Some estimates ran as high as 30 million in 1800. By 1889 at near extinction, about 1000. Recovery: 200,000 by 1994.

homa. Because of the suffering and number of deaths enroute, their trek became known as the *Trail of Tears*. By this time many whites had come to the conclusion that the only way to "solve" the Indian problem was by *genocide*, though this word had not yet entered our language. There were some estimates that when white men came to the Americas there were around two million Indians in what would become the United States and the southern third of Canada. The Indians themselves set the estimate much higher. At their lowest population there could have been only around a hundred thousand. Some tribes had been wiped out completely by such diseases as small pox, measles and tuberculosis to which they had no immunity at all, and those who survived were made almost helpless and hopeless by alcohol and starvation. At government boarding schools, they were further demoralized by making them dress, act and talk like white children and were severely punished if they failed to conform. Their gift-giving ways and their concept of no private land ownership were ridiculed. They were even robbed of their names so that many today have ones that are combinations of *two English first names*. Then came the —cruelest blow of all — the near extinction of the buffalo, their main means of livelihood for their nomadic way of life. In the United States the making of treaties was blackmail, for almost without exception, the ink was hardly dry before the terms were broken. A Quimper friend, **Jim Cross**, now living in **Victoria**, did some research for me on Canadian Indians. From the Canadian Encyclopedia, p. 1038 follows:

> "The development of the treaty system throughout much of western Canada was based as much on economic pragmatism as it was on any particular legal view of aboriginal rights. During the 1870's the U.S. government was spending over *$20 million* a year fighting plains Indians. This amount was larger than the entire budget of the whole central government in Canada; with these facts of finance before them, federal officials chose to rely heavily on treaties to bring about a relative degree of acquiescence among the 35,000 Indian inhabitants of the territories scheduled to be opened up for settlement."

Jim added this personal note: "As a kid I was fascinated with the stone tent rings which abounded on the plain just above the steep coulee banks. There were also some Indian graves on the farm. I was curious, but did not feel they should be excavated."

Indian arrow heads were found by almost all of Quimper's early settlers, but the dust storms of the thirties uncovered many more.

One of the last things tried was that of *assimilation*. Indians would be *treated as if they were white* so that eventually they would, it was hoped, lose their identity as a race. They were given help with tools and instruction on how to become farmers.

Those who adapted, were given high praise and held up as examples. In one account an encyclopedia stated this program was quite successful as "many Indians, even of the warlike Sioux, became successful farmers."

It was hoped that with the success of this program, the reserves, or reservations as they are called in the States, would no longer be needed. As it is now in the United States (I do not know about Canada), white people *cannot buy* reservation land, but they *can rent* it, so, as one drives through, there is little if anything to indicate to you whether you are on Indian land or not.

I've often wondered what would have happened had Indians been given a *large enough* tract of land while there were still enough buffalo, to have enabled them to preserve their way of life.

Though on the whole, all methods have failed dismally, judging by their rate of unemployment, alcoholism, lower life span, etc, there are some bright spots. It is now estimated by some that the Indian population is at or near what it was when white men arrived, and it is good that now many are even recovering pride in their identity — instead of being ashamed of it. They are becoming again what they once were, a people with a *proud heritage.* And the white race is at last seeing some things from the Indian point of view — twenty-twenty hindsight, some would call it.

And of course they are no doubt right, up to a point. But it has been demonstrated that much can be done to bring back fishing, lumbering, mining and even hunting when there is the *will* to do it. We note the recovery of Lake Erie as but one example.

Sometimes distance, in both time and space, is needed to get perspective. *Distance* was, in fact, already playing a part near the turn of the century. In a beautiful big hardback Mom won in England for perfect Sunday School attendance, Indians were portrayed in a much kinder and more honest way than was true in the West. And in the Americas, how wonderful it is that at last these people are having their craftwork recognized and sold at prices compatible with its real worth!

Now what of religion? Just recently I read of an Indian who had been told in his youth that to be a Christian, he had to give up his "heathen" ways. But after much struggle, and still being condemned by many traditionalists, he is now a minister in the Methodist church. For himself and his ministry, he has been able to bring into harmony the Indian's belief in the Great Spirit, the Story of Creation and their moral teachings, with the essential tenets of the Christian Faith. How many of you have heard or sung the beautiful Christmas carol, " 'Twas in the Moon of Wintertime" with its haunting old French melody and words that fit an Indian setting? This carol was composed back in the 16th century for the Huron Indians and in their language by a Jesuit priest, **Father Jean de Brebeuf**. (Once, many years ago, I was privileged to play the piano for just such a portrayal of Jesus' birth.)

And Indians are the *good guys* now, sometimes even *better* than whites in a few recent movies!

We may not *see* buffalo around to remind us of the old Indian way of life, but we *do* see *Pinto ponies* and *Appaloosa horses*, both breeds developed by Indians from horses brought to the New World by the Spaniards in the early 1500's. They carried the blood of their Arabian and Barb ancestors and are small, quick, fast and have great endurance. To begin their spread north to the plains, some escaped, while others were stolen. There are in fact, still some bands of these wild horses roaming the West, known by such names as broncho, cayuse and mustang. The best of those captured are broken and sold, while poor ones usually end up as pet food.

One can easily see how an Indian would put such high value on his horse, sometimes even above his wife and children, for these animals had transformed their lives. How familiar to us is the picture of an Indian riding bareback, drawing his bow to send an arrow into that massive beast at his side. Is it to Indians, I wonder, that we owe a *halter-broken horse* that will *stand still* in *that* very spot when his rider dismounts and lets the reigns fall to the ground? In the chapter on vignettes in this book, you'll read about a pony named **Buck** that had this sort of training as well as neck-reigning by which one could give a horse direction by simply laying the reigns to right or left across the mane. When riding bareback as the Indians did, knee pressure can also steer a horse.

In our Fourth Reader we had a true story which illustrated just how much a certain Indian Chief thought of his horses. **Mrs. Lajimodiere**, the first white woman to make her home in the Canadian Northwest, was approached by him as he tried to buy her beautiful little fair-haired blue-eyed boy. First he offered *one* horse, then *two,* and finally *one of his own children.* She was, of course, horrified, and burst into tears. That ended the bargaining. This episode is only one incident in the intriguing story of this French-Canadian pioneer woman.

The Hudson's Bay Company

In order to get more information than one usually finds in text books or encyclopedias on a particular subject, I wrote to the Hudson's Bay Company. In response **Anne Morton**, head of Research and Reference in Winnepeg sent me "A Brief History of the Hudson's Bay Company" ©1990, compliments of **The Beaver Magazine**. **Judith Beattie** is the H.B.C. Keeper of the Archives. And in the August 1987 **National Geographic** there is a 38 page article titled "Canada's Fur Trading Empire". From these and other sources, I will excerpt a few portions I found particularly interesting or which related to *our* area in some way.

The texts were very informative and interesting, but the maps, pictures and diagrams alone give us a fascinating glimpse of our prairie history and the integral part played in it by the Hudson's Bay

Company. If you like this lesson in the form of these maps, just refer to ones titled Prairie Provinces ©1994; Great Lakes ©1987; Native American Heritage ©1991; Canada's Vacation Lands ©1985.

Since the hey day of the fur trade, this large on-going company, the Hudson's Bay Company, has undergone significant changes: **1)** incorporation in 1867 into the Confederation; **2)** by the Rupert's Land Act of 1868, whereby Canada compensated the Company by a payment of £300,000 and 1/20 part of the land in any township settled within the fertile belt, the boundaries of which were defined as the U.S. boundary on the south, the Rocky Mountains on the west, Lake Winnepeg on the east and the North Saskatchewan River on the north, plus 50,000 acres around the Company's posts. Thus, on a map of our Quimper district, you will find the HBC initials on a certain section. As trading posts diminished greatly in number, in their place some well-stocked department stores, catering to the requirements of the general public, have been built in some major cities. The first opened in Winnepeg in 1881 and was nicknamed "Ali Baba's Treasure Trove" because of its "exotic foods such as lobster, anchovy and Russian caviar; Rose Point lace from Brussels; silk lingerie from Switzerland; bolts of English woolen cloth; fine hunting guns; musical instruments and colourful snowshoe costumes," all in addition to the great variety of everyday goods.

After WWI, almost 400,000 more acres of farmland was sold, but the company retained the mineral rights to land sold after 1910. This, in 1927, opened the way for their involvement in oil exploration in Alberta.

Just prior to the changing of the name **The Fur Trade Department** to **Northern Stores** in 1959, the HBC began to serve as buying agent for **Inuit** carvings, a service they still perform today. They also own and operate four major retail companies; **The Bay, Simpsons, Zellers** and **Field Stores** and you can still buy those beautiful woolen **Point** blankets. To commemorate their 300th anniversary in 1970, they built a full sized replica of the **Nonsuch**, an early day trading vessel. After sailing the English coasts, the Great Lakes and the waters of the Pacific Northwest, it was placed permanently in the Manitoba Museum of Men and Nature in **Winnepeg**.

Women in the Fur Trade

If you want a glimpse of the feminine side of this huge industry, read **Sylvia Van Kirk's "Many Tender Ties"**. Marriages between Frenchmen and Indian women were so common that eventually there was a new race, the **Métis**. These unions were of two kinds — those sanctioned and performed by the R.C. clergy and those which were known as "after the custom of the country." Not many such wives lived within the fort or post. Most families lived around the outside in what was called a *guard area*, but all were doing similar work as before, gathering and preparing furs for trade, making leather clothes (moccasins are comfortable, but don't last long), gathering berries and roots, making pemmican, sewing hides together for tepees, gardening, drying fish and taking care of the family. Their work may have been a little easier, but *one* other thing surely *wasn't*, for, from here on, they would have to live in *two* very different cultures. The change-over began as soon as she arrived at the fort as a bride, when she was expected to adopt a white woman's mode of dress, especially if she was one who would live inside the fort as the wife of a Company man of authority. I tried to imagine a scene with this taking place so here is a mini drama. I will call the husband **Pierre** and the wife **Little Wing.** (He has courted her at camp and been granted her father's permission to marry her, so somehow they have managed to communicate over the language barrier. The men at the post prepared for this *transformation* by keeping white women's clothes on hand and some bolts of cloth.)

Pierre: Oh Little Wing, I'm so glad you are here with me. I know we'll be happy together and our little ones — surely we will have some won't we — will see the best in both your people and mine. It will be difficult for us both in many ways, but harder for you than for me. We can't speak each other's language too well yet, but I know a little of your tongue and it won't be long before you'll be able to talk French just fine. Meanwhile sign language will have to do sometimes. I know you will be lonesome so there is no reason you can't go back and visit your people once in a while. You'll still work very hard here at the fort, but at least you won't have to pack up that heavy tepee, load it and all the other stuff and move all the time.

Little Wing: Yes, you are right. I will try to be a good wife and a good mother to any children we have. I know many of my people's ways to help if we get sick or have accidents.

Pierre: Come now into this other room. It is time for you to give up your Indian way of dress and put on these clothes that white women wear. I am sure they will feel strange to you at first, but you will soon get used to them. So now you must undress. (No doubt Pierre has looked over the shelves of clothes and picked out ones he think will fit her.)

Little Wing: Yes, but it makes me feel sad to do this.

Pierre: I know it dear (or whatever term of endearment was common in those days), but it must be. Also, we must have you wash all over. Here is some water in a basin and some soap. (I've never read whether or not Indians had soap — there are so many details of everyday life that are missing. And what did they dry themselves with, some cloth they wove or a soft piece of leather, dry grass, or what?) It is doubtful if Pierre was all that clean himself — standards of today not yet in place.

As she washes, Pierre has been laying out some clothes with his back to her to give her a bit of privacy. Bras and bloomers are still far into the future and according to this book, Indian women didn't wear underclothes — at least nothing resembling white women's undergarments, anyway.

Pierre: Here try this on (he hands her a sleeveless cotton vest that reaches to her thighs). That's fine isn't it?

Little Wing: Yes. What comes next?

Pierre: This. It's called a corset. Come. I will help you put it on, though I have never helped a woman put one on before.

They get her into it and he is busy with the back lacing after she has managed the hooks and eyes.

Little Wing: Don't pull it so tight, Pierre. I can hardly breathe.

Pierre: Yes, dear, but I know it is supposed to be tight so your dress will fit right.

Little Wing: Oh, I'll never get used to this! And how will I ever be able to work with it on? I won't be able to bend over to dig roots or gather moss or anything. And I know it isn't good to bind one's body like this. It just isn't natural.

Pierre: Well maybe so, but we don't have any choice in this matter. As my wife you simply have to wear these clothes.

Little Wing: Well, what's next.

Pierre: This petticoat comes next and then a dress. Here's two or three dresses. Which one do you like best?

Little Wing: Well, I suppose I'll take which one fits me best. I'll try this one on first. (It fits.)

Pierre: Now it's time for shoes and stockings. Here try these.

Little Wing: No! I am going to keep my leggings and moccasins. I simply can't put my feet in those shoes, and even if I could, I wouldn't be able to walk in them. You won't *make* me wear them, will you?

Pierre: No, I see some of the other Indian wives are keeping theirs, too, so I'll not insist on it. Besides, these shoes look so uncomfortable anyway, and your moccasins and leggings are so pretty with all that lovely beadwork you put on them. And did you notice that some of we white men even are wearing moccasins? It's hard to get regular shoes from Montreal and often they aren't the right size either. So Little Wing, we shall both wear Indian leggings and moccasins. Does that make you happy?

Little Wing: Oh yes, Pierre, and thank you. Can we go now and meet some of the other Indian wives? I must learn what I am to do here, though I'll still have many of the same jobs I had before, tending to the babies round about, preparing food — cutting up meat and drying it, gathering berries for the pemmican, preparing the furs for trade and so on. I'll try to learn to cook some of the foods *you* like that we Indians don't use, but I'll bet you'll become fond of many of our Indian foods, too. We'll have the best of both worlds, won't we? But when I make mistakes, because I don't know your ways, please don't laugh, Pierre.

Pierre: No I won't except when we are able to laugh together, Little Wing. Oh, you'll have to put your hair up soon like the white women do — but that will do for another day.

(Métis and Indian women were an essential link between successful fur traders and the Indians and sometimes helped to avert real clashes.

End.

The Hudson Bay Company men had more marital and family problems than the Norwesters because marrying native women, was more frowned upon in British society, especially after the merger of the two companies. Many had left wives and family back in the old country during their tour of duty in the West. Those who did take Indian wives and establish families had another problem. When they retired, often they would have to abandon their families at the fort to go back home. French men seldom went back to their former home to live even if it was only as far as Quebec. Both men and women suffered emotional turmoil over these mixed up, responsibilities and loyalties. Later, when **British** women came to the West, there was conflict of a different kind. Very few could adapt to this harsh life and their loneliness was often unbearable. Many considered themselves *superior* to both Indian and Métis women which led to further disharmony. In spite of all these negative aspects, it was gratifying to read of many *good* marriages and *harmonious* homes in these situations where it was hard to set up what we might call a more natural home life within their own race and culture.

Two Distinct Differences

In many ways the train of events in the West ran in similar paths on either side of the border, but with at least two significant differences. One was the fact that *slavery* existed in the States prior to the Civil War and Canada was the place of *refuge* if they could possibly get there. The *Underground Railway* and the name **Harriet Tubman** are synonymous. I remember so well when my sister, **Nellie** and I were taken for a drive in southern Ontario by **Stan and Mary (Donald) Atherton** and Stan saying, "*That* is the *very* spot at which the Underground Railway ended!" How can we ever imagine the scenes of joy that took place right there! One time when I had a fairly lengthy stopover at the airport in Calgary, I naturally headed for **Cole's** bookstore. There I found a paperback reprint of an 1856 book "Fugitive Slaves in Canada" all in first person narratives. The other big difference centres in western rather than eastern Canada. It is an integral part of the story of the **Mounties**. Their organization and their *Great Trek West* from **Dufferin,** Manitoba to **Fort Walsh** in what is now Saskatchewan, in 1874 is one of the most enthralling law enforcement accounts you can read — only 300 men to establish and enforce law and order in such a vast territory. There were six troops each identified by the color of their horses — bay, dark brown, chestnut, grey, black and light bay. Each had some 8 pounder field guns, beef cattle, cows and calves, wagons, and carts containing provisions, ammunition and farm implements. The main body went to **Ft. MacLeod** and a smaller detachment to **Edmonton**. It wasn't long before they won the respect of the Indians by successfully putting a stop to outlaws from Montana called **Wolfers** who had been taking advantage of them. According to **Wallace Stegner** in his book *Wolf Willow*, it was "these red coats who became a fitting symbol of what made the Canadian West different from the Americans in that they had become triply effective now that the American cavalry had become an abomination to the Plains Indians. **Mounties** stood for friendship, protection and righteousness of the law for *all*."

Today the **Red Coat Trail** is a well marked east-west highway which passes only a few miles north of our rail line through Aneroid and Ponteix.

Captions:
1. A settlement on the Red River. Lord Selkirk naming the parish of Kildonan, 1817. "The Parish shall be Kildonan; here you shall build your church, and that lot is for a school."; **2.** The great march of the North-west Mounted Police; **3.** Twenty-two Clydesdales, Percherons and Belgians pulling a genuine freighter wagon, a load of freight, a rack of feed and a tank of water. This is a portrayal of the actual type of hitch used by freighting teams in the late 1800's in southwest Saskatchewan. This freight wagon is one of 400 horsedrawn vehicles in the collection of the Western Development Museum and its branches at Saskatoon, North Battleford, Yorkton, and Moose Jaw; **4.** The Red River cart was used as a means of transport across the prairies before the days of railways. Owing to the difficulty of procuring iron, wooden pegs were used in place of nails, and the tires of the wheels were bound round with strips of fresh buffalo or ox-hide, which shrank when it dried and held them tightly together. These carts were very noisy.

Surveyors of the 49th

To begin his chapter on the surveying of the 49th parallel, Stegner in *Wolf Willow* asks, "Have you ever read an exciting frontier story about a surveyor?" Your answer as his, would be "No", as there seemed to be none. Therefore, his account makes *number one.* The chapter he called "The Medicine Line" is engrossing. This odd title came from the fact that the Indians were so pleased with this survey *line* that it was like *good medicine.* At this time, many United States Indians, including 800 Nez Perce, had come across to "Land of the Red Coats" for refuge. In fact, there were about 800 Teton lodges near **Fort Walsh** only a few miles from the site of the Cypress Hills Massacre. When the Mounties came "the ground was still white with human bones and skulls."

On the great importance of establishing a frontier border, Stegner had this to say, "Borders draw lines in a number of ways. Here one body of law stops and another begins. Cultural divisions take shape. Ecological and physical demarcations become more real such as the boundaries between woods and plains, plains and mountains or mountains and deserts. Each side creates its own brand of lawbreakers, especially smugglers, bootleggers, and black marketeers, and that any real inequity or disparity between the laws of Canada and the United States starts a flow of contraband in one direction or the other." His family's homestead was on the Canadian side of the border from 1914 to 1920 at a time when Canada was "wet" and Montana "dry". As a young boy he watched smugglers at work — mostly at night, and in stormy weather. He would "see the lights of Marmons and Hudson Super Sixes, so heavily loaded that springs were down to the axles as they groped their way in the grass and mud, all in low gear, leaving ruts eight inches deep." (Are some still visible, I wonder.) Until *the line* was in place, this area was more a *zone* leaving open the speculation that *this prairie country* was a "natural inevitable extension of the States." In August of 1874, joint survey parties met and Canada was now truly a country stretching from sea to sea. It wouldn't be many more years before two trans-Canada railroads would enhance this sea to sea join.

Still, the surveyors themselves remained unsung heroes in spite of enduring the very same hardships of weather, terrain, insects, terrible alkali, or worse yet, buffalo urine-polluted water; near starvation for both themselves and their animals (because prairie fires wiped out vegetation); broken equipment; worn out clothing, loneliness, frustra-

(Continued on page 68)

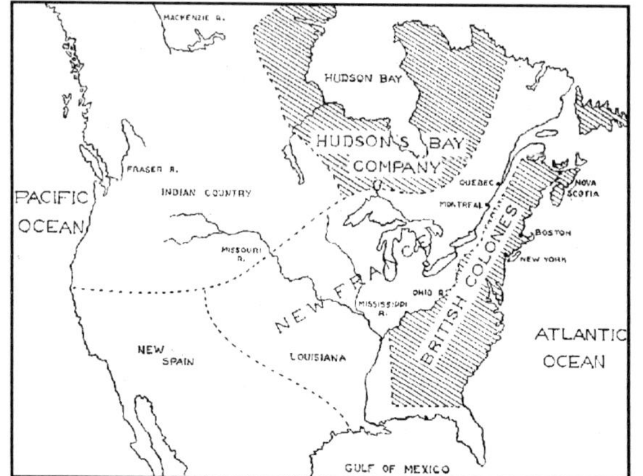

North America, 1713. Shaded areas are British. Cape Breton remained French.

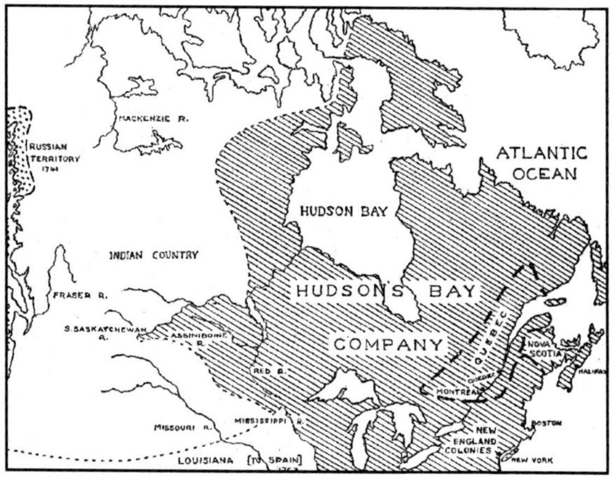

British North America, 1763. Shaded areas are British.

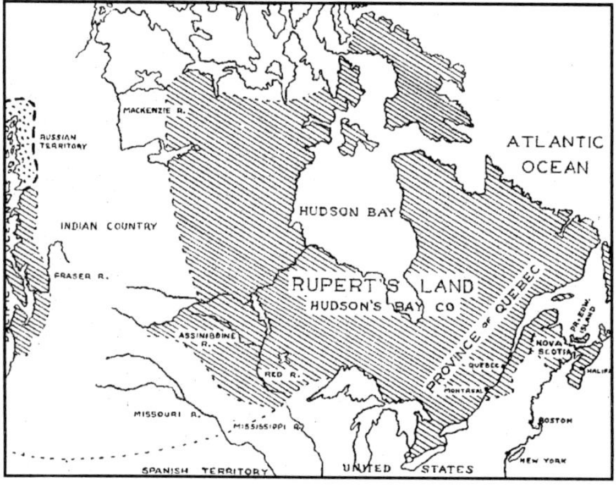

British North America, 1783. Shaded areas are British.

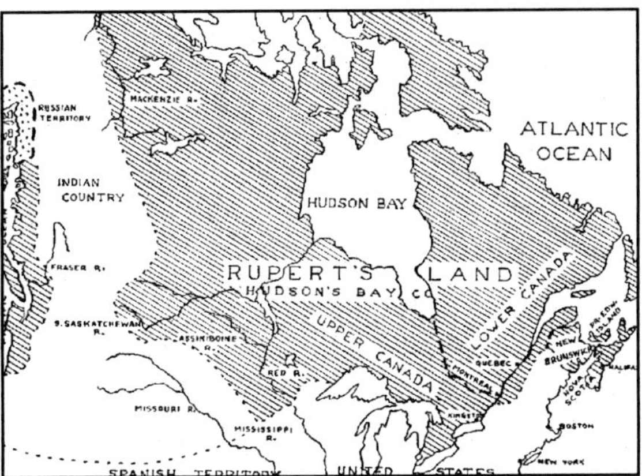

British North America, 1791. Shaded areas are British.

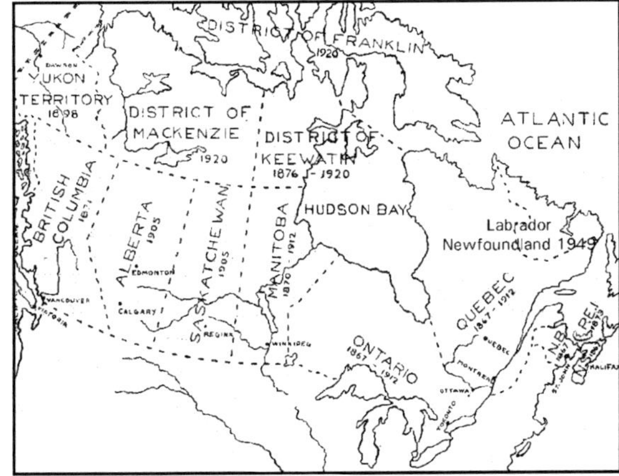

Dominion of Canada, 1949.

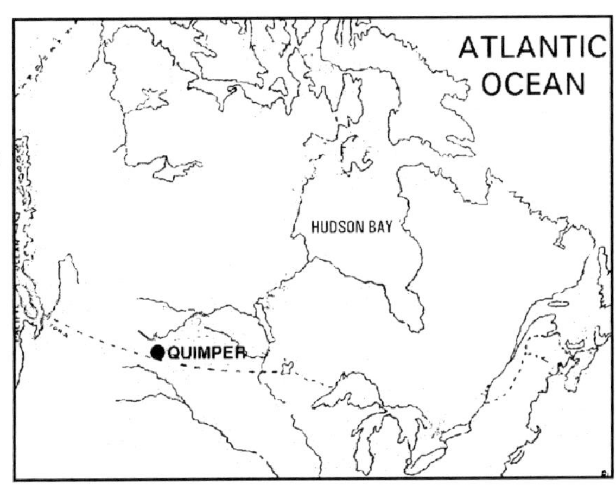

Headwaters for two river systems were in our area: The S. Saskatchewan and Nelson draining into Hudson Bay and The Frenchman, Milk, Missouri, and Mississippi draining into the Gulf of Mexico.

tion and discouragement — just as explorers, traders and missionaries about whom there are stories in all the history books.

Yet *all residents and travellers* of this area had similar troubles as confirmed by this author in these quotations:

"(1)Mosquitoes were so thick that they formed 'moving crusts' around the eyes of horses and oxen and sometimes animals were so weakened from insect attacks they died."

"(2)In their icy camps, they would hear the gunshot reports of willows bursting as the sap froze."

"(3)In some areas so many buffalo had been killed in such a short space of time that nature could not take care of the decomposition fast enough and they had to 'push their way through the carrion stink of a way of life recklessly destroying itself'."

But, lest we blame white man exclusively for this carnage, Stegner pointed out that the Métis would "kill six or eight a piece and then the women would take the tongues and hump ribs and leave the rest of the carcass to rot."

How great a debt of gratitude we owe those few individuals who, in the nick of time, rescued the last remnants of these magnificent animals! And never can we ever begin to comprehend the depth of despair and sadness of Indians over this loss of their way of life and their spiritual heritage.

The English language has been enriched by the adoption into it of many Indian words or expressions, and Indian place names are so common that we seldom give a thought to their origin. French, on the other hand, has by intent been preserved in its pure form. Parisian French (this the kind we had in our high school text) and French Canadians have a number of differences mainly because ties between France and the New World were not strongly maintained. I remember when **Geraldine Lallier** was going over the French lesson in my text book with me, she would often say "But we French-Canadians say it this way." At home we used to try to use French for things on the table sometimes, but we never got far, I'm afraid. We lacked any real commitment to learning French, I regret to say.

Looking at the full page of foods and other things (page 54) so common for us today we rarely give a thought to how we got them. Some became part of *our* diet before they crossed the Atlantic. For instance, Mom, when she came to Canada, was surprised at us eating corn on the cob. In England it was still just pig feed, she said.

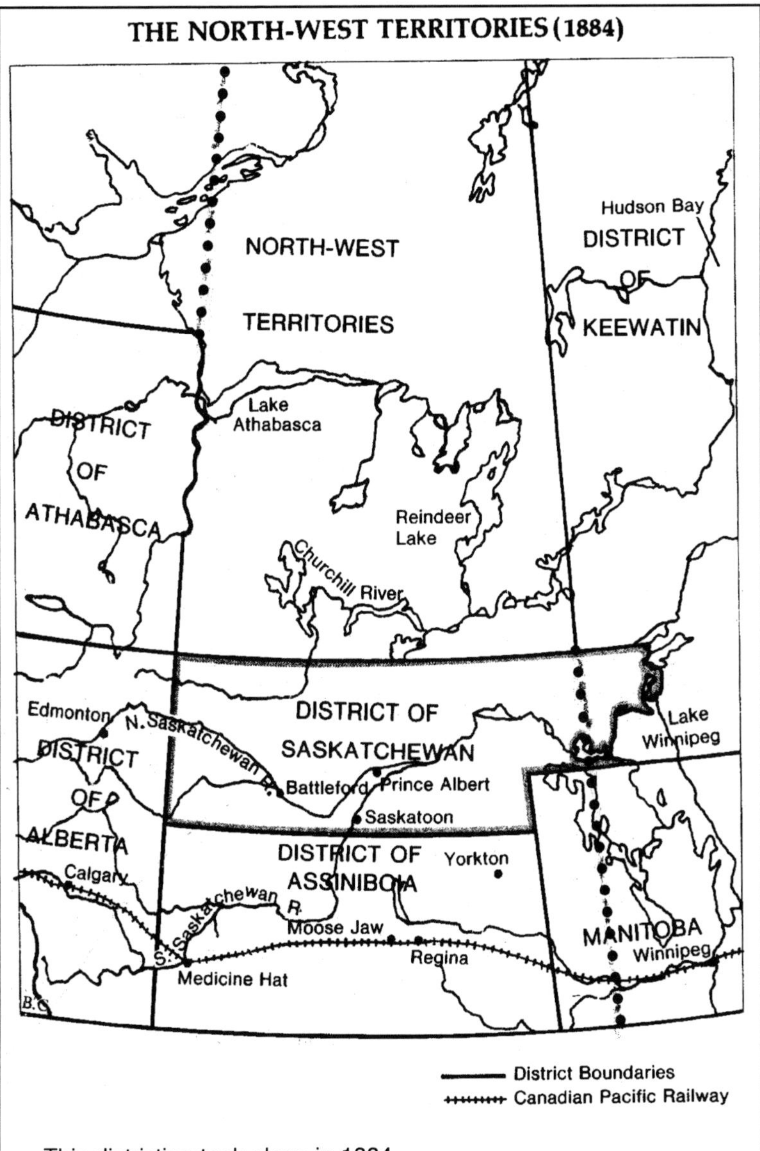

This districting took place in 1884.

Based on a map from J. H. Richards and K.I. Fung, *Atlas of Saskatchewan,* p. 10, (University of Saskatchewan, 1969).
• • • • Shows future Saskatchewan boundary.

I do hope that because of these quotes from *Wolf Willow* you will waste no time in getting this book for yourself. Its graphic descriptions will bring into sharp focus just *what was going on* only a few miles south of us at the time Quimper School was getting underway.

Other Race Relations

It may seem odd, but I never saw either an Indian or a black person till I was almost grown up, and as for orientals, the only ones we saw were the men who had a café or laundry in every little town. How sad that we never seemed to question *why* these men had *no family* or how lonesome they must have been! I don't know that it was the *full* explanation, but there was great fear of the yellow race overwhelming the white race if wives were permitted to come. China's over-population would, they felt certain, spill over to the West if that door was opened.

After slaves did reach freedom in Canada, it didn't mean that they were welcomed with open arms and hearts by the majority of white Canadians. They have suffered much discrimination in Canada also, though Canadians have probably thought themselves better than Americans who had *that* blot of slavery on their nation.

In one district where I taught, a young black woman came to keep house in a home where the mother had left. Only the father and his youngest son, my Grade One pupil were there. We became quite good friends so that eventually I felt I could ask her how being black had affected her life. She was very much overweight and her reply was "I hate being fat much more than being black." But when she was at a social at the school, I felt it was her *color* that made people avert their eyes more than her figure.

The Railroads

Until I read the **Time Life Book** "The Railroaders" I didn't realize how limited was my knowledge on this most vital aspect of our lives on the prairie. Trains had arrived at our towns of **Aneroid** and **Ponteix** *before* those of us now in our 70's were even born, so we could never appreciate the excitement of that *first* smoking, whistling, bell-ringing monster approaching from the east and clanging to a halt with those hissing, steaming brakes. What a blessing! No longer did our fathers have to travel those terrible long tedious, even dangerous, miles to **Swift Current**, and our mothers would now be able to get to town, once in awhile, to shop, visit, or go to church. The soon-to-be train service had, you see, triggered the building of towns all along its

In the old photograph above, Donald Smith (who became Lord Strathcona) is shown driving the last spike in the Canadian Pacific Railway, at Craigellachie in the Rockies, Nov. 7, 1885. After years of disheartening difficulties, Canada was at last united by a transcontinental railroad. In 1871 British Columbia joined the Dominion on condition that the railway reach them within 10 years — a project most thought physically impossible and would never pay for iteself. Without it, there was high chance B.C. would join the United States.

anticipated route. Sometimes a wrong guess meant the quick death of a new town or, in some cases, its wholesale move to get *on the line.*

On almost every page of this big hardback there is a photo, a map or diagram, a painting and even ads or cartoons. The stories and pictures of getting tracks and locomotives *over* or *through* the Rockies are awesome. The exact procedure for laying track was most interesting, especially as we pictured our dads being on the work crews doing it. I didn't know till I learned it here, that triple decker work cars were common on some lines and sometimes there would be contests between work crews on how fast track could be laid. They said the record still stands — 643 miles of track between April 2 and November 19, 1887. Some track laying had to be guarded by soldiers — who, of course, had little to do if some police action was not being required at that time — so they sometimes provided for their own on-the-road home-type entertainment. One troop took their own band along.

Some wild and crazy celebrations took place as a certain goal was reached. Once in 1866 "celebrities were entertained with a buffalo hunt and a man-set prairie fire." Indians were generally not pleased with this marvel of technology cutting across their land and sometimes they fought it vigorously. They attacked workers, put grease on the tracks and sometimes set prairie fires.

The invention of *rotary snow plows* saved much work, time and frustration for with it they could clear as much track in an hour as a *bucker* could in a day. This was graphically portrayed, when in 1867, it took 12 engines with a bucker to get through a drift similar to one that in 1890 was cleared quickly and efficiently with the rotary in about an hour.

The inside of passenger cars could span the gulf between fantastic luxury and basic four walls, benches and little else. In vignettes you will read about some experiences of Quimper families on these settler trains. In our youth we didn't travel in luxury but we *did have* decent seats, lights and heat, and, on the main lines, diner and pullman cars. Maybe we didn't think of it as very fancy, but to our parent's generation, I'm sure, it had this qualification.

But as rural schools were coming to an end, so was train passenger service. Buses, cars and planes were coming into their own and finally, trucks would eliminate much freight train service. Some long freights with electric engines still travel the branch lines, but depots are gone and the train often doesn't even stop at a little town. Even trans-Canada train service is gone, though a few partial runs still take place through either very scenic or heavily populated areas. (We have the set of two videos of this last trip.)

Toy trains are still a hobby, but mainly for men who perhaps worked on trains. And how often nowadays does a little boy ask Santa for a train?

Political History

Canada's political history is summarized by the maps and captions a few pages back. They show which European countries claimed major areas, the transfers of ownership which took place in treaties made at the end of wars and the dates of establishment of provincial boundary lines from 1867 onward until the Dominion of Canada was its full width of today. Perhaps soon we will need another map as it seems likely that it will not be long before more of the North West Territories will acquire provincial status. However, these maps do *not*

REFERENCE-OUTLINE FOR STUDY OF CANADIAN HISTORY

I. **Prehistoric times:** Indians cross from Asia over Bering Strait I-107-9, 141 (Eskimos E-484)

II. **Discovery and early exploration** C-101-2, A-197, map A-199: the "Beardmore Viking" C-101

- A. **Later Vikings reach the New World** N-356-8, C-101: Leif Ericson E-479, picture A-197
- B. **Early Indian tribes** C-101, maps I-109, 134, table I-135-6: Eastern Woodland I-117; Mackenzie-Yukon Caribou Hunters I-112; Northwest Fishermen I-112, 131-3; Eskimos E-481-2
- C. **Rediscovery by John Cabot (1497)** C-101-2, C-8-9, N-165: sights Cape Breton C-130
- D. **Search for a Northwest Passage** A-200, C-102: Henry Hudson H-511; Frobisher and Davis A-200, P-418, table P-419
- E. **Basis of French claims in North America** A-200-1, C-102: Jacques Cartier C-145-6

III. **Founding of New France** C-102-3, A-200-1

- A. **Champlain at Port Royal and Quebec** C-102, N-374-5, C-207, pictures Q-14, C-103
- B. **Maisonneuve founds Montreal** C-102, M-476-7
- C. **Habitants (French farmers)** C-102-3, Q-8
- D. **Government** C-103: Frontenac F-349
- E. **Mississippi and Great Lakes region explored** A-201, M-389, G-209: Marquette and Joliet M-113, J-438; La Salle L-128-9; Hennepin H-380
- F. **Cadillac founds Detroit** D-97, C-10
- G. **Early fur trade** F-373-6: Hudson's Bay Company C-103, H-512, M-90, picture C-104

IV. **French and British conflict** C-103-4, chart H-415

- A. **British claims** N-166, N-375: Acadia A-5-6
- B. **The first intercolonial wars:** King William's War K-57; Queen Anne's War Q-15; King George's War K-56
- C. **The final conflict**—the French and Indian War F-333, S-117, A-6: Wolfe wins Quebec W-211, M-473; Canada ceded to Britain by the Treaty of Paris (1763) C-104, S-117

V. **A century of British rule** C-104-8

- A. **American loyalists (Tories) settle in Canada** C-104, N-164, N-375, O-459, P-498, S-18
- B. **Exploring the West** C-104, M-15, M-90
- C. **War of 1812** W-11, C-105, O-459, T-173
- D. **Canada-United States border treaties** G-208, V-497, M-56, T-263, maps U-423, N-280
- E. **Struggle for self-government** C-105-6, M-15, P-107, B-22
- F. **Effect of American Civil War** C-106-7, 108, C-374
- G. **Founding the Dominion** C-107, M-6, T-244

VI. **Dominion and expansion** C-107-8

- A. **British North America Act of 1867 creates the Dominion of Canada** C-107
- B. **John A. Macdonald's first Conservative government (1867–73)** C-107, M-6
  1. Rupert's Land purchased from Hudson's Bay Company (1869) C-107, H-512; Louis Riel and Red River Rebellion R-120, C-107-8; Manitoba becomes a province C-108, M-90
  2. Relations with the United States C-108, C-95
  3. Canada reaches the Pacific C-108: British Columbia enters the Dominion B-333
  4. Struggles to build a continental railway: scandal overthrows Conservatives C-108
- C. **Alexander Mackenzie's Liberal government (1873–78)** C-108: North West (later Royal Canadian) Mounted Police C-108, R-138
- D. **Conservatives restored to power (1878)**—Macdonald's policy C-108: Canadian Pacific Railway C-108 (Strathcona S-483, picture C-109); rebellion in Saskatchewan C-108; Bering Sea controversy C-109
- E. **Wilfred Laurier's long Liberal administration (1896–1911)** C-109-10, L-164
  1. Immigrants settle Prairie Provinces C-109: Alberta A-154; Manitoba M-91; Saskatchewan S-53
  2. Gold discovered in Klondike and Yukon C-109: Yukon separated from Northwest Territories Y-394; Alaska boundary dispute R-286, C-109
  3. Relations with the United States C-109: reciprocal trade agreements C-109 (Laurier supports L-164; Borden opposes B-268)
- F. **Robert Borden forms a Conservative government (1911–20)** C-110, B-268-9
  1. World War I C-110, B-268-9, H-513: Ypres W-259; Vimy Ridge W-262; Passchendaele W-263; Amiens W-266; Cambrai C-110
  2. Suffrage extended to women (1918) W-215

VII. **Between two World Wars** C-110, chart H-415

- A. **Progress toward self-government** C-110; Mackenzie King, Liberal prime minister K-54-5
- B. **The depression years** C-110, S-53, A-154, K-54
- C. **New political parties** C-110: socialism in Saskatchewan S-52, 53; Social Credit in Alberta A-154; social laws in British Columbia B-333
- D. **Statute of Westminster (1931) recognizes autonomy of all British Dominions** C-97, C-110, B-335
- E. **Trade agreements with the United States** C-110

VIII. **World War II** C-110-11, W-284

- A. **Canada and United States establish Permanent Joint Board on Defense** C-111, R-274, W-289
- B. **Industry expands to meet war needs** C-95, C-111
- C. **Alaska (Alcan) Highway** C-111, Y-394, R-217
- D. **Campaigns and leaders** C-111, picture W-307: D-Day W-316; St. Lô and Falaise-Argentan W-317, picture W-317; drive through Germany W-318, 320

IX. **The postwar period** C-111, chart H-415

- A. **Federal District of Ottawa created in 1945** O-511
- B. **Bretton Woods and San Francisco Conferences**—Canada joins the United Nations C-111
- C. **St. Laurent replaces Mackenzie King as prime minister and leader of Liberal party** C-111, S-18
- D. **Newfoundland, together with Labrador, becomes the tenth province** N-165, L-92
- E. **Last formal ties with Britain cut**—term "dominion" dropped C-97; British Privy Council replaced by Canada's Supreme Court C-97, 111
- F. **Canadian forces fight in Korea (1950–53)** C-111
- G. **Vincent Massey, first Canadian-born governor general, succeeds Alexander** C-111
- H. **Canada and the United States build radar warning stations to defend North America** C-111
- I. **St. Lawrence Seaway Project approved by the United States** C-111

(For bibliography, see Canada.)

(Only through the 50's.)

give names of Canada's political leaders, nor information on the forms of government or the courts of law, and neither can you read from them stories of the different ethnic or religious groups that make up the population of Saskatchewan. But all this information is easily obtained by those who wish to study these aspects of the history of our province. On page 657 of the May 1979 **National Geographic** you can see the main ethnic settlements in Saskatchewan together with the dates they took place. One however, is not there, the Ponteix Hutterite colony just a few miles southwest of Quimper.

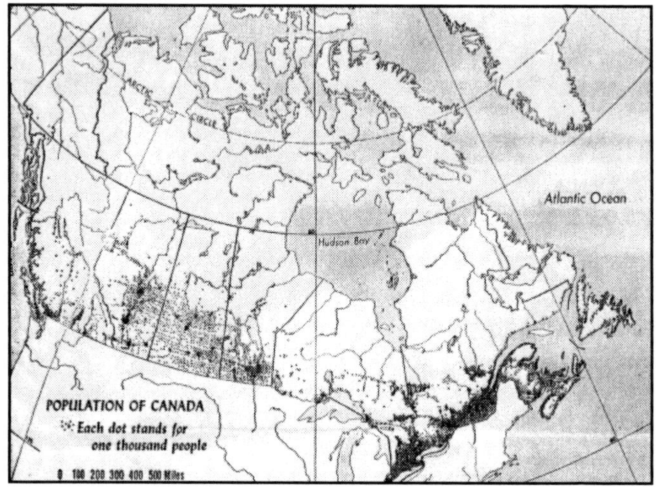

POPULATION: Though this is not an up-to-date map, the general character of Canada's population dispersal has not changed.

Métis

Métis peoples had little land or other legal protection prior to 1938 when laws acknowledged their squatters' rights. The book "The History of the Métis Nation in Western Canada" by **A.H. de Tremaudan** and other publications and trends helped them uncover pride in their heritage. Many live in the northern parts of the provinces and have developed a distinct culture which combines elements of Cree, French and English languages, religion and economic-industrial-trade activities. For example, they do a dance called jigging, which mixes the reels of Scotland and France and the chicken dance of the Cree.

By 1988 they hoped to win court cases that would give them full constitutional rights.

Rules for Teachers, 1872

1. Teachers each day will fill lamps, clean chimneys.
2. Each teacher will bring a bucket of water and a scuttle of coal for the day's session.
3. Make your pens carefully. You may whittle nibs to the individual taste of the pupils.
4. Men teachers may take one evening each week for courting purposes, or two evenings a week if they go to church regularly.
5. After ten hours in school, the teachers may spend the remaining time reading the Bible or other good books.
6. Women teachers who marry or engage in unseemly conduct will be dismissed.
7. Every teacher should lay aside from each pay a goodly sum of his earnings for his benefit during his declining years so that he will not become a burden on society.
8. Any teacher who smokes, uses liquor in any form, frequents pool or public halls, or gets shaved in a barber shop will give good reason to suspect his worth, intention, integrity and honesty.
9. The teacher who performs his labor faithfully and without fault for five years will be given an increase of twenty-five cents per week in his pay, providing the Board of Education approves.

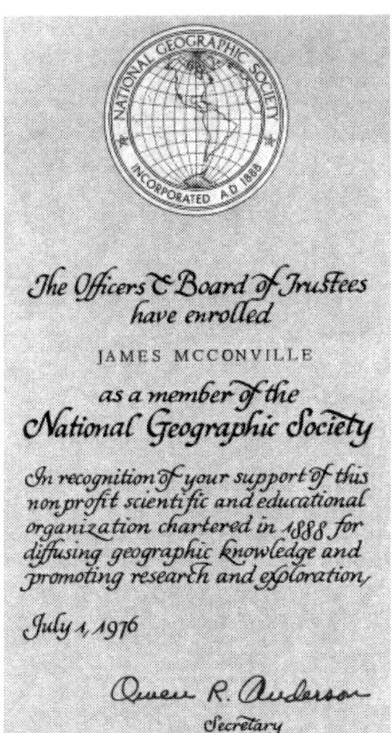

NATIONAL GEOGRAPHIC SOCIETY
INCORPORATED A.D. 1888

The Officers & Board of Trustees
have enrolled
JAMES MCCONVILLE
as a member of the
National Geographic Society

In recognition of your support of this nonprofit scientific and educational organization chartered in 1888 for diffusing geographic knowledge and promoting research and exploration

July 1, 1976

Secretary

We found this among Dad's treasures. One of the saddest days of the Depression for Dad was when he had to give up his beloved Geographic subscription.

The **National Geographic** has carried some excellent articles on Canada — the best for our own province being "The People Who Made Saskatchewan" in the May 1979 issue.

Many original old Geographics are available from the Society. They range in price from a 1914 one at $36.00 to a 1979 one at $2.65. At these prices maybe some of you have a little "gold mine" on your bookshelf!

(Author Unknown, from "Mingling Memories — History of **Wapella**, Sask. and District". This gem found by **Karen McConville Atherton**.) When I taught in the 40's, we were about halfway between these 1872 rules (I presume these were similar for Canadian and American teachers) and some very different ones for teachers in the 90's. From our own memories, we realize just how *liberated* we teachers were even then.

The Juke Box

My father often used to say:
"My boy don't throw a thing away:
You'll find a use for it some day."

So in a box he stored up things,
Bent nails, old washers, pipes and rings,
And bolts and nuts and rusty springs.

Despite each blemish and each flaw,
Some use of everything he saw;
With things material, this was law.

And often when he'd work to do,
He searched the junk box through and through
And found old stuff as good as new.

And I have often thought since then,
That father did the same with men;
He knew he'd need their help again.

It seems to me he understood
That men, as well as iron and wood,
May broken be and still be good.

Despite the vices he'd display
He never threw a man away,
But kept him for another day.

A human junk box is this earth
And into it we're tossed at birth,
To wait the day we'll be of worth.

Though bent and twisted, weak of will,
And full of flaws and lacking skill,
Some service each can render still.

From **A Heap O'Livin'**, ©1916

Bibliography

Wildflowers Across the Prairies, ©1977, F.R. Vance, J.R. Jowsey, J.S. McLean
Charlie Farquharson's Histry of Canada, ©1972, Don Harron
Mrs. Mike (A Mountie's Wife), ©1947, renewed 1975, Benedict and Nancy Freedman
The Miracle Planet, ©1990, P.B.S., T.V., Bruce Brown, Lane Morgan
Learning from the Indians, ©1973, original 1908, Wharton James
The Railroaders, ©1973, Time-Life Books
Indians of the Plains, ©1954, Robert H. Lowie
The Broken Cord, ©1989, Michael Dorris
Fugitive Slaves in Canada, ©1856, Benjamin Drew
Crying Wind, ©1977, Crying Wind Autobiography
The Lonely Road, ©1961, Sigurd Olson
The Red Record, ©1993
Wolf Willow, ©1955, Wallace Stegner
I Heard the Owl Call My Name, ©1973, Margaret Craven
From Sea Unto Sea, ©1959, W.G. Hardy, Canada 1850-1910

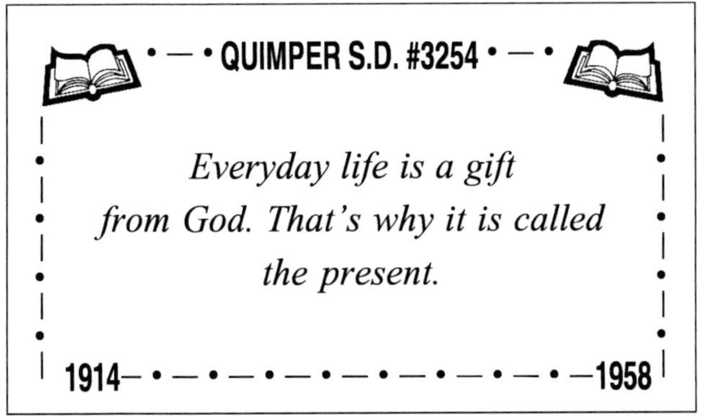

Earth's moths rust and thieves cannot reach the treasures your heart stores up in heaven. — Matt. 6:19-21 (paraphrased)

3 — Daily Living

Quimper Gathers Itself Together

Constant cooperation between parents, teacher and children was necessary in rural communities, sometimes to the point of survival, especially in severe winter weather and later on in the dust storms of the 30's. When Quimper school opened in 1914 even phones were a thing of the future and very few cars were to be seen as yet. Only one year had elapsed since a branch rail line had reached **Ponteix** and **Aneroid**. And for only two years prior to that, had another line to the north reached **Pambrun**, **Neville** and **Vanguard**, which had cut the 65 mile trip to **Swift Current** in half.

From the beginning of Quimper's settlement, pioneers knew the value of spiritual well being, so church and Sunday School always had high priority. Still another essential was a balance between work and play, both such broad topics that I found it difficult to place many of the stories and even pictures, because the line between *work* and *play* is sometimes quite blurry. Remember Tom Sawyer and his friends?

Though there were numerous and profound changes in the years 1914 to 1958, there were as many aspects, I believe, that remained essentially *unchanged*. Many jobs in field, yard, garden and house were being done in 1958 almost as they were in 1914.

If the old saw, "*Idleness* is the Devil's workshop" is true, I'm sure he had little to do when he chose to work in Quimper! Likewise, the problem of *boredom*. That *word* was not even *in* our vocabulary — loneliness, frustration and fatigue, yes, but boredom — no.

A Find

The cover is gone, also a number of first and last pages, so it is impossible to know where, when, or how Dad got his mini-mini farm encyclopedia. It has *everything* in it you'd *expect* to find for mixed farming, plus a lot of stuff that really surprised me — how to cast (or throw) a horse or a cow; how to organize a beef ring; how to tan hides; the possible use of yeast to treat a cow's infertility; a legal section with a question and answer section (including all sorts of laws for the farmer and his hired man — but *nothing* on a hired girl (he was a *man,* she a *girl*, no matter their age). To top off this amazing little-in-size, but packed-with-facts book, there is **Canada's History** from 1497 to Feb. 17, 1919 — all on five pages!

Perhaps this picture and information (copy is in actual printing size of book) will remind those our age of something we had better *know* back then, but will be absolutely *useless* today. What would young folks do now with a car that had *no self starter* or *turn signals?* They would surely say that would be living in the Dark Ages!

CRANKING THE FORD

Almost every local paper tells of some one getting a wrist or some bones in the hand broken by cranking a car. If you will take hold of the crank in the right way the chances of an accident are greatly lessened. The illustration shows the right and the wrong way of

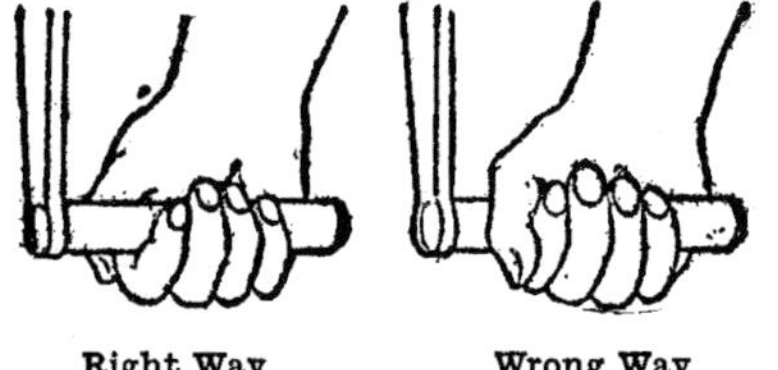

Right Way **Wrong Way**

gripping the handle. A very little practice will enable you to crank as well this way as by taking hold so a "kick back" is sure to break a bone. Keep the thumb back of the crank handle, then if the engine "kicks" the handle is jerked out of the hand and no damage done.

Getting Around

Settlers such as the Crosses and McCoys came from Down East in settler's cars. Most homesteaders for our area got off at either Moose Jaw or Swift Current. Many spent a short time working in the city — perhaps at their old occupation, carpentering, lathing, shingling, butchering or whatever they found to do in the booming economy — before hunting for a homestead site either by being taken in a wagon or buggy by some one already *at* their claim or sometimes even heading out on foot. I always wondered how in the world they could begin to find a *tiny* marker in that sea of grass, but I never ran across any stories telling of much difficulty in this regard. They would step off the right distance *from* a marker and then hunt in the vicinity till they

Aneroid Station 1922.

Jan. 13, 1947, first train to Aneroid after a blizzard had blocked the railway for two weeks.

found it. Sometimes they used lengths of cord to be more accurate, or, if they were in a vehicle, the circumference of the wheel could determine the distance. After a site was found, a wagon and team of oxen or horses might be purchased back in town after they had filed for their claim and probably an exemption, too. It was believed that a half section could provide a good living, but many hoped to buy the homestead quarter of another whose land adjoined theirs to make a better working farm. This was especially important if part of their land could not be cultivated for one reason or another. I do not know if it was true of any man in Quimper, but some were even given *scripts* for land because they were veterans of the Boer War. It was necessary to have an overnight stopover between **Swift Current** and the homestead. It might be at the Mennonite village of **Blumenof**, in a pitched tent, or even using their wagon box for a shelter.

Not long after arrival the farmer would get that simplest means of conveyance imaginable — a stone boat. I often wondered how this name came to be — the *stone* part yes, as there was the never ending job of picking stones, but *boat*? That was strange, I thought, as this "boat" would never be propelled by oar or paddle. On snow, of course, it was easy pulling, but how hard it dragged on bare ground! It seemed to me they could have made some kind of a wheeled undercarriage for the summer months. There was very little clearance under a stone boat either, so when you went over a stone that *didn't* clear, you had a rocky ride for a minute. Also, the jiggling might cause you to lose quite a bit of water out of a barrel. A stone boat stand-up rider required special skill as starts and stops were pretty jerky. I distinctly remember so well how proud I was of myself the first time I was able to remain upright without losing my balance. Women and children would usually have boxes provided for them. (There was no hay baling then.) In winter this arrangement, along with a good lap-robe, made for quite a comfortable ride.

For winter time many would just lift the wagon box onto a bob sled and the buggy top to a set of runners. Sometimes the weather played tricks on this arrangement — especially if a chinook came up while you were some distance from home. How well I remember just such a day! A chinook had completely taken the snow off the high narrow grade just out of Ponteix, so, thinking it might be easier pulling in the ditch, Dad decided to try this. The slush, however, was much deeper than expected and the horses floundered shoulder deep in it. I was so frightened. Oh the relief when we got back on the road at the far end!

Some joked that if a chinook came up, the front runners could be *on snow* and the back ones *on dirt!*

Cars preceded trucks by a few years, but by the mid 20's almost every family had a car. Ours was an **Overland** sedan. Other early car names I recall in Quimper were **Model T's**, **Maxwell**, **Dodge**, and **Grey Dort**. Probably my readers could name others.

Then came the Depression. Gas became too expensive and of course, a car requires lots of other outlays too. Some did keep the car in running order, but often more for emergencies than everyday travel. In the worst dust storms, when horses refused to face into them, fathers would come in cars to pick up the children and bring feed for the horses, which would be left in the barn overnight. Driving was done very slowly with lights on.

There were two other ways farmers dealt with transportation at this time. One was to convert cars into "Bennett" buggies. (**R.B. Bennett** was Canada's Prime Minister and people were not feeling kindly towards him, as though he were to blame for their troubles.) The engine would be removed to lighten it, and a hitch put on the front, thus making it a very comfortable rubber-tired horse-drawn vehicle. Some kept only the chassis, so it served as a flatbed.

It was *long* on *looks* but *short* on *performance*. It was very hard to start and noisy, two qualities, I suspect, which earned it the derisive nickname of the *cement mixer*. Our Overland, 1924.

A really stripped down Bennett Buggy, 1936.

An Anderson cart made by Ed McCullough for his kids.

Others used just the back axle and wheels and called their rig an "Anderson" cart — **J.T. Anderson** being Saskatchewan's premier at this time.

Because it was cheaper — and more fun, too — young people would chip in money for gas for a truck — often McCoys, Uncle Sams' or Cross's. Trips to ball tournaments, dances and day outings to Lake Pelletier were thus made possible and affordable.

Airplanes of course, were seldom seen until after the war. Most of us can recall the day when a small plane was going over the schoolhouse and the teacher excused us all to run out and look at it. I had my first ride in 1941 in **Tacoma** — in a little two-seater Cessna. What a thrill! Now, it would be unlikely that any Quimperite had yet to have their first ride in the air. (I'm glad they're just called "planes" now — so we don't have to worry over whether we should write aeroplane, airplane, air liner or whatever, and on the ground, *automobiles* became just *cars*.)

Public transportation by bus was, by the 40's, starting to compete with train services, sometimes enabling one to get to places more directly or to some destination not on the rails. Busses were not of the best quality though, and roads not what they are today either, so breakdowns were frequent. In 1946 the *Saskatchewan Transportation Company* was organized after negotiations with *Greyhound Bus Lines* and local lines. When Quimper closed and children had to be bussed to town, there were some real headaches — both with the conveyances themselves and contending with the rural roads — snow in winter and mud in summer. Eventually, there were so few rural pupils that bus service was discontinued altogether. High school students would be back to the pre-depression days set-up and would board in town. Others, such as the Crosses might move into nearby towns or the city, or even change their occupation to accommodate their school-age children.

The back spring has come through the floor! That's my trunk on the top — with all the books in it. Maybe I contributed to the overload! (1945, just west of Moose Jaw.)

Communication

In early days rural post offices were common. Quimper was served by three such — Wallard (was it a town — it had a store!), **McCullough's** and **Uncle Sam's**. **Phoebe** remembers walking up the road to greet **Tom Claydon** coming for his mail. I don't know the year it took place, but by the mid-20's all rural post offices were gone and each family had a mailbox in town. The position of postmaster often went to a war veteran.

When we could send our voices via that special thing on the kitchen wall and wires on poles throughout the whole country, we figured we were next door to heaven! None had any inkling of today's advancements — faxes, cordless phones, e-mail, cellulars, etc., but I dare say no new technology equals the thrill to modern folks that the phone brought to us.

Such sophisticated technology is all around us today that even the most extraordinary developments quickly become everydayish. Remember the wonder of T.V. and everyone being glued to it for hours on end when men walked on the moon? Yet it wasn't long before a lift-off hardly got a line on an inside page.

Nearly fifty years had elapsed after **Alexander Bell's** invention of the phone in 1876 until Quimper folks got those wooden boxes with the crank on the right side, the receiver hang-up on the left, double bells at the top and a little slant shelf at the bottom for a note pad.

Every town had its switchboard operator — always a young woman it seemed. Each system had many lines. By 1927 the *Ponteix Rural Telephone Company Ltd.* had 160 subscribers, and by 1935, a total of 28 lines.

You could call on your own line with a designated number of long and short rings. Ours was line 5 ring 5. A long ring was a full turn or a little less and a short was about a quarter turn. Of course, everyone on the line could hear the ring, but politeness dictated only the one being rung was to answer. To avoid ringing in on others, you checked for openness before ringing. There were many tales — funny, sad, tragic, or just ordinary — that related to these party lines. Some lonesome folks might listen in just to hear human voices. Others were tuning in to hear some gossip. "Rubbering" was the common term for listening-in. In our home it was strictly taboo, but in my husband's home district near **Simmie**, it was an *accepted* form of community togetherness. They called it a real time saver! If one was going to town, any neighbor could cut in with a request to have their mail picked up or something to be bought at the store. If it weren't for rubbering, they said, the town-goer would have felt obliged to call these neighbors separately.

Then there was the general ring — one long, long ring by which Central could get everyone to lift their receiver and get all sorts of messages — announcements of sports events, shows, funeral notices, disasters, the circus or Chautauqua coming to town, weather and road reports, calls for help in case of accident or sickness — and so on. When you rang Central, and if time wasn't pressing, you might have a little chat with her before she plugged in the connector for who you were calling. Also, the operators, when not busy, would visit with each other. These girls had to have a very high sense of propriety as they knew everyone's private business.

Long distance calls (not counting short-distance ones like Quimper had between its two halves) were not too satisfactory and were almost exclusively for *bad news* — usually the death of a relative. These calls almost always had a lot of static and sometimes the voices were pretty faint and far away. To improve reception for the one *getting* the call, rubbering folks would hear, "Would all those listening in please hang up so that there will be more power for the one for whom this call is intended?" This was followed by a lot of clicks! Yes, phone service is high-tech nowadays, but we lost that personal neighborly touch with the demise of the party line.

In the Pontcix IIistory Book on page 147 is the list of all subscribers on the 1935 Ponteix Exchange along with their party line number and ring.

Saskatchewan was, in 1966, the third province in Canada, and one of the largest areas in the world, to give its rural customers automatic dial service.

Letters used to be the most common means of keeping in touch with those at a distance, but for short, quick messages, one would send a telegram. That continual clicking (the Morse code in operation, in case younger folks might wonder what this is) in the train depot was the telegraph. Otherwise, quietness reigned except at train time morning and afternoon.

It is very difficult for young ones of today to get a grasp of the contrast between horse and buggy days and this computer age. One of my favorite books is "A Touch of Wonder" by **Arthur Gordon**, though its theme is seeing *wonder* in *common* things in nature and in people rather than in scientific marvels. After all, our bodies, especially our minds, are the biggest wonder of all, and the more we learn about them, the more we realize the truth of the Bible description that we are "knit together in our mother's womb" and are "fearfully and wonderfully made."

In a large area of southwestern Saskatchewan **The Magnet** newspaper was looked forward to weekly, from its inception in 1913 to its demise in 1960-61, with only time out for the Depression, when its owner, **Thomas Manning,** simply couldn't make "a go of it" after the 1929 collapse. In the 30's Manning did whatever printing jobs he could get, as well as other types of work, one of which was being Registrar of Electors for the **Maple Creek** Constituency. In this capacity he worked out a system for accurate voting lists which would be continually updated. For 15 years, which included the decades of the Depression, he served on Aneroid's Village Council and school board. A complicated system of checques — which never saw the bank — relief vouchers, arrangements for boarding the school teachers, coal for the schools, taxes, groceries and repair services was worked out. It was a bookkeeper's nightmare, but received high praise from

The News Magnet

VOLUME XXVI No. 40 — ANEROID, SASKATCHEWAN, THURSDAY, JULY 31, 1952 — CANADA $2.00; U.S.A. $3.00

NEWS OF OUR NEIGHBORS

Kincaid

Mr. and Mrs. A. Baldwin and family of Hamilton, Ont., are guests of the former's parents, Mr. and Mrs. F. Baldwin.

Hazenmore

There will be service in the United Church on Sunday, Aug. 3, at 11 a.m. Miss Irma Magee in charge.

40th Anniversary Celebration Proposed at Board of Trade

Aneroid & District Board of Trade held its July meeting in the theatre on Monday night with a small number in attendance. H. M. Manning presided, with A. W. Wright recording

Crowd Enjoys Baseball Tournament When Vanguard Wins Round Robin

Only a fair sized crowd attended the Aneroid baseball tournament on July 23 in spite of perfect weather. Only first, between Vanguard and Aneroid when the former won by 4 runs to 3 in the 11th inning. The first four innings

BUSINESS ENTERPRISES

8 Elevators
1 Bank
1 Hotel
1 Doctor
1 Printing Office
1 Photographer
1 Baker
1 Harness Shop
3 Garages
3 Implement Dealers
1 Drug Store
1 Barber and Pool Room
1 Picture Show
1 Butcher Shop
2 Confectioneries
4 General Stores
3 Hardwares
2 Lumber Yards 3 Drays
1 Real Estate and Insurance
3 Cafes 2 Livery Barns
2 Blacksmiths
1 Co-operative Store

The News Magnet

A weekly newspaper published in Aneroid and circulating throughout one of the best and most prosperous farming districts in Saskatchewan makes it the cheapest and best medium through which to interest prospective customers.

JOB PRINTING
of all kinds neatly and promptly executed.

YOUR BUSINESS IS SOLICITED

DISTANCES BY AUTO ROAD

	Miles
Regina	183
Moose Jaw	158
Assiniboia	63
Morse	63
Herbert	54
Gravelbourg	49
Shaunavon	53
Swift Current	66
Gull Lake	104
Maple Creek	166
Ponteix	8
Medicine Hat	233
Calgary	437
Banff	522
Lake Louise	559
Cranbrook, B.C.	724
Kingsgate	772
Spokane, Wash.	909
Seattle, Wash.	1098
Portland, Oregon	1286
Vancouver, B.C.	1413
Havre, Mont.	196

This clipping from an early day Magnet gives you some idea of the number of diverse businesses in most of these small prairie towns and the distance table on the right shows their interest in both those near and far-away places.

Saskatchewan's premier **J.M. Anderson** saying the Department of Education would have had no problem financing if other districts had been this hard working and resourceful.

After the war, he was joined, when resuming his business, by his son, **Gordon**. The business prospered. Gordon married **Loie Murray**. The father died in 1955. Five years later, his own health failing, Gordon hauled the equipment to Edmonton to sell it. The family then made Edmonton home. Thus ended a newspaper business which had been a mainstay of a service area that stretched from the U.S. border to the south, Assiniboia on the east, Shaunavon on the west and the main rail line to the north.

From only *two* pages of *one* **Magnet** I will list some of the items covered — just enough to give you the flavour: weddings, showers, business news items, ads and notices of all kinds, world current events, a column of jokes — "Funny and Otherwise", recipes, nature's oddities, archeological news, seasonal work schedules, a comic strip, and tidbits in any little space left for them. It is interesting to note the cost of an ad — first insertion, two cents per word, minimum 50 cents — each subsequent insertion, one cent per word, minimum 25 cents. In England and sometimes in Canada, the Salvation Army is called the **Sally Ann** and an appeal for funds was on the front page. You could even order fresh flowers from a Moose Jaw flower shop through agents along the rail line. An Ottawa notice told of cheaper rates on the railroad for Eastern Canada workers to come west for the harvesting of a predicted good crop. There was even an item from **Huntingdon**, England, telling about a split vacation for school children so they could help with potato harvest.

We think special borders on ads are fairly modern, but on just one page I counted *four* different ones. There was also a variety of printing styles, thus giving it an attractive appearance.

Food and Water

A homesteader had no idea when filing on a claim whether his land would have good water on it or not. Many suffered bitter disappointments as well after well was either dry or had terrible water. Some would finally just give up and resign themselves to hauling it from a neighbor's who had been fortunate enough to get good water. We had excellent water at the foot of the hill in our yard. We would always go for a pail of cold water just before the men came in from the field. On a hot day men hauling grain to town would often stop in for a cool drink. For a supplemental supply, another well was dug nearby, but it too, had good water.

Our first well had a pump house on it and so did our Uncle Sam's, but for some reason I do not know, the second was left open. However, when our new house was built in 1924 and all the plumbing was done for an inside bathroom, dreams took a nose-dive. The well dug near the house had very bad water. However, the well itself served another purpose. To keep it nice and cool, Dad suspended the can of cream just above the surface of the water.

For most farmers, ice for everyday use was not common, but if one had a dam like **Oscar Foss**, blocks of ice would be cut in the dead of winter and stored under straw in a nearby granary. It was this ice that made possible that scrumptious homemade ice cream at com— munity picnics.

A no-name creek ran kitty corner through our farm — from Morin's at the northwest corner to the alkali flat — that spot which featured heavily in choosing the location of the school. In early days this creek ran all the time, and when it was high in the springtime, it was a real worry for our parents. Later on when the land was under cultivation, it might only run after a flash flood or just a little in the spring. Sloughs left behind when the creek stopped running were wonderful places for

Some of the essentials for keeping clean in olden days.

us to play — rafting and wading in summer, and skating, sliding, sled pulling in winter.

Most people got soft water via a rain barrel at a roof corner or, in newer houses, a cistern under the cellar. In winter snow melting was common — especially for hair washing. A pan on top of the stove and the reservoir on the side, both filled with snow, would be a common sight.

Though we appreciated the cool, fresh water, Mom made her own root beer, which was so refreshing on hot days.

Everyone grew a garden. You might have to water it a lot, but if you could beat the drought, grasshoppers, potato bugs, cutworms, gophers, etc., you would have lots of fresh vegetables and a bin full of potatoes for winter. Maybe other families had root cellars, but we didn't. I do remember us trying to preserve carrots in sand, but I don't recall this being very successful. I guess we didn't do it correctly. Many housewives canned lots of vegetables, but not us. I think Mom was too scared of botulism. But many jars *were* filled with canned beef, pork and chicken. Wives were proud of their butter which, along with a crate of eggs, often helped pay for the groceries. For winter when hens weren't laying, big crocks of water-glass preserved eggs, but these were used mostly in baking.

Mom used to also pack cooked steaks in a big crock — layering them in with melted lard. When butchering was done at freeze-up time, meat was cut and wrapped and would stay frozen all winter on tables in a granary. For fresh beef in summer months, most districts as did ours, had a beef ring. Each family in turn would supply the animal and after it was butchered, all would come to get their share. A system was worked out so that all choice portions would be shared fairly.

Small fruits, mainly strawberries and raspberries, were grown by most folks and rhubarb plants were found in most gardens. The only wild fruit we had was saskatoons, which were picked along the **Pinto**

Creek. These berries are delicious fresh and no better pies or cobblers can a cook turn out than with saskatoons! In the hard years this was sometimes the only fruit that got canned. Most English people are very fond of fruit and ours fit the pattern. In good years, as each came in season, and was shipped from the **Okanagan**, we would get some. It was hard to prevent much of it disappearing before getting into the jars! Somehow, even in the worst years, Mom would manage to fill quite a few jars with fruit. But *one* fruit fits *neither* of these categories and that was apples. Oh, the aroma that filled the house when two or three boxes of McIntosh apples were brought in each fall! I don't recall us ever having any other variety. I'm sure we all ate our apple a day and more, and **McIntosh**, in the opinion of many of us, especially we who are now in our 70's and 80's, is the best cooking apple there is. You can read the fascinating story of this apple in the old Canadian Fourth Reader.

We didn't have fish very often. In fact, about the only kinds I remember are finnan haddie and canned salmon. During the Depression some kind people in the Maritimes sent boxes of fish — probably salted cod — but sad to say, they neglected to send along instructions on *how to cook* it, so much of it was wasted. When word of this got back, following shipments included instructions and recipes.

The food in homesteading days didn't have much variety. Our Mom, who was used to lots of fruit in England, missed it greatly in her first years in Canada — especially oranges and bananas. With frustration in her voice, I can still hear her saying, "Salt pork and prunes!" However, she had quickly learned to like and lavishly use the plentiful dairy products and eggs, but they too, were bad as she gained weight on this diet.

Clothing

In the early days practically all clothes were ordered from Eatons, though **Mr. Lorenzino** in the general store in Ponteix did stock a few bolts of cloth. I think there were about as many kinds of cloth then as now, but of course, few of what we call man-made materials. When one thinks of it, differences between *natural* and *man-made* are not all that definitive as *both* use basics provided by nature, whether from animals, grasses or chemicals. Great amounts of time and money have been spent to impart certain characteristics to fabrics — for instance, preshrunk, no iron, permanent creased, fast dyed, waterproof and so on. Oh how we females dote on some of these! Prior to 1958 we had few such advancements to enjoy. The one that comes quickly to mind is the no-iron materials. When we went on a trip in 1954, our daughter **Milla** and I had our first no-iron blouses and skirts. And it was around this time that they came out with *lifetime* socks. I must admit, we were a very skeptical lot when we first saw *this* ad. However, it was enticing enough to overcome skepticism and we got some. They really did wear and wear and wear! Up until this time few women attended a Ladies Aid meeting without taking along their darning baskets.

Until perma-crease pants came out we battled those wire pant creasers for work pants, and good trousers had to be steam pressed. Pleated skirts were a bug-bear! I remember I had one dress I really liked, but it had all around *pin* pleats — well named as it took forever to press those pleats — pinning them to the ironing board cover as you went. ("Pin" really meant small, so I'm making a play on words here.)

Flowers in Field, Garden or House

Prior to Dust Bowl days, wild flowers abounded on the prairies. The variety of color, shapes and perfumes was probably as great as you would find anywhere — crocuses, wild roses, buffalo beans, gaillardia, bluebells, buttercups, primroses, scarlet mallow, daisies, violets, black-eyed susans, clovers, goldenrods, coneflowers and, of course, Saskatchewan's provincial flower, the red lily. In the beautifully illustrated book "Wild Flowers Across the Prairies", by **Vance, Jowsey and McLean**, ©1977, you will see many, many more even than these. One of my favourites we called grandfather's whiskers, but which this book calls a three-flowered aven. Some of course, including our emblem lily, were more common where there was more moisture, nor did we find lady slippers. Few would classify a thistle as a lovely blossom and the Russian thistle flower would get no praise from anyone, I'm sure, in spite of the fact that if you look at these miniature flowers without prejudice, the variety of colors and dainty shapes is intriguing. We didn't have cactus on our farm, but on the coulees to the south there were plenty of prickly pears in yellow to pinkish orange.

Most of these wild flowers were no longer found in our area after the 30's, as many had their roots simply blown away and of course, cultivation of the land took many others. But most, if not all, of these varieties still bloom in other areas of the prairie and the recent establishment of the **Grasslands Park** near **Val Marie** will surely help many to recover.

Even throughout the 30's, Quimper gardeners refused to do without flowers and would spare enough water to grow many of them in their gardens. We didn't grow many flowers, but I learned the names of a lot of them when I visited at **Bjores**. Because of their garden, those in need of a cheerful bouquet would seldom go without, and arrangements would frequently be seen on the teacher's desk during the week; or on this same piece of furniture bedecked for a church service. **Alcide Dumont's** garden was not only *his* pride and joy, but because of his generosity, especially with his gladiolas, special events such as weddings, pilgrimages and R.C. church services were well supplied.

A favourite of mine with the sweetest perfume was always in Aunt Phoebe's garden — minionettes.

Now let us step indoors. I don't remember a single home without house plants. Some of the favourites were geraniums, begonias and coleus. Mom had a big flowering maple. Beautiful bell-like blossoms hung randomly all over. **Wilma** in **Dawson Creek** still has hers started from a slip Mom gave her.

Green plants indoors, we've learned recently, are very good for the air and aloe vera is excellent first aid for burns, so prairie women were promoting good health, too, if unwittingly.

Many of us took real delight in *pressing* flowers, but except for the naturally drying everlastings, I do not recall us *drying* any of them, though I've seen in museums and old houses some beautiful, elaborate dried bouquets — some in frames, also. They are faded, of course, but still very beautiful.

Nowadays it has become an "art" to make *new* things look *old*, but one thing they can't imitate is those fly specks on everything — especially old photographs! Another reason the good-old days *weren't*!

Most old-time methods of fighting flies have gone, including swatting in public places, but *one* is still around — those sticky coils. We hung them in our Young Life food booth at the fair last year.

Rural Electrification

A day to remember! The day when all rural Saskatchewan got public power! In 1949 legislation was passed to provide rural electrification and that year 1,100 got connected — by 1955 25,000 and by 1964, 65,000. Prior to this the only power on farms was from either a wind generator or a Delco light plant. We had a Delco. It was a 32 volt multi-battery set-up with a gasoline motor. How well we remember that, as the batteries discharged, our lights got dimmer and yellower — until when those two little white balls on the end of the row of batteries got near the bottom of the columns, Dad would start the engine. Immediately we had bright lights again. Before farms got public power, only the few with a Delco had a yard light. A number of appliances were made to run on this 32 volt plant, but all we got was the washer.

Gas irons were fairly common, but most women were still using the old sad irons you heated on top of the stove. As the one you were using cooled down, you went over to the stove for a hot one. You just interchanged the clip handle. Women could very accurately test the temperature by a quick spit-on-finger touch-the-iron. Few ovens had a thermostat on the front either, but this lack was of small concern to women who were used to a coal and wood stove. They *knew* the temperature by simply opening the oven door and putting their hand inside.

Medical Services

One of the real hardships of rural life both then and now, is the difficulty or impossibility of getting quick medical service. Doctors and nurses travelled to homes instead of patients going to town as a rule, but this began to change for Quimper folks when Aneroid got their Cottage Hospital. This was where both Rob and I were born. But by 1923 Ponteix had its Gabriel Hospital (I didn't know it by this name until I began working on this book — we just called it the Ponteix hospital), so my sister Nellie, five years younger than I, was born there.

I do not know what the sickness was (I suspect a woman in labour, but such things were not spoken of openly in those days), but I do remember one blizzardy night. This family lived quite a few miles south of us and we were 9 miles from town. A sort of relay set-up was established by phoning ahead. Horses would go as fast as possible, and at each stop a fresh team would be ready. I do not remember the outcome — whether the woman made it or not.

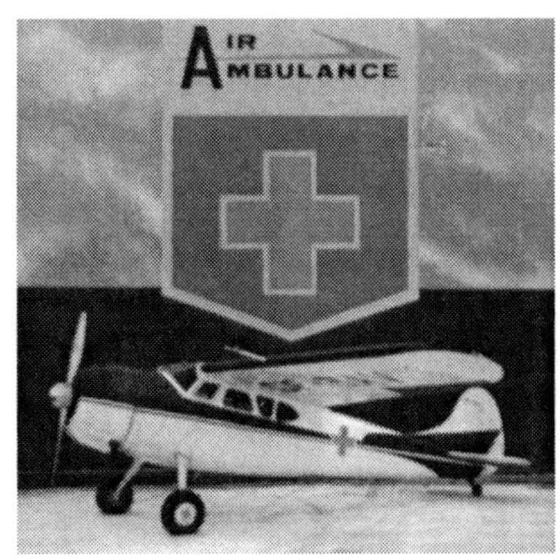

Common problems of that day seldom encountered today and just contended with at home were boils, styes, and what was called "sleep" — a yellowish crust which formed on eyelashes during sleep.

On February 3, 1946, Saskatchewan inaugurated an air ambulance service titled Mercy Flights.

Three former members of the armed services were the crew — pilot **Keith Malcolm**, flight engineer **Donald Watson** and nurse **M.E. Gleadow**. For northern parts a second plane equipped with skis and pontoons went into service. By March of 1955, 6677 patients had been flown on these planes, which landed on highways, fields or lakes. This wonderful service no longer exists, sad to say. I never heard why it was discontinued.

Nurse holding Egbert, son of Dr. Kitchen on porch of Cottage hospital 1918.

Gabriel Hospital in Ponteix. Built in 1917.

Aneroid Cottage Hospital served the early settlers until the bigger Ponteix Gabriel Hospital was fully operational. A rich lady in France granted a considerable sum towards it providing it bore her son's name. The Sisters of Notre Dame took the responsibility of building and equipping it. The Health Department subsidized it with 50 cents per patient per day. It was barely in operation when it had to handle the horrendous care of flu patients — this plague lasting until March, 1919. **Dr. Kitchen** and **Dr. Lupien** got little rest — often only what they could grab as they were driven from one house to another.

In 1967 the hospital was closed and the building used for other purposes. However, in 1966, the construction of a Union Hospital was already underway so, as the old hospital closed, the new was opened. The cost was $160,000.00, of which the provincial government granted $33,183.00 and the federal $30,372.00. A Manor and Foyer (nursing home) now serve senior citizens.

Rob was chairman of the Ponteix Union Hospital Board from 1973 to 1976.

Dr. Osborne was the resident dentist in Ponteix from 1924 to 1940. From then on dentist services were mostly by itinerant dentists coming on certain days from Shaunavon and Swift Current.

Dr. Laflamme was the chiropractor in Ponteix for many years and served the community in many other ways also.

Many of us can attest to the high professional skill of both of these men, and no medical person could receive higher praise for their work and compassion than **Sister Mary** — one of the founding sisters of the Ponteix Hospital.

Depression and Dust

It would be impossible to give any sort of overview of daily living without making a fairly definitive set of time periods, because each so clearly had its own characteristics. Nevertheless, the one which stands out most distinctively in everyone's mind is that of the Depression — sometimes "Great" preceding it. It began with the collapse of the stock market in October of 1929, but for prairie folks it really began with the first of many horrendous storms, called black blizzards. The price of wheat dropped from $1.50 a bushel in 1929 to 29¢ in 1931 and even to 19¢ a year or so later. These figures from the memories of those who gave them — don't quite agree with *official* statistics as given in Archer's "Saskatchewan — A History", but *accuracy* is secondary to what happens when markets collapse. Prices paid for eggs and butter bought so little in groceries it was hardly worthwhile to take them to town. It wasn't long before almost everyone was on relief. The Relief Commission set up in 1931 arranged for securing and distributing food, fuel, clothing, shelter, medical care, livestock food, machinery repairs, oil and gas, seed wheat, etc. At first, all help was in loans against the farmers' land, but when it was clear debt repayment was absolutely impossible, a Debt Adjustment Board was formed which virtually wrote off almost all debts. School teachers' wages had been placed against the farmers' taxes also, so when debts were cancelled, those who had boarded the teachers had done it free in a crazy sort of way.

I remember Dad and Mom trying to get a set-up whereby they would get 10¢ a day, I think it was, from ratepayers for board money, but it fell through. In some districts, the teachers simply had to spend a couple of weeks at each home in the district, but in Quimper this was not even seriously considered, as teachers *wanted* to stay put at our place and would pay whatever they could out of what little cash they got from time to time. I don't remember if any of them were on relief also, as I was in my first year of teaching.

Once when Dad had been asked to help sort relief clothing, someone else on the job said, "Jim, you really need a sweater, I see. This one looks as if it will fit you." He was persuaded to take it. But a couple of days later Mom was saying "Never again will we accept *any* relief clothing." They were so humiliated — the sweater belonged to **Mr. Elliot**, the storekeeper in Aneroid, who was a fellow sorter, so, in tracking it down, *everyone* would know just *who* had it.

Prairie folk had been used to getting the good hard anthracite coal from Alberta, so it was a real come-down to have to use the soft lignite coal from **Instow**, just a few stations west of Ponteix, or **Estevan** in eastern Saskatchewan. Wood was used very sparingly — mostly just for kindling.

Various methods of field management were tried to battle soil blowing — planting caragana hedges, strip farming, contour furrowing, rod weeding, listing and discing rather than plowing. Manure was placed *on* the land instead of being burned in piles. It was hard on aesthetics too, as farmers had always been so *proud* of their summer fallows being *clear* of weeds.

Merchants in town had extended credit to farmers for food, machinery repairs and other necessities, so they too, had to be helped by the government rather than sink under bankruptcy.

Sometimes a good car was simply put into storage with hopes for next year. (The term "next year" in fact, came to be the most common two words on everyone's tongue.)

Those with poetic ability turned out many highly descriptive or poignant poems — some of which you can read in the history books most towns put out when celebrating Saskatchewan's 75th Anniversary in 1980.

It was remarkable and high tribute to those who stuck it out on these devastated, eroded, desolate looking farms long enough to see the days of their recovery beginning in 1938.

Statistics may seem rather dry, but when translated into *living* them out in personal lives, they mean much more. In "Saskatchewan a History", by **John H. Archer**, I read these words: "Saskatchewan suffered to a much greater extent than any other province of Canada; the average per capita fell by 72 percent; in 1932-33 wheat prices fell to the lowest level in 300 years; farmers forced to sell thin cattle and low-grade grain could get a *bill* for transportation and other charges rather than a cheque; the drought of the 30's was more severe and more prolonged than any which preceded it in recorded history; recognizing the terrible unemployment problem as national, the Bennett (federal) government passed the Unemployment Relief Act on September 22, 1930; in 1931 almost all the settled area of the province, south of the South Saskatchewan river, was a crop failure area; the railways waived freight charges on some 577 carloads of food and supplies donated by Ontario and the Maritimes; strict policing of unemployed young men riding the freights failed to prevent them riding back and forth across the country; in 1937 the Dominion-Provincial Youth Training programme was initiated with courses offered at Saskatoon, Regina, and in local centres; the Prairie Farm Rehabilitation Act was passed in April 1935 and in only two years sixteen community pastures had been established each with 6,000 to 25,000 acres and dug-outs and dams became common throughout the Palliser Triangle."

Lest these facts make it appear that all was sad and dreary in the 30's, you'll see the other side in following chapters. And in no account of these years and previously, can we miss the telling of stories about some big companies and their services to us. If you were asked to name but five, I'm sure you would all come up with different lists except for *one* — **The T. Eaton Company**. The other four I would name might be **Watkins**, **B.C. Sugar**, **Neilsons**, and **Rit Dyes**. I enjoyed researching these businesses and hope you will enjoy in turn a few of the things I learned. Each one wrote to me, not only to answer a few of my specific questions, but to send me interesting materials.

The Timothy Eaton Company

Who could forget the thrill each spring and fall when that wondrously fat Eaton's catalogue came in the mail? Family members almost needed to choose lots to see who would get it first. It was even referred to somewhat irreverently as the "Homesteader's Bible". Apparently there was a hundred percent "recycling" way back then as *not one* surfaced for me to use as I tried to write this story! The nearest I came was part of a sale catalogue, from the thirties I believe (the *year* was missing). Eaton's Archives sent me a number of sample pages though, and other things, so with these sources, plus memories, I have worked up possible orders that *could* have been in three *representative* years.

South of the border another huge mail order house was operating also, but I never heard expressions of *affection* for it as for Eaton's — satisfaction, yes, but not affection. This personal touch often showed up in the correspondence that went back and forth between the company and their customers. Dad had saved some notes from an article

(Continued on page 100)

Heating: 1) coal and wood cookstove; **2)** portable kerosene heater; **3)** front room heater. **Lighting: 4)** a table gas lamp (a school room had a similar hanging one), coal oil lamps were used in all other rooms but the front room. **Travel** : **5)** everyone had at least one trunk for trips — between times other uses were: storage, supplemental shelves or wardrobe and often for kids seated at the table. **Fun**: **6)** an accordian, mouth organ, violin or guitar were found in many homes; **7)** almost all folks played cards.

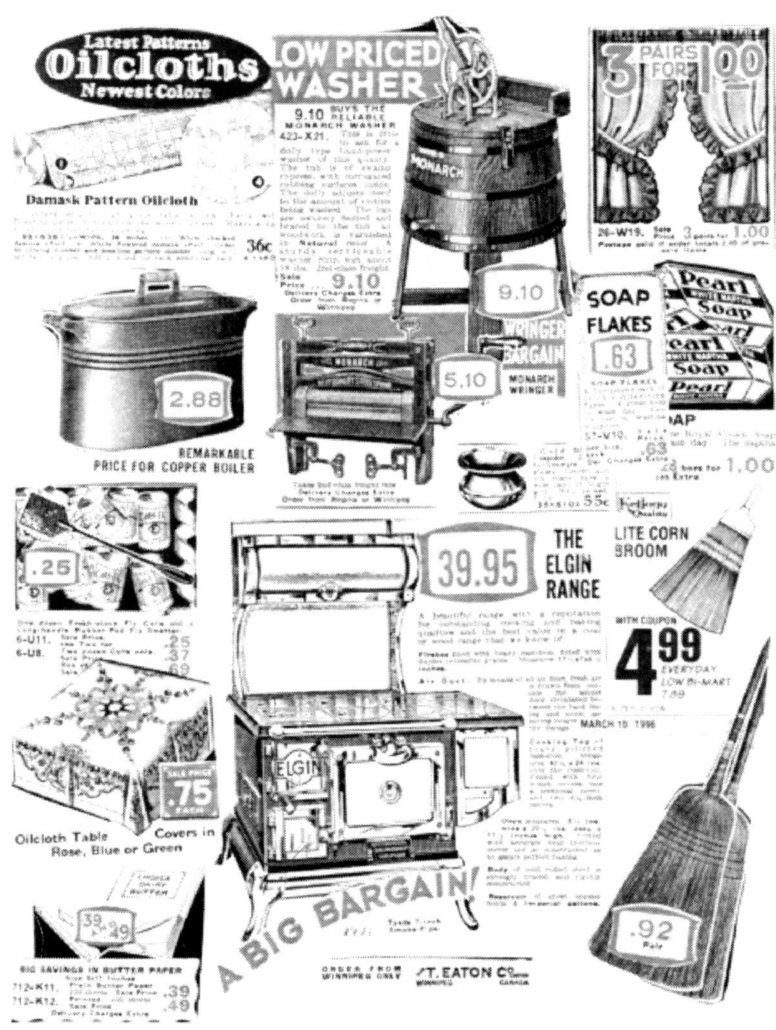

generations. It is very difficult for everyone today to grasp the tremendous changes that have taken place, not just in the first half of the century — the main focus of this book — but perhaps the even faster and still more revolutionary changes since the half way mark. It would be interesting for grandparents and grandchildren to go through some of *today's* catalogues and have it pointed out that some things are just the *same* as always in many respects, while other items were never *dreamed* of in those bygone

years. For females, or as they used to be called "the fairer sex", it can be pointed out that with such freedom in today's clothes, we are now at liberty to wear almost any style we wish and not be "out of style" — a terrible stigma in past eras — if your dress hem was not the right height; your hair style out of line with the narrow dictates of fashion; the wearing of hat or gloves either "in" or "out", the size of the heels of one's shoes off the norm — even just how much of your skin that

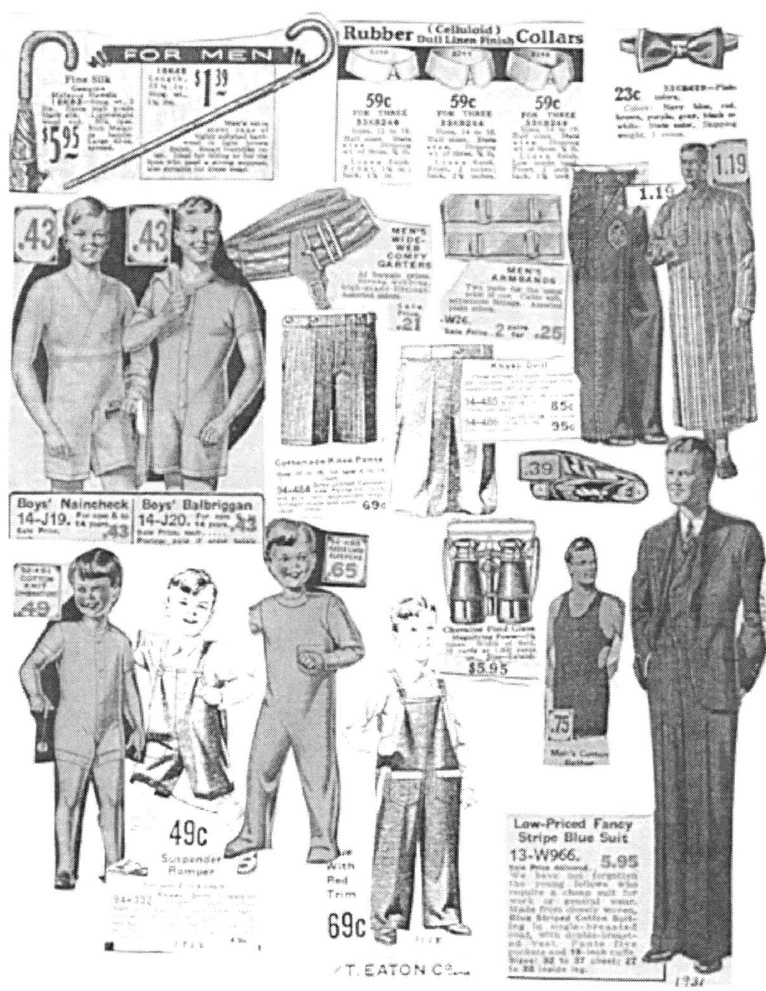

showed. All were non-negotiable. Even the *colours* one could wear were narrowly defined. For example, a widow had to wear *black* for a certain length of time after the death of her husband and older women were confined to black, navy, brown and grey. On and on it went!

Men's fashions haven't changed much except that casual dress is much more accepted, even in formal settings, than previously. Nevertheless, a well-dressed business man is more apt to get a certain job if he shows up in

Also, women's hats, hair and dress styles are very easily identified. The 30's can be spotted probably more by the *prices* of items than anything else, as both the company and their customers were suffering from the Great Depression. Few marriages were taking place and the birth rate took a drastic dip. More potent factors determined what was being ordered by mail from the T. Eaton Company.

These pages can serve as real conversation pieces for bridging the

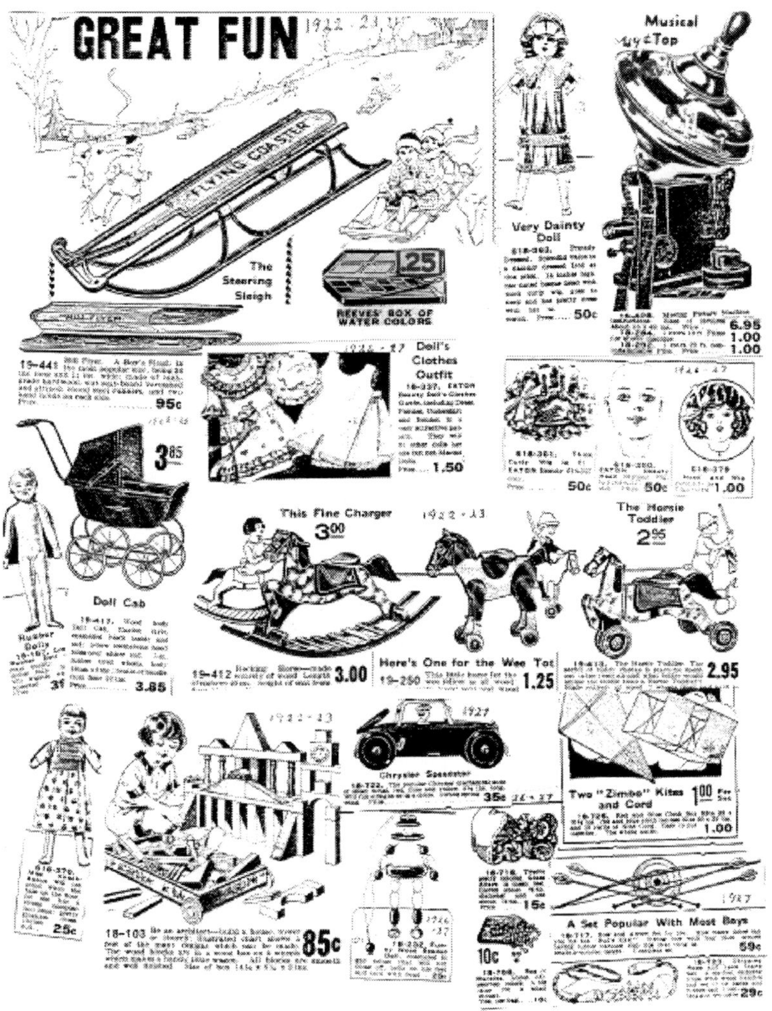

Fold out pages are a *collage* of items found in Eaton's catalogues in widespread years. They are not in any sequence, but are partly in groupings. As you look at the prices of items and the styles of clothes, you will no doubt detect that some are for the teen years (prior to 1920) when many homesteaders were bachelors, but, married or not, farm operations and household needs dictated what was being ordered. In the 20's most were married and things for wives and children probably dominated the ordering.

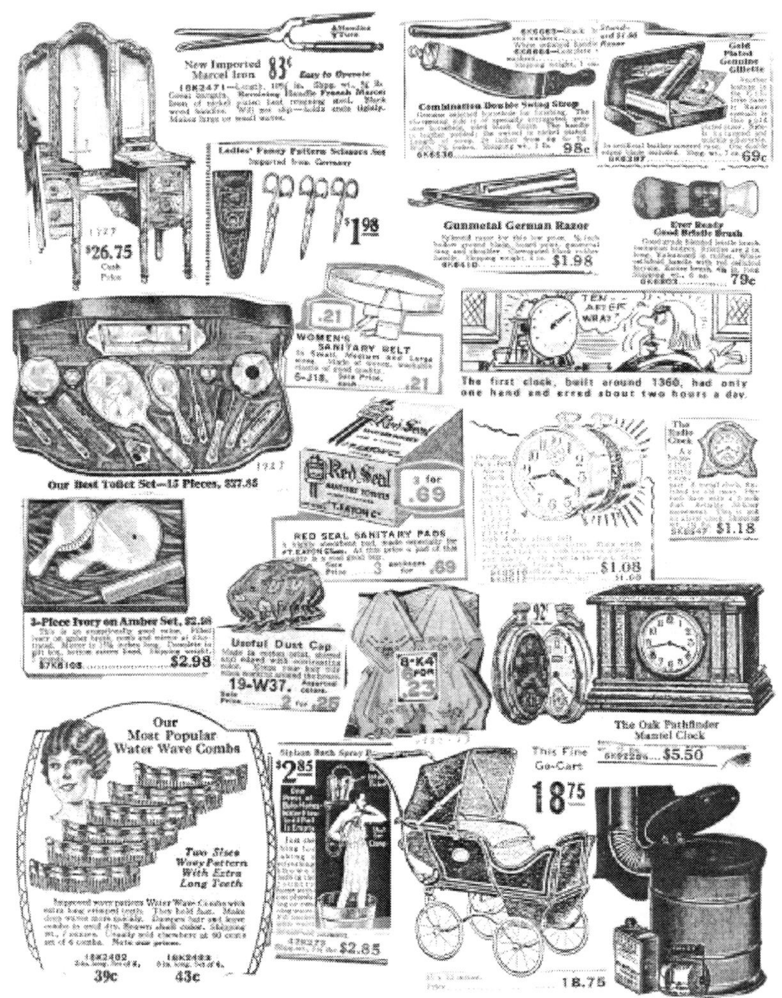

a suit and tie and dress shoes and with an acceptable hair cut.

It is hoped that older folk have saved at least one of those big fat catalogues which are no longer put out by any of the big mail order houses. They will be a real novelty to young ones now accustomed to the flyer types that often come with our daily newspaper.

Yes, you could even order a house or barn by mail!

These three lists are indicative of what a Saskatchewan farm family (1 and 2) might have ordered from Eaton's in these representative years while column 3 are some things a young teacher might have ordered with her first paycheck.

(1) 1914	(2) 1927	(3) 1939
little wagon	6 rolls binder twine	dress shields
toy train	6 gunny sacks	lady's coat
high chair	1 pair men's felt shoes	lady's hat
nursery chair	1 pair lady's dress shoes	lady's galoshes
home barbering set	washing machine	back seam hose
home doctor book	cream separator	brown & black shoe polish
Eaton Beauty doll	boot black	garter belt
hanging parlor lamp	2 pair child's sleepers	corselette
gramaphone	2 children's garter waists	lined leather mitts
gramaphone records	set of men's military brushes	lace collar & cuff set
gramaphone needles	1 pair men's high buckle overshoes	2 yards gingham
washtubs, wash board bench & wringer	radio	mirror brush & comb set
bluing (cakes or bottle)	kerosene heater	vanity set and runner to embroider
dash churn	indoor closet (toilet)	6 embroidery skeins
1 lb. butter mould	Hawkeye box camera	6 rolls Dennison crepe paper
butter papers	curry comb and brush	boxed silk hose
bottle butter coloring	tinker toys	Hohner harmonica
4 sets work harness	mechano set	box of stationary
1 set buggy harness	singing top	bottle blue/black ink
horse muzzles	lady's coat and muff	box straight pen nibs
man's union suit	lady's corset	blue and red correcting pencil
razor, strap, mug and brush	upright piano	1 pair dress shoes
10 yards flannelette	soap flakes	1 pair stamped pillow cases

that was, we believe, published in the Saturday Evening Post a long time ago. These have been lost, but we still remember our side-splitting-laughter every time he got them out. The examples of misspellings, misplaced phrases, reasons for returning goods and so on were simply hilarious. It was said that Eaton's could have written up *life stories* of some of their customers from the orders sent in — first those from their parents growing up years, then an engagement, the wedding, the first baby, subsequent children, all progressing through the years till they were grandparents themselves.

Eaton's stood by their guarantee at all costs, it seemed, no matter how ridiculous the complaint with returned goods. Here are two such examples: a woman who ordered a coat, found it *too* long, shortened it — *too* much — and sent it back with the complaint that it was *too* short. Another returned a brooder after using it one season, saying they didn't need it any more!

Many rural schools had bazaars, raffles, etc., in order to earn money for their Junior Red Cross Society. If you sent a letter of request for craft materials, Eaton's would send *free* a *big* box of all sorts of things — odds and ends of laces, ribbons, remnants of fabrics and oilcloth, weaving materials, etc. Such generosity and kindness on the part of a huge mail order company provided the teachers with a very appropriate setting for the children to learn to write thank-you letters, don't you think?

Catalogues also had numerous secondary uses — teachers used them as teaching tools — helping immigrant children to learn English; hockey players used them for shin pads; new farmers could even learn how to prepare seed for planting or how to harness a horse; little girls made whole sets of paper dollies with beautiful wardrobes — all from Eaton's catalogues. By folding pages a certain way a catalogue could even become a doorstop.

If a customer didn't know a shoe or glove size, all they needed to do was trace around a foot or hand. If an item ordered couldn't be supplied, something of higher value was substituted, and if change was due the customer, they received a slip stating the amount of credit for the next order.

If your hand writing was good, you could, if you lived in **Toronto** or **Winnepeg**, get a job addressing the thousands of letters and parcels that went out each day.

Later, the **Hudson's Bay Company**, **Simpson's** and the **Army and Navy** offered some competition, but most Eaton's customers remained loyal. However, modern highways and the kind of prosperity people enjoyed after WWII gave them the opportunity to shop more in person, so in 1976, Eatons closed their mail order division while still retaining retail stores in a number of large cities.

Timothy Eaton did not believe in Sunday shopping. I do not know what year it was discontinued, but in the sixties it seems to me, the drapes were still being drawn on store windows so as to prevent even the *sin of window shopping*!

One unique service to rural school districts was this: from a list with the ages and sex of all children in the district along with a suggested price you wished to pay, Eaton's would send a most wonderful selection of gifts to go under the Christmas tree the night of the concert. But in the worst of the Depression years they added their *heart concerns* for those districts hardest hit. They asked that this same type of list be sent in but these gifts would be *their* gift. I got a beautiful fleece-lined sweatshirt.

In the 40's they instituted a really novel idea called "The Personal Shopper Service". If you wanted to be *exclusive* and *not see yourself coming* as they said, in a dress just like the one you had on, because you *both* liked *that* one in the catalogue, you could do this: cut out or sketch a dress style you liked, say which colours were your first, second and third choices, and give your size. Soon would come a dress that just fit your dream. It had been selected by your Personal Shopper in Winnipeg. Once I ordered one each for my sister and myself, hers to be my Christmas gift for her. We were both elated with our dresses and old snapshots show us frequently wearing these dresses.

A wonderful article on Eaton's was carried in the Oct. 8, 1992 issue of the "Western People" newspaper magazine. Among many interesting things I learned here: in their first department store in Western Canada in Winnepeg, which opened in July of 1905, there were tables where women could make out orders to be delivered later that day by vehicles drawn by beautiful high stepping horses; there was a restroom and a nurse on full time duty; there were telegraph services and a place to check your hat and suitcase; the pennies for change that other companies scorned, were deposited in containers near cash registers and donated to charity; phone ordering was introduced and they had their own printing plant, also testing and research bureaus; they sponsored writing contests for high school students and had annual banquets for high achievers; for a radio program they sponsored, they sent talent scouts out into rural areas. All this and the list went on!

It would be almost impossible to have the Eaton story without telling a few things about the life of its founder, **Timothy Eaton**.

He was born in **Ireland** in 1834 to a farm family. His father died two months before he was born, and his mother when he was only 14. Most of his eight older brothers and sisters had by then already emigrated to **Canada**. At age 13 he was an apprentice to a storekeeper in a neighboring town. His employer was a severe demanding man — a *negative* example of what young Timothy vowed *never* to be were he ever an employer. His siblings welcomed him as he arrived in Canada and they all worked beautifully together in establishing businesses in the little town of **Kirkton**, **Ontario**. A move to bigger **St. Mary's** provided challenge, competition and incentive for his retailing skills and here he met his wife, **Margaret Beattie**.

Buying the Toronto Jennings Dry Goods store in 1869 led to opening the T. Eaton Co. Toronto store at 176 Yonge St. This was only the first of moves which led to business expansions. Catalogues were now being distributed and the store had Canada's first passenger elevators. They soon had their own factories also. Eatons was the first company to have employee holidays and to continue to pay wages in both world wars to its employees in the service.

To conclude my Eaton story, here is an anecdote from a National

Geographic: May 7, headlines screamed, "Lusitania Blown Up by Germans, Loss of Life Reported Slight. Remained afloat 12 hours." The next day headlines were *different* — at least the sub-headings. "Probably 1,260 dead; sinks in 15 minutes." But a *tiny bit* in the text as quoted in the April 1994 National Geographic caught my eye. "As the ship went down, one of the giant funnels sucked a woman down inside, only to blow her out again in an explosion of steam. Covered with soot, she survived." Then in a letter to the editor in the August issue, these words jumped out "Riddle of the Lusitania". A lady, **Pauline Welch** of Toronto, Ontario, was thanking the Geographic for ending her husband's scoffing, that her **Aunt Josie (Josephine Burnside**, the daughter of Timothy Eaton) *was this lady* and that the reason she was on the Lusitania was that she and her daughter were traveling (Americans use only one 'l' in this word) overseas to visit the grave of the son she had lost early in World War I. The daughter, Iris, was drowned, but Aunt Josie had lived into the 40's.

(The T. Eaton archives are now stored by the Archives of Ontario in Toronto. A listing of their main inventory was prepared and sent to me by **Linda Coban, Lorraine O'Donnell, Tom Belton, Carolyn Heald** and **Larry Weiler**. The main dates go from Timothy's birth in 1834 to the year 1977 when **Fredrik S. Eaton** took over as President and CEO.)

The B.C. Sugar Company

We cannot purchase Rogers Golden Syrup in the States so we stock up when we're in Canada or friends or relatives bring some when they come. I'm looking forward to someday, at the invitation of **Joanne Denton** on behalf of this company, visiting their museum in Vancouver, B.C.

I wrote requesting the recipe book I read about on a jar of syrup, but told them, too, of my book project, hoping they'd send me a little *brochure* on their company's history. But along with the recipe book and personal letter, came a *hard-*

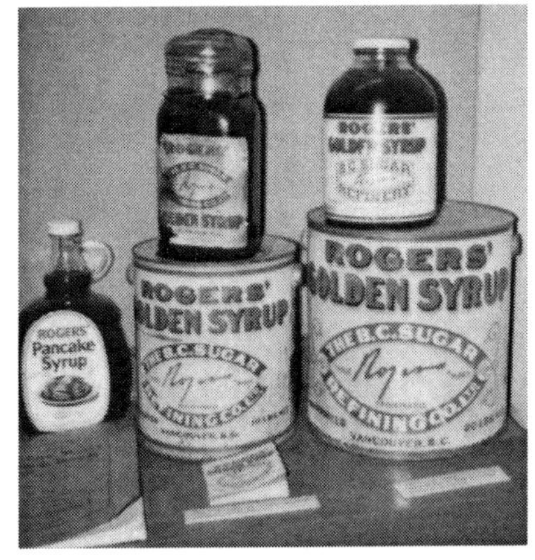

Close-up of containers over the years. Oldest, a glass jar with wire cage holding the top in place. Not shown here is the container used during WWII — a cardboard one with a crimped metal top.

back put out to celebrate in 1990 their century of history, and some polaroid pictures to use if I wished. The author of the book is a Saskatchewan man now living in Vancouver, **John Schreiner**. It is ironic, is it not, that it was an *American* who founded the company, yet their products are *not* sold in the States? The business has been in the family continuously except for one ten year period.

Benjamin Tingley Rogers was a brash twenty year old when he began the company — the first in British Columbia *not based* on logging or fishing. They had what the author says was a "roller-coaster ride" as they contended with "rivals, soaring and dipping prices, union squabbles, skirmishes with the Mormon Church, strikes, and wartime restrictions."

And, in spite of warnings on how *bad* this beloved sweetener is for us, most of us died-in-the-wool fanciers still pour it generously over our pancakes; use it as an ingredient in cakes, cookies, puddings, cake icings and put sweet toppings on our ice cream.

Throughout the era of rural schools, thousands, maybe even millions, of lunches were carried in Roger's Golden Syrup pails. So common were these on the prairie scene, that author **John Charyk** titled one of his coffee table books "Syrup Pails and Gopher Tails". On the jacket front you'll see a boy carrying his syrup pail lunch. The tight lid and strong handle made them very satisfactory even for carrying milk to or from a neighbor. (They included a copy of a letter by a lady who had done just this when a child.)

One of my special childhood treats was brandy snaps — how they got this name is a mystery as there's no brandy in them — and from the recipe book I turned out my own batch. They tasted just as good today as they did those long years ago!

There were many interesting anecdotes throughout the book, but I'll quote just one: "Founder B.T. Rogers was a wealthy man in only ten years and he kept his youthful exuberance as evidenced by the fact that on June 22, 1906 he was stopped and fined for the ?th time. He'd just 'whipped around a corner in his Pierce Arrow sedan and speeded up to *seventeen* miles an hour, a full *seven* miles above the urban speed limit!'"

In this book you'll learn of close cooperation between the C.P.R. and these sugar refinery entrepreneurs. The railway wanted stable industries on the west coast so that many products would be loaded on their trains. At this time sugar consumption was growing dramatically. A former *luxury* was now becoming a *staple* and at a price people could afford. Because the company's interests were inextricably linked to the baking industry, and because sugar and flour are two of the most important ingredients in baked goods, there was constant, sometimes not too smooth dealings with sugar cane, sugar beet, and wheat growers. The intensive stoop labour required in sugar beet fields, in Alberta especially, were constant problems. Finally, the development of a good

Top: Refinery employees, about 1891; many worked a lifetime at BC Sugar, including members of several families.

monogerm seed plus machinery that could do most of the field labour, and wheat varieties with good yields, helped stabilize the smaller labour force needed. These all in turn, led to a more constant market.

Without the many Japanese who had been evacuated from the coast, plus prisoners of war and conscientious objectors supplying field labour, sugar rationing during WWII would have been much more severe. In fact, "the Japanese", said one sugar company field hand, "saved our bacon." (Little did we think when we were using our sugar coupons just *who* was doing the field work under trying working conditions to supply us with our sugar.)

After the war a number of European immigrant refugees fleeing Russian advances had their transportation paid by UNRRA (the United Nations Rural Rehabilitation Association) when they came to work in the Alberta sugar beet fields. Then, when this labour pool dried up, many native Indians from northern Alberta and Saskatchewan became the mainstay.

The latest venture of the B.C. Sugar Company is their step into the chemicals and petroleum industries.

They started with *cane* sugar, went to *beet* sugar, and finally ventured into this very different field. But for those of us whose chief interest is *sugar* — the main word in the company title — we hope they stick with sugar products also.

In 1995 the name was changed to "Western Operations" in order to have the company name and products name uniform.

Watkins

- *A company motto: The talent of success is nothing more than doing what you can do well and doing well whatever you do. Longfellow.*
- *For a cook-off for their 125th celebration four employees spent almost six months sifting through 15,000 entries. The five finalists had their winning recipes printed in the heritage book.*
- *Joseph Watkins hired his first assistant, 14 year old George Smith, who retired in 1947 after more than 60 years with the company.*
- *Grace was J.R.'s only surviving child and would have become the company head in 1911 at her father's death — if she had not been a woman.*
- *I'll bet few know that for a short time in the early 20's Watkins sold auto supplies, tires, inner tubes, spark plugs, etc.*

J.R. Watkins, Founder of the Company, 1840-1911.

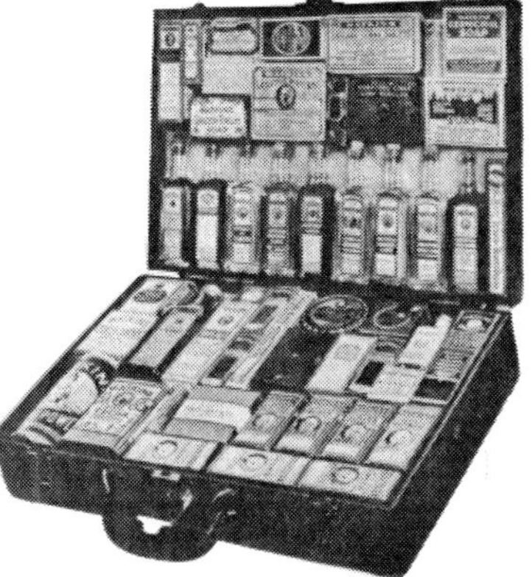

This is the kit the Watkins man would have brought into your home in the 20's. All of us in our 70's and 80's now will still recognize many of these products.

Many peddlers at our door today may not get a welcome, but I'm sure the prairie housewife in the early days welcomed the sight of the store-on-wheels coming down the dusty road. She was no doubt running low on a variety of the products he had in his kit — spices, extracts, medicines, etc. — many she couldn't get in town, and with the superior quality she'd come to trust. Besides, they had a wonderful guarantee — if you were *not satisfied* for any reason, when you had used down to a *trial line* on a bottle, you were to just keep it for his next visit and get

Left, this is one of many of the conveyances used by Watkins. In 1993 their museum opened and in it you will see one of these wagons as part of the 125 year history of Watkins.

Right, during World War II Watkins devoted, at various times, as much as 90 percent of its productive capacity to the needs of our armed forces. "Keep Fighting Fit — Care for Your Health for Your Country" was a slogan often used by Watkins.

your money back. This line is still there today.

This company began in 1868 in **Plainview, Minnesota** with *one* man mixing up bottles of liniment in his own kitchen, bottling it in his woodshed, and delivering it by horse and buggy. Now, Watkins is the "largest, oldest institution of its kind in the world," but they had some huge climbs, and disastrous falls in the interim. To quote from a 125th anniversary book: "Watkin's history is one of phenomenal growth and decline, untold wealth and bankruptcy . . . brilliant leadership and disastrous mismanagement." Today, under **Irwin Jacobs'** headship, and with a superiour, independent and cooperative sales force, they are forging ahead in great strides.

One of their workers is a man I welcome at *my* door with a far greater selection of products than the peddler of old — but with the same old guarantee of customer satisfaction. And he brings me an appointment calendar, too, which pictures all those yummy things I can make with Watkin's products. One calendar also had a page of household tips, a metric conversion chart, plus first aid and stain removal charts.

I'm grateful to Watkin's corporate staff for sending me not only their 125th anniversary book, but copies of a number of pages from their old, old *Almanacs* and their *Home Doctor and Cook Book.* I'm sure Quimperites have old copies of these books in some dusty corner — but they will find *none* after *1948*. for shortly after that the company went modern with their advertising — full color ads in magazines, T.V. shows, booths at fairs and so on. They now sell more than 375 items and have nearly 70,000 representatives and directors in the

In 1913, 12 horses and six teamsters were needed to transport the ice making machine to Gladstone.

global market. But it's not all serious. You can still find jokes, riddles, pithy sayings, party ideas, and tidbits from folklore, such as how a Watkins Vice President's wife, under an assumed name, finally got the company to publish her cookbook; and oodles of other items to *keep* you looking at a Watkin's calendar for *other purposes* than just the date.

They may not have been too accurate by today's scientific standards (but meteorologists still make goofs, don't they?), but how many farmers consulted that old Almanac for planting schedules and weather forecasts as they tried to decided what job would best fit the day? And if you find one of those old books, you'll be lost to the present for an hour or two, I'm sure.

William Neilson

To my door one day in 1995 came a Federal Express lady with a big long tube package together with a paperback book and personal letter fastened on the outside. Inside was a beautiful big plastic map of Canada.

The book was the hundred year history of this company whose name was on many of the candy bars that were such a treat when Dad or Uncle

Frank brought a bag of them home from town for us kids. And many, many years later, this is the name I look for when buying some *Canadian* candy bars. (Note: In the 90's Neilson began exporting a selection of Canadian products to the United States and other global markets.)

So how come the map, you are wondering? Well, in one of **John Charyk's** books I read of a most unusual way this company *advertised* their chocolate bars. They would supply maps of Canada and the World free to any school upon request, the only stipulation being that the *names* of the candy bars *not* be covered up. I wondered if my memory were playing tricks on me as I could remember no such maps in Quimper or on walls of schools where I taught — until I learned that this program was only begun in the 50's. It was this unique idea for advertising that prompted me to write to Neilson's.

Now for a few fascinating tidbits gleaned from this book written by William and Mary Neilson's great-great-grandson, **John Pellowe**: Scandinavian **Nilson** was changed to Scottish **Neilson**, though the reason remains unknown. Actually, because milk and chocolate are two of the main ingredients in confections, especially ice cream and candy,

The author happily anticipates what is in this odd package.

this story interweaves three industries — dairying, ice cream making and candy production. **William**, the oldest son of John and Mary was in 1867 a journeyman millwright living in Toronto and fascinated by the machines that turned out bricks of ice cream. In 1875 he married his American sweetheart, **Mary Eva Kaiser**. Five children were born to them. Their second, **Morden**, eventually became head of the company. Due to William's failed attempts in the retail business, the family was desperately poor, a fact testified to by Morden 25 years later when he recalled having to squeeze his feet into his mother's shoes as he had none of his own. During these years of financial distress, Mary Neilson built up a business selling her homemade mincemeat and milk from their few cows. The milk was delivered door to door by Morden dressed in those old button shoes and his father's cut off trousers.

The tide began to turn on May 24, 1893 when they sold their first block of ice cream. Eventually, Neilsons would be satisfying sweet tooths in 14 countries around the world. But the rise to fame and fortune was anything but fast or easy.

William had bought two old hand-cranked freezers — the kind used at Quimper picnics — the ones that needed *real muscles* during the *final* stages. Twenty years later Morden recalled those days, telling fellow businessmen, "I was in charge of preparing and cranking the mix, but it was those freezers that broke our hearts. All that hand-cranking! Besides, father believed that the *speed* of the freezer should be *gradually increased* until the climax was reached in a *frenzy* of speed. You can imagine the strength needed by those of us who did the cranking!" That first summer, using only the purest cream, Morden cranked out 10 to 20 two gallon buckets of ice cream a day. The 3,750 gallons brought in more than $3,000 — the first *real cash* the family had seen in years.

Because the ice cream business is quite seasonal and there was the necessity of providing year-round jobs for employees, the company went into the chocolate business in 1906. Later, because it was impractical to juggle employees between these two operations, from 1925 on they were made independent of each other.

On their own printing presses they ran off beautifully illustrated catalogues — showing specialties of the season; all the different flavours and shapes of chocolates; fruit and cough drops. A photo might show a beautiful team of Percherons hitched to their ice cream delivery wagons. In **Toronto** they also worked with the city's tram operators for speedy deliveries.

Mary Kaiser Neilson — the wife to whom goes credit for being the driving force in her husband's company.

The Great War brought with it many problems — the securing of needed ingredients such as sugar and chocolate; workers being sent to **Europe** to work in munitions and men going into the service. But because emotions and sentiment are at high levels in war time, one way to show love and concern for Canadian soldiers was to include elaborately wrapped boxes of chocolates in care packages.

Morden had had to take the helm in 1915 after his father's sudden accidental death. There had been a great outpouring of love and respect because William Neilson was able to greet so many of his employees by name. They felt they were *friends* as well as *workers*. This was quite a feat, for in a 1912 picture, there are over 300 people. Family members who have carried on the business maintain this same very close relationship with employees. Morden, in fact, had a company party at Christmas time for all of them and, it was said, spouses also. Bonuses for the company's success were given out, as well as ones for individual performances. The Second World War brought the same problems as had WWI but personal tragedies brought even closer ties within the business — so much so, that when Morden suffered leukemia in the 40's, over a hundred people at the factory were lined up to donate blood for him. Just before his death he used the last of his strength to visit the homes of all donors.

The stories behind the many different candy bars is a fascinating story in itself. And have you noticed that the name **Neilson** is on the *tiny milk containers* you get with your cup of coffee in a restaurant as well as quite a number of other products we use today?

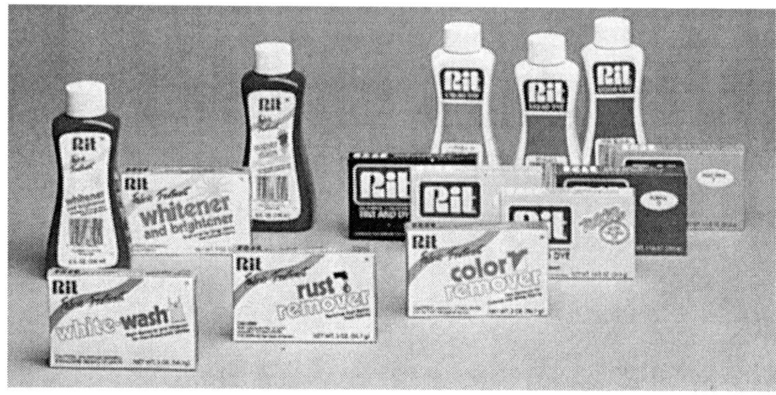

Rit Dyes

What a significant part this company played in our younger days! After Mom had worked long and hard getting those pictures and the printing off those 100 pound flour and sugar sacks, then it was time for little Mary to select the color she would like for her dress. And not only did Rit Dye brighten up a dull off-white world of fashion, but Rit *whitener* and *dye remover* played their parts, too. By using them, housewives could be spared the shame of hanging out a tattletale grey wash.

When I wrote to the **Rit Dye Company**, they very kindly sent me samples of today's products. I like their motto: "With Rit everything old is new again." Their charts on *Common Laundry Dilemmas* and *Fabric Care Basics* come in handy, too. As I thought of fabric dyes, I realized how grateful we ought to be for *colorfast* materials — this being a fairly recent technological advance. In fact, once in awhile even yet, one can get hold of a garment that lets the color run. Remember those jokes about the pink long johns? They were *no joke* for a housewife and it was a lot worse if something that would be in *plain sight* and was supposed to be *snowy white* accidently got dyed any other color. Somehow it has always seemed strange to me how it is so *easy* for dye to *run into* something but so hard to get it to *run out*!

Jeff was soon to graduate before we took him on the trip. (Our other four are in a picture on page 330.)

Yes, the curtains at the window; the dress on the little girl; the shirt on the man's back and numerous other things in most any home, have that cheerful bright hue (or that dark practical one so the dirt won't show), all thanks to Rit dyes. (Rit is a registered trademark.)

World Travel

When young folks left the Old Country to homestead in the West, they no doubt hoped to get back to visit in a few years, but for some their goodbyes were either for many, many years — 40 for Dad and Mom — while others like the Shaddocks, got back home for a visit in just a few years. Still others made a trip back before marrying and raising their family as did Dad in 1913.

During the Depression, trips for pleasure were non-existent. Young men, desperate for work, searched everywhere and by any means possible — on foot, on horseback or as rod-riders on trains. And then there were those making family moves — up to the **Peace River Country** or back **East**. When most farm animals were shipped north for the 37-38 winter, some Quimper bachelors travelled with them and cared for them as well as they could.

I marvel at this picture taken in England in 1913, when my dad-to-be came home with my mom-to-be's elder brother, Walter. *Somebody* got *everybody* together — parents, all eight offspring, spouses, grand–children and a friend who I guess was just there! The teen boy is my Uncle Frank born when Grandma was 49.

We, those settlers' children, though, are different. Many of us have visited places all over the world. The Stensrud travels have not been as extensive as that of some Quimperites, but by borrowing an idea from other grandparents on a Carribean cruise, we have taken our grandchildren, one at a time when in their mid-teens, on a trip. Somehow we went in different directions with each — Jeff to Alaska, Jake to Hawaii, Angie to Mexico and Eric down the St. Lawrence. However, we now have a two-year-old grandson, Andy, and a little sister joined him in August, so we'll have to be pretty spry old folks if we are to carry through with them, eh?

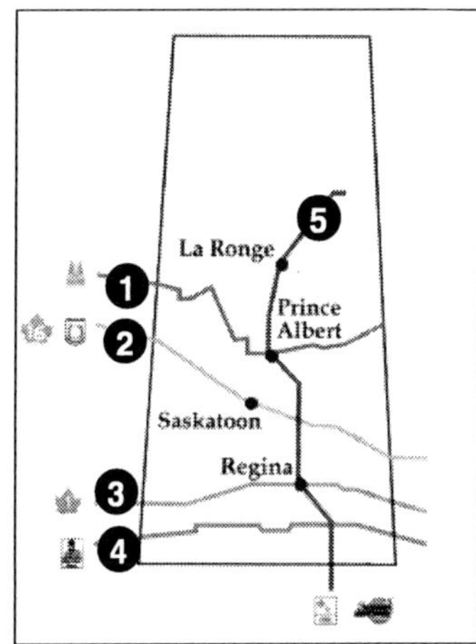

Saskatchewan has four cross-province highways. **1)** Northern Woods & Water Route (#9 & #55). **2)** Trans Canada/ Yellowhead Highway (#16). **3)** Trans-Canada Highway (#1). **4)** Red Coat Trail (#13). And one **5)** international north-south highway (#35, #39, #6, #2/102).

Our House

We play at our house and have all sorts of fun,
An' there's always a game when the supper is done;
An' at our house there's marks on the walls an' the stairs,
An' some terrible scratches on some of the chairs;
An' ma says that our house is really a fright,
But pa and I say that our house is all right.

At our house we laugh an' we sing an' we shout,
An' whirl all the chairs an' the tables about,
An' I rassle my pa an' I get him down too,
An' he's all out of breath when the fightin' is through;
An' ma says that our house is surely a sight,
But pa an' I say that our house is all right.

I've been to houses with pa where I had
To sit in a chair like a good little lad,
An' there wasn't a mark on the walls an' the chairs,
An' the stuff that we have couldn't come up to theirs;
An' pa said to ma that for all of their joy
He wouldn't change places an' give up his boy.

They never have races nor rassles nor fights,
Coz they have no children to play with at nights;
An' their walls are all clean an' their curtains hang straight,
An' everything's shiny an' right up to date;
But pa says with all of its racket an' fuss,
He'd rather by far live at our house with us.

From **The Path to Home**, by Edgar A. Guest, ©1919

Bibliography

Saskatchewan A History, by John H. Archer ©1980
Saskatchewan A Pictorial History, by Douglas Bocking ©1979
Nothing to Make a Shadow, by Faye C. Lewis ©1971
A Touch of Wonder, by Arthur Gordon, ©1974
Butter Down the Well, by Robert Collins, ©1980
The Gift of Sky, by Linda Ghan, ©1988
Barefoot on the Prairie, by Ferne Nelson, ©1989
Chronicle of a Pioneer Prairie Family, by L. H. Neatby, ©1979
The Dog Who Wouldn't Be, by Farley Mowat, ©1957
Muddled Meanderings in an Outhouse, by Bob Ross, ©1974

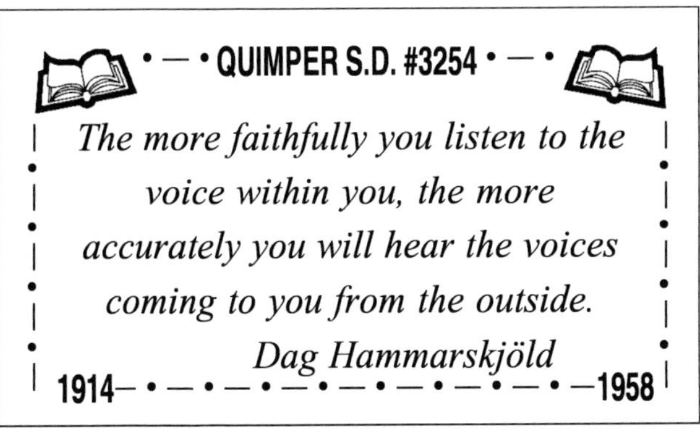

• — • QUIMPER S.D. #3254 • — •
The more faithfully you listen to the voice within you, the more accurately you will hear the voices coming to you from the outside.
Dag Hammarskjöld
1914– • — • — • — • — • — • — • —1958

Share your belongings with the needy and open your home to strangers. — Rom. 12:13

4 — A Wider View

It would reveal a lack if the Quimper story did not look a few miles in all directions from our own district's borders, so for this chapter we will take a brief look at the next door neighbor school districts, the Glenvern area, and the two municipalities and towns of our vicinity. I will also include a few personal stories that tie in with this wider view.

Bordering School Districts

Our surrounding school districts clockwise were **Royer**, **Erinlea**, **Pinto River**, **Hulbert**, **Westerleigh** and **Atoimah**. Royer #4384 was not formed until 1920. Erinlea was named by a resident who wanted to remember old Ireland. Pinto River #3281 was formed the same time as Quimper and was often called "Raymond" as **Joe Raymond** had sold the district two acres for one dollar. Hulbert #107 was named after homesteaders **Henry** and **Clara Hulbert**. Westerleigh #3357 was named by **Mrs. Hilling** in honor of her old home in England. Atoimah #4201 is **Hamiota** backwards as a number of its earliest settlers were from Hamiota, Manitoba. When Stove Lake School was destroyed by lightning, Atoimah was moved there in 1956.

Erinlea opened the same year as Royer to our north, both six years after us. Erinlea closed 12 years before Quimper so it was only open 26 years compared to our 44. One of Quimper's long resident families, the Donalds, came from Erinlea.

The Pinto River school became a Community Club House after the school and site were sold to them for $200. Erinlea's teacherage became **Hilton Eddy's** shop in Aneroid.

There were some especially interesting interactions between Pinto River and Erinlea. In 1943 the Pinto River enrollment was so low that for 15¢ per day per family for each school day Erinlea would take their pupils. After two years Pinto River reopened and in another two years their enrollment was boosted by pupils from *their* neighbor, the **Warren** district. Pinto River finally closed for good the same year as did Quimper. Both were then in Shaunavon Unit 7, but Pinto River soon joined the Wood River Unit 6 into which the Quimper School building was moved. Rather a strange interweaving, don't you think?

Glenvern Hall

Mrs. George (Florence) White kept a diary on Glenvern Hall from the dream of it in 1929 until Quimper put on the first function there on December 27, 1929. The land was donated by **Jim Vandergrift**. The foundation was dug June 24 and 25. Then work was stopped for regular farm work until October. The building went up in November with the chimney for it being built by brick mason, **Mr. Corbin** from Aneroid. Men donated all work and women the meals and lunches.

The name was derived from half of the names of two municipalities, **Glen McPherson #46** and **Auvergne #76**.

I remember Mom saying that as the hall was in the last stages of being built, some high spot had to be reached to fit something into place so Dad, being the smallest in stature there at that moment was boosted up on some shoulders to do the job.

January of 1930 saw the first wedding — **Harold Adams** and

Glenvern Hall, South of Ponteix.

Another view of Glenvern Hall.

AT GLENVERN HALL

FRIDAY, DECEMBER 14TH, AT 8.30 P.M.

The PONTEIX PLAYERS

will present the 3-act comedy drama:

"LOVE'S MAGIC"

THE CAST OF CHARACTERS IS AS FOLLOWS:

JOHNNIE LACOURSIERE	Robert Gray	Hero of the Play
OLIVER ROUSSEAU	Gene Mason	Villian
ELIE NEAULT	Harry	The Cook's Husband
VERNA KANE	Susan	The Maid
IRENE GAUTHIER	Hulda and Clementine	Mistress of the House
DOROTHY KOURI	Harriet	The Cook
HELEN HOFFMAN	Victoria	The Heroine

PLAYING TIME TWO HOURS

A LUNCH ——and after the lunch—— **A DANCE**

This is a complete change of program. There are many reasons why you should all attend this show. It is all home talent and should be encouraged. You get so much more for your money than any other place or entertainment can give you, and you will meet all your friends and neighbors. What would you do if it were not for Glenvern Hall? So give us your patronage.

Bring Your Own Lunch. We Supply Coffee.

MUSIC BY THE YOUNG ORCHESTRA

Violet Merritt, followed later in the month by that of **Bill Holt** and **Mary Kinney**, a Westerleigh school teacher.

In February of 1930 the Hulbert, Westerleigh and McKnight districts met to form the **Glenvern United Church** congregation.

The official opening was held on May 23, 1930. Sports Days, dances, concerts, plays, church services and political meetings were frequent. Later the **Square Dance Club**, the **Glenvern Cooperative Association Ltd**. and **4H Clubs** met in the hall.

In the 50's the hall got a new floor and a new furnace, but in 1985 major renovation took place. The inside was painted, the ceiling low-

(Continued on page 121)

Glenvern Community Hall

OFFICIAL OPENING

Friday, May 23rd, 1930

Programme

1. The Maple Leaf
2. Chairman's Address
3. Address .... Inspector Chatwin
4. A. W. Murray .... Our Country
5. Community Singing... "My Country 'Tis of Thee"
6. Miss Ellen Hanson .... Glenvern Hall
7. Mrs. A. Young .... Musical Number
8. E. Lane, Jr. .... The Indian
9. Debate: "Resolved, that morality increases with civilization," W. Lloyd. affirmative; Miss Farnsworth, negative.
10. Everett Baker .... Co-operation
11. Community Singing..... "Blest be the tie that binds"
12. Farm Organization .... R. M, Glassford, U.F.C.
13. Wheat Pool .... J. W. Vandergrift
14. [illegible] .... Finis Hulbert
15. .... Buffalo Horn
16. .... Lamb .... The League of Nations
17. Kenneth Hoffman... "The challenge of our country to the youth of today"
18. .... Hulbert .... Musical Number
19. Mrs. J. H. Veitch .... Musical Number
20. Douglas Robins........ "Advantages of a hall to the people of the community"
21. Vic McCarthy ....
22. Mrs. A. E. Andrew........ Song

Supper from 5.30 to 8. **Lunch after programme**

DANCING

Admission $1.00 **Children under 12 years 25c**

I've heard that one Glenvern lady saved all the flyers from early programmes. If this collection is still in existence, to get them bound into a booklet would make a wonderful souvenir.

Come To..... **Glenvern Hall**

FRIDAY, JANUARY 19th, 1934

A Play by the WAR[illegible]TO PLAYERS, en[illegible]led

"Wanted: A Mother"

A Comedy Drama in Three Acts, by Lillian Mortimer, entitled

"The Road to the Right"

CAST OF CHARACTERS:

Camilla Ray, an orphan in search of a mother ..... Hope McDonald
Billy Ray, her brother ..... Frank Ulm
Pansy Black, an ebony treasure ..... Lois Murray
Mrs. Lily Mason (mother), a good imitation of the real thing ..... Evelyn McDonald
Dick Mason, alias Daddy John Harrison, not what he seems ..... Ken. Murray
Sheriff Theodosia Flicker, the law in petticoats ..... Barbara Paterson
Skidwell Flicker (Skid), the sheriff's husband ..... Mac Murray
Kay Ellison, with a problem and a secret ..... Norma Paterson
Ralph Gladden, in love with Kay ..... Alf. Raymond
Jim Smith, an ungrateful son ..... Paul Froyman

Time—The present. Place—A small town in New Jersey.
Time of playing—About two and one-half hours.

Lunch

After the play

and then a

Dance

Bring your own lunch
We furnish the coffee

Admission:
Adults 15c **Children 10c**

Don't miss this! It is good, and the price is so low that it is practically free.

GLENVERN HALL COMMITTEE

It was about 1930, according to **Ormand Young** that their orchestra began playing for dances — free for a couple of years, until Mr. Vandergrift suggested they get 25 cents per night to help pay for their music.

The name of the players did not copy well, but my guess is that it was Warinto because when I looked over the actors' names, they were from either the Warren or the Pinto River District.

In any case, this and the Ponteix poster indicate that the Glenvern Committee sought out talent from quite a wide area.

Programme . . .

for evening of May 23rd, 1941

AT GLENVERN HALL

Opening remarks by the Chairman

1. A short play by Stove Lake School
2. Musical number by The Young Orchestra
3. A Short play by McKnight School
4. Singing by Mrs. James Green
5. A number by Miss Betty White
6. Singing by Miss Patricia Kouri
7. Westerleigh School
8. Musical number, Hawaiian guitar and accompaniment.
9. A short play by Quimper School
10. A talk by Charlie McCoy
11. Singing by the Hulbert sisters
12. Hawaiian guitar and accordion
13. Singing by Patricia Kouri
14. A Speaker is expected also.

— Glenvern Hall Committee

The Ponteix History Book has a copy of a 1936 program at Glenvern — a four act comedy drama, "Little Miss Jack." It was put on by The Ponteix Players with music for the dance following by the Young Orchestra. Maybe they weren't making expenses, or had nothing for the Glenvern Hall fund, as I noticed that in 1934 Adults were 15 cents, children 10 cents, but in 1936 Adults were 35 cents, and children 15 cents. However, in 1930 The Depression hadn't hit full force yet, so for Glenvern's first play, put on by The Quimper Dramatic Club on March 28, with music by the Robins Orchestra . Adults were 75 cents, children 25 cents.

ered and circulating fans installed. The balcony was turned into a storage unit. They held a contest for a theme as part of celebrating Glenvern's new look. **Tara Gillis** won with "A meeting place for friends."

At a 40th Anniversary dance the Old Time Fiddlers played and donated the proceeds to the Hall. On November 8, 1988, **Eldon** and **Jean Finell** came back from Regina to celebrate their 40th anniversary.

It has taken the cooperative efforts of a great many people to keep everything going all these years and it is hoped their theme will remain relevant for many years to come, thus bucking the trend of community events now being in the towns. (Please check my suggestion following the Foreward on page viii.)

James and Maude (Ferguson) Vandergrift

To most people in an around Ponteix **Jim Vandergrift** would be "The Father of Glenvern Hall". Though he had no title as such, everything that took place there was part of his life. And even though wife, **Maude,** wasn't as visible around the hall as Jim, she was behind him all the way. It was Cananae's loss and our gain when Jim lost his homestead there by a late return from working in the gold mines of northern Ontario. (Note: Cananae was a school district north of Aneroid.) He used his South African script in 1909 to get land in the Glenvern area. Maude came from Oldham N.S. Their farm grew to two sections with well-equipped machinery and buildings.

Some Aneroid Folks

Blair, Corbin, Boyce and **Elliott** are four names that pop up very frequently as you read the history of Aneroid. All their roots were in England, but Blairs and Elliotts came to homestead in 1910, after a number of years in Ontario. The Blairs had set up a store and post office in their farm home but soon both were moved into town to become Aneroid's Blair and Elliott General Store. To this same area two Boyce brothers came to homestead. It wasn't long before Aneroid had its first wedding — **Ernie Boyce** and **Laura Blair** on Dec. 25, 1913. Laura taught two years at the sod schoolhouse so the other teacher listed, **Ida Blizner**, must have only taught a very short time as this school was only open two years. On Jan. 12, 1915 the stork carrying baby **Ted**, barely beat **Dr. Kitchen** with his horse and stone boat to the Boyce home. Three years later Ted got little brother **Reg**.

The 1918 flu may have left their mother weak for she passed away with T.B. (tuberculosis — often called consumption in early days) in

1924. In 1929, Ernie married a second time, but she too preceded him in death in 1962.

Ernie Boyce at 93° and **Lucy Corbin** at 98 were King and Queen at Aneroid's 60th celebration. (Lucy lived to 101+ and for her 100th birthday party Mom asked me to make a birthday card as no such cards were in the store. In fact, I don't see any even now, though more and more are living to the century mark and beyond.)

Ernie served his community in a great variety of ways, some of which were: handy man, veterinarian, member of the Aneroid and Rural Telephone Board, Trustee of the Consolidated School Board, judge of many events at the fairs, butcher for the beef ring, and long-time member of the Saskatchewan Wheat Pool.

Elliotts had four children, **Ruth, Harold, Jack** and **Lorna**. Harold married a childhood classmate, **Margaret Watson**, in a double wedding with Margaret's sister, **Evelyn** and **Murray Bourne**. (It was in the Watson home that Rob and I took a few piano lessons just before scarlet fever hit our home. On its heels followed the Depression so there were no more lessons.) Ruth became a nurse and Lorna was Town Administrator for 25 years. Jack at age 14 lost his life as the result of a hockey game accident.

A little **DeBruyne** baby, **Lottie,** weighed in at one pound at Aneroid in 1912 — her cradle a shoe box — but she grew up healthy. She and her brother, **Harry**, got a shock in May of 1922 when they arrived home from school. Their house had burned down.

Fletcher and **Mary Walls** were very community-active homesteaders near Aneroid. She was one of the few women of that day who drove a car. Fletcher had a big Rumley separator, cook and bunk cars and a straw supply rack. They burned straw in the Rumley instead of coal as some did. He helped organize early grain grower organizations and finally the Wheat Pool. Mary was active in the Methodist church which later became part of the Union Church. He was Justice of the Peace for about 40 years. At one time he had around 50 horses — having become convinced horse farming was more efficient than with the huge engines and equipment. This family got connected to Quimper when their son, Kelso, married a McConville girl, Minnie.

Minnie was badly burned in 1944 when a gasoline iron exploded. They celebrated their 50th in Lethbridge in 1992, the first 50th of our generation that many of us attended.

Casey and Alice Empey

This family was also early Aneroid settlers. One man's misfortune was another's fortune. Casey got a quarter that had been abandoned along with the pre-emption beside it. Mother Alice had her hat blown away as they were going to their claim — the first experience, no doubt, of many with prairie winds.

Some Glenvern Folks

Henry and Clara Hulbert

Farmers tried to protect themselves from prairie fires with a ploughed strip around the yard. In the district named after them, Clara Hulbert's husband, **Henry**, was away hauling wheat when a fire was heading their way. Clara took her three little ones, their best clothing and hand-made quilts to the strip. The house didn't burn, but a cinder set fire to the clothing and bedding, and month old **Dayton** in his carriage got some slight cinder burns.

When this little boy grew up he married **Juliette Pord**. They were both musical and became members of the Swift Current Old Time Fiddlers Band. (I have two of their tapes that I enjoy from time to time — I keep a tape player on my kitchen counter.)

The Young Family

... but they grow old just like the rest of us! But let's think of the young at heart instead of the chronological years. **Ormond**, the only surviving member of **Albert and Edith's** offspring lives in Hawaii with his wife **Dorothy**. In 1984 they, as guests of the Kaulapapa Lions Club, fell in love with Hawaii and its people. However, they felt there was a resemblance between the isolation and loneliness of the lepers who had been banished to the island of Molokai and that of the homesteaders — the main difference being that the former were *sick*, while the latter were a *healthy, sturdy* lot on the whole.

Hospitality in their beautiful modern home south of Ponteix plus music wherever they were, were hallmarks of this family. The Young Orchestra often played at Glenvern Hall.

George and Maude Paterson

In 1921 when **Aylmer Boulter** was teaching in the Warren District, Mrs. Paterson, a nurse, was very concerned over the high number of children with diseased tonsils and adenoids and decided to do something about it. She persuaded a Regina surgeon to hold a tonsil-adenoid clinic at the school. Desks were stacked up, mattresses laid down and the rudiments of an operating room set up. The teacher said he did not remember how many operations were performed that day, and he believed that the number included some from other nearby districts. He commented, "This sort of thing would probably shock doctors today, but I saw no setbacks in the children and many were helped."

Worth and Marjorie (Hulbert) Hunt

Worth gave us some interesting details on what riding the rods was all about in Depression years, when many simply didn't have the price of a passenger ticket. He himself was trying to save enough money to get married, so chose the rods to get from **Ontario** back to **Ponteix** in 1931. His definition of this mode of travel was "finding a spot to sit on top or anywhere on the train's side or back where you could find a place to hang on." Though police were supposed to prevent this sort of riding, they were fairly lenient if it was done on a freight. Nevertheless, Worth and another fellow chose to try it on a *passenger* train. He had had his trunk shipped on this same train. They managed to elude a police with a flashlight for awhile, but when caught, Worth credited his ability at "talking fort", along with a little bribery, with not getting thrown off. He handed over his watch, whereupon the conductor said "Sit still and don't say a word." He did just this for the next hundred and fifty miles.

Worth was good on the drums and in the late 20's and 30's played with the **Robin**'s and **Young**'s orchestras at Glenvern Hall. He excelled at ball and hockey also, until he had the accident in which the tip of a willow stick pierced his left eye. He married Marjorie Hulbert in 1933 and for three years they were at the Community pasture west of the Westerleigh District. During WWII, when Worth was working at DeHavilland Aircraft in **Toronto,** he also played the drums two or three nights a week. After the war they lived in many different places, did various kinds of work, and took many world-wide trips, finally coming to rest in retirement years in **Ladner**, B.C.

Henri Liboiron

What are the first words you think of when you hear this name — historian , archeologist, plesiosaur, museum, Gouverneur, Niska , collector, geologist, Napeo, cemetery-restorer, etc.?

This remarkably interesting man wrote a number of articles for the Ponteix History Book and has moved his private museum from his farm home near town into Ponteix where it is now known as the **Heritage Museum**. Here you will see his models of a buffalo pound and an early trading post, as well as a huge collection of Indian artifacts. He will tell you how he loves to visit schools. (We wonder how many of these children will be inspired to become archeologists). He may even give them a sample of some pemmican he has made and you can be sure they will hear about the exciting discovery of a plesiosaur that has been nicknamed Moe (see pictures, page 324).

Though they won't ask about it, they will notice a deep scar on his forehead. When he was a youngster he had a brain tumor which invaded the bone of his skull, deforming it. A childhood friend grew up to become **Doctor Douville**. Henri was, according to this sensitive doctor, "teased unmercifully by other children who didn't understand", though he and other friends did their best to protect Henri. Dr. Douville added that "despite these problems, he became a renowned and highly respected archeologist."

Henri, with a bit of help from a few others, restored and documented the Gouverneur Cemetery. The last funeral there was in 1926 for homesteader **William Allen**. The 1918 flu had taken two adult sons, a daughter-in-law and three very young grandchildren. His widow left after the funeral never to return to this place of such bitter memories.

Of the many stories about Henri, I must tell just one more. It came to Henri's attention that the town of **Gouverneur** in **New York** state claimed to be the *only one* in the western hemisphere. In a convoluted account you can read the whole story in the Ponteix History Book on pages 94 and 95, Henri sent a copy of a page from an old atlas showing "our" *Saskatchewan Gouverneur*. The point was conceded, but Henri graciously said that though it was *not true* years ago when our Gouverneur was still a little but thriving town west of Ponteix, now that it was no more, the *other* Gouverneur now had a correct claim to being what they had claimed to be all along.

There may be another connection between these two towns, also, as *our* town was named after a C.P.R. man, **Isaac Gouverneur** and he and a **Mr. Ogden,** who was vice president of the Canadian Pacific from 1901 to 1928, were both from the same local area of New York state where *their* Gouverneur is.

Other Nationalities

Names other than of French or British origin were hard to find in the indices of the Aneroid and Ponteix history books, but there was a sprinkling of Scandinavian and German names. Though I'm not able to identify the nationality of some, it was clear that Central and Eastern European families were very scarce in our area. To represent this small minority in our midst, I have chosen to speak of but one Polish family (in the Quimper vignettes you will read of Quimper's Dutch family), one with a Scandinavian background, and one of German.

Karl and Julienne Schkwarck

Both husband and wife were born in Poland. In 1922 Karl came to Aneroid as a section foreman on the C.P.R., but he left the railway to farm. Twelve children were born to them. The youngest died when only 14. All the others married mates who did not have last names that appear Polish.

Having different customs and language made it very difficult and strange at first, but they must have been made to feel welcome seeing as they became an integral part of their community. We wonder, too, if their neighbors adopted some Polish customs and foods or if some Polish folk dances could even have become a feature at social dances.

The stabbur, a two-story storehouse of common use in Norway.

Allan and Geraldine (Nostbakken) Oliver

It was a recent pleasure in my life to meet this couple and visit at their home near Aneroid. All sorts of interesting things came to light. Gerry had been next to the last of Quimper's teachers, though, because of not having a teaching certificate, she was called a Student Supervisor. In her home district, the teacher she had for many, many years, refused to put on a concert, so the one she put on at Quimper was both her *first* and *last*. Gerry and her classmates, no doubt, felt cheated out of this particular joy of a rural school life — especially when they attended concerts put on at other schools.

The Olivers now combine farming with other involvements, such as Boy Scouts, Girl Guides, the Co-op and their Lutheran Church. Allan was elected to the legislature representing the **Shaunavon Constituency**. This interesting couple has built what may be the only one of its kind in Canada, a Norwegian Stabbur. It was a common type of storage building back in the old country.

Allan is now reeve of Auvergne Municipality #76.

Fred and Anna Ruehs

The Rueh's roots were in Germany but they arrived in the Aneroid area in a settler's box car from Nebraska in 1920. Anna had packed her best china in wooden barrels (something you never hear of nowadays). At the entry point of **Portal** they were informed that their box car was being condemned and that everything had to be moved to

Does this building bring back memories? Remember writing our departmental exams here? Some former Quimper students attended High School here, too. (Aneroid Consolidated School)

Aneroid, Saskatchewan

Just a Good Town in the Best Kind of a Farming District, Where a Million or More Bushels of Good Wheat is Grown Each Year.

Good Settlers **Good Markets** **Good Schools**

You are invited to look this district over if you are looking for a farm.

MORE SETTLERS NEEDED

As seen in the "Magnet".

another car. For this transfer, the railway people lost all sensitivity and perspective. She had also brought some lard and honey, which they simply threw on top of the china, smashing all of it in front of a heartbroken lady. They also had a buggy, and on top of it they threw the gang plow ruining it also. Luckily the 1915 seven-passenger Studebaker and some of their smaller pieces of farm machinery and household effects came across safely, and at sales shortly after their arrival, they were able to buy enough other necessities to get started. The land, however, was very rocky. With the intention of removing later all the stones the plow struck, they began marking them with laths, but even after going for an extra supply, they didn't get them *all* marked. But so many *were* labeled that some laths had to be removed to get the team of horses out of the field!

Another disappointment came when the boys were given orders

not to play ball on *Sundays*. (Blue laws were still in effect at this time in Canada). It wasn't *Christian*, they were informed.

The Ruehs and their descendants have taken an active part in the community in education, sports and politics.

Though those of the Ponteix and Aneroid history committees did the major work of searching through old minutes for nuggets of interest, I have chosen some from *their* lists that I would like to pass on second-hand (or should I say third hand?) to you. I'm only selecting those up to 1958.

Aneroid Highlights 1913-1958

1913 — Secretary's salary $300.00 per year
— Constable's salary $150.00 per year
— Cost of iron bars for wooden jail $4.80
— Health officers wage per year $50.00
1914 — Cost of land for a cemetery $75.00
— Cost of plots $8.00-15.00 depending on size
— Cost of getting a grave dug $4.00
— $500.00 borrowed from bank at 9% interest
— Purchased a Chemical Fire Engine $750.00
— Nuisance ground leased, fee $5.00 per year
— Land purchased from C.P.R. for townsite for $350.00
— Cost of auditing village books $2.50
— Cost of single 25' lot, $12.50
— Paid Mrs. Blair 75¢ for a Flag for Better Farming Committee
— 30 band instruments purchased from W. Blair $300.00
1915 — Aneroid hotel owner Mr. Cleveland paid for funeral of his bartender, who was accidentally shot and killed in the bar by a policeman (story page 10 Aneroid History Book)
— Taxes cancelled on all property owned by active servicemen
1916 — $2500.00 borrowed from bank to build hall-theatre.
1917 — Driving vehicles over sidewalks prohibited
— License given for a pool hall and bowling alley. Boys not allowed to work here
1918 — Mrs. Lillie, A. Hatcher, Quong Tong — restaurant licenses
— Motor vehicle speed limit in village 8 m.p.h.
1920 — $6000.00 borrowed from bank for electric power plant
1923 — Madden issued license to sell milk in village
— New broom for jail 90¢
— Curfew at 9:00 for school age children
1925 — Two silent policemen erected on Main Street
— $50.00 donated to women's club to buy cinders from the C.P.R. for cemetery walks (why not a gift from C.P.R.? is my thought)

1926 — $500.00 spent for wooden sidewalks
1927 — Single jail cell purchased for $225.00
— City will provide a suitable site for 60th Battery
— Secretary to acknowledge gift to pioneers from H.R.H. Prince of Wales
1929 — Shaunavon Electric to supply light and power
1930 — $5000.00 to be borrowed from bank for cement sidewalk
1931 — Relief paid $1737.57
1932 — Rate of pay for men to gravel streets 30¢ per hour
1933 — If boarding the teacher, the amount could be applied to taxes
1937 — A $4.00 train ticket to Regina to councillor for business
1941 — Old Rex Cafe to be used for Salvage for Paper campaign
1942 — School to have Tag Day for Milk for Britain Fund
1945 — A $300.00 grant to Aneroid Legion building fund
1947 — Mayor $3.00 per meeting Councillors $2.00
1949 — Dept. of Highways instructs Village to remove the "Welcome to Aneroid" sign off the highway (I wonder what this was all about!)
1951 — $2500.00 purchases a Chevrolet Fire Truck
— 12 man volunteer fire brigade organized
1953 — Fire siren purchased.
— Grant to Aneroid Memorial Skating Rink Fund to erect a covered rink
— Books audit $134.00 (Remember $12.50 in 1914?)
1957 — Street lights converted to Mercury Vapor Lights
NOTE: Please refer to the Aneroid History Book for other minutes from 1958 to 1980 (the year they published their history book).

Excerpts from Ponteix Minute Books, 1914-1958

1914 — First meeting of Village of Ponteix in Quebec Bank
— Doc Kitchen — Medical Health Officer $50.00 annually
— James Innes, $395.00 to build fire hall and jail
— Arthur Marcotte — for village legal advisor $400.00 per year
— Fines for drunks 1st $3-5; 2nd $10-20; 3rd $50.00 (what about *more* than 3?)
1915 — J. O.K. La Flamme, Secretary-Treasurer, $150.00 per year.
— Borrowed $6000.00 for town hall, sidewalks, fire apparatus scale and cemetery
— E. Matte — secretary $200.00 a year
— Nuisance ground — $200.00
— $25.00 to recruiting officer for 202nd Battalion
— By-law regulating operation of automobile for livery purposes
1916 — R.M. of Auvergne and village discuss telephones
— Under Alex Thompson Village streets to be lighted
— Mr. Thompson's engine making too much noise, remedy it or source will be removed

1917 — Bowling alley licensed to Grimes Bros.
— Tenders sought for cleaning, removing and emptying all PRIVIES, work to be done at night May to Nov., every 2 mos. Nov. to May
— Constable authorized to order 32 calibre revolver and shells and 2 sets automatic hand cuffs
— Letter to Health Commissioner regarding names of firms where "closet pails" can be bought together with dimensions generally in use in the province
— Tender for outhouse emptying to Chris Solback; rates private ones $1.00 a mo., hotels and restaurants $3.00 a mo., council to furnish buckets for same
— Asked priest if church bell could be used as fire bell if needed
— Tax rate 1˚ mills Patriotic Fund
— Grant of $124.00 for aid in hospital maintenance and construction

1918 — Authorization for installing street gasoline pump at edge of sidewalk
— Pleasure expressed that Dr. Lammaure will come to Village to practice dentistry. (Inducements) convent, 130 pupils, 3 room school, 32 bed hospital
— Curfew for 16 and under off streets 9:00 p.m.
— Letter of thanks to Madame Jos Cousin thanking her for her devotion and care of people during the influenza epidemic with no remuneration whatsoever

1919 — Grant of $100.00 for Committee of Returned Soldier's Reception to buy free tickets for them on sports grounds, theatre, etc., July 3, 4

1920 — Borrow $11,000 at 8% for fire engine $5700.00; 800' of hoses at $1.30 per foot — $1040.00; 3 cisterns — $3000.00 and suitable building $1260.00

1921 — Two special constables to look after needs of quarantined persons (what was this for, I wonder?)
— $529.86 grant to Ponteix Hospital

1922 — Dr. J.O. Lupien, Medical Health Officer, $75.00 a year

1925 — Catholic Church to ring curfew bell

1926 — Land purchased from C.P.R. for amusement ground and skating rink

1927 — Borrowed $10,000.00 to construct skating rink and 2 sheets curling ice

1929 — Dr. L. Beaudoing, Medical Health Officer, $75.00 per year

1932 — Council will write a certain ratepayer (I guess they decided to save him face!) to keep his dog at home as he is a menace to women and children of the village (he didn't bother men or they didn't want to admit it, I guess!)

1932 — Relief orders for the needy to be issued to merchants
— $177.50 grant to Gabriel Hospital

1934 — Wilfred Liboiron appointed fire chief $83.00
— Permission to P. Potvin to operate a mink fur farm
— No waste water to be thrown in streets or lanes
1936 — Trees for village streets to be ordered from Wadena Nurseries
1937 — Speed limits within village 20 m.p.h. (about the same 60 years later!)
1938 — $300.00 authorized for new cement sidewalks or repair of old with labor to be done by tax payers as possible and credited to their taxes
1940 — Franchise to Dominion Electric for power and electricity for 10 years
— Carloads (how many?) of cinders ordered from C.P.R. in Moose Jaw for use on streets
— Christmas lights $45.00 to be installed permanently
1942 — Secretary authorized to accept Victory Bonds for taxes
— Lee Fong closed his laundry business
1946 — Milk Control Board approved selling prices, 11¢ per qt., 6¢ per pint, 4¢ per ˚ pint
1948 — Debenture $6000.00 to complete War Memorial, curling rink and rec. centre
1952 — $455.00 to Saskatchewan Power for village share of lights in business area of building
1955 — 300 watt luminaries to be 250 watt mercury vapor lights
1957 — Village becomes TOWN OF PONTEIX
1958 — $62,800.00 for installing water and sewer in town. Rates: water $3.50, sewer $3.00

Rural Municipality of Auvergne #76

As with naming a school, the procedure for a municipality name was similar, so from its first meeting in 1913 a list of seven in order of preference were: Auvergne, Beaudevert, Desautels, Dunnell, Excelsior, Quimper and Westerleigh. It's interesting to note that Quimper's Dunnell was there, that Quimper was a sixth choice and that the first three were French names. Also you will remember that Albert Dunnell was the reeve — the same man who was Quimper's first school board chairman.

Choosing from the list of excerpts by **Shirley McKenzie**, again I will only go to 1958. From then until 1988 see Ponteix Yesterday and Today Volume I, pages 35 and 36.

1914 — Formation of school districts
— Wages, man holding scraper $3.00; man and team $5.00 for a 9 hr. day
— Bounties, $1.00 prairie wolf; $10.00, adult timber wolf; and $1.00 for pup
— Arrears to appear in The Spectator and the Aneroid Magnet

1915 — $1.00 per meeting paid to Quimper School for use of school for meetings
— Refuse application for grant for hotel in Aneroid
— By-law to prevent cruelty to animals
1916 — All school instruction to be in English only in the province and in Canada
1917 — A vote be taken from each school district not yet open to see how many willing to open April 1st to Nov. 30th
1922 — Request to department not to reduce grants to schools only open 160 days instead of the 210 required in School Act
1924 — Motion for office site to be Ponteix
— Jan. bounty of 3¢ for gopher tails
— June — bounty reduced to 1¢
1925 — Feb. and March meetings held in Aneroid, balance in Ponteix
1927 — Price of road dragging 40¢ per mile
— $350.00 grant towards cost of maternity hospital in Aneroid
1928 — Bounty of $1.00 to finders of patches of sow thistle or Canada thistle (I can remember Dad fighting a patch of Canada thistle by covering it with tar paper)
1929 — $200.00 grant to help a teacher attend summer school in Chicago providing teacher remain in R.M. for 2 years (I wonder if anyone went)
— Purchase of 60 h.p. Holt Caterpillar tractor and 12' Russel grader for $8430.00, cat operator paid $1.00 per hour
1930 — $100.00 donated for cost of memorial gates at Aneroid cemetery
— Sept.: borrowed $10,000.00 to purchase relief supplies
— Oct.: borrowed $50,000.00 for relief supplies of fodder, coal and flour
1931 — Aneroid maternity hospital closed (I never knew Aneroid had such a hospital. I wonder how many Quimper babies were born in it in it's short 3 or 4 years of operation.)
— R.M. to get 2 carloads of potatoes if free freight can be arranged
— Cattle and horses may be shipped to Eaton's Ranch at Cando, Saskatchewan at 60¢ and 70¢ a lb. per month respectively
— Rate payers to be contacted by general ring regarding meeting to discuss methods of controlling soil drifting
— Borrow $2000.00 to send men north to harvest hay supplies
— Stock to be sent to Marwayne, Alta or The Pas, Man.
— Special meeting in November to request gov. assistance to run schools to year end and then close for first 3 months of 1932
— Due to crop failure, gov. bonus $1.00 per acre needed
— Cost of transporting hay from The Pas $2.75 per ton
1932 — Council protests closing of Gouverneur C.P.R. station
— Recommend supply of seed for fall seeding of rye to alleviate soil drifting
— Request gov. assistance for binder twine and repairs

— Relief Commission approves advance 1 ton coal per approved applicant, request 50% hard coal
1933 — Arrange to import firewood from North
— By-law prohibiting burning of straw
1934 — Dept. of Agriculture recommends setting up committee for grasshopper campaign
— Request $900.00 grant from gov. to provide hospital, medical and nursing home care for one year (I didn't know they had nursing homes then)
— Urge, along with R.M. #46, gov. to build a highway from Mankota to Val Marie with connecting link to highway #13
— Urge gov. to have Lac Pelletier organized as a public recreation and pleasure resort ("Lac" is French for "Lake" in English)
1937 — Requested assistance to send haying outfits to Man.
— Ordered 2000 bags of flour
1938 — Ordered 1 car of Thatcher seed wheat @ $1.75 per bu.
— Requested P.F.R.A. to investigate implementation of community pastures
1939 — E.E. Boyce authorized to vaccinate horses against encephalomyelitis (sleeping sickness)
1940 — Paid anti T.B. League $500.00 in addition to $200.00 already paid
— Order prohibiting hunting or killing weasels
1944 — New D7 80 h.p. Caterpillar purchased $6,970.00
1945 — Due to shortage of fuel, coal to be rationed according to distance from town
1947 — Barn from Lemay farm to become part of Ponteix skating rink
1948 — Opposed legalization of sale of margarine
— Tabled petition of 95 ratepayers requesting services of bilingual secretary-treasurer
— Anyone receiving social aid to be prevented from patronizing beverage rooms
1952 — Heavy road damage due to flooding
— Recommend trapping of weasels be limited to male of species if possible (I smiled at this for how would one catch in a trap only one sex? Maybe some kind of box trap so females caught could be released?)
1956 — Contract made with Ponteix Snow Plow Club for opening roads
— Purchased a Gestetner duplicator (price not given — this is first mention I see of any sort of duplicator)
— Approved joining the Ponteix Senior Housing project (Manor)
1957 — Secretary salary $3000.00 a year
— By-Law: farmers warned that willful negligent farm practices could result in action for damages (burning stubble on light land and causing soil drifting)
1958 — Tax roll converted to card system

Councillors of the Municipality of Auvergne, 1931. L. to R.: Fletcher Walls, A.C. Browning, Henry Stringer, Jim Lamb, Ed Shaddock, Gjert Nostbakken, Geo. Corbin, Jim Donald, and Ken Hoffman.

Here are names of reeves and secretary-treasurers of Auvergne #76, but not up to present:

REEVES OF THE MUNICIPALITY

Dunnell, Albert	1913-1915
Lane, Ernest K.	1916, 1920
Raymond, Joseph A.	1917
Murray, Andrew	1918-1919
Eddy, Gordon S.	1921-1923
Shaddock, Edwin G.	1924-1931
Walls J. Fletcher	1932-1936
	1954-1966
Stringer, Henri	1937-1941
Gillis, Joe A.	1942
Wright, Arthur W.	1943-1947
Lamb, James	1948-1953
Lallier, Rene J.G.	1967-1970
Finell, Eldon	1971-1972
Ruehs, Gerald	1973-1976
McKenzie, William	1977-1982
Oliver, Allan R.	1983-

SECRETARY-TREASURERS

Edwards, Henry Charles	1913
Andrew, Lewis M.	1914-1916
Hilling, R.L.	1917-Mar. 1924
Cameron, E.	1924-1925
Browning, A.C.	1925-1948
Lapp, Ray C.	1948-Mar. 1954
Past, William	1954-1957
Hornung, Art (acting)	Oct. 1957-June 1958
Thurmeier, S.M. J. (supervisor)	Oct. 1957-June 1958
Roberge, Lucienne (acting)	June 1958
Johnston, Ken (supervisor)	June 1958-1959
Jackson, J.A. (supervisor)	1959-Aug. 1960
Roberge, Lucienne	Sept. 1960-Nov. 1973
Wolff, Charles	Dec. 1973-Jan. 1977
Howes, William S. (interim)	Feb. 1977-July 1977
Faucher, George	July 1977-

The Auvergne Wise Creek Community Pasture

In 1935 Parliament passed the Prairie Farm Rehabilitation Act (P.F.R.A.). On 67 sections of sub-marginal land, the Auvergne Wise Creek (these two municipalities had parts go to the pasture) pasture was established. Most of this land had been abandoned by farmers. The few remaining were moved to better land not far away or to an

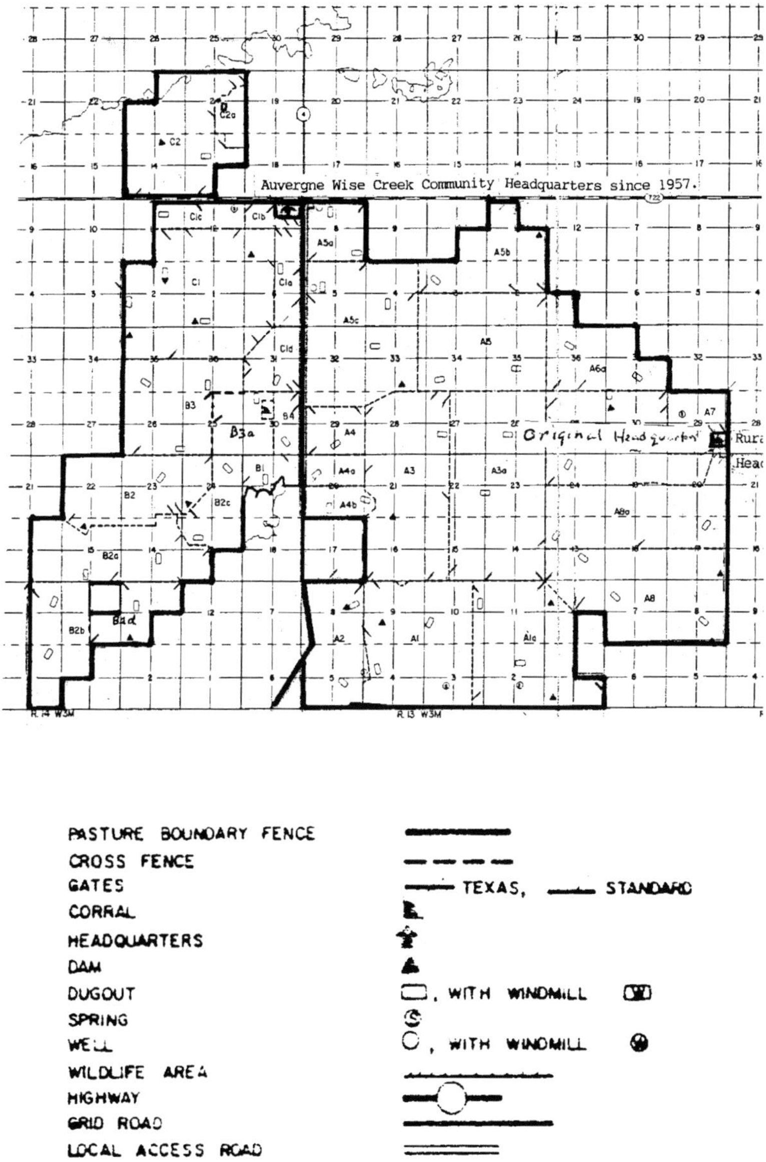

Auvergne Wise Creek Community Headquarters since 1957.

Original Headquarters

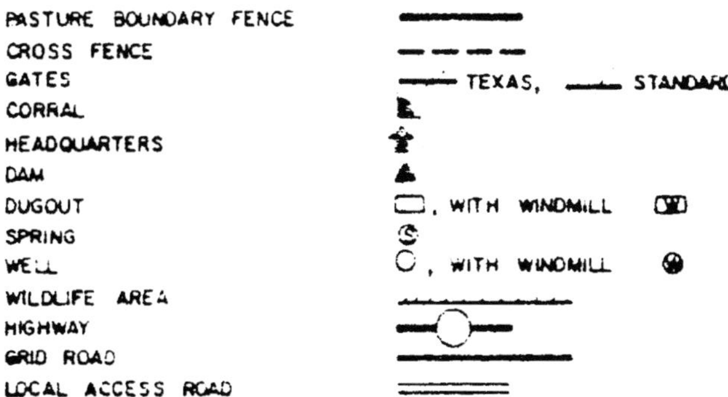

Auvergne Wise Creek Community Pasture established by the Prairie Farm Rehabilitation Association, P.F.R.A.

irrigated project at **Rolling Hills**, Alberta.

These pastures are an excellent example of PFRA conservation policies at work as once barren areas have been returned to grass. At first both cattle and horses were in the pasture, but from around 1960 only cattle were accepted. The PFRA owns around 50 bulls and rents another 30 from pasture patrons.

Bread and Jam

I wish I was a poet like the men that write in books
The poems that we have to learn on valleys, hills an' brooks;
I'd write of things that children like an' know an' understand,
An' when the kids recited them the folks would call them grand.
If I'd been born a Whittier, instead of what I am,
I'd write a poem now about a piece of bread an' jam.

I'd tell how hungry children get all afternoon in school,
An' sittin' at attention just because it is the rule,
An' looking every now an' then up to the clock to see
If that big hand an' little hand would ever get to three.
I'd tell how children hurry home an' give the door a slam
An' ask their mothers can they have a piece of bread an' jam.

Some poets write of things to eat an' sing of dinners fine,
An' praise the dishes they enjoy, an' some folks sing of wine,
But they've forgotten, I suppose, the days when they were small
An' hurried home from school to get the finest food of all;
They don't remember any more how good it was to cram
Inside their hungry little selves a piece of bread an' jam.

I wish I was a Whittier, a Stevenson or Burns,
I wouldn't write of hills an' brooks, or mossy banks or ferns,
I wouldn't write of rolling seas or mountains towering high,
But I would sing of chocolate cake an' good old apple pie,
An' best of all the food there is, beyond the slightest doubt,
Is bread an' jam we always get as soon as school is out.

From **The Path to Home,** Edgar A. Guest, ©1919

Bibliography

Going West With Annabelle ©1976, Molly Douglas
Along the Old Melita Trail, ©1965, Isabel McReekie
Remembering the Farm, ©1977, Allan Anderson
Welcome Home, ©1992, Stuart McLean
Me and the Model T, ©1965, Roscoe Sheller
My Discovery of the West, ©1937, Stephen Leacock

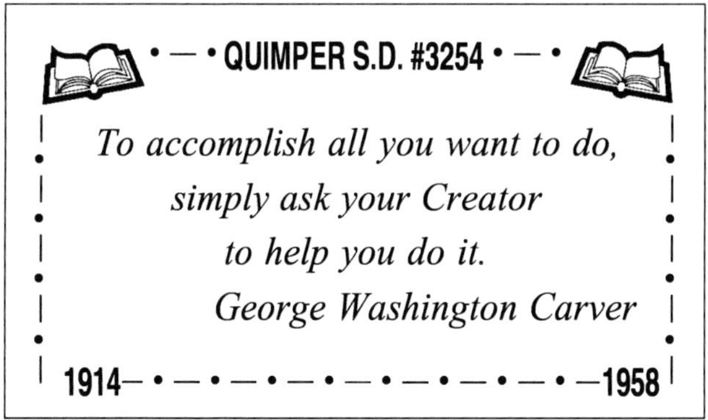

• — • QUIMPER S.D. #3254 • — •
To accomplish all you want to do,
simply ask your Creator
to help you do it.
George Washington Carver
1914–1958

A merry heart is good medicine.
Gloominess is a slow death. — Prov. 17:22

5 — Quimper Vignettes

It will be assumed that most people who read my book will either have their own copies of the Ponteix and Aneroid History books, or that they know where to access copies in order to get the dates of births, deaths, weddings, etc., for any of those whose stories I've chosen to put in vignettes. For others, I trust the stories will stand on their own because of their wider appeal, many having lived in the same era and under comparable circumstances. I have, however, taken the odd tale from these books, but most have been gathered from other more personal resources — letters, phone calls, visits and in some cases, family writings given to me. These vignettes are in random order, many in first person. There will not be stories for *every* Quimper family, but I'm trying to have most represented in at least a picture even if only in a group. Nevertheless, there are a few individuals of whom I was unable to get *any* picture. Such missing links seem hard to understand, especially when one has so many of others.

In reviewing materials for this vignette chapter, one thing became very clear. *All* the ones who sent me their stories, *all* those I got over the phone, and *all* those I found in the Aneroid and Ponteix history books agreed on at least *three* things: that Quimper School and the district it served held many positive memories for them — with its concerts, dances, young people's meetings, Sunday School, church services and, for most, the school days themselves; that Quimperites cared about each other and showed this in many ordinary or extraordinary ways; and that they had cordial relations with neighboring districts. Such recollections made it somewhat easier to pick out those which would fall into place more easily in this chapter.

(I was delighted when my printer, Abbott's Printing, made mini-mini Quimper schools to indicate these different vignettes!)

Box Car Travelling. Earl Cross, in his memoirs written in 1970 for his grandchildren, but which he kindly sent copies of to some old friends, which included my parents, told many tales of his early years in Saskatchewan and of his family's trip west from **Peterborough,** Ontario in a settler's box car in 1909. Because his dad had been a semi-invalid most of his life after being kicked in the head by an unbroken horse, added responsibility for the move fell on the mother's shoulders and his teen aged sons **Bert** and **Earl** and younger sister, **Minnie**. From Toronto on, the whole train was made up of settler's cars — about 70 or 80 of them, with a number of cabooses at the end for women and children and one for the crew. In their car they had 3 horses, a number of chickens, a dog, an expecting cat, and their household effects. Also on the train were men who looked after the stock enroute. Regular stops were made along the way to purchase fodder and refill water barrels. The family was upset at their cat's disappearance at one of these stops, but they hoped some lonely people would take her in. In Ontario their partly open box car door let them look out at the passing scenery — numerous dog teams pulling loaded sleighs on the still frozen lakes and rivers, many of the drivers, Earl said, being Indians. They were relieved, after passing through Ontario, Manitoba and Eastern Saskatchewan still with much snow, to find spring had arrived in Swift Current just ahead of them.

. . . almost 30 years later, Earl, his wife, **Mildred**, and their two children were going *back East* — this time his oldest son **Jim** with him in the box car, and his wife, Mildred and younger ones, **Alison** and **Richard** coming by car. For Jim it was an adventure, especially milking the cows in the swaying box car. They survived on cold meals except for one tin of hot beans ingeniously warmed for them by some kind railway yard worker by spraying the tin with a steam hose.

Perils of the Trackless Prairie. From where settlers got off the train at **Moose Jaw**, or more likely **Swift Current** for Quimper settlers, there were no fences as yet, and very likely no road of any kind. For a few miles out of town — maybe even as far as **Blumenof**, they had a wagon trail of sorts, but it would gradually peter out and they would be relying on their sense of direction and their compass, or if they were caught travelling at night, which would be infrequent, the north star. (I read of one smart father who *plowed* a strip from home to the school for his children's guide). After arriving and setting up a shelter of some kind on the homestead, a lantern on a post or a coal oil lamp in the window were sometimes actual life savers. Now let us return to Earl's memoirs.

A couple of days after arriving in Swift Current and staying with friends from Peterborough who had come a little while ahead of them and had rented a house there, Bert and Earl and their father set out for their claim. The first day out they had to ford the swollen Saskatchewan River. Their first night they spent in a tent they'd brought along. The second day saw them arriving at the little French-Canadian settlement of **Notre Dame**. There were still 11 miles to go, but their father was so ill they unhooked the wagon and headed the 54 miles back to Swift Current. They rested a day and set out again, but this time all five of them. Now Earl tells their story in first person:

"Father, Mother and Minnie were in the democrat. Bert and I with the wagon. We soon found it was too heavily loaded, but we struggled on until about 20 miles from our destination. Then we unloaded part of it and left it by the side of the road. At the homestead we all spent the night in our tent. Next day Bert and I headed out to pick up our things. We knew we would be late getting home, so Mother said she'd hang the lantern on a stake by the tent to guide us. All went well until we were about 10 miles from home and darkness was setting in. A bright light was filling the sky to the southwest. It wasn't long until we realized we were right in the path of a prairie fire. On our way out in the morning we'd noticed that at a spot not too far from where we were, a settler had done some plowing, and we felt we would be alright if we could reach here. We forced our tired horses to their limit and did reach this safety spot — just in time to help this French-Canadian homesteader carry all his belongings from his shanty onto the plowed ground. The fire swept by, driven by a 40 to 50 mile an hour wind and fed by the deep thick growth of grass. We helped the man beat out the flames backing up against the wind, and then helped him carry his effects back to the shanty. By now it was pitch black, but in our concern for how the others had come through the fire, we left immediately with only the stars to guide us the remaining 6 or 7 miles. Insects, known as timber ants, build their houses out of short dry pieces of sagebrush and these were still burning. But when we got to within about 3 miles, we were able to distinguish the steady light of the lantern on the stake in our valley homestead. Our folks were safe as they had backfired. Minnie had been left alone in the tent while

Mother and Father went about 5 miles south to **Pinto Horse Creek** for some drinking water. However, no grass had escaped the fire, so we turned our horses loose and they managed to find little patches of grass in an alkali flat about two miles away. Grass is scarce in alkali so the fire had left a little here and there. (*Yes,* this is the *same alkali flat* so many Quimper stories centre around.)

But one night we got a driving snow storm and in the morning we were unable to find them. Knowing they would drift with the storm, we finally found them about 10 days later. They had found some grass the fire had missed. However, our **Billy** was dead. He had choked to death by getting his hind foot in his halter and the rope had strangled him. This was a serious loss to us as two horses could do very little in breaking up the tough prairie sod. However, by now the grass had grown enough to allow us to tether the remaining two horses close to home."

Breaking Sod. A team of *four* horses or oxen was considered necessary. So what could a homesteader do if he lost, as did the Crosses, some of their team? Sometimes they would combine efforts with a neighbor in order to get enough animals to make up the necessary team or they would try to buy others to take the place of those they'd lost. Back now to Earl's account: "By the spring of 1910 we had only **Jerry** left, but Father had bought two oxen. Needless to say, they didn't like working together. Jerry was humiliated at having to slow his pace to that of **Spot**. (Somehow Earl didn't mention the other oxen by name or how it worked in the team.) When he was especially disgusted, he'd try to bite Spot who in return would use his blunted horns to dig into Jerry's flank. With his previous owner he'd had three other oxen to work with, and did fine. With me and the extra work load, he would simply lay down when he got tired and look at me with *that* look of, 'What are you going to do about it?' It took me some time to figure out how to get him on his feet and working again — a fire of sage brush twigs under him! One day I heard of a farmer who wanted an ox to fill out his team of four after one had died. Father finally agreed to sell old Spot. I was delighted. And it was good for Spot, and his new owner also, for he settled right in to working well once again."

I've read other stories also, about working with oxen which had a mind of their own. If a slough was nearby or the flies or mosquitoes were especially bad, they simply pulled implement or buggy *into* the slough and stayed there till *they* got ready to get out again, no matter how exasperated this made their driver.

Mosquitoes. There's many a tale, and most of them only too true about mosquitoes. As one fairly representative, here is Earl's: it happened around 1910. Earl went with a neighbor in the wagon to

Notre Dame to get some kerosene and eggs. His mother had baked bread for the neighbor who had come to pick it up. The day-time travel had been uneventful, but it was getting dark as they started home and mosquitoes were out by the millions. The oil would have spilled and the eggs would have broken if he'd set them down in order to fend them off — so his torture continued for the duration of the wagon ride *and* for the 4 miles he still had to go after getting off the wagon. (What a boon would have been the insect repellent of today!)

For some unknown reason, mosquitoes seem to prefer certain people. My sister **Nellie**, for instance, over me. I remember well going home from school one day getting hardly a bite, and poor Nellie was covered. Some are affected more by the poison too, and their faces swell up from bites. But, many or few, scratching them into oozing sores is almost impossible to resist, they itch so badly.

In spite of all the misery they caused, some wags would try to work a touch of lightness into the situation. Made up especially for tourists were "photo" post cards — with these creatures in *human* size!

A Later Storm. In 1937 a terrible hail storm at Lake Pelletier had Jim's grandma screaming so loud from fright that Jim wondered if it was this experience plus other aspects of those awful years which made her head back East and persuade her daughter and son-in-law to go, too.

Smoking and Drinking. Though I cannot speak for our R. C. French Quimperites because we did very little socializing with them, it

Left, Jim and Alison, 1952. Right, Mother Mildred with great grandchild, about 1994.

appeared to me that smoking and drinking did not carry the same moral implications with them as these habits did with many English Protestants, particularly those who had a Baptist or Presbyterian background.

Dealing with *health* issues of either or both, was far into the future, and smoking was part of the *male* world only. Most of us never saw a *woman* smoke until after the War. Many, if not most, of the older men smoked, as they had begun the habit in their youth. It was as sad then as always, that money which *should* have gone for food and other things, was going up in smoke, and though, as I said, health implications were seldom voiced, it was obvious that the coughing and other manifestations were the result of tobacco, and that early deaths of some Quimper men were the direct result of this terrible addiction. Nevertheless, I must admit, we went along with it in such ways as giving cigarettes and cigars for gifts and we kids doted on those metal cigarette boxes, the wooden cigar boxes and the special premiums that were part of it all. I remember them having a series of beautiful little silk birds and flowers. Besides, those little roll-your-own packets of cigarette papers were wonderful for tracing!

Dad loved his pipe, but even more — cigars. But once when we'd mailed him a box for Christmas, he had an odd and rather frightening experience. Without being given a reason, he was called down to the post office and put in a separate room all by himself. Eventually he was let go — still with no explanation. We speculated that for some reason they suspected drugs were being smuggled in with those cigars. Needless to say, we sent no more such gifts.

Dad was a pipe smoker until in his 70's when he was in a hospital ward with three other men. Though he wouldn't give up his pipe for all our mother's frustrated complaints during the Depression, he did give it up while he was in the hospital. Strange to say, it didn't seem to bother him a bit, and when he got home, he tossed out all his smoking paraphernalia and never smoked again.

At our Quimper dances there was *no* liquor, and as far as I can remember, none of the fights that sometimes took place in other places where drinking was done. In fact, most of us can recall the night when two young men arrived at a Quimper dance with liquor on their breath and bottles besides. They had hardly arrived when they were gone — literally — tossed out and told not to come back.

However, many of Quimper's young folks in the 40's found themselves in other locales or situations where *both* of these habits were common, and as a result, many took them up. So for many years, right up until the 70's or 80's, smoking held sway in a lot of homes and gatherings. Finally, many joined the trend of these latter years and succeeded in becoming ex-smokers. I don't know what percentage of our district's people smoked, but I believe that by far the majority never did acquire the habit — perhaps due to the good "anti-" influence of living in Quimper in their youth.

As for drinking, I'm not aware of any from our district who had a problem, but maybe that's because I was mostly unaware of its presence. There was no liquor in our home except a bottle of brandy which was brought out only at Christmas or New Year's and then only the grown ups had a tiny glass of it. It had been a real problem in Dad's home in England and no doubt this sad situation helped him decide that it *wouldn't* be a problem in ours.

In Trouble. A personal anecdote that will give *you* a laugh at *my* expense — except that as I've shared this with others such as with a church group on a day tour, I laugh about as hard as they do. This goes back to grade school days when we were playing ball at recess time. Ordinarily in an "honest" game I would be playing field, short stop, third or pitching, so playing *first* was "not my thing" as they say today. Our side was *in* the field. The batter hit the ball and with the fleet feet I had in those days, I was down at second in jig-time. Another fielder got the ball and was going to fire it to first for a hoped for *out.* Where is she?? It was a minute before either others or myself figured out just what had gone wrong!

And Again my absent-mindedness caused trouble, but this was not a Quimper event. It happened at a school where I was teaching and there was no phone. As you know, a teacher gets asked to do many things that have *no relationship* to her job. I was asked to be a go-between for the message that a boar was to go from one farm to another. You guessed it. I forgot! I was *not* well thought of for a while when found out!

Mary Donald's Story. By the time Mary was a Quimper teenager she was "Dee" to distinguish her from three other Mary's in the district. Not all of her story is here in vignettes as some parts of it fit better in other chapters, but here we'll have her tell some stories in her own words.

"When I was little we lived in a **Switzer** house in Quimper — then another Switzer house in the **Erinlea** district — and finally back to Quimper where we were for much of my school life. When I was four the doctor came from town for the birth of my little brother, **Gordon**. They told me he came in the Doctor's little black bag — a slightly different "stork" story, eh? (How different from today's openness on such topics!)

"Cellar steps, usually led to by a trap door in the kitchen, were an ever present danger. I remember my falling down them once and cutting my face very badly on the edge of a tin can in which Mom was starting a plant. Grandma Cross put me on the table to tend to my face. It should have been stitched, but in those days one seldom went to the doctor's, so I have a scar from this accident.

The Donald family about 1942.

Albert and Sarah Dunnell. Daughter, Eva, tells about their family: "Mother came from Belfast, Dad from Ontario. They were married in **Winnepeg**. I was born in 1913. I had twin brothers, **Victor** and **Gordon**. **Mrs. Innes** was Mother's midwife for us. Victor died in 1915, and Gordon later, with pneumonia. Seeing as we left Quimper in the early 20's, their graves in Aneroid were cared for by our kind friend, **Mrs. McCoy**." The Dunnell and Innes families live in B.C. and Alberta and keep in close touch.

Joe Cyr: He had just come in second in a three mile marathon (Uncle Frank was first). 1929. Notice those awful hats!

Suzanne Morin's Story. "We were a Parisian French family rather than French-Canadian. Dad served in the military in France from 1903 to 1906, forming in those years a lifelong friendship with **Jean Thomasset**, who persuaded him to emigrate to Canada. By 1908 Dad was on his homestead in the yet-to-be Quimper district, doing what most were doing to prove it up. A promise to his father before leaving France found him back in the French military. In 1915 he was severely wounded and was a year in the hospital. In 1916, he got married and in 1917 they arrived in Ponteix. My older brother died shortly after birth with the 1918 flu. I was born in 1920, and in 1925 I got a little sister, **Odette**. Dad's health was still not good, so he had to give up farming. He was the Ponteix postmaster for 26 years. Odette helped him in the post office. She is a published writer specializing in preserving our French heritage. Their son **Charles,** married **Leanne Shaddock** — thus uniting grandchildren of Quimper homesteaders.

Tom Claydon, Ed and Fred Shaddock, Uncle Sam, Frank Morin, Uncle Frank, Aunt Phoebe, Mrs. Shaddock, Uncle Tom. Children, Alice, Evelyn, Minnie, Walter, Ethel. Circa 1920.

Herb and Ailie McCoy.

"Mary has asked me to tell the story behind my attending Quimper School in Second Grade. My Dad discovered that I really knew no English even though it was a required course at the convent. Most of the nuns were from France and often knew very little English, so they had to rely on the French-English textbooks. One evening when I was reading my English aloud and following along with my finger, supposedly — my finger would *not* be in the *right place*. I had just memorized the whole thing. Later, when I was supposed to be in bed asleep, I heard my parents talking downstairs. It was all coming up through the vent (a common way in those days to get heat upstairs). Dad said 'That child doesn't know a word of English.' Mother, with her own limited English, couldn't believe this. She said it sounded alright to her. But Dad knew it was true and announced 'We're going to have to do something about this.' And he did. He arranged for me to board at McCoys from Monday to Friday. He would take me there on Sunday afternoon and come for me on Friday night. McCoy's hired man, **Joe Cyr**, was French and had worked for Dad before Mr. McCoy. As part of the plan, he was forbidden to say *one word* of French to me. This made me furious. Dad was proved right my very first night at McCoys. There were nine of us at a long table. Mr. and Mrs. McCoy, Wilma,

Charlie, his wife Nellie, their two children, Willard and Aileen, Joe and I. They were having corn on the cob and Mr. McCoy asked me to pass the salt. I didn't understand, and said 'No thanks.' — in French, I presume. Then a minute later I got up and walked to the other end of the table for the salt. Thus my training in English began with the word *salt."* (I asked Suzanne how it was that she now spoke with *no accent* and could pronounce the 'th' sound, a sound not in the French language and therefore few can say it.) Suzanne's story now continues: "Wilma is four years older than I am and every day going to and from school (we had a half mile walk before catching a ride with Bjores) she would drill me on every word she could think of with the 'th' sound. She showed me how to put my tongue between my two front teeth so as to make the correct sound. I'll always be grateful to her for teaching me. When given the choice of a separate bedroom or to be with Wilma, I chose to be with her. This was no doubt a good idea for a number of reasons, one of which is that we would talk together and I would be learning more English all the time.

"Then came the day when the Quimper Sunday School children would be singing at the *big church* in Aneroid. I was so glad my parents let me go and sing with them as in those days it was very rare, for we as Roman Catholics, to be permitted to go to a Protestant church." (And though Protestants were not forbidden by their church to go to a R.C. church, they very seldom did. Isn't it wonderful that such restrictions are no more?)

Here is Suzanne's little ending to her school story: "I should have gone into Grade Three back at the convent, but they put me in Grade Four. Mother was very angry." (Suzanne and I both wondered about this fairly common practice. It created a silly barrier between contemporary aged kids and, of course, they would miss some of the prescribed work for that grade.)

Suzanne also told me how her Dad and Mom had appreciated the warm welcome given to them as newlyweds. "Before going back to France to serve his country as he'd promised to do, he had made such good friends of so many Quimper homesteader neighbors, that when bride and groom stepped off the train on a very cold night, many were there to greet them. After one night in town with **Lacoursieres**, they were invited to stay at the **Shaddocks** until their own house had an addition on it. This would be mostly Mr. Shaddock's work as he was a carpenter and Dad was still walking with two canes. Mrs. Shaddock knew no French and Mother no English, but somehow they managed and became good friends in spite of this difficulty. Dad had to hire his farm work done that year, but in December he went to Rochester where he had a successful operation. Later however, he got a leg ulcer which forced him to quit farming. They went back to France to live, but after getting his ulcer healed with some special ointment, they were soon back at Ponteix and it wasn't long before Dad got the job of postmaster. Dad died in 1961, but Mom lived to be very nearly 100." (I regret being unable to find a picture of the Morin family.)

The Symingtons. Don will tell us some of their story and then his younger sister, **Dorothy**, will add a little more.

"Dad came from Scotland. He married **Nan White**, whose family had been among the Barr colonists. I have an older sister, **Margaret**, an older brother, **Tom**, and a little sister, **Dorothy**. We were nearly 4 miles from Quimper and only about a mile from **Royer**, but Royer wasn't built until 1920 and a lot of kids around there were big, but had never been to school. We asked and were given permission to still go to Quimper, but for only *one* more year. By then most of these older French children had dropped out of school so it was more like an ordinary school. Their teacher this first year had no less than 44 pupils — 43 of whom were French speaking. On top of this load, she gave, without pay, a half hour's religious instruction after school.

At Quimper there was a slough about three-quarters of a mile west of the school and the teacher used to let us boys go over there to swim at noon. She would ring the bell early enough for us to get dressed and back to school on time. (Don was the only one who mentioned this special privilege for boys.) "Margaret married **Frank Simpson**. It was very sad when their baby girl died. That was the second death in our family. Dad had died from consumption. He was buried on such a cold day that the minister asked the men not to take off their hats for the customary show of respect. We left the farm not long after this."

The Symington family prior to the arrivals of Don and Dorothy.

Dorothy: "I remember the fun Nellie and I had together. At the dances at school, we would do our own little thing between the grown-up dances — feet close together, hands joined, leaning back and going round and round, sometimes getting so dizzy we'd fall down. But it was fun. Nellie and I were a mini-sized bride and groom at my big sister, Margaret's, shower.

A snapshot of us shows we were not very happy in our roles. Sometimes I got to stay overnight with Nellie. We had fun playing hop scotch in their old house they called the shack. Once when Mom was in a play, I was left at the Tom McConvilles. We made pull-taffy. I'd never seen anything like that. It was fun and tasted good, too. Sometimes I got to play with **Dorothy Gammie**. Her grandparent's old sod shack was still standing and we got to play in it. In 1933 Mom, Tom and I left for **Leask**, Saskatchewan.

The McCulloughs — as told by their daughter-in-law **Madge**, who, as **Miss Rogers,** came to Quimper to teach in 1932 and to board at our home.

"My in-laws-to-be, Jim and Annie, were from Ontario. They arrived at their homestead in 1912, so were founding members of Quimper School. They had a post office in early days. Retirement years were spent in Moose Jaw.

"My life in Quimper in the 30's has many fond memories. My home was in eastern Saskatchewan in bush country so the prairies were new to me, but what was really hard was the dust storms, black blizzards, as they were sometimes called. And neither was I familiar with snow blizzards because in my home country trees prevent winds from getting the sweep that piles snow into drifts. In 1934 I became Mrs. Ed McCullough which made it a bit awkward for the children at school to call me by my new name." (Being in school at this time I don't remember the problem, I guess we just went on calling her Miss Rogers — until in later life when she was just 'Madge' to all of us. Sometimes this new way — which some still consider disrespectful in certain circumstances — of addressing people by their first names,

James and Annie McCullough. Their son, Bill, and his wife, Lottie, often hosted Quimper young folks on visits to Moose Jaw in the 30's and 40's.

does solve certain problems.) There are a number of pictures and stories about the McCullough families in the Aneroid and Ponteix history books. In Aneroid's, page 319, you'll see the only *inside* picture I've run across for Quimper. Such a lack puzzles me as there are numerous ones for other places. It would have been so good to have had one of the inside of our school.

The Ed McCullough family in 1946.

Back to Madges, first person story: "In our courting days Ed often walked me home from school to the McConvilles, but this one evening after a ballgame, I had told Mary I would ride home with them — but she forgot. It took awhile to sort out *why* I had been stranded at school. She was embarrassed when she realized her goof, but added somewhat philosophically and prophetically with a knowing smile, 'It won't matter much when I get old and forgetful. It will just mean that I'm forgiven with a little more understanding and sympathy — I hope.'

"Quite often Mary would stay after school so we could walk home together. One very cold blizzardy night, our facing the storm *together* might just have saved us from tragedy. We took turns leading while the one behind held the front walker's coat over her head. How welcome the kitchen light that night!

"In 1943 we would begin a period of 15 years of dual living — farming and politics. Ed served three terms for the C.C.F. (**Cooperative Commonweath Federation**) in **Ottawa** representing the **Assiniboia Constituency**. We were proud of some of the things we accomplished — especially the establishment of Saskatchewan's socialized medical system which set the pattern for all across Canada, eventually.

"We bought land around beautiful Cannington Lake, which we developed into a year-round resort with good fishing, cabins, boats, a children's playground and a miniature golf course. Over the years we have welcomed many old Quimper friends to our home and resort. As they arrive they are struck by the many oil wells pumping at our place. What a contrast between our early years of marriage with their *real*

Quimper school at the miniature golf course. 1980.

poverty and today! We even hitch-hiked once back to Ponteix.

"Now we live in luxury in our retirement years — mainly with money from our oil. We built a beautiful big log house and in the 70's and 80's did a lot of travelling — **Britain, Israel, Germany** and **Switzerland** to name a few. Until we built our new home, we lived in one of the oldest of Saskatchewan's houses. We had done a great deal of renovating and remodelling of it, so with this in mind, I wrote an article titled 'House Makeover' and won a small prize from the magazine **Resort Weekly**. Back to Quimper days: When Ed and I were married, the Quimper women made up a hand-written scribbler full of their favourite recipes. I treasured it and used it often." (I now have this tattered recipe book. Madge thought an old Quimper gal might value it more than her own children or grandchildren.) "One of the nicest happenings of my long teaching career took place at Quimper. In the depths of the Depression, high schoolers were struggling, even though they had the correspondence courses. Ordinarily there was no school in January, but in 1933 a deal was struck. They would go to school that month; parents would donate coal, I my time and the district would pay my board. It worked beautifully! All of them passed department exams that June."

A Knight in Shining Armor. One morning **Old Nell**, the Tom McConville school horse, fell on the ice as they were going to school. She got up finally, none the worse for wear, but the shaft was broken. Farm boys were usually ingenious and **Roland Dumont** was. He repaired the shaft well enough so Isabelle and Olive could drive home after school.

Theo Claydon's Story. Theo chose to feature the alkali flat for her anecdote. Here it is in her own words:

"Our road to school was one of the longest any of the children had to travel and without doubt, the very worst. Just before we came to the bridge, there was this alkali grade. Alkali mud is like no other. It sticks to your shoes like glue — every step you take puts another layer on your shoe. You could get very tall walking through alkali mud — except the stuff squishes and oozes in all directions. Every time you pull your foot out of the mud it makes a 'glup' sound.

"Going to school by horse and buggy was a somewhat different experience. The mud would clog up the buggy wheels and the horses had to 'glup' their way through it using *four* feet instead of *two*. On one memorable occasion, the Dumonceaux children and we were crossing the alkali. We had the buggy and they had a wagon. The harder we tried to get across, the more the vehicles sank — until we had to unhitch the horses and lead them to school about three quarters of a mile. Of course, we were late for school, as we quite often were, on account of alkali mud.

The Tom Claydon family.

Theo, me, Audrey, and Rob at the 1985 Claydon reunion in Ponteix.

"In the dry season, alkali was *still* a problem. The dust would swirl up from your footsteps or blow off the buggy wheels. This caused your eyes to sting and water and your skin to dry and crack. There are many things I miss about the 'good old days' at Quimper, but not the alkali woes."

Here is a good spot to add one of my own alkali stories. When alkali mud dries, it is *very hard*, so by the time the bumps are pulverized into dust, it is almost time for mud again. One time Rob decided on a different solution — enter the *ditch* at the *beginning* of the grade and climb out at the bridge. This was a bit scary as the grade was quite high, but at least it was smooth travelling.

They say there is good somewhere in everything, But I think one would be hard pressed to find any Quimperite speak well of *that*

Part of the Bjore family. Alice and Raymond missing.

alkali flat.

Alice Bjore. "I don't remember why, but my older brother **Louis** and I started school together. I recall Dad asking for a road through the **Dick Edwards** and **Dumont** places because, without it, we had *seven* gates to open and close in going through those two farms to get to school. Also, we got the blame if *others* left the gates open. It was all a real headache. **McCoys** and **McKenzies**, too, wanted such a road. If our school had been in the far eastern part of Saskatchewan, we wouldn't have had this problem, as there, early surveying methods made road allowances *every mile east* and *west,* the same as north and south. I never read the year or the reason for the change.

"Dad had a severe upper back injury. When atop a load of grain, he didn't clear an overhead door at the grian elevator as he drove in. He suffered much pain and gradually was bent almost double. He was bedridden for a number of years before he died.

Dorothy and Alice. When in their latter teens, these two Quimper girls found themselves in the same big city — **Regina** (did you know its first name was **Pile of Bones**? Its new name was chosen by the then governor-general the **Marquise of Lorne** who named it in honor of his wife's mother, **Queen Victoria**). Alice was there taking a course in hair dressing and Dorothy was going to business school. Dorothy's big sister, **Connie**, was in Moose Jaw General Hospital for three years of nurses training.

Wilma and Mary. Two other Quimper girls also found themselves living in the same city — **Moose Jaw** — Wilma was working out and I was going to Normal School. I don't know if Wilma was as fond of chocolate as I was, but she went along with my "extravagant" idea — a split-in-two nickel candy bar each Saturday afternoon. Wilma was in the audience when our room put on H.M.S. Pinafore. She said afterwards that she could hardly believe that that was me as Little Buttercup. It was a strange, but very pleasant experience to me to "be" someone else.

Windsor, and Brantford, Ontario and Winnepeg. These cities made quite a few link-ups with Quimper folks. **Alice Bjore** and **Mickey Collins** were married in Windsor in 1943, as was her younger sister **Alma**, and my brother **Rob**, the same year. Later when Alma died with polio in 1953, **Karen** went to live with her Aunt Alice and Uncle Mickey, who by then were back in Saskatchewan, but in the **Pinto River District**. Karen, husband Bill, and their **Jennifer** and **Andrew** now live in Winnepeg.

Because Frank had had machinist's training in England and his skills were needed in the war effort, he and Mary also moved to Ontario. However, it was not long before he was stricken with cancer and died there, leaving Mary with three little ones to raise. This tragedy brought help from both sides of her family. The **Donalds** moved east, but to **Brantford** rather than Windsor, and our **Aunt Mag** went East too, to help out.

In earlier years Winnepeg was the scene of a number of weddings for couples heading to Quimper — Dad and Mom, Shaddocks, Benders, and Dunnells, and probably others. It was in this city, also, that a young Quimper couple, **Alice** and **Gerald Robins**, lost their little son, **Dougie,** to a kidney disease. After the War **Louis Bjore** became a city worker in Winnepeg. He had done such outstanding work for so many years that when he died, Alice received a letter from **Frank Hamilton M.P.** (Member of Parliament) with high praise for his devotion to his family and community, his work, and for serving his country in the Royal Canadian Air Force in WW II.

Many, many years later Windsor again touched Quimperite lives when Nellie and I attended part of a folk dance festival there. We were made so welcome and felt so safe in this big city, that at midnight on our last night, as we waited to catch a bus at 12:30, we wandered the streets and enjoyed an ice cream at a sidewalk café. For the next few days we had delightful visits with Mary (Donald-Atherton), her now grown family and grand children, and in **Cobourg**, a visit with her **Aunt Mildred**, another Quimperite. To top it off, our old **Lallier** friends drove about 300 miles from **Black Lake**, Quebec, to Cobourg so we could visit together at Mildred's. It was wonderful, but all too brief.

Adams and Gunters. In the Dirty Thirties some of the **Adams** and **Gunter** families moved to the Peace River District, settling near the town of **Dawson Creek** — Mile "0" on the Alaskan Highway. A nearby town **Poucé Coupé** is where **Seth Gunter** celebrated his 100th birthday in 1987. He and his wife, **Mary**, had homesteaded in 1912 in what would become the Glenvern District south of Ponteix.

When I spied the name **Evodia** in the Gunter story, my mind took a leap back to childhood. Her mother had come to help my mother one spring. Evodia was a bit older than Rob and I and therefore a lot wiser! She informed us that all eggs that rattled were rotten — so we proceeded to "test" a bunch of setting eggs. They tested rotten — so we broke them all — thereby greatly diminishing the number of little chicks that would have been hatching out soon!

Russel, or **Curly**, as he was called, a brother of Seth's, but ten years younger, was a real cowboy. In fact, he published a book "The Mustang Wranglers." In it he tells of he and four other young men in the dry year of 1931 driving 100 horses to greener pastures at **Poucé Coupé**, B.C., a trek of 1400 miles. Curly had a horse, **Diamond**, who was famous for his many tricks. (I wonder if his book is still available. I'm sure it must tell which tricks Diamond could do.) Another of Curly's publications was his account of a terrible hail storm in 1914.

Two people who got little or no coverage in the Aneroid or Ponteix books were **Oscar Foss** and his housekeeper, **Molly Horner**, though there are a number of referrals to Oscar by others, as it was at his place Quimper held many picnics. Molly was a good-natured lady, and kept the inside-the-house-action on track. I was told that she later

Here we are commemorating this get-together in Cobourg. Therese, Nellie, Velva, Julienne, me, Geraldine, Mary, Mildred.

moved to the coast, married and had son, but I was unable to track down any more of her story than this. Also, I don't believe she is even in a single group picture I have.

The Kelmans. This Scottish family, whose six children were all born before coming to the West, lived in Regina and Indian Head a short while before their arrival in Quimper. The parents and children all took an active part in community life. **James** lost his life in WW I in 1918; **Maggie** married **Jack McKenzie**, but died when their fifth child was born; **John** never married, but farmed the home place; **Charlotte** (Lottie) married **Andrew Gammie**; **Mary** — **Howard Broley**; and **Alex** — a Quimper teacher, **Ruth Bush**.

The event that all Quimperites remember is the evening their house burned down. Alex told me on the phone how it happened. Here are his words: "All of us but Dad, who had decided to work longer in the field, had gone to a ball game at McCoys. The house was on fire before Dad came in from the field. In trying to find out later what caused the fire, it was discovered that the coal oil stove had been left on *high*. We never told Mother this as it would only have added to her grief. In just two weeks with Herb McCoy in charge, our neighbors and friends built us a new house — far better than the one we had — but of

Oscar Foss.

Below, Jack McKenzie and second wife, Annie. His first wife, Maggie, is found in only a group picture. Below right, Mr. and Mrs. Kelman.

course we missed our pictures and other mementos."

I never heard them play, but Lottie said her brothers would often take their accordions under their arms, walk to the neighbor's and play for folks to dance in the kitchen. Lottie also told of a stream near their house where John could "lie on his stomach and catch trout with his hands." But Alex's violin playing I remember *very well.* He learned to play this difficult instrument wonderfully well from a correspondence course! His talent was on display at Quimper's dances with him on the violin and **Kit McCullough** on the piano. He was often part of musical evenings in our home also.

Another trait of Alex' was his humorous streak. He was what I call, "Quimper's Red Skelton," though of course, this comedian we hadn't heard of yet. How well I remember Bessie and I often being helpless with laughter.

Minnie and George Loken, 1927.

George and Minnie Loken. George's family came from Norway, but only he came to live in the Quimper district. Here he had found the *reason* to stay — **Minnie Gammie.** George was a painter. It was he who painted our new house. He was also a violinist — often playing for dances at Erinlea.

But it is Minnie's story I want to tell here. What a frightening experience for a little girl! Here are her words: "Dad and my brothers were digging a well. A chicken fell into it. They didn't have a windlass, so the dirt was lifted out hand over hand with a bucket. I was only six and therefore small enough to be let down. They *made* me do it and wouldn't bring me up again until I got *that* chicken."

The Gammie family.

Minnie's first home was a dug-out in the side of a hill, but winter in such a house was too damp for the mother, so the next winter, they lived in a house

These five brothers and sisters finally have a get-together.

whose owner was away working. This lasted until they got their sod house built — this, the one that Mary Donald remembered playing in. Actually, the dug-out came *second* — their very *first* being a rack covered with a blanket! One wonders how many would never have left the Old Country had they not been lured west by pictures of "nice homes and flowing wheat fields." Her mother also suffered from hay fever — a rare complaint in those days.

The Shaddock family, Ed, Emily and Dennis.

The Newel Post. This incident did not take place in Quimper, but it happened to one of us — **Mrs. Robins**. I can hear her laughing yet. When coming downstairs in some fancy hotel, her hand sliding on the bannister came to rest on a smooth knob — a newel post, she supposed — until it moved! It was a man's bald head!

The McConville Families. The three brothers Sam, Tom and Jim and their families are all written up quite well in both the Aneroid and Ponteix books, so I will tell a few stories here that are not found there.

Their sister **Nellie** married **Percy Kirkpatrick** and their home in **Vancouver, B.C.** was a second home to all the prairie relatives. Another younger sister, **Evelyn**, didn't marry and remained in England. How delighted we all were when she made a trip to Canada! She had been a faithful letter writer to all her nieces in Canada and each of us had been given some of her lovely crochet work.

The Tom McConvilles didn't homestead. He had been in the navy and married an American girl, **Ellen Roberts**, and they lived in

The Sam McConvilles with their Maxwell 1923.

The Jim McConville family in front of the shack not long before moving to the big, new house.

Uncle Tom and Aunt Ella, 1945. Walter recently came upon some Glenvern programs his mother had saved: **1)** An Arizona Cowboy. **2)** The Clay's the Thing. **3)** Area Belle

Mom and Dad on their 50th anniversary. Mom died Feb. 28 of 1976, so they just missed their 60th by one week. Mom lived to 88, Dad to 96.

New Westminster. When they came to Quimper with their two little tots, **Walter** and **Minnie**, they didn't have a house of their own for two years, so lived in the shack with our family during that time. We have often tried to imagine what it was like — *two* families with *four* little ones probably still in diapers (diddies they were called) with *two* women of such different backgrounds and temperaments in such a crowded space and with *no* modern conveniences.

Because our parents and the **Shaddocks** were such good friends and close neighbors, it was a "clan" of four. If you had asked any one of the *fifteen* McConvilles or the *one* Shaddock, **Dennis,** what they remembered best, I believe most would have answered "the Christmas parties." That meant *three* each season — affairs which lasted from dinner at noon till the wee hours the next morning. Being brought up side by side, these cousins and Dennis had kept in close touch with each other over the years.

Herb and **Allie McCoy** were both born and raised in Quebec. Herb scouted a number of areas in Saskatchewan in 1907, finally in 1908, filing on land he'd selected in the Quimper-to-be district. One of his many jobs in 1907 had been with a land locator for which he drove out men looking for good land just as he was doing, from Swift Current, so he had an inside track! The land he'd chosen was surveyed, but not yet opened for settlement, so the family had a sojourn on a purchased quarter near Swift Current. **Charlie** and his mother had come by train a couple of weeks after his dad had arrived with a box car full of four horses, one cow, a collie dog, and their household effects. At the homestead, after a shack was built, Charlie remembered as a little tot with his mother, putting out sacks in front of his dad on the plow so the furrow would be *straight.*

One day on their way to church, which was being held in the Indianola sod School, they got stuck in an alkali flat. (Another one!) He had to unhitch the horse before he could get either horse or buggy out of the mud. In the process, he gave vent to his quick Irish temper. They never continued on to church — his mother reasoning that the sermon would not have done much good considering the mood he was in.

Herb became one of the first *employers* hereabouts, my Uncle Sam having worked for him before getting settled on his own homestead just a mile west.

Uncle Sam married his English sweetheart, **Phoebe Rustige** in 1907, so were also among the earliest homesteaders. While their husbands were away working from time to time (Dad and Uncle Sam helped build the railway from Swift Current to Vanguard), or doing any job to earn cash — usually with the aim of getting more land near their homestead or the adjoining pre-empted quarter, wives would be left on their own with the children. I'm sure Allie and Phoebe got together to visit when their husbands were gone.

Walter McConville left home in his early teens to work in Ponteix as an assistant to the reeve, **Mr. A.E. Browning**. He boarded with a French family. They were a lively lot and there was a lot of enthusiastic bilingual conversation and singing. To one tune they had as many impromptu verses as they could dream up. Perhaps he was unconsciously building up to writing a *whole* book in *rhyme*, "Talara by Teaspoon" ©1992, in which he tells of his years in Peru working for an oil company. Walter has received a number of awards for this and previous writings.

Alice Bjore tells this anecdote: "One day one of our neighbors, **Charlie Heamon**, came to borrow a gun to shoot one of his horses which he was really disgusted with for continually getting out of the fence. Mom talked him out of it by persuading him to give it to the Klein family instead. He agreed and this horse took them to school for many years. I guess he liked his new home better than his old one. Maybe Charlie had not been good to him which made him try to escape."

Mr. and Mrs. Lallier at son, Joe's, wedding.

Lalliers. I will single out here but three of the many special memories of the Lallier family. (1) Geraldine was the outdoor girl and I, not being very good with horses, always admired how she could handle that wild team she drove to school. (2) I don't know how musical all the family was, but I can hear yet Ernestine and Julienne in a lovely duet "What are the Wild Waves Saying." (3) Many of you will know that I gave piano lessons for many years — a little finger exercise that I taught all of them was one I learned from

Geraldine. I believe she told me she'd learned it from a nun at the Ponteix convent.

The Kleins. Mina has written for the Aneroid History book a lengthy account of their family.

The Klein family before the last three girls were born.

I found it interesting to read again there of life in Holland; their decision to come to Canada in response to Canadian ads in their home town; their dreams as they saved up money for the trip; the reason they were *not* on the Titanic; celebrating Nellie's birthday at sea — but mother not feeling very well being about eight months pregnant; a May snowstorm upon arrival at Ponteix; their happy, but hard, first years on the homestead, first in sod shack, then a two roomed house with an upstairs; while welcoming more little girls into the family with their Daddy being midwife — until a terrible blow befell them — a widow and six little girls without a daddy due to the 1918 flu. What a desperate time this was, but gratifying also to learn of help from neighbors, family, friends and their church. In 1914 the grandpa on their mother's side sold his Dutch property, came to Canada and homesteaded just south of them. Later he sold it and moved into the Klein home — a joy and a help to both his daughter and six grandchildren. In 1920 a single man, their Uncle Cornelius, came from Holland also and stayed to help with the farm until 1927. The older girls attended a Swift Current convent in winter and Quimper school in summer. The younger ones had all their public schooling in Quimper. The family enjoyed community events and appreciated the school having been moved south so they had *only* three miles to go to school, instead of four! They especially loved the new dresses their mother made for the Christmas concerts.

Marguerite and Jeanne had just lost their mother and a baby sister. In Mrs. Klein they found a kind and loving foster mother who boarded them until their father remarried and they were of school age. They had been treated just the same as her own six girls. English was spoken in the home, so they had to relearn French.

(From Gertrude I learned the cross-arm method of taking off a blouse or pullover sweater — easier than the English way.)

Mr. and Mrs. Goffinet.

Just recently I read how johnny cake got its name. It's a corruption of "journey", but the word *cake* with it led me astray. To me *cake means sweet tasting* (though we have potato cakes so this sweet idea isn't a constant, is it?). We kids often traded lunches — my trading partner often being Gertrude — her nickname Trouda. In grape season we always traded because I liked her concords and she liked my red ones. But the johnny cake trade was, as they say today, "something else". I don't remember what I traded for it, but once was its *first* and *last* trade! I didn't like that cake then and still don't!

The Goffinet Family arrived in Quimper in 1926 with their seven children, the oldest five having been born in **Belgium**. The two youngest, **John** and **Joe**, born in Winnepeg, were the only ones to attend Quimper School. An older sister, **Marie**, had died in the 1918 flu.

This family, like the Klein's, were booked to sail on the Titanic, but they were late and didn't make the sailing of this ill-fated ship.

John, in 1934, went to B.C. to live and in Kelowna had his own excavating and bulldozing business and was the prime mover for a golf course there. His widow, Gertrude, resides in nearby Grand Forks.

Joe married a Ponteix girl, **Yvette**, who was very sports minded. They moved as a newly married couple to the Goffinet farm in Quimper

John and Gertrude Goffinet, 1934.

Joseph Goffinet family.

in 1945 They operated it till 1975.

Yvette's curling team —mother, sister, a friend and herself — have won bonspiels in **Shaunavon** and **Swift Current**.

In the 80's Belgian and Canadian relatives visited each other, first here and then over there.

The Quimper farm is still operated by the Goffinet family — Joe's and Yvette's daughter, **Rose**, having married another Quimperite, **Bob Dumonceaux**.

An Embarrassing Moment. This is one I will let **Bill Busch** tell in his own words: "One day I went to town with Uncle Jim (my parents became his aunt and uncle when he married Ethel). I'm very fond of weiners and succumbed to temptation when I bought a whole dozen I'd spied in the butcher shop window, dreaming of roasting them at school after the children had gone home, when the furnace fire would be just right. The magic moment came. All rational thought left me. The whole dozen disappeared! Then a very disturbing thought hit me. This was Friday night and there would be some *special* on the supper table. There was! Another of my loves — home canned jellied chicken. I valiantly tried to eat at least some, but it was quite evident I was "*off my feed*". Then when I turned down *apple pie*, Aunt Martha was all for calling the doctor. Finally in great embarrassment, I apologized profusely — the whole episode ending with her extracting a promise from me to have no more private weiner roasts."

Both **Ethel** and **Bill** gave me much material for my vignette chapter, so I have to be very selective in choosing which to pass on. I've chosen but ten condensed to one-liners, first Bill's, then Ethel's.

BILL...

(1) ..playing a violin duet with Allan Claydon who "accidently on purpose" was passing his bow under my nose or into my ear.

(2) ...one stormy night when visiting Donalds, we had to stay the night — "six of us lads sleeping (?) crosswise on a double bed."

(3) ...missing riding with my new bride because I was too busy helping pull other cars out of the mud.

(4) ...having my fiance's sister, Isabelle, observing me teach as part of her Normal School training.

ETHEL...

(5) ...riding to school on the handle bars of my teacher's (Charlie McCoy) bike.

(6) ...standing in the corner for talking and have George McKenzie come to keep me company.

(7) ...Frank Adshead (our softball team manager) running around the bases before a game handing out sticks of gum.

(8) ...thrilled being asked to play on the Ponteix team in their game against Swift Current, but feeling disloyal to our Quimper Orioles in yellow and black as I donned the red shorts.

(9) ...jumping to catch a high ball — and landing on a still fresh cow plop.

(10) ...making my first cake at Mrs. Claydon's while she was washing her hair to get it ready for me to finger wave. I saved up four quarters so I could buy a yard of material to make myself a dress.

The Dumonceux Family in 1938 moved onto the Lallier farm. The parents were from Belgium where he had lost his first wife. In Canada he married a Royer school teacher. They had 14 children, all of whom attended Quimper.

The Percy Claydons. There are stories elsewhere about this Scottish family who just lived a quarter of a mile from the school. They were all very active in our community.

Mr. and Mrs. Percy Claydon.

The Dumont Family. Both parents were from Quebec. It was Mr. Dumont who had the threshing outfit that came to our place, and we read elsewhere in this book of *his* wonderful flower garden and *her* love of music and other interesting things about this family.

Mr. and Mrs. Dumont.

Rob and I Become Painters. In his words: "One day we found a partly used can of green paint — just right, we decided, for the pump — handle and all. When Dad came in from the field and went to water the horses, he wasn't too pleased, and when we got to the house, neither was Mom. We were a mess from head to foot. Need I say that traces of that green paint lasted on *us* for *days,* maybe *weeks,* and on the pump itself for *years.*"

A Late Compliment. Another in Rob's own words: "Mary has told you about my first school days. Yes, my shyness led to me repeating Grade One, but later a kind-hearted teacher moved me up to be in the grade with others I'd started school with. About 50 years later, when I was visiting a former Quimper teacher, she introduced me to her daughter as her best student."

A Gasoline Lamp Explodes. Again in his own words, Rob tells of this tragedy: "In 1935 our family was visiting the **Robins** one Sunday evening. Supper was over and we were all in the living room singing hymns with Mary playing the pump organ, when the gasoline lamp exploded, spraying burning gas over three of us on the settee right below it. Mom and I were both badly burned, but Mrs. Robins died the next morning. I believe that only my youth and having on my Sunday best suit, vest, shirt and tie, which covered me up enough to prevent more serious burns, saved my life. We were taken to the Ponteix hospital where the nuns, especially **Sister Mary**, took such good, loving care of us. I heard later of the rumors (remember Quimper's split phone lines?) which flew everywhere the next day, one being that if I lived, I would be blind. Though my eyes were swollen shut, they had not been injured — but this was not true of my hands and ears. I had plastic surgery later in Regina on my ears, and x-ray treatments on my hands, but worst of all was the pain when scar tissue formed to close off my ear canals and I had to have them lanced. Mom's arm and hands got her worst burns and she never again wore a short sleeved dress. I probably owe my life to our teacher at that time, **Ken Miller**, who rolled me in a carpet to put out the fire." (Though I read of some Central European people who lived at some distance from us and who knew of the cold water first-aid treatment everyone knows of today, it was unknown by any of us when this fire took place. I've often wondered how different the outcome might have been if all those who were burned had had cold water from a nearby well pumped over them *before* that horribly long and painful 10 mile ride to town.)

Other Fires. When we think of the homesteaders, often there were no warnings of any kind of a prairie fire headed their way — nothing but the horrifying red glow in the sky to the west — a signal to get onto the fire-guard strip around the farm buildings. Later, a safe place was summer fallow land.

During my fifth teaching year, a fire got away from some men burning weeds and one of them ran to the school with a warning. Horses were quickly hitched up and we all went to the summer fallow just behind the barn. The fire got part way into the school yard before they got it out.

It was ironic that our family, under Dad's very vigilant eye, took *no* chances with fire, while some others used to start a morning fire in the cook stove with a tiny bit of kerosene, but not Dad. And yet it was *our family* that suffered through one of Quimper's worst fire accidents.

I remember once when Rob was playing with matches and tossing them out his upstairs bedroom window. Dad caught him and he got a lesson on fire he wouldn't forget. Dad touched a burning match to the end of his finger. Again, how ironic that Rob would suffer such terrible burns.

There was still the idea, even into recent years, that Christmas tree lights should be *real* candles. This was no longer the case at our Quimper concerts, but one teacher did have us do a drill, carrying candles — Dad was horrified that a teacher would be so lacking in safety measures.

Mom was used to an open fireplace in England and missed seeing the fire burning when all they had on the homestead was the coal and wood cook stove. So one day she just lifted the lids so she could *watch* the fire — a *no-no*, Dad quickly informed her, when she told him of it — danger of poison gas from coal not yet fully ignited, or of an explosion, even.

But one time Mom and Dad were fighting a prairie fire at the northwest corner of our place. Luckily a slough was nearby, so they could dip their bags in it, the better to beat back the flames. I don't remember them saying how this fire got started or how they happened to see it in time to get it out this way.

Just recently I learned that a sod barn Dad had in the early days burned down.

Square Dancing. Newcomers to square dancing no doubt find it hard to catch the words of the caller. When Mom attended her first dance in the Quimper Schoolhouse, and a man was standing on a chair "doing his stuff", Mom, thinking he was surely drunk, leaned over to Dad and said, "Why doesn't someone throw him out?" Caller **John Kelman** wouldn't have appreciated her remark, would he?

Karen McConville. "When schools were first consolidated, and snow plow clubs not yet organized, neighbors took turns with their cars to get their children into town. We children were packed like sardines. Once when **Joe Goffinet** was driving, he was *gunning* it to get through a big drift ahead, but the drift proved rock solid and the car, going *into* it, ended up sitting sideways on the top."

Becoming Beautiful. Cousins **Olive** and **Nellie** had heard that oil would make hair shiny and pretty, but what *kind* of oil could they use? Sewing machine oil should do it. The results were hardly satisfactory and a *lot* of soap and water was needed to restore these two drowned rats to some semblance of normalcy.

Even so, the recovery was much quicker than other more common childhood attempts to perform tasks best left to older ones with some barbering skills. Though no picture was taken (who really wanted to remember?), I can still "see" my little sister with her self-done haircut.

The School's Drinking Water. When the school was in its first location, **Walter** was the water boy. Their well was the pulley and bucket type. **Minnie** recalled one day when, as his helper, she accidentally let the rope slip, causing the full bucket of water to pull his hand right up into the pulley. No broken bones, fortunately, but a sore hand and a sister who felt badly for causing his misery.

In its second location, **Rob** took water to school — for 15¢ a day. A can that held about two pails just fit in the back of the buggy. I don't remember how many years he did this, but it was a long time.

The Red Booties. I loved the little red booties Mom knitted for me, but the *reason* for them was not good. I was a little kid walking home from school when some big boys were riding their horses and trying to see just how close they could come to us, showing off to each other, I suspect, but it all went *beyond close.* A horse stepped on my little toe. I was taken to the Ponteix hospital. The story of just how *badly* I was hurt escalated of course. I had only lost the *tip* of my toe, not the *whole* toe. However, I couldn't walk to school for quite awhile, and I dreaded the stinging iodine treatment each day. But my Mom won a little girl's heart with her knitting needles.

Beginning a Business. Cousins **Minnie** and **Andy** decided one spring to raise their own chickens. Believing a big fat rooster could cover more eggs than a hen, they caught one, plunked him on top of about two dozen eggs and quickly put boards on top wieghted down with some good sized rocks. But *he* didn't want to be a *mother* and they were disgusted with his poor performance. What a mess too, with all those broken eggs! And, needless to say, *mothers* weren't happy with this budding poultry business either.

The Robins Family. Robins rented the Shaddock farm. One very cold winter day **Jean** persuaded me to ride double with her on their pony, **Buck**, over to her big brother **Vic**'s, about 5 or 6 miles away. We'd only gone a mile when we were so cold we decided to stop at

Joe Cyr, Cousin Andy, Elmer Robins, Uncle Sam, Gerald Robins, Aunt Phoebe, Mrs. (Ethel) Robins, Cousin Evelyn.

Beliveau's for a warm up. No one was home — but people didn't lock their doors then, so we went in for awhile before going on our way. I wonder if they ever knew they'd had visitors.

The Robins family were all very musical. They played for many, many dances at Glenvern Hall. Two neighbors, **Cliff Andrew** and **Worth Hunt** often played with them. Most people wouldn't consider a piano a *portable* musical instrument, but if there was no piano where they were going to play, they simply put oats in the bottom of the sleigh to cushion the bumps and took it along. Jean said that when she moved down East in 1951, she could still vacuum oats out of it!

Elastic Breaks are Embarrassing. Though *sewn-in* elastic has nowadays practically replaced the thread-through type, I'm sure a great many other older females could share similar embarrassing moments related to thread-through with its built-in problem. Because of the action at the join resulting in a break, a pair of bloomers could suddenly drape one's ankles. For fielders in a ball game, a nearby gopher hole might prove a ready place to stuff one's fallen bloomers. (We were often playing in dresses rather than long pants or shorts, especially if it were just a recess or noon-hour game.) My *break* came during outdoor exercise at school one warm day. A quick grab through my dress saved the day as I tried to sneak *out* of class and *into* the school.

More McCoy Stories. Wilma and I have kept in close contact since we were Quimper school kids, though she was Rob's age, therefore one grade ahead of me. We teen-aged girls often spent two or three days staying at each other's home during summer holidays. Wilma's big brother, **Charlie** (he was her teacher when she was in grade two and both agreed he was harder on her than the other kids — not wanting to be accused of playing favourites with his little sister), had ping pong set up either in the yard or in the loft of their big barn. And there was **Johnny**, Wilma's own strawberry roan horse, the first of many horse-loves in her life. In fact, a common thread in McCoy family stories is devotion to horses (Madge also often mentioned their mutual love of horses).

McCoy's had the only *named* farm in Quimper, "Happy Hollow".

The McCoys departed from the traditional in another way also — in the color of their farm buildings. Buff was a good choice as it made the name in black stand out very well.

But in all these years Wilma and I have only visited each other twice at our respective homes — in **Dawson Creek** and **Yakima**. However, letters, phone calls, gifts and snapshots, etc., have helped to bridge this mileage gap.

Charlie was in Quimper's *first* class and his daughter, **Marilyn**, the youngest of their four, was in the *last*. The oldest, **Willard**, taught school in Calgary. **Aileen** became a registered nurse. To set her course in this direction, she told me of this incident: Mrs. Bjore (in another story you read of this lady making stuffed Mickey Mouses for sick children) made some cream puffs and took them to **Fernand Dumont** who was in bed with rheumatic fever. How his eyes lit up when he bit into this delicacy, an almost unheard of treat in those days! Aileen, then and there, decided she wanted to do in life whatever it took for *her* to bring similar pure joy to the sick. She would become a nurse.

Terrance died in 1962 in Germany and is buried in a military cemetery there. **Marilyn** got a degree in Business Administration and now lives in Calgary. In 1968 the last McCoys left the Quimper district when Charlie and Nellie retired in **Saskatoon**.

Almost without exception those who wrote their Quimper story for me, told of picnics at **McKenzie**'s and **Oscar Fosses** —the scrumptious home made ice cream; swimming in either Shaddock's or Foss' dam (we called the *water* the dam) and trips up to Lake Pellitier. McCoys were the only ones I remember who spent *weeks* up there, first in a tent, and later in an old cook car, converted, in Aileen's words, into a one-room lakeside cottage. As with most rural kids of that day, bakery bread was a real treat, but Aileen thought it a special treat for her Mom in a different way — a welcome respite from bread baking at home. McCoy's first boat was a simple rowboat, "The Bluebird". Later they got a little bigger one with an outboard motor and called it "The Clipper". This name was also on their "cottage" and in Quimper's colors, yellow and black. (I remember stenciling and painting this sign on it before it went up to the lake.)

Aileen thanked her Dad, her Grandpa and **Bert Cross** for serving on the school board and getting the teeter-totters and swings. (Yes, *they* were due appreciation from *all* of us for we surely spent a lot of recesses and noons on them.)

Kids today would have difficulty getting excited over one incident that was so memorable to Aileen. Her Dad came home from town one very cold winter day and with a flourish and a grin produced from under his heavy coat a stick of *celery*. The warmth of his body had kept it from freezing.

Depression Woes. At first in the Depression, not all farmers had given up hope of things getting back to normal soon, but they *were* feeling the pinch of not being able to afford gas, repairs, or license plates for their cars and trucks. To make matters more difficult, they (the government) had colored the gas *purple* to designate its use *exclusively* for tractors. What to do? Well some took a chance and used some purple gas in "wrong" tanks and some travelled at night as best they could *without lights*. Understanding Mounted Police were as lenient as they dared be and still keep respect for the law. Aileen recalled them getting stopped one night when a truckload of young people was off to a play practice — in the dark. There was great relief when he let them off with just a warning.

Temptation. We had the Travelling Library at our house and Aileen dredged up her fight with *sinful* thoughts one time when they'd come over for books. She spied a dolly tea set. Oh, how she wanted it! She even confessed to thinking of how she could *hide* it if she *took* it. But stealing, she knew, was very wrong. Integrity prevailed. Her parents must have seen her longing looks, for that Christmas, Santa left her a little tea set — which she still has.

Only Ten Left. Now we'll hear a little from Marilyn as she recalled the last days of going to school at Quimper with about 10 pupils and only four English speaking. It was not a very happy or inspiring time in her school life, but at least, she said, they were not plagued with the drugs and violence of today's classrooms. It was an innocent time. Tree planting on Arbor Day had seldom, if ever, taken place at Quimper, but usually the teacher organized a yard clean-up. The kids would spread out, take their distance and be responsible for picking up litter in their pathway. (Marilyn didn't tell me how she felt about the school closing and getting bussed to Aneroid, but I'm sure it would make for a happier more fulfilling school life to be with more children and have a greater variety of activities both during school hours and at recreation time.)

Everett and Ruth Baker. In Chapter One you read of a visitor to Quimper School shortly before the school closed. The "reason" was left blank, but just recently I ran across what could have been the explanation. Had news reached **Everett Baker** that a young woman from her adjacent school district was teaching here and he just decided to call in, wish her well and give her a bit of encouragement? Also, elsewhere in this book, you can read more information about both this teacher, **Geraldine Nostbakken** and her illustrious caller.

Turn now to page 254 and you will see a picture of Everett and his wife, Ruth. Both were very influential province-wide as well as locally — Minnesota's loss being Saskatchewan's gain. Much of his work and personal philosophy are found in two books he authored, "Working Together" — on co-ops, and "Trails and Traces", his portrayal of of Saskatchewan in color photography. As head of the Wheat Pool, he had covered a great many of its miles with his camera always at the ready.

Did you notice the logo at the top of the Indianola School plaque on page eight? Yes, he was founder and first president of this society. And if you have travelled the **Red Coat Trail Highway**, the markers you see all along the way are there because of his efforts.

Everett and Ruth lived out their strong convictions in fighting against alcohol, prejudice, and complacency. The establishment of the **Pine Cree Park** in memory of the Indians who once lived in the area was one concrete example. As others also came to value some of his ideals, they named a nearby coulee in his honor, **Baker Coulee.**

Quimper vignettes could, I'm sure, go on and on — maybe a whole new book's worth —but, for now, they end here.

A Sunday afternoon gathering at our place. Circa 1940. Not long after this Mr. Bjore (on the left) would be bedridden. I'm not in the picture, so guess I was the photographer .

The Stensrud Family in 1961 in Yakima, WA. Milla, Roy, Dad, Mom, Carl and Jimmy.

Jim asked us to drop the "my" when he was in his teens and then went back to it later! He is the one in light suit. He was killed in an accident in 1977.

The Mother Watch

She never closed her eyes in sleep till we were all in bed;
On party nights till we came home she often sat and read.
We little thought about it then, when we were young and gay,
How much the mother worried when we children were away.
We only knew she never slept when we were out at night,
And that she waited just to know that we'd come home all right.

Why, sometimes when we'd stayed away till one or two or three,
It seemed to us that mother heard the turning of the key;
For always when we stepped inside she'd call and we'd reply,
But we were all too young back then to understand just why.
Until the last one had returned she always kept a light,
For mother couldn't sleep until she'd kissed us all good night.

She had to know that we were safe before she went to rest;
She seemed to fear the world might harm the ones she loved the best.
And once she said: "When you are grown to women and to men,
Perhaps I'll sleep the whole night through; I may be different then."
And so it seemed that night and day we knew a mother's care —
That always when we got back home we'd find her waiting there.

Then came the night that we were called to gather round her bed;
"The children all are with you now," the kindly doctor said.
And in her eyes there gleamed again the old-time tender light
That told she had been waiting just to know we were all right.
She smiled the old-familiar smile, and prayed to God to keep
Us safe from harm throughout the years, and then she went to sleep.

From **The Path to Home,** Edgar A. Guest, ©1919

Bibliography

One Man's Journal, Herbert Driscoll, ©1983
The Home Children, Phyllis Harrison, ©1979
Barefoot on the Prairies, Ferne Nelson, ©1989

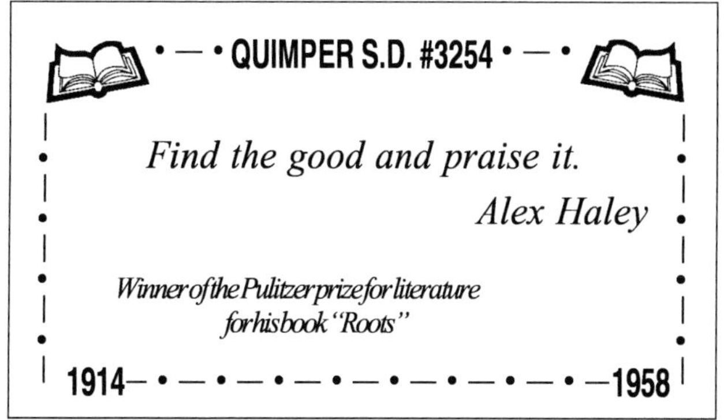

• — • QUIMPER S.D. #3254 • — •
Find the good and praise it.
Alex Haley
Winner of the Pulitzer prize for literature
for his book "Roots"
1914— • — • — • — • — • — • — • —1958

In God's sight be a worker who is not ashamed of your work. — 2 Tim. 2:15

6 — The Work-A-Day World

Railroad Work

Somehow I don't remember Dad ever talking about he and Uncle Sam working on the railroad, so as I give here some of the details of this job, I do not know just which particular thing they did, or if they switched jobs from time to time. Supposing a work train was similar in Canada and the States, here is a description:

A work train consisted of a locomotive, coal and water tankers and flat cars loaded with ties and rails. The engine had conveyor belts on the sides to bring the ties to the front. Men with teams and wagons would take the ties off and lay them in position. Then a man operating two cable drums high above the engine, would pick up the rails and lower them onto the ties. Spacers were then put between the rails and a few spikes driven in to keep everything in place until 30 or 40 men at the back of the train would drive in the rest of the spikes. At the end of the day the men took the conveyor belt off and the train backed up to camp for supper and loading supplies for the next day.

Some work trains had triple decker bunk cars for their crews (refer back to page 71), but I couldn't find out if these were used in Saskatchewan.

Quite often the C.P.R. chose to lay rail a few miles north or south of where settlers expected it to go, thus making double profit on the land they sold on either side of the railway — first for *farmland* and the second

Not a shack, but a house. Built by Crosses about 1909.

A bachelor's basic sod shack.

time around as *lots* in the town. This explains why many little towns which mushroomed just *ahead* of the line ended up having to move lock, stock and barrel, as did Notre Dame, to become Ponteix.

Building

Very old people can tell you their personal experiences from actual tent living to being in as modern and beautiful a house as you can see anywhere. But now in their 80's or 90's, they may very likely be living in a retirement or nursing home. Most my age never even *saw* a sod shack though I learned to my surprise that two Quimperites actually got to play in the 20's in the then still standing Gammie sod house. In finding pictures of quite a few "soddies", it was interesting to note the great differences in sizes, neatness of appearance and, by word descriptions, what the *insides* were like — much variation there too — dirt or wooden floors, skin or glass windows and so on. Norwegians had built sod houses for hundreds of years, but I didn't read of anyone in our district learning special skills from any such settler in a nearby district. A sod house was in some ways *superior* to a tar paper shack, being warmer in winter and cooler in summer, and, with certain improvements over the basic, could be made quite aesthetic and homey. Though I never read of it, it would seem a sod shack (before drying out anyway) would have provided protection from a prairie fire. But it seems that even a small drafty tar paper shack was higher on the status ladder, so most men, as long as they were bachelors anyway, built one of these. Then, with marriage in the offing, most strived hard to have *her* come to a frame house — if only one or two small rooms. But soon, with such limited space, the next step was often a two bedroom lean-to. However, these additions, lacking any attic space or insulation, and often on the north side of a house as ours was, were really a headache, especially on cold winter days. Doors to these rooms were often kept closed during the day — probably to save fuel. Hot water bottles might have been put in the bed just before bedtime and I doubt if they fully undressed and donned nightclothes. Upon awakening in the night, the pot would be dragged out from under the bed and used, on the floor — (hard to imagine — awkward to say the least) — but far better than having to go outdoors. And what of tending to babies or toddlers in these tiny bedrooms *with* their parents? Then in the morning, for privacy, doors might be kept closed while a fire was started and the kitchen and front room heated up to a reasonable temperature. After breakfast, when doors had been open awhile, the frost-laden walls and ceilings became a dripping mess. I can remember so well the job of mopping up to

Step One in building the McConville house — digging the basement with horse drawn scrapers.

In progress — the McConville house, Aunt Mag, Mom, Fred Shaddock, Grandma, Uncle Frank.

The Jim McConville house.

McCoy's house, circa 1925.

prevent the beds getting sopped with the drips. Well, as you can guess, dreams of better housing of some sort would be taking shape — either improving what they had, or building a brand new house. The 20's saw most Quimperites make such improvements. One exception to this familiar pattern was the Shaddocks, as Ed was a carpenter by trade and right away had built a very good house (still in use today), for his bride to come to in 1916. As far as I remember, theirs was the only house in Quimper with a den and a dumb-waiter.

A tar paper shack — one step up the housing ladder.

There was a saying that "If the husband was the *real* boss, a *big barn* went up first — if the wife, it was the house." Well, I don't know about this theory's authenticity, but the Jim McConvilles got a big house and the Sam McConvilles a big barn and the McCoys got one of each! Whichever came first, no doubt a family hoped the *other* would soon follow. Uncle Sam, in fact, had a basement and foundation all ready for a new house. Then the Depression hit and all building came to a screeching halt. Later, as tractors replaced horses, big barns were no longer needed. When prosperity and bigger came into being in the late 40's and 50's, huge metal quonsets for those monstrous tractors, combines, etc. were the order of the day and round metal grain storage units supplemented or took the place of wooden

A typical lean-to house. Barely visible on the right the basement and foundation for a new house.

granaries. Cars bought in the 20's had made small one-car garages a common sight, but as shacks or these small garages were replaced with something better, these old or inadequate buildings came into other uses. Our shack turned into a workshop and grain storage. And where milk or cream had to come under more stringent standards, a milk house would be built between house and barn.

Late improvements — the quonset, double garage and new truck.

In the first few months of settlement, outdoor toilets and chicken houses (sometimes sod at first) were very soon in place, all pretty much alike from farm to farm. The chicken house was often painted red like the barn and granaries, while the toilet was more apt to match the house. In later years, both of these buildings would become obsolete, first the outdoor privy when indoor plumbing came into being and then the chicken house, or coop as it was called, when farmers went into grain farming exclusively or they moved away, leaving the farmyard deserted.

With all these tremendous changes, the *looks* of a *familiar* farm yard was no longer even a landmark in more recent years, leading some of us who were heading back to our childhood haunts, to suffer the humiliation of getting lost in broad daylight when only a mile or so from "home"! This was more likely to happen if the *house* was gone — torn down as was Uncle Sam's or hauled into town and beautifully remodelled as was Uncle Tom's. Luckily for us Jim McConvilles, our beloved big old house is *still there* and well kept. I wonder how many times this house has been painted over the years! As far as I can remember we were the only ones that had a corrugated metal barn. It has long since been unused by cattle, horses or pigs. But stepping inside, your heart gets a few tugs as you see reminders of those olden days — some old harness, the remains of mangers and stalls, the nail on which the lantern hung and so on. We can recall each horse's name and which stall was theirs. In the cow barn we see the old milking stools, and in the pig pen in the corner, that old trough into which we would throw some chop (ground oats), and then dump over it that mixture of most everything from the house which came under the name of *slop*.

Not only *looks* bring back memories, but also *sounds* and *smells* — calling the cows with "*Co* boss *Co* boss!", the chickens with "*Here* chick chick chick, *Here* chick chick chick" and the pigs with "*Here* pig pig pig." We had no calls for horses or turkeys though. To coax a horse, you had a pail under your arm with a bit of chop in it. For turkeys, which we considered pretty stupid birds, you just did what you had to do — fed and watered them and hoped you could somehow shoo them inside if a storm was coming. Even farmyard smells are nostalgic for some, I've learned, but not for me! I confess that even the smell of warm milk was not pleasant to me and the smell of manure and chicken-house droppings was even worse. And then there were those other repugnant, but necessary, sights, sounds and smells of butchering days — the sound of the gunshot that downed a steer —

A number of farm wives work at jobs in town also — Doris McConville here working at Kouri's in Ponteix.

the squealing of a pig being dragged across the yard; the growing heap of chickens as each had had their neck wrung, turkeys strung up to bleed, and so on. I was grateful not to be brought up on a ranch, for seeing and hearing that horrible business of branding would have been worst of all. I've seen pictures and read of branding times being *happy social* events, but I never could understand having a gay time with such suffering going on. Being a girl I was never in on any of the castrating which had to be done, and, as with many girls of our day, the business of breeding was also shielded from my eyes whenever possible. In fact, even the *births* of farm animals were hidden from me and I must admit I felt unfairly treated when I had to *milk* the cow *after* a calf's birth, but never was permitted to *see* the birth. Perhaps it was a good thing that I became a city girl!

Raising Chickens

Some farm women got incubators, but we never did. Mom liked looking after setting hens and baby chickens and I did too. We used a nearby granary for this rather than building individual coops as did some others. We had a couple of rows of attached boxes with lids on leather hinges. We would let out a few at a time to feed and when these were back on their nests and the lid down, we'd let out a few more. There is something very fascinating about seeing chicks hatch, and few things prettier and nicer sounding than a mother hen with her baby chicks. It is, of course, more *efficient* to use an incubator, but the thrill of doing it *nature's* way is something few children of today will ever see. Another job I always liked was gathering eggs. To get an egg from under a hen which didn't want to get off her nest, we used to lay a stick across its neck, grab its tail and pull it off. But I saw others use a kinder method — put an elbow in front of the hen's beak and just reach under her for the egg.

After we had set enough hens for the amount of chickens we wanted to raise, broody hens were denied becoming mothers by being put in a long slotted box hung on the outside of the chicken house. In two or three days they would be "off the cluck" as we said, and turned loose. **Bud** tells me that at their place, broody hens were put in a sack and hung on the clothes line awhile.

Well Digging

There were no deep wells in the early days as all were dug by hand. Some used a horse to help. Bud told me of their smart horse, **John**, who would walk out from the well far enough to haul the pail on the rope to the surface for dumping and then would back up to the well edge to let the pail down into the well to be filled once again.

Lest one think that pioneers were all “paragons of virtue”, as they say, I read of a couple of scoundrels. They were digging a well and had quit for the day. That night they dumped a couple of barrels of water into the well, showed the farmer next morning they *had* water, collected their money and left!

Witching — indicating black magic might be involved, or divining — maybe God had a hand in it — in searching for a spot for a well had both adherents and skeptics — until, in some way not yet figured out even today, water was found. Some insist it is a special gift for a few while others believe anyone can do it with know-how and faith.

Though I’m not saying much about field work, I will tell about one fall during the Depression when we were harvesting what little crop we had. I was Dad’s “hired man”. This meant I was stooking (shocking in the U.S.), not a job I liked because I was getting sunburned and stuck with Russian thistles, and that shadow took *forever* to point straight north so I could go in for lunch. Finally, I hit upon a good idea — I stooked at night by moonlight. This was my first pay job. Dad gave me $5.00, which was no doubt very hard for him to come up with, so I really appreciated it.

In the garden and in the rows of trees we worked so hard to grow, I would ride our good old **Ruby** and Rob would guide the cultivator. Sitting on the back of a horse that is pulling is a very different sensation than being on one that is just walking along. Planting, hoeing and harvesting the vegetable garden was everyone’s job, but it was we kids’ job to knock those potato bugs into pails having soapy water in the bottom to drown them. Otherwise they crawled up the inside and you had to keep pushing them back down.

So let’s go indoors now and describe some housekeeping jobs — some that are no longer a part of many farm women’s lives today. In fact, her grocery list now might be an exact duplicate of that of her town friend.

Canning

To get ready for the chickens just killed out in the chicken house, we would have a couple of big wash tubs full of boiling hot water down in the basement. Holding these chickens by their feet, they were dunked for a minute or so to make plucking easier. Oh how I hated the smell of this! Next, they were all taken upstairs and hairs singed off with matches. Then came the operation that I would do anything to get out of, and Mom, bless her heart, always indulged me — so I have reached the age of 77 without having had to clean a chicken! (Remember when chickens and turkeys in the butcher shop were strung up with their heads and legs still on and their innnards still in there? When I was working for my board and room and going to Normal School, I didn't have the price of a trip home at Thanksgiving and thought sure I was going to *have* to clean the turkey and I was dreading it. Then — saved! The lady of the house said "Oh that's a dirty job, I'll do it.") After Mom had cut off heads and feet, cleaned and skinned them, I would help cut them up and stuff pieces in the jars. Mom only put in drumsticks, thighs and breasts. As I look back, I can't recall what we did with so many necks, wings, and giblets, but I'm sure they all got used somehow in soups, pot pies, chicken and dumplings, etc. When the jars were filled, water and salt were added and the jars put on racks in the copper boiler and cooked for *hours* — three or four, if I remember rightly. This canned chicken was served cold on hot summer days. Our cool basement kept it jelled. (In Yakima in years past I was able to get some canned chicken — a whole one in a 46 oz. can — that *tasted* just like Mom's, but it just fell apart, so didn't look appetizing. Now it's no longer on the market. I've written to the company asking them to carry this product again, but no luck! So if you want to have such delicious canned chicken, you'll have to do as I've started to do — can your own.

Now a word about canning beef: basically this was similar as for chicken, but the heart, liver and tongue would be wrapped and put out in the granary and frozen, the butchering having been done late enough in the fall so freezing would be constant the whole winter.

But the product that needed the most jars at our house was fruit. I liked all the phases of this job and it gave me a chance to eat some as I worked!

Clothes Care

How we wash, iron and mend our clothes and household linens is one aspect of housekeeping that has changed about as much as anything we do. It used to be done on a very strict time table — wash Monday, iron Tuesday, mend Thursday and darn the socks anytime you sat down to rest! Tallying up the hours each week for just the care of clothes makes us wonder sometimes how women had time for all the *other* jobs to be done concurrently or on Friday and Saturday.

Karen McConville by a barrel of water on a stoneboat. Clothes washing about to begin.

Remember the nursery song, "Here We Go Round the Mulberry Bush" with each verse an action related to a certain task on a certain day of the week? Of all these portrayals of caring for clothing, most familiar is the picture of a tired, harried woman bent over her washboard with children all around needing her attention. But in this picture there seemed to me to be so many missing details that might be of interest to younger folk, or that could bring our own nostalgic remembrances into clearer focus, that I decided to go step by step through the care cycle, centreing on the most likely routine for when a lot of women had a wooden-tub-hand-agitated washing machine and a little girl, like me, old enough to help a bit. Also I am choosing a warm summer day with only a note at the end to tell how the job would be different on a very cold wintery day. **1)** Hitch up the "Old Grey Mare", by whatever name, to the stone–boat and head for the well. **2)** Pump as many pailfuls as needed to fill the barrel. **3)** Put boards across the top and weight them down with two or three rocks. **4)** Haul it to the house. **5)** Unhitch Dobbin, put him/her in the barn and hang up the harness. **6)** Put more coal in the cookstove as it has surely died down since being lit before breakfast. **7)** Put the copper boiler on the stove and add two or three pails of water and don't forget the lid (everyone knows a lidded pot boils faster). **8)** While it heats, do other jobs — tend to children, make beds, wash the dishes or whatever. **9)** Gather and sort clothes into piles — whites, light-colored, lingerie, dark colored and wool things — which will shrink if not given special care. **10)** Into the boiler of water slither some washing soap (some women made their own, but at our house we used good old Fels Naptha). **11)** Add a little lye (I don't remember how much). **12)** Put the whites in and punch down with a cut off broom handle. **13)** Drag the washer from its storage corner to the centre of the kitchen. **14)** Set up the wash bench and tubs. **15)** Attach the wringer (if not *part* of the washer) to the washer. (It was on a swivel so you could swing it in place). **16)** Dip the clothes from the boiler into a pail with your stick and dump into the washer. Add some water from the boiler, but leave enough room to enable you to add sufficient cold water so you can dip your hands in without burning them. (Young ones of today are often amazed at the temperatures we older women can tolerate). **17)** Agitate a few minutes with the back and forth handle on the side of the machine. **18)** If not already done, now is the time to put cold water into the two tubs. **19)** Add bluing to the last one (cake or bottle — be careful how much as it is very concentrated). **20)** For each batch in the right order — whites, colored, lingerie (if not washed separately by hand) table cloths, towels, dark colored things, work clothes and small scatter rugs — follow this order — 1) agitate; 2) wring; 3) first rinse; 4) wring; 5) second rinse; 6) wring and let fall into clothes basket. If you were working alone you had to pick the clothes out of the machine with your left hand and feed the wringer while turning the wringer handle with your right hand. This was difficult enough for a right handed person, let alone one who was left handed. When all done don't forget to release the pressure on the wringers. They'll last longer and won't stick together between washings. **21)** Hang clothes on the line (some took time between each batch to hang clothes so that on a really nice breezy day, the light weight things would be dry by the time later batches were ready for hanging). **22)** If clothes line space ran out, a nearby fence would suffice for work clothes, rags and rugs. Some left the clothes pins on the line, spaced as you might use them (as I do today) — while others always put them in a clothes pin bag which they slid along the line as needed or — they had a clothes pin apron which was kept in the

Is he playing or working?

house from washing to washing. (A favourite gift was an embroidered clothes pin bag or apron.) Oh — I forgot to tell you about *starching*! During the first phase of the whole job, you find time to stir some Niagara laundry starch in cold water (spray starch was a product of the future). Add enough water for perhaps a quart (you gauge the amount of starch and water by how many things you need to starch and how stiff you want them to be — it all came with practice and experience). Watching it carefully, cook until it boils and becomes clear. Then set it aside to cool until you are ready to use it. As you hang the clothes, you separate out the ones to starch, doing them in the order of how *stiff* you wanted them, until near the end, articles would be getting very little starch. This was in the days before commercially stiffened collars and cuffs on some men's shirts, so you gathered the collar and cuffs in your hands and dipped *only them* in the starch. Some men were so fussy over their shirts that wives, daughters, or hired girls leaving wrinkles in when ironing were in trouble! On top of this, some even insisted on their shirts being *folded* and *buttoned* to look just as they did in the store! Back to this clothes-washing-starching business — when you hung up the starched things you had to be alert, as a bit too much breeze would undo your starching job. After all the clothes were washed, you used the wash water for two more jobs, to scrub the kitchen floor — usually on your hands and knees so as to do the best job especially in the corners — and the outdoor toilet.

Most women in town or country just *had* to be *proud* of the wash on the line. Your standing in the community depended on it! Some women even hung clothes in *precise order* and *fashion* — all the good shirts beside each other, all the towels just so, and so on, but my Mom was not this particular — and neither am I, I must add. However, the Dirty Thirties put a crimp in this standard and, in fact, the whole set routine. Wash day could be any day when you thought at breakfast time that the wind wouldn't blow, or not till late afternoon anyway, so you could get your wash out and in before disaster struck. If that happened too suddenly, you might end up having to do the whole job over again.

A little sidelight — Mom was in the hospital for a serious operation in a Dust Bowl year and Aunt Mag came to keep house. She finally decided *not* to have curtains at the windows at all because of all the dust. Finally, in complete exasperation, she would exclaim "I don't know why in the world they ever took this country from the Indians. It wasn't worth it!"

A habit begun in bachelor days and which Dad carried out into his 90's was to fold his pants just so and put them under his pillow for a simple overnight pressing.

Back to the 20's and a regular wash day — if all had gone well and you'd even snitched a little *rest time* in the middle of the afternoon, it's now about 4:00 p.m., so you bring all the clothes in and go through another sorting job — those needing ironing, or mending, socks needing darning, and towels and underwear to be folded and put away. Now you tend to the ironing stack. On the table, work your way through the pile, sprinkling each piece with warm water either by finger dipping and shaking as we did, or like some others using a bottle with holes in the stopper. As you finish each piece, you roll it up tight and deposit it in a big bowl, perhaps, or let them set in a pile till you finish and wrap the whole lot tightly in a big towel so moisture would spread evenly throughout by the next morning.

(It was believed, and perhaps they were right, that clothes hung out and frozen stiff would dry faster when brought in, so it didn't matter how cold it was, you hung out the wash. But what a miserable job! I decided when I was my own boss I would *never* do this and I haven't!)

Ironing, Mending and Patching

Men are in the field; beds made; dishes done; meals planned for or partly prepared — it's ironing time. Seeing as the stove has to be kept going at a good clip to heat the sad irons, very likely the whole dinner is either *in* the oven or ready to go in. Get the ironing board set up and put the three irons on the stove. Thinking it next to impossible to do this job well sitting down, many women always stood to iron. However, when Mom got an ulcer on her leg and could only iron if sitting down, this became the way we always did it from then on. If you plan very carefully, you can get by with very few jump-ups. The main thing you have to know in ironing is the required temperature for each material. The ones needing the highest temperature you iron first — then, as your iron cools, you take the others in corresponding order. The handle of a sad iron is interchangeable, so when your iron is too cool, you get another hot one from the stove. In our kitchen in the big house, Mom had a board on a pulley. All the ironed things — the flat pieces anyway, were put on it until the next day to finish drying out. Shirts were just hung on chairbacks for a little while.

If you had washed lace curtain panels or a lace tablecloth, you would have had another job. Such things would have had some starching very likely. Some women had special drying racks, but at our house we just took them one at a time and with two people — one on each end — each gathered their end, half into each hand, and see-sawed back and forth gradually letting loose of the gathers in their hands. It was surprising what a good job this did in straightening the weave to ready the article for ironing. But oh how we treasure the no-iron lace materials of today! And then there were those beautiful white embossed linen "company" tablecloths and matching serviettes. Oh the time it took to do a good job ironing them! No wonder oil cloth was the everyday eating surface! We were glad when plain broadcloth or rayon tablecloths came out. They needed ironing, but one didn't have to be nearly as careful with them as with the linen ones.

Now let's look at the mending basket. In it you would find many skeins or tiny spools of cotton thread and little balls of wool — different enough in color variety, and types of thread to make good matches with all the socks and stockings that needed attention. There was also a pin cushion with needles of many sizes and a small pair of scissors. Woe betide anyone who took mother's scissors from the basket and didn't put them back! Some women used a special darning knob, but we just stretched and held the sock just so. One who could darn a hole so it hardly showed was given high praise. Also if you didn't make it smooth, it could lead to a blistered heel. It behooved mother and daughter to get that basket emptied prior to the next wash day!

And what about patching? Every home had a bag of left-over fabric scraps and, because most garments were home made, you could usually make an exact match. Some women even made men's shirts and pants, but Mom and I didn't tackle them. I guess we figured they were somewhat beyond our degree of sewing skill. Again, learning to do a very good job of patching would gain you praise and gratitude, especially if the article you had mended was for "good" or "dress". In fact, if one was especially skillful, they might be able to earn a little money as their fame spread. (Iron-on patches came much later.)

But not all patching and mending was of this type. *Strength* superceded *looks* when it came to men's overalls, duck bags, mattress covers and binder canvases. These of course, were sewn with very heavy thread, often linen, a very rough, difficult and dirty job.

Perhaps this little anecdote should have been in the vignette chapter, but it fits here too seeing as it pertains to patching: Though she had worked in a corset factory in England and could handle a sewing machine very well, sewing was *not* one of Mom's loves, and of all *kinds* of sewing, one of the lowest on the totem pole was mending overalls. This story got lots of laughs *later*, but at the time it was no joke. Mom had cut two nice patch pieces out of the backs of the legs of the *pair of pants* she was about to *patch*!

Even men and school kids learned a few basics of sewing. A wintertime job for men was getting all the horses' harness in shape for spring. For sewing, the linen thread was often of double strength or more and waxed. An awl was needed on this job as one couldn't push a needle through thick leather. But why do I mention school kids you may wonder. Well it's because almost every night a softball would have to go home with somebody for a sew-up. We had both inseam and outseam balls and we soon learned the type of stitch needed for each. And the kid had better not forget to take it back to school next morning as it was unlikely that there was more than *one* ball to play with!

Making Butter

Mom, being a city gal, had never seen butter made and had no idea that you had to *wash* it. However, it wasn't long before she was proud of the quality of the butter she made and would be offered the best price in town for it. Now, seeing as butter making is seldom, if ever seen, by those of our younger generations, and to help we older ones recall those "dashing" days. I'll describe how it was done.

In the days before having a separator, the milk was put in big flat pans on a shelf underneath the kitchen table. Next morning you skimmed the thick cream off the top and put it in the churn. It was saved for a few days until you had it about a third full. Then you put the dasher in, slipped the lid over it and started that up and down motion. Time to get butter could vary greatly. The cream on the sides of the dasher gathered in the hollow shaped lid, and when it was looking like whipped cream, you knew you were nearly done. A

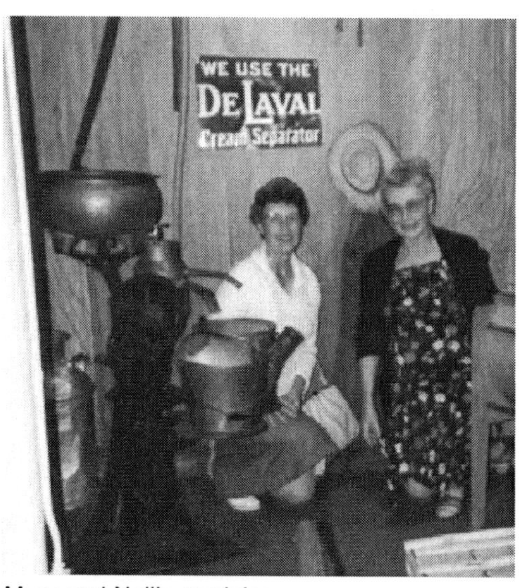

Mary and Nellie reminisce.

few more dashes and you would have butter. Take the lid off and, with the dasher, make a sort of circular motion to get the butter to gather into a lump. (Many people like buttermilk to drink and it is very good for pancakes, cakes, cookies, etc.). Take the butter out of the churn with the paddle and put it into a big round-bottomed wooden bowl. With the coldest water you could find (remember we had no ice, so it was what you got fresh from the well), you washed the butter — probably about three times — until the water was clear. Then you made up pound prints with a butter mould and special paper, making sure your wrapping was straight and wrinkle free. Enough was saved towards the end for home use — the table and baking. I enjoyed butter making on the whole, but especially my chance to make different designs on the pats reserved for the table.

A separator, of course, eliminated the overnight pan settings, as you let the cream spout put it directly into the churn or a bowl which you then emptied into the churn. In Depression years when the cows had been eating Russian thistle, the cream would be thin and often take a very long while to churn. On hot days though, I really didn't mind a bit as we churned in the cool basement and I would sit and read at the same time. Mom used to laugh and say she knew how the story was progressing by how fast or slow the dasher was going. Rob, however, when he had to take a turn, wanted *everyone* to know just how miserable and tedious this job was so he would count the strokes and announce in a *loud* voice at each hundred mark. "One hundred, two hundred", etc., until he, at last, got butter.

Care of Sunday Dresses

Most of our good dresses were of crepe material. Spots and underarm perspiration stains spelled disaster. In desperation, if you decided to wash the dress in soap and water, it required a very skilful ironer to stretch it back to the right size. Dunking these dresses in a pail of gasoline out in the yard was one home dry-cleaning method.

Hair Care

Our well-water was excellent for drinking, but not for hair washing so we usually used the soft water from the cistern, or in winter we melted snow on top of the stove. We frequently added a little vinegar or lemon juice to the final rinse to make our hair soft and manageable.

We always thought that those who had naturally curly hair were very lucky. If you were not so blessed, you got your curls in a number of different ways, usually with just water, though we did have our own brand of gel. (Remember our school beauty parlor?) Young folks may laugh, but rag curls were probably a lot easier on the hair than some of the commercial curlers used nowadays. To make a rag curl you just lay a short strip about three inches long and a half inch wide on a section of hair, roll it up and tie the two ends together at the top.

When I was about twelve, my hair acquired some natural curl much to my surprise and delight. I remember one evening when my teacher, Mrs. Ellis, did my hair up in finger ringlets, a pleasant time for both of us.

Other methods of acquiring curls in those days before permanents — wave combs, finger waves, spit curls, or curling irons. A marcel iron made two or three bumps and hollow waves at one time. Both it and a regular curling iron were heated by holding them inside a coal oil lamp chimney. You wiped the soot off before using it on your hair, of course. I was still too young when these hot irons came into being, but I used to watch the teachers who boarded at our home fix their hair with them.

On a nice day this job went outdoors — out of the housewifes' way and one less clean up job to do. Dad is in the middle at the back. The little girls are Phoebe and Maude.

Men's styles remained quite static during the first half of this century, while women broke out of their Victorian shell in the 20's, mainly with the advent of bobbed hair. This was so radical that some marriages were even threatened by it! It was almost as disruptive as when boys went for long hair so many years later. But again the old pendulum swing theory began to operate so that now just about any style for either sex is tolerated — up to a point I have to add. Still excepted are those that most of us consider outside the boundaries of general acceptance. We still stare and make some pretty emphatic negative statements at that *colored* hair — not colors that *nature* could have given, but say green, purple, etc. As for women — long, short, straight, curly, bleached, etc., doesn't get any reaction. Nevertheless there were a few styles of the 50's that most of us can recall our teenagers spending a lot of time and effort on to get *just right* —

beehives, big Afro's, and frost-streaked, for examples.

It is an interesting little mental exercise to think of — even to list or sketch — all the different hair styles one has had over their lifetime.

Now for a few lines on *barbering*. There has always been the question of a do-it-yourself with family or neighborhood abilities, or the professional way. In our day there were barber shops for men and boys but, until bobbed hair came in, women didn't need a barber's services. At the barber shop men would indulge themselves in what Dad always said was a real treat — being shaved by a professional. Some regular customers even had their own mug kept there. Those lathered or hot-towel-wrapped faces were a common sight to those of us peeking in the window as we strolled by on the street.

Did you ever wonder why the barber pole was red and white and why it is twisting around? These unique poles captivated me almost as much as those gas pumps with the markers showing how much gas was going into the tank followed by that bubbling liquid filling it up again in readiness for the next customer. But why this sort of a pole? In the days when common people could not read and write, each profession or trade had its logo as we would say today. A barber was one who performed minor surgeries, or did patient bleeding, so his "come-in" had red to represent a bandage being wrapped around a white arm. The word "barber" comes from the Latin "barba" for "beard". Folks could *see shaving* going on through the window but with his *pole* besides, he was set up for *both*. Another "way-back" tid bit is this: In the days of wigs, a big part of his job was making them and then keeping them cleaned, curled and powdered. (I wonder if they had a shaved head under the wig?) Peasant men probably didn't ever have their hair cut except for whacking some off if it got too long. A style of some men today — a pony tail, was common judging by long-ago pictures.

Then, coming nearer to the modern era, beauty shops opened up — but only for women. They sprang up in every little town. Here women got shampoos, shingles, bobs, or other cutting styles, plus the curls or waves dictated by the fashions of the day. (Marcels were named after the French hairdresser M. Marcel). Then came permanents, done only professionally for many years prior to home permanents.

At our home Frank was the barber until I took over. I watched him intently and to this day, follow pretty much the methods I saw him use. If you want to be a home barber, it is good to have a "willing victim" to practice on! Mom was mine. Then Dad let me cut his and one time Rob, in desperation, allowed me some limited snipping on his! With the aid of my three-mirror bedroom dresser, I also cut my own hair. In fact, I am plain addicted even now, to a three mirror arrangement. I complain all the time when travelling that one simply *can't* maneuver hotel or motel room mirrors so as to see the *back* of one's head! Solution — husband holds one just so!

It used to be back at Quimper that spring had surely arrived when some boys showed up with shaved heads. And do you remember the ridiculed "bowl" hair cuts? But now in 1996, just *such* haircuts are "in"! Another modern aspect of professional hair care is unisex hair salons. I'll never forget the day Jim came in saying he'd just had his hair *styled* —and for $8.00 yet! I could hardly believe what I was hearing.

So, once hair was shampooed, cut, curled and styled either at home or in a shop, how was the "do" preserved for everyday? For women in the pre-bob era, dust caps were worn during the day and hair was let down and braided for the night. I've often thought how clever our mothers and grandmothers were to be able to put their hair up in some pretty elegant styles. Hair nets and hair pins saw a lot of use also. Short hair, though, put an end to hair pins, so we got the kind of pin that *would* hold bobbed hair — bobby pins. From then on the variety of clips and hair ornaments has been almost limitless. However, we few women who have chosen some long hair style are still in the minority and both *grey* bobby pins and *invisible* hair nets are very hard to come by. This problem seemed strange to me until I realized so many older women wear their hair in the very short curly style, which requires neither pins nor hair nets.

Men used to use brilliantine to make hair stay put and be glossy. Sometimes, for especially unruly hair, vaseline was used. For healthy hair, lots of brushing was considered essential. Women, no matter how tired they might be, would usually do their 100 strokes before turning in and I well remember seeing Uncle Walter do his stint with a pair of military brushes — a popular gift back then.

Over the years, for both sexes, styles of both dress and hair have often followed movie star looks — so much so, that certain styles even took the *name* of the actor or actress who introduced them. How many little girls with straight dark hair longed for a Shirley Temple head of blond curls, or a teen-aged boy a pompadour? Years later wasn't it the movie star Veronica Lake that introduced long, straight hair draping over one eye?

Jobs Seldom Done Now

Here's a few not mentioned previously, maybe you could add more:

(1) **Shoe Polishing** — We all had a box with black and brown

Nugget polishes (remember that ingenious turner on the side to open it?); perhaps a navy blue paste also, and liquid white and black with sponge tipped applicators.

(2) **Carpet Beating** — usually done only at spring-cleaning time. The men were asked to get rugs on the line and then it was the kids job to do the beating until no more dust was flying out.

(3) **Everyday Carpet Cleaning** — We would spread on damp tea leaves, let set for a few minutes and then gather them into a dust pan with either a whisk broom or a damp rag.

(4) **Waxing Linoleum and Hardwood Floors** — The kitchen inlaid was usually scrubbed on hands and knees and the dining room one just wiped with a damp rag. For many years we only had the paste wax which had to be applied with a rag and let dry for about 15 minutes before polishing. Polishing the hardwood one in the dining room was fun, as we kids donned woolen socks and slid all over the place to do the job. Later we got liquid wax which you poured on in patches and spread around with a sponge mop and then let it dry. But no matter the kind of wax used, those shiny floors were downright treacherous, and scatter rugs on them were accidents just waiting to happen. They did have non-slip patches you could put on the back of these rugs, but as I remember, you didn't trust them very far. Even yet I still am apprehensive as I step out on today's beautiful shiny (but mercifully non-slip) floors.

(5) **Chambermaid Duty** — taking a slop pail to each bedroom when you made beds and emptying into it the contents of those pots under the bed or in *that* cupboard.

(6) **Calcimining** — the bedroom walls and oil painting the other rooms. (Oh how wonderful are latex paints!)

(7) **Cleaning Stove Pipes** — unhooking them from their ceiling suspension wires, taking them outside and *very* carefully tapping and brushing them to get the soot to fall out, then rejoining and rehanging them.

(8) **Cleaning the Soot** out of the cookstove through that little trap door under the oven.

(9) **Turning Shirt Collars** — an easy, quick job with a razor blade and the sewing machine.

(10) **Exchanging Sleeves on Sweaters and Jackets** — so worn elbows would be on the crook of the elbow instead.

(11) **Turning a Coat** — taking it all apart and putting it back

together with the *inside* becoming the *outside* so it looked like you had a new coat!

(12) **Slitting a worn flat sheet** down the middle and sewing outside edges together with a flat seam for a "new" centre section.

Note: School girls learned the basics of hand sewing, the stitches required for different jobs and how to cut out and pin together for a simple garment. There were no sewing machines at school, so all such sewing had to be done at home. Most boys didn't take sewing, but Alice remembered her big brother, Louis, making a potholder or something in school.

A Different Job

Now I will tell you of one job which was not commonly done even back then, as far as I know. By the late thirties silk stockings were on the market, but they were expensive, especially for Depression era customers. Runs even now are bad, but then they were much more traumatic. I don't remember where I got it, but I had a special little gadget with which to mend runs — one thread at a time — a bit like crocheting. I needed glasses long before I got them with my first teaching paycheck, and this job was very taxing on my eyes along with my reading for Normal School. However, seeing a little badly needed cash in my skill, I offered to mend other women's stockings at so much an inch. But my business didn't last long for I soon decided my eyesight (I was getting headaches too, of course) was worth a lot more than that cash pittance. Besides, I didn't feel it was time well spent seeing as *studies* were to be top priority next to whatever I *had* to do to earn my board and room.

Cleaning Wallpaper

As I said, all decorating in our big house was in calcimine or paint so I was not acquainted with wallpaper cleaning. I wonder if other Quimper homes used this product — a sort of dull pink spongy material that came in a can. You took enough out at a time to make a comfortable sized ball for your hand. Then you made a swipe down the wallpaper and lo and behold the smudge dirt was now *on your ball.* You worked it *into* the ball and made another swipe — continuing in like fashion till the whole room looked wonderfully clean. This was one of my jobs when I worked for board and room in Moose Jaw when attending Normal School.

Papering

Do you remember Lucy and Ethel doing some papering in one episode of "I Love Lucy"? My sides ached and tears ran down my cheeks as I watched this show. Humor reaches its height, I believe, when it relates to some personal experience.

Because we had no wallpaper in our new house, and in the shack, I think Dad and Mom or whoever was around to help, papered *after* we were in bed, I had never seen it done. My husband, on the other hand, *had seen* his mother paper lots of times, but was too young to help. So — picture us tackling a kitchen papering job — including the *ceiling*, in a little house we bought shortly after coming to Yakima. I knew, or course, that one did the ceiling first! You can guess the *conversation* and the *result* with the very first strip! It wasn't long until Bud was out the door, blaming *me* for not doing it right! I was on my own and *determined* to get *that paper* up one way or the other. I figured I could handle pieces two or three feet long so that ceiling had joins and overlaps staggered to resemble brick laying. I was quite proud of the fact that by the time, a few hours later, when Bud came home, that *that ceiling was papered.* It stayed up, too. I often wondered what new owners years later thought when they noticed that odd papering job. Today's pre-pasted paper eliminates a novice's first problem back then — making non-lumpy paste and spreading it quickly and completely enough on the back sides.

Cobbling

I liked cobbling shoes. With a last set Dad had, no doubt, bought from Eatons, some thick leather, a shape knife to cut out the soles to fit the shoes you were about to mend, a box of shoe tacks and a hammer, you were ready to cobble. Sometimes you could simplify the job by buying ready-cut soles and heel lifts in town.

I don't remember how many new soles were put on before the uppers wore out, but probably two or three. However, during the Depression even new leather soles were out of reach and a good many cardboard inner soles were in use.

The word *cobble* has acquired a negative meaning somehow. Was it because this was a job poorly done so often I wonder?

Schoolwork

Art was one of my favourite subjects and we did have quite a varied course of studies on it — the color chart, free-hand drawing, lessons on perspective and shading, etc., but we were not given much help on being original nor in sketching from *actual* objects and scenes. We had booklets with pictures of many famous paintings to develop our art appreciation. We were taught how to analyze the picture and to learn about the artist. We often put our artistic talent to work in other subjects also, in props for concerts, the blackboard seasonal borders and the school newspaper.

At the end of Normal School, I was quite flattered when Mr. Gagne, my art teacher, asked if he might keep a couple of my efforts to show his next class — but I wished afterwards, packrat that I am, that I still had those pictures! I enjoyed also serving as one of four art editors for the yearbook. One certain thing though, was that I was *not* asked to contribute any rhymes! But as I glanced, just now, through the little character sketches for each of us, someone for Mary McConville said "She is cheerful and yet wise, she succeeds at what she tries, she shows her talent in her art, and always does her given part."

It would be nice to think I'd always lived up to such a complimentary jingle — but, of course, I didn't. It makes us wonder, too, how often we have failed to say something nice to or about others when we had the opportunity. Then again, one of the real joys of my writing hobby is having the chance now and again to hand out some well deserved compliments or thank yous.

School Music

Quimper, as did almost all country districts of our day, had a number of piano players. When Madge was teaching, every Friday afternoon the words of a new song would be put on the blackboard and we would copy it into our scribblers before learning to sing it. At Normal School we were taught to use a pitch pipe plus the old-fashioned doh-ray-me for the tune, for school singing. I wonder how many teachers made use of these! The music theory text book was one of the dullest, most impractical that I've ever seen — a harsh judgment on my part for sure, but in support of my opinion I greatly doubt many school children came to *love* music through *that* text. It made many *simple* things so *complicated*, it's hard to believe — such things as how to identify key signatures, how to determine what sharps or flats went with each, how to find the three basic chords for each key, and so on.

Nellie and Hilda hard at the trigonometry — but apparently, enjoying it on a lovely day outdoors.

Etudes

One of the best hand-me-ons ever to come my way was a whole boxful of **Etude** magazines. They proved invaluable to my piano teaching for years and for *constant* enjoyment. My neighbor, **Frances Lockwood**, gave them to me way back in the 50's.

If anyone has a collection of these from their first to last publication, I'm sure they have a fortune at hand. I do not remember where or when I first saw this magazine, but it could have been that Frank found one or two at some second hand store in Regina. But I do know I fell in love with them immediately and used them frequently in giving my little sister her first piano lessons, and Rob and I found some of our favorite duets in them — including one Mom always asked us to play, "El Capitan".

Palmer Writing

Today's school child would get some surprises in a number of back-then classes, but especially ones in cursive writing and in learning to print. Sloppy sitting in one's desk was never allowed, but during writing practice, posture was stressed even more — feet flat on floor, back straight, left arm curved just so, with hand resting at the top of the paper or scribbler page, and the pen (a straight one) held exactly so-so in one's right — the tips of thumb, index finger and third finger the correct distance from the tip with the index finger rounded. The *exercise* itself was either put on the blackboard or, if you had a Palmer workbook, it was there for you. Though few attained completely what was called *freehand* writing with *no finger* action — most achieved a combination of them which in turn led to relaxed muscles as well as a certain degree of speed. The exercises at the beginning of the lesson consisted of totally free arm movements some of which were:

If we felt a bit "fancy" or artistic, we would turn out free arm doodle pictures such as trees, people, buildings, or designs, etc., but I don't remember such originality being encouraged very much.

Then came practice on certain capital and small letters. At the conclusion of such specifics there was a bit of wisdom to write out — a motto, a proverb or perhaps a verse from a poem. The teacher was always on the lookout for such gems. Instead of this always being on the blackboard, pupils might be told to find something in their reader. For example, Grade Four's might turn to page 254 to find this:

Teach me to feel another's woe;
To hide the fault I see;
That mercy I to others show,
That mercy show to me.

Writing class might last about 10 minutes and while in progress, the teacher would travel throughout the room observing and helping each child individually as needed. At the end, as at the conclusion of all seatwork, scribblers would be stacked opened at the right place face down on the teacher's desk to be graded by her at noon, probably, or after school. It was always tempting to use the noon hour to correct these books so as to lessen the time required for it after school. But with me the desire to go and play with the kids often won out and I came to believe that this was best, after all, for the kids, as well as myself. Next morning, these scribblers would be handed back to their owners. To me this seemed a very orderly way to preserve work done, not only to show clearly the *rate* of progress in each subject, but to serve for ready review. For this work method, it was necessary to have a scribbler for each subject. Up to grade three, all work was in pencil and in printing rather than cursive writing. At the top of the blackboard or on some stretched out heavy paper, would be *correct* capitals and small letters. No variations were allowed. This was so ingrained in our training, that it almost gives us nightmares to see what is not only *allowed* nowadays, but *encouraged* as a sort of indication of originality. We cringe, too, when we see a pen held in *any fashion* but the *correct* one. Any child who turned out something like this: CHildREN, obEy youR pARENTS iN tHE LORd, foR tHis is RiGHT, would surely have received an F grade, and told to do it over again — even if it meant doing it during their recess or noon hour.

There was little to no tolerance for the left-handed, either. It was firmly believed by most in those days that, because we live in a right-handed world, it was best to be "fitted" into this world, if at all possible. Nowadays this coercion would almost be called child abuse. But a changeover was taking place, if I remember correctly, in the late 30's. I know that when I was teaching, there was little or no such pressure. However, perhaps I should note that it is difficult for a right-handed teacher to teach certain things to a left-handed child — writing, cutting with scissors, and so on. How well I remember during the War when we were not only *encouraged* to knit for the war effort, but almost shamed into it. I learned the basics, but never became much of a knitter and — trying to teach a Grade Two left-handed girl to knit was double frustration!

The Enterprise System

Though this was the basic philosophy behind the way we were being taught to teach at Normal School, I don't ever recall hearing this name for it. We had a number of American professors and much of what we were taught was far more suitable to a town school than a country one — especially the method of objective testing with its true or false, multiple choice and fill-in-the-blank tests. Just recently I read a very enlightening article on this concept, which is still extensively influencing today's school system. Only now is it finally being acknowledged that many children have, because of it, fallen through the cracks and thus lack some real basics. It was thought that with some *enterprise* or *project* all the *basics* would fall into place as the work progressed to completion. But for slower pupils especially, it just didn't happen.

A whole new set of texts came out for my first year of teaching and I remember trying to figure out why the standards were being lowered as was so obvious, especially with the new speller. It was so *easy* as to be practically useless. The idea that we want all children to

Bernard in Grade One learned to read by dictating to his teacher how to run this steam engine. When she read it back to him, he realized what the printed word was all about. He simply could make no connections to **Jerry, Jane, Laddie** and **Snow.**

succeed academically so their self-esteem won't be damaged seems laudable at first, but what it came down to, though not stated of course, was that we began to cater to not only those with lower abilities, but also to those with less drive and ambition. Putting it bluntly, the saying fit, "If you aim at nothing, you'll hit it every time."

Another example was with the readers. Old ones had their faults, of course, especially those for the higher grades, but I feel certain that most children who completed Grades 1 through 5 with the Canadian readers came out with higher reading skills than those who studied with the Highroads to Reading. Though I didn't realize it at the time, the memorizing of poetry had, at this time, fallen into disrepute. I admit we learned some poetry better left out of those old readers, but think of the joy we have even today as snatches or even whole selections come to mind, or if songs, we can sometimes still sing *all* the verses.

In some ways I think the changeover was an illustration of the old saying, "They threw out the baby with the bathwater." They should have preserved more of what was *good* under the old ways and made corrections where they were obviously needed.

Nevertheless, it is true that chidlren who are going to succeed will do so no matter what system they are under, and some will fail for the same reason. It is also true that wise teachers will adapt their teaching methods to the needs of their pupils. In our rural schools, I believe there was more opportunity to do one-on-one teaching, especially if the enrollment wasn't too big.

Nowadays, perhaps, this is a real advantage with computers — the pace can be adapted to the learner and steps of advancement can be carefully laid out and monitored.

Wouldn't it be wonderful if leaders in education could somehow rescue some of the good old values and methods and pair them with some of these fabulous new technologies? And it will always be true that the best education for any child will take place when parents, teachers, society and students are *all* in tune with each other.

Two movies which feature classrooms in operation are "To Sir, With Love" and "Mr. Holland's Opus". Both graphically illustrate the almost magical changeover that can take place in that same room and class when the teacher and the students come to respect each other and work harmoniously together so that real learning can take place.

Tied Down

"They tie you down," a woman said,
Whose cheeks should have been flaming red
With shame to speak of children so.
"When babies come you cannot go
In search of pleasure with your friends,
And all your happy wandering ends.
The things you like you cannot do,
For babies make a slave of you."

I looked at her and said: "'Tis true
That children make a slave of you,
And tie you down with many a knot,
But have you never thought to what
It is of happiness and pride
That little babies have you tied?
Do you not miss the greater joys
That come with little girls and boys?
"They tie you down to laughter rare,
To hours of smiles and hours of care,
To nights of watching and to fears;
Sometimes they tie you down to tears
And then repay you with a smile,
And make your trouble all worth while.
They tie you fast to chubby feet,
And cheeks of pink and kisses sweet.

"They fasten you with cords of love
To God Divine, who reigns above.
They tie you, whereso'er you roam,
Unto the little place called home;
And over sea or railroad track,
They tug at you to bring you back.
The happiest people in the town
Are those the babies have tied down.

"Oh, go your selfish way and free,
But hampered I would rather be,
Yes rather than a kingly crown
I would be, what you term, tied down;
Tied down to dancing eyes and charms,
Held fast by chubby, dimpled arms,
The fettered slave of girl and boy,
And win from them earth's finest joy."

From **The Path to Home,** Edgar Guest, ©1919

Bibliography

Confessions of an Immigrant's Daughter, by Laura Goodman Silverman ©1939, 1981
Land of Pain and Promise, by Harry Piniuta, ©1978
Set of Four Books by Charles Earle Funk
A Hog on Ice, ©1948
Heavens to Betsy, ©1955
Horse Feathers, ©1958
Thereby Hangs a Tale, ©1950
Butter Down the Well, by Robert Collins, ©1980

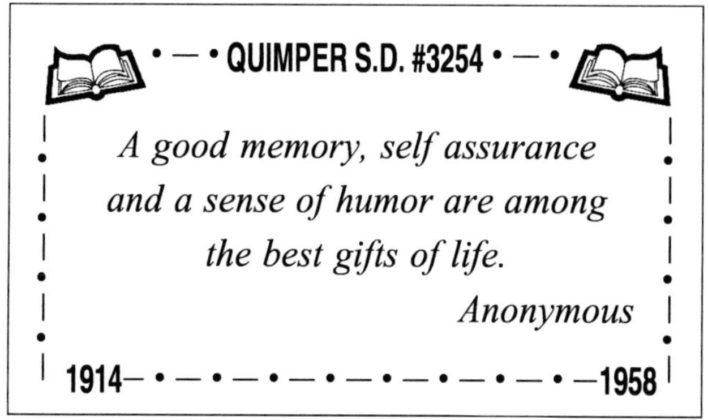

They were singing joyful songs, dancing and playing instruments. — I Sam. 18:6

7 — The World of Play

Those of you who have read my "ash" book may recall me talking to my friend, **Adelle**. Her remark "Mary, you are doing so much *work* to put this book together." My reply to this widow with a half-acre backyard, "What do you call what *you're* doing in your yard?" We agreed — the line between work and play becomes blurred when one is engrossed in their hobby. Just so with *this* book. Each chapter has its own special kind of joy as I write it, but putting together this one on *play* brings back so *many* happy memories that it will be very difficult to hold it to any allotted number of pages.

Baby and Toddler Play

By the time Quimper School opened, there were not only children of school age, but many babies and toddlers. Parents from many different backgrounds had brought with them their lullabies, finger plays, stories and perhaps some toys if they had arrived with children. Others had sent orders to Eaton's, but for the most part, toys and other amusements would usually be homemade by parents, live-in relatives or hired help — balls, wheeled toys, kites, windmills, bow and arrow sets, sling shots, etc. Imagination and ingenuity had full sway. Most children had a number of brothers and sisters, so with parents having to work such long hours, it was good they had each other to play with.

What little kid doesn't like to wear a mask? Milla is being an old witch riding her broom.

Was there ever a kid who didn't love to dress up in their daddy's or mommy's clothes? This is Dale Kelman trying his daddy's on for size.

A modern day child, Andy, loves his old-fashioned toy.

Nevertheless, from the beginning parents *found* time to play. Mothers sang lullabies to little ones. (Did you ever listen carefully to the words of some of these? I read one time that these *harsh* words, but sung in a *sweet* voice, may have been one way women vented their frustrations. And those nursery rhymes — some were apparently disguised political railings as peasants didn't dare say *openly* what they *really* thought about their rulers. Still others held some medical advice — remember Jack's hurt head? One who studied the origins of these rhymes said it was likely that "Ring Around a Rosy" was describing the Black Death when children at play suddenly fell dead. But let's dwell on happier thoughts.)

Little tots were bounced on a knee to "Ride-a-Cock Horse"; little fingers or toes became little "piggies" and laughs burst forth as the last little pig went wee wee wee all the way home; the little mouse still ran up and down the clock as it struck one; Humpty Dumpty still fell off the wall — all these little rhymes said or sung to matching actions. (Such wonderful interaction is completely lost, I believe, in a little one with their tape player or even the very best of T.V. programs.) Peek-a-boo and Pat-a-cake have never lost their charm; a pan and spoon drum set was always at hand; a table draped with a blanket became a tent; a cardboard box became a sleigh, with dolls and teddy bears or sometimes a real puppy or kitten the passenger; a string of smaller boxes became a train, and the stuffed foot of a sock became a ball. Unsophisticated kinds of fun were the order of the day.

But as time went on, more *bought* toys showed up. Dolls could even open and close their eyes, and when bent over, could say "Ma Ma". Then we got ones which could cry, wet and finally, today, a pregnant one! But as with many toys, technical advances often rob children of their imagination. There is much more variety and spontaneity when little girls are playing house and talking *for* their dolls than listening to their

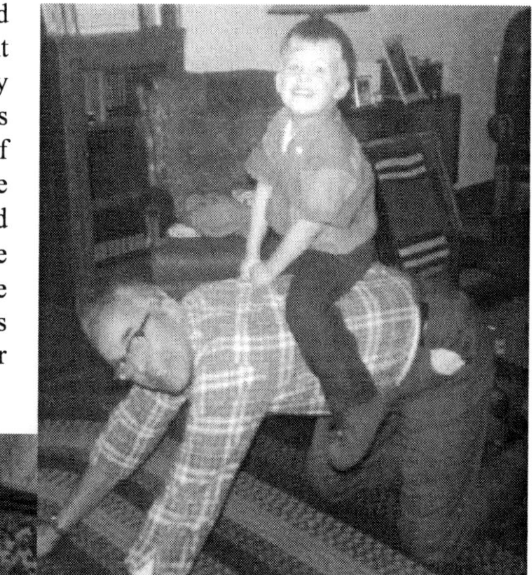

Above, Grandpa makes a good horse, says Jeff.

Left, Jeff gets a ride by his "team" of horses, Jake and Angie

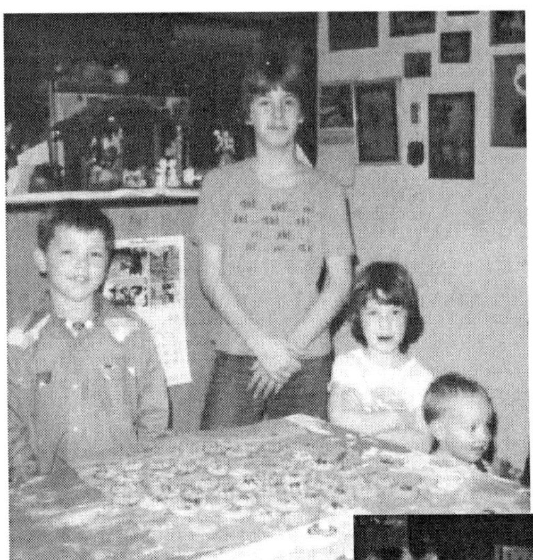

Above, fun with grandchildren. Each Christmas they would choose a different category, cookies, bread, pies, etc.

Right, It would be easier to make the "chair" if the two boys were a little nearer the same size and the seat wouldn't be quite so tippy either, but they're still having fun.

dolly on tape.

How sad that a little boy was ridiculed for wanting to play with a doll! What golden opportunities were lost to instill in him the attributes of a good father he should be as a grown up! A little girl was somewhat better off in wanting to play with boy's toys. They were called *Tom boys,* but somehow this term didn't have the intense sting of a boy being called a *sissy*. At least it seemed this way to me, for I could play with Rob's mechano set, train, tractor, etc., and only hear a mild rebuke such as "Why don't you play with your dolls?" When I was about five, Mom and Dad, I think, decided to have a last try to win me over to dolls by giving me a lovely doll in a doll carriage. I don't remember what I did with the doll, but that carriage was wonderful to straddle and ride down the hill on! I don't remember it breaking either. Another proof of just how *strong* a lot of toys were back then is a little Model T Ford Bud used as a roller skate! He has it still and it's as good as ever, although now it is just a conversation piece in our front room.

Paper Dolls

Though I didn't care much for dolls as such, *paper dolls* I was nuts about. It was lucky for me that **Connie** and **Dorothy Claydon** were older

Water coloring fun at Grandma's. Angie wore this little hat *all* the time. Her cousin, Jake, is by her side.

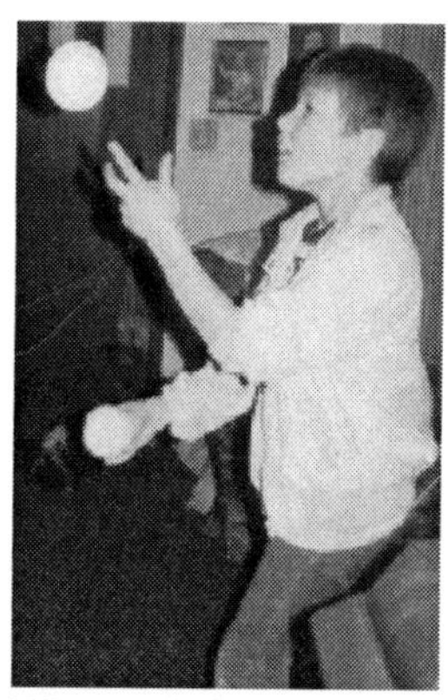

What kid hasn't tried to be a juggler?

than I, or maybe they didn't care much about them, but oh how I enjoyed the page of Dolly Dingles their mother saved for me out of her Pictorial Review! Besides these, I had boxes full of my homemade dolls and oodles of clothes for them.

Grace Drayton was originator of Dolly Dingles in 1913.

Perhaps it was because this type of doll led me to draw, cut and color to my heart's content, that I liked them so, and they were also good when playing alone. Just recently I read the most interesting article on the history of paper dolls and I can't resist passing on here a few things I learned: In France they were a form of advertising for aristocratic women's clothes — the *real* thing being much more cumbersome and expensive to show. Some were quite large and became children's toys when they got to be the worse for wear. Books and books of paper dolls were put out about famous people, movie stars and sports figures. In mint condition, such books or good examples of homemade paper dolls (usually a mother's efforts, rather than a child's) could be quite valuable today.

A Special Toy

Most of us can remember *one* very *special toy* we had. For me, it was a teddy bear which Rob and I could carry on a "conversation" with. By wiggling its tail you could make the head say "yes" or "no", so we took turns asking questions and giving answers. Eventually he had little hair left.

Remember the poem in our Canadian Reader Book II — "The Lost Doll". I shed tears of sadness at her loss and tears of joy at the finding. Though its beauty was gone, it was still to her "the prettiest doll in the world."

Good Toys

Recently I read one person's opinion on ideal toys, and though I agreed with most of what was said there, I decided to make my own list. Here it is:

1. *Versatile* — So a child can turn their imagination loose.
2. *Durable* — Few things more frustrating than broken toys.
3. *Age Adaptable* — It is wonderful when those of different ages can all participate in a game.
4. *Safe* — For the age its intended for — discernment needed.
5. *Pleasing Appearance* — I don't believe in fostering ugliness.
6. *Character Builder* — It is an aid to learning good manners, sportsmanship and ways to express feelings.
7. *Is Art* — Encourages taking part rather than just spectating.

As one thinks back to their own childhood, isn't it the toys and activities that meet these different criteria that you remember best? Even the element of danger, when under reasonable constraint, added something to the overall enjoyment. For example, Rob and I had *real* sling shots, *real* bows and arrows and *real* darts — all things frowned on today, but which, with precise instruction by grown ups, and very careful supervision at first, enabled us to enjoy many hours at these pastimes.

Another activity Rob and I were challenged with was stilt walking — on homemade ones, of course. There was something very exhilarating in "being" so much taller than one really was. Many years later with our own children, one of the best toys was tin-can stilts — 46 oz. juice cans with rope handles.

In researching games, I found that string play — we didn't have a name for one that Dad used to play with us, which I learned later is often called the cat's cradle — is of very ancient origin and played in many different parts of the world. Today with *no string* being used in stores (remember those big rolls of brown paper and the huge cone of string fed by a pulley system with which each storekeeper speedily wrapped and tied each item? I still break thread and string with a little twist of the finger I learned at the small store in Wallard my Uncle Frank ran for awhile in the 30's) and velcro replacing shoe laces, children may not even *see* string in their daily lives. Do you recall also

Sam and Jim McConville, cousins, enjoy playing together.

those boxes which held a ball of string with the end hanging out the bottom, or the separate ball which *grew* and *grew* as a thrifty mother added on *every* piece that came her way?

The debate is endless on whether a child should ever have guns or other war toys. We let our kids have cap guns and water pistols, but drew the line at most others.

Outdoors

I've often said that a child who grows up without a little *hill* to play on or the *four* seasons in the year, has been deprived. On both scores we were most fortunate, so here's accounts of how we took advantage of them.

Rafting

I must tell you of one rafting incident. Rob and I had made a raft and this day I was giving Nellie a ride. Apparently I didn't "dock" too smoothly at the big stone, for she tumbled in head first. I think it was too shallow to be dangerous, so when I fished her out, she ran to the house crying, more scared than hurt. Mom was having Ladies Aid that day so everyone soon knew what I'd done. But Grandma was living with us then, so a bit of comforting and some dry clothes soon set things right.

It was a sad thing at our house that Grandma's reasoning, though I understood it later, alienated we older two from our young sister. We had *each other* she felt, so Nellie *needed* her. In her eyes, this little girl could do no wrong, but if she *did do* something bad (turning the oil barrel tap on one day, for instance), it was because of *our* bad example or influence.

Snow

I remember when I was about eleven, a lady from Australia was on the **Chautaqua Circuit**, and when she said she'd never even *seen snow*, I felt sorry for her — no snowball fights, no snowmen, no snow houses, no sleigh rides, no fox and goose game and not even the wondrous experience of actually seeing those tiny, intricate, delicate six-pointed stars landing so softly on one's dark coat sleeve!

Down Hill Fun

Rob and I earned ourselves a little wagon by getting enough gopher tails to pay for it and I don't ever remember it breaking with all its hard use. Years later Nellie, who is five years younger than I, enjoyed hauling our big dog **Sandy** around in it. To make riding down the hill a bit more challenging, we dug little ruts for the wheels of just the right depth and on a curvy trail. We would try to get down the hill without tipping over or jumping the track. Another kind of fun on our hill was to curl up inside a barrel and roll down. In winter of course, there was no counting how many times we sledded down that hill.

School Fun

Now let us look at the many things we enjoyed at school, winter or summer, inside or out. Blizzards were miserable to endure, but in their wake they left drifts which provided some special ways to play. By digging toe holds in the lee side of a drift, you could climb it like a ladder. When you crested, you slid down the other side in the paths made by "trail blazers". A wide drift could accommodate many such slides side by side. Also, this snow was packed so hard you could cut it into big blocks and build an igloo. In our Book II Reader we could *see* how to make an "authentic" one, though I don't remember *any* we built looking much like this one! If the snow had fallen gently and at the right temperature, the fun was of a very different sort. Probably the first thing we did was play Fox and Goose. (We said "goose", but grammatically we should have said "geese".) We would tramp out two big concentric circles equal distance from each other with many "spokes" going from the centre *safe spot* to the outside circle. To play the game, one, the fox, would try to catch the others — the geese. As each was tagged, they became a fox, the last caught being *It* for the next game. If you stepped out of the pathways, you were out of the game.

And, of course, there were snowball fights — two-somes, free-for-alls for many, team contests, or a more formal game with forts and a limited number of snowballs. When I was teaching, I had two stringent rules which saved a lot of tears: 1) no one was to have a snowball thrown *at them* if they didn't want to play the game; 2) no *packing* a snowball.

A third thing we did, but not as often, was blanket tossing. It could be done in summer, as you can see here. It was fun to get tossed like this.

That's Alice Bjore up in the air. Blanket toss at Lake Pelletier. Picture courtesy of Alice Collins.

If winter weather was too bad for outdoor play, we had lots of indoor games to choose from — a variety simultaneously going on in different places — the basement, the cloakrooms, at desks or on the blackboard. The Erinlea School also had a basement and the Donalds had come to Quimper from there bringing with them what I think was probably the most unusual kind of fun for us girls. With the aid of a box or a boost up from another, you grabbed the cross braces between the rafters. Then you did hand-over-hand to the other end, turned around and came back. You can imagine the blisters if at first you didn't work up to how far you should go! There was quite a bit of room in the basement, so others might be playing such games as "Mother May I?", "Statues", "Red Light, Green Light", "Dodge Ball", "Jacob Rachel", "Imitations", "Pin the Tail on the Donkey", and so on. Seeing as the *furnace room* was strictly the boys' hangout, I can't say what was going on in there! Upstairs, using the cloakrooms and the school room, games like "Clap In Clap Out ", "I Spy", "Blind Man's Bluff" and "Musical Chairs" might be underway. At spare spots on the blackboard (you had to have teacher's permission to rub out anything) four two-some games were very common — "Hang the Man" (we never thought about this gruesome name — it was just a word game with us), "X and O", "Initials" and "Trails". These last two were played on a grid of equally spaced tiny circles. In Initials, you only claimed a square where you could complete it with one line.

In Trails, you put X's on any two circles and the opponent made a trail from one to the other. In subsequent plays no trail could be crossed. These games were of short duration and could be completed in one recess time.

Sometimes, if the bigger children were doing something else, desks would be pushed back against the walls and all the younger ones would play those old singing games — "The Farmer in the Dell", "Looby Loo", "Go In and Out the Windows", "London Bridge" and so on, either to piano accompaniment or just their own singing.

Now let us suppose it's nice summer weather. The teeter totters and swings would all be on the go and a ball game, too, very likely. Usually sides chosen up in the morning would last for the day. The bat would be tossed between two self-appointed captains to see who got first "at bat". There was a certain amount of position switching by players, but most got to play where they preferred. The odd game of *hard ball* was played with only the bigger kids allowed to play. Usually this was for boys only, but probably because they needed them to get enough for teams, they did let girls play with them sometimes — **Mary Donald** and **Freda Bender** being lucky "choosees"! (No that word *isn't* in Websters — I just coined it this minute!)

By the time ones about my age were playing, it was always *softball*. (However, a new *softball* was *not* soft and only the catcher and the first baseman had a mitt, as a rule.) But regular ball was not the only ball game we played. Others were "Scrub" or "Work Up", "Five Hundred", or, with no diamond or bat, "Keep Away". Most ball games require a certain number of players, or somewhere near that number, for even a pick-up game, but Five Hundred or Keep Away could actually be played with as few as four, but the usual number was more than this. In Five Hundred one threw the ball up in the air and batted it towards all the others stationing themselves randomly in the field. Each kept their own score and the batter tried to aim to all as fairly as possible. A fly was 100, first bounce 75, second bounce 50 and a grounder 25. Attaining 500 gave you the bat. Keep Away is self-explanatory — each side throwing a ball to ones on their team and the other team trying to intercept. It was just a free for all with no scoring. If little ones were playing, they were given easy tosses and the chance to throw without the usual interference.

Top soil piled up against the page-wire fence around the school yard, loaded with Russian thistle seeds and bathed in warm spring rains and sunshine, sprang into lusty green life. Teacher Bill reasoned

"Why not some vegetables?" This was greeted with downright apathy. These kids had their own idea. They were turning this fence dune into well organized farms. Weeds were all pulled and fields seeded to various grains. Roads were constructed between them and "vehicles" (mere blocks of wood or some toy from home) were travelling about. But soon they were drivers needing much more skill, as they guided small hoops along with T-shaped tools made of laths. Though the unwritten traffic rules usually worked, just as with grown-ups, there were collisions and arguments over who was at fault. Bill wisely let them settle these tiffs on their own.

But one day they got tattled on by some girls and his intervention was required. A couple of boys had caught and put crude harnesses on a "team" of gophers and were trying to hitch them to a little wagon. Gophers are very hard to "domesticate" and besides, they have sharp teeth, capable even of piercing leather gloves. A killjoy teacher ordered the release of the captives and the wounded boy home to get the bite treated. They were quite cooperative when they understood the danger from infections and even rabies.

Sportsmanship

Sportsmanship was held in *very high regard* in our day. A *braggy winner* or a *poor loser* were equally frowned on whether by a team or an individual. Every ballgame at a tournament ended with the rousing cheer with hands upraised in praise — "Hip Hip Hooray", shouted three times with the losers getting the same acclamation. After a hockey game, as I still see done today sometimes, the two teams skate in a line going opposite ways shaking hands with each opponent in turn. I never have been to a curling game as it only came into popularity after I'd left home, and as far as I know, was never played on our rural rink. I do not know if they have any special ceremony or cheer at the end of a game. From the Ponteix history book: "**Joe** and **Evette Goffinet** and their curling team, **Dennis Shaddock**, **Bob McConville** and **Lloyd Lamb** in 1963 made it to the curling finals in **Yorkton**, Sask., and curled against the **Richardson Brothers**. Even though they lost the game, they gave these pros some stiff competition."

Here is an anecdote connected with curling: At the last school I taught, the man of the house at Logans where I boarded, was an avid curler and each winter would be gone for a week or more to the Winnepeg Bonspiel. Wherever I boarded I would usually help with dishes or other household tasks, but at bonspiel time when Mrs. Logan had the cows to milk while he was away, I would don coveralls and go out and give her a hand. Once, one Saturday morning just as I was preparing to go out and help milk, the Browns arrived (I had three of them in school — the youngest, Hilda, in grade two). She was flabbergasted. She had no idea a *teacher* could *milk a cow*!

Below, Kit and Maude — the nucleus of a girls' hockey team?

Quimper's hockey team: Bert, Ed, Alex, Frank, Earl, John and Wellington.

History of Hockey and Baseball

Directions here on *how* to play ball or hockey would be *superfluous* to say the least, but I thought it might be interesting to give a little of the history of these two games.

Field hockey preceded ice hockey by hundreds of years, maybe thousands, as it is believed to be of ancient **Persian** origin. But an ice game may have been played in northern **England** as early as the 18th century.

The game as we know it, is of **Canadian** origin — probably at Kingston Military College, **Ontario** in 1876.

In 1895 it went across the border to **Maryland**. Until artificial ice made its appearance, the game remained almost exclusively Canada's. The Stanley Cup was donated by **Lord Frederick Stanley** in1893 when he was governor-general of Canada.

Quimper hockey team in action.

Above, back row: Marie, Catherine, Jack, Walter, Willie, John, Louis, Maude, Nellie; Front: Dorothy, Albert, Andy, Rob, Freda. Quimper kids ready to play ball (And you boys think it's "modern" to wear your cap backwards?)

Right, Quimper School ball team, 1937, Robert Mc., Jim McC., Arnold, Roland, Jim C., Evelyn, Alma, Walter, Allan.

Though on ice, players are not on skates. They slide smooth, heavy granite stones towards goals or tees at either end. Brooms are used sometimes to vi–gorously sweep the ice in front of the "kettle" to get it to go farther. Four players make a team or rink. The game originated in Scotland and is its national game. The Turners of Weyburn, Saskatchewan, have an extensive curling museum.

Top: we were just the Quimper "Q" team; and bottom: we go "modern" with shorts and a *real* name. Our colors, yellow and black, remained the same.

Quimper's Orioles: Wilma, Alma, Mary D., me, Ethel, Alice, Jessie, Kit, Evelyn, Isabelle.

I am not much of a spectator sports fan, but with Quimper's hockey team, that was *different*! Next day after a game I would be hoarse. And how vivid are our memories of all the other goings on on game days — shoveling the snow; ice-scrapings between periods being tossed over the fence; we females skating out there between times or after the game; putting on and taking off skates in the cook car pulled up beside the rink, and sometimes having coffee and cake after a game. Not all the men engaged themselves in getting the ice ready for the next period, so for some of us, particularly we who were not too confident in our ability to skate without falling, what a pleasure it was to have someone like **Bert Cross** (he was short too!) take us for a partner and go round and round. Such abandonment of apprehension and the pure joy of skating as we leaned on those strong arms!

As Canada's national sport is hockey, that of the United States is *baseball* — along with its *younger brother* (that *term* is *in* my encyclopedia) *softball.* Its history is much more difficult to trace than that of hockey, there being so many games with some similarities, as played mainly in England and the United States. It is, however, a matter of record that the game received a *standard* set of rules in 1845 when **Alexander Cartwright** organized the Knickerbocker Baseball Club of **New York**. His basic rules have met with very few changes over the years, none of them significant. Modified games of baseball, played both indoors or out, eventually were merged to come under the name of *softball* which was given its own set of rules in 1933.

Hop Scotch

Very little space or equipment was needed for this popular game. If you were playing indoors, all you needed was a piece of chalk — outdoors, a sharp stick — and in either place, little flat, pebbles, pieces of tile, or some just-right-sized pieces of heavy glass. It required a reasonably "straight" eye as you chalked or scratched the outlines of the mini-playing court. Two, three or even four *could* play, but two was probably best. You could even play solo if you wanted to. It was a game of skill, not chance — jumping accurately enough so as not to step on a line, keeping your balance while you stood on one leg to pick up your "piece" and throwing well enough to have that piece land where you wanted it to and stay put in that spot.

I wondered if this children's game came from Scotland as the name seems to imply, so off I went to the encyclopedia. Wrong! It came from **England** and the *Scotch* is a corruption of *scratch*, because you scratched the playing diagram with a stick. In some versions of the game, pieces are kicked rather than thrown, I learned.

Skipping

This was one of the most popular things with girls. Sometimes it was a twosome activity with them facing one another, but at school it was more often a group affair, sometimes with only one rope, other times the more challenging two ropes going opposite direcitons. Many rhymes were chanted as we skipped. "Salt" was slow, "Pepper" was fast. One day in a bookstore I saw a hardback on these skipping rhymes.

Tennis

As far as I remember there was no other Quimper tennis court than the one at our place, and this, as with so many other things in our district, was the brainchild of my Uncle Frank though financed by the Quimper Young People's Group. Court lines were made with wide, white, light canvas strips fastened down with big "U" shaped staples. The net and tennis rackets were no doubt ordered from Eaton's. Gophers sometimes tried to *share* our court, but they were quickly "informed" that we wouldn't share with them! A new hole quickly had a trap set for the invader. We played so frequently that we became reasonably good players. Many, many years later our kids were quite surprised that "mother", for awhile anyway, could even beat them at a game!

At one school where I taught, there were not enough pupils to play ball, so we set up a court in the school yard. Though I don't know for sure, I believe we may have been *exclusive* for a rural school with our tennis playing.

Most homes didn't have a room big enough for a regulation size ping pong table and, even if there were room, where would you have stored it when not in use? We didn't let this stop us from playing this delightful inside game in the winter. We simply made the kitchen or dining room table as long as possible with its leaves and pretended it was "authentic".

Most "indoor" games were of the quieter kind — card games galore with a regular deck or with all those specialized ones for kids, "Old Maid" (even our *game* had what we call today a mean-spirited name), "Authors", "Travel", "Alphabet", etc. We had many board games, also. "Ludo", "Snakes and Ladders", "Racetrack", and, of course, checkers. But even *quiet* games could get mighty noisy. One even had the *built-in noise* factor — the card game Pit. We first played it at Uncle Tom's — *upstairs* — so the grown ups playing whist at the kitchen table downstairs could still play! This game is supposed to be the stock market exchange which in *real* life *is one noisy affair*, so ours was true to form in this respect! Later — much later, that is — I found this old card game at a yard sale, but looking brand new. I tried to introduce it to our kids and grandkids, but for whatever reason, I never quite figured out, it never really caught on. Maybe its previous owners had had the same problem!

Tag

What fun that tiny word brings to mind! With its many adaptations to age, ability and circumstance, all could participate from the simplest form of chasing one another, and when caught to reverse roles; to all the games with sets of rules such as "Prisoner's Base", "Pom Pom Pull Away", "Anti I Over", and so on. In between we had poison tag, three-deep and touch tag.

Races

These too, can cover the gamut from the simplest, like a line up, a signal to start, and a run to the goal at the other end, to the highly coordinated relay races. Again, you have many novelty in-betweeners — sack race, potato race, three-legged race and so on, which were always part of community picnics. We, who were fast runners when we were young, could always earn an extra ice cream cone or two. At Quimper picnics I could come in first — only if my cousin **Alice** were not also in the race.

I must tell you of a funny race between another teacher and myself when our two schools were having a field day. Someone came up with the novel idea of the two *teachers* having a race. I was game and so was she, but we had no idea of each other's ability. Well, you know a cardinal rule in a race is *not* to look back to see where your competitor is, so at the starter's voice "One to get ready, two for the show, three to get ready and four to go" (no starter gun in those days!), or an alternative "On your mark, get set, go." We were off. In about three steps, Connie had simply stopped in defeat, so I ran the race by myself much to everyone's hilarity.

Bowling

Real bowling only took place at alleys in town, but rural kids had what might be called *Human Ten Pins* — ten people lined up at the far end of a yard space or room facing the bowler who had 3 medium sized soft balls, perhaps sponge rubber ones so common when we were of school age. The "pins" could only lift one leg to prevent getting hit and all pins were of equal value in scoring. Everyone took turns as pins or bowlers.

Some old time games and toys, however, have surely stood the test of time — "dominoes", "tiddly-winks", "tinker toys", building blocks, checkers, chess, marbles, etc. They may diminish in popularity for a period of time, but they always come back. I think this will also be true of some later toys we didn't have as kids, such as yo-yos, hoola hoops, and pogo sticks. Still later, other wonderful toys and games came on the market — Etch-A-Sketch, Spirograph, and Scrabble, for instance, or take-offs from these originals. And some card games are as popular today as when they first appeared, or even more so — bridge and pinochle, for example, while other card games so popular in our day seem to be "gone" — whist for one.

Rob and I had one game that I've never seen anywhere else — even in a museum — "Bloxo". It was played on a small board with peg holes in it and was for only two players, a sort of combination tic-tac-toe and checkers. Opponents had red or green pegs and markers (toothpicks we colored for the tiny holes to mark where we had made three in a row).

Word Games

These have such great variety, it's hard to know where to begin, but it will help when I narrow the field to those learned mostly at school, simply because so many come under the heading of *educational.* We didn't perhaps remember all the names that went with them — serious sounding terms such as anagrams, acronyms, synonyms, etc., but a wise teacher made many of them into word games. However, we didn't pigeon hole *education* or *just for fun.*

Today, perhaps part of the fault lies in labeling. Reading is *work* because you *have* to do it for school classes. *Educational* T.V. isn't watched simply because it isn't fun. Certainly, learning some things can hardly be made attractive enough to become play, no matter how they're "packaged" — but isn't the opposite also true that in those things which *interest* us most, nothing can be more pleasurable than *working* in that field — so that even the dinner table and the clock are forgotten? When this happens, has it gone over that fine line from *work* to *play?*

I suppose this is basically the philosophy behind hobbies. Sometimes a hobby gets turned into a business which *can* work out well, but often it goes the other way. What was *play* becomes *work.* Close to home — writing is *play*, but marketing it is *work.*

Now let's chat a bit about some things *all* agree are *fun* — jokes, riddles, puns, etc., Many are based on what is done with words as they are misplaced, misspelled, mispronounced and so on. Somehow I think the art of telling jokes and funny stories is going downhill as more and more people depend on professionals on T.V. with their one liners or half hour-sitcoms. This is sad in my opinion for when they are at the *personal* level, there is much interaction between talker and listener, and in a group setting, everyone gets caught up in the spirit of it all. Spontaneity and laughter are *contagious* — so much so at times that even the usually shy and reticent may instead be led to share their own hilarious or embarrassing moments.

Singing and Whistling

City living for *most* of us, and radio and T.V. for nearly all of us, have drawn a line between singing and whistling *at* daily tasks, and *watching* others in more structured formal settings. Does a woman sing as she loads the dishwasher or dries clothes in the drier? Most appliances make a noise of some kind when operating, so one's own spontaneous music-making seems almost incongruous. This is true for the farmer in the field also. His tractor is noisy, so perhaps he's listening with headphones on to tapes or to the radio. This was one of the biggest changes, I think, that came about when tractors replaced horses. I know Dad often said his love of field work took a nose-dive when this took place, for he had sung to his horses and was sure they enjoyed it, too. And though Dad was more apt to *sing* on the job, my two uncles, Walter and Frank, would usually *whistle.* Later on, this trait of happy spontaneous whistling, though not maybe recognized at the time, was one of ways Bud was becoming the *one* for me! But again, other things robbed us both of this pleasure — he in *the doing* and me in the *hearing*. City life or being in the service and whistling were simply incompatible and that habit was lost.

Let me tell you of a couple of personal experiences along this line:

Quimper Players in "Treasure Farm", 1928. Notice the little boy at the left on the stairway. That's Jim Cross whose parents were in the cast. It was said he knew everyone's lines so well he was the unofficial prompter.

Mary Kelman in costume for a play.

When I was going to Normal School, I wasn't yet far enough removed in time, space, and circumstance to have weaned myself off singing as I walked along, so when I was coming home from Normal School and houses were not too close together, I would be singing — not very loud perhaps, but singing nonetheless. But as I approached my boarding house, my already soft singing had dwindled to barely a hum. **Mrs. Payne** said to me one day "How come you're always humming?" Well, as I said before, this lady had a grating personality, so you know thereafter my humming too ceased before reaching the door.

The other incident took place after I was back to country living again. I was teaching school, and when all was quiet after the kids had gone home, I would often be singing away. Now when one supposes there is *no listener* other than the mouse which might skitter around the schoolroom, one may try, as I did, to sing something entirely out of the range of their musical ability. In this case, it meant that I, with a naturally *low alto* voice, was singing at the top of my voice one of my favourite pieces which I'd heard so many times on our gramaphone — "Lo, Hear the Gentle Lark" by high soprano **Galli Curcie**. If you know this aria and this singer's voice, you can guess how unmatched I was! Then came an ominous silence. The secretary and another school board member had been listening at the door! They tried to tell me they'd been appreciating my effort, but I wasn't convinced they were *not* saying this tongue-in-cheek as the saying is today, and my very red face was my reply rather than a "Thank You".

I can't leave this section without a few words about Mom and her singing. It was practically nonstop except for sleeping, eating or sewing, or later on, when "The Lux Theatre", "Amos and Andy", or "Fibber and Molly" were on the air. Often, if she didn't know the right words, she would just make up some, because a la-la substitute just wouldn't cut it, as we say now. When confronted with her hilariously unmatched words, she would just laugh as heartily as her critics. But only secular songs got this sort of treatment, not hymns, for she knew their words.

I can still hear her singing coming down the hall on Easter Sunday morning, "Christ the Lord is Risen Today". I remember, too, how much she liked "The Little Drummer Boy" when it first came out.

I never realized till much later in life how many songs and hymns I know all or most of the words to — many learned just by hearing Mom and Dad singing. Others were memorized at school as we enjoyed Friday afternoon singing or as we practiced for concerts. Still others I made a conscious effort to memorize as I walked to and from school. And what a joy all these musical memories are — not just songs, but instrumental tunes also. I seldom sing aloud now and I never could whistle, but if my mind is not on something else, they are being sung or played in my head. At times I am troubled with insomnia and one of the best "sleeping pills" is to concentrate on some "head" singing — for instance going through the alphabet with either secular songs or hymns.

When you hear *opera* what do you think of — a high class performance on the stage or do you automatically put "soap" in front of it, and if so, how come? I don't know how "opera" got in there unless someone was trying to make a very definite distinction between *high class* and *low,* but we know how the word "soap" got there because the very first one, **Ma Perkins** in 1933, was sponsored by Oxydol.

Two of my favorite radio programs were "Walter Budd and his Blossoms" and the "Calgary Old Time Fiddlers".

Early Settlers

It was strange what people were appealed to by the high class, high pressure, often much too flowery, even untruthful posters, which popped up in western Europe when the west was first getting settled. The results were the basis of many hilarious stories, others only too tragically true as these people, with no experience at *any* type of *farming* or even *manual labour* of any kind, would file on a homestead and become farmers. Nevertheless, the percentage of failures was surprisingly very low. I mention this here because it was often these people who brought some refinement to many country districts. Some instead had been professional musicians or educators in the old country, or Eastern Canada. So thanks to such as the **Edwards** family, **Mildred Cross**, **Minnie Claydon** and others, Quimper had its play directors, singing teachers, dance instructors and, in one who married into the Edwards family, even a piano tuner. Somehow, as we look back on just who settled where, we wonder if, in our 20/20 hindsight, we saw the Hand of the One who was making arrangements behind the scenes, for somehow the mix was just what it ought to be for a harmonious, practical, cooperatively, culturally-varied community.

Hobbies

In previous chapters in this book, particularly the one on vignettes, there have been a number of hobbies mentioned, but to have a chapter titled "The World of Play" and not give this topic more coverage wouldn't seem quite right. Usually we think of a hobby as something done by one's self, but if skill and enthusiasm are shared, a little group or club might result. Sometimes we learn in our old age something which took place when we were young. I was so surprised when my cousin **Phoebe** told me Mom had taught her to crochet.

And some of us love to write. (We now routinely disobey what we learned in school that we were to *love people* and *like things)*. So now I say people "loved" to get Mom's long newsey-just-as-if-she-were-talking-to-you letters. Limitations in punctuation, spelling and grammar due to only a Grade Four education made her feel trapped or humiliated at times. Nevertheless, she passed on to all three of us her love of writing, Nellie and I for sure, and Rob, too, I think, seeing as he wrote some good articles for both the Aneroid and Ponteix History Books. Now we dream that this enjoyment of *hers* may someday become the hobby of some of her grandchildren or great grandchildren.

Continued on page 226

Alice carries on the quilt making of her mother. I wonder how many quilts the Bjores made in all.

A sample of Phoebe's lovely crochet work.

Almost all overstuffed furniture was protected with these three-some crocheted sets.

Crocheters are always looking for new patterns — does this one qualify for some of you?

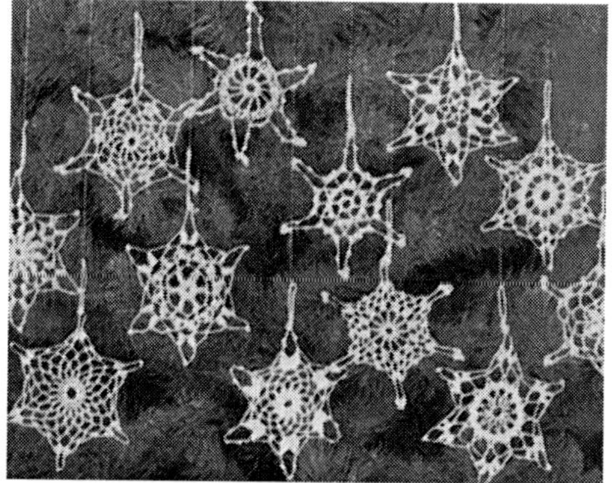

Above, all crocheters try new ideas. Snowflake ornaments are still popular. Right, three gifts in one! For our 50th, a doily from Phoebe, a dried bouquet from Dorothy F. with flowers which had dried naturally in a bouquet from Hilda added in.

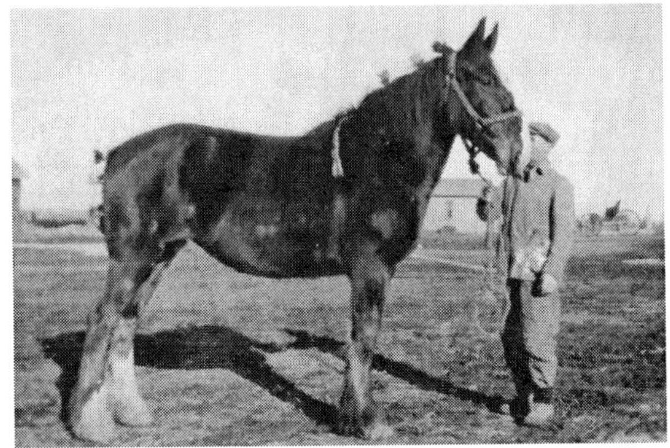

Dad with a new auction purchase. I remember the roses and ribbons woven into the horse's mane and tail. Circa 1923.

WESTERN JACKALOPE

The first white man to see the singular fauna speciman was a trapper named George McLean in 1829. When he told of it later he was promptly denounced as a liar. An odd trait of the Jackalope is its ability to imitate the human voice. Cowboys singing to their herds at night have been startled to hear their lonesome melodies repeated faithfully from some nearby hillside. The phantom echo comes from the throat of some Jackalope. They sing only on dark nights before a thunderstorm. Stories that they sometimes get together and sing in chorus is discounted by those who know them best.

Left, have you seen one? Trying to get a gullible one to believe a tall tale is a specialized hobby.

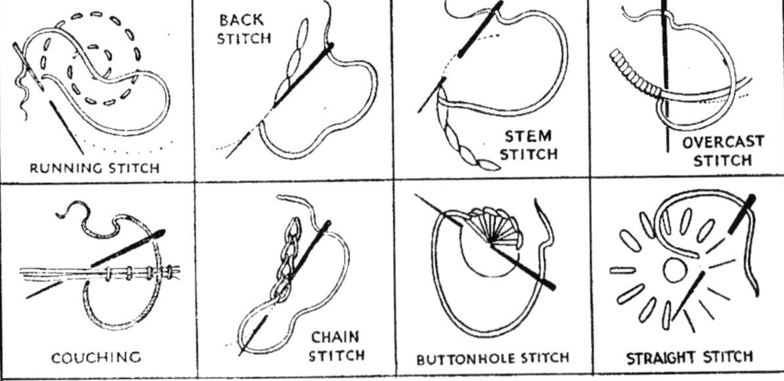

It would be the rare teen girl who did not learn embroidery. Many articles that went into her Hope Chest would show her handiwork. Some drew original designs, but most relied on already stamped things ordered from Eaton's catalogue, or they sent to needlecraft companies that advertised in the weekly newspapers.

I was only one of many who was given beautiful gladiola or other flowers from Mr. Dumont's fabulous garden.

No one knows how many Mickey Mouse dolls Mrs. Bjore made. Any sick child for miles around got one, and, of course, grandchildren each received one.

A hired man at Uncle Sam's built this darling little house. I remember even the door and windows worked.

Are nicknames fun? Well, yes, apparently, in the T. McConville family — Walter the giver and Olive the receiver. He called her his little green olive, she tells with a laugh.

Indulging my hobby of reading on a visit to Ed and Madge's at Manor.

Because there are few joys in life that can compare with that of having *our children* come to share the things that bring *us* so much pleasure — it is sad, that the inspirer has often passed away before getting a glimpse of such fulfillment. This was the case with my writing hobby, as Mom had died before my ash book was published.

It has been interesting, as I've perused many of the home town histories, to see the great variety, not only of occupations, but of avocations, and yes, hobbies, of those who have succeeded the pioneers. One of the down-sides of a pioneer's harsh life was often the lack of time or means to have hobbies. For the most part, excellence at their work had to give them their sense of self worth and joy of living. Even now, sad to say, quite often people reach retirement years before they take up a hobby. Hardly a magazine or newspaper comes out nowadays without some article extolling the benefits of a hobby. And there are few I find more interesting than those featuring certain people and their hobby, often an unusual collection or skill. I do not know enough second and third generation Quimperites to mention their hobbies, but seeing as I'm focusing on my parents' and my own generation, theirs are the hobbies I tell of here. We didn't think of certain specialties in cooking or sewing as hobbies, but I think they were. For instance, being known for certain cakes, cookies, pies, candy, or all-around excellent cooking put this stamp on their products. And turning out unique quilts, rugs, cushions, dresses, hats, etc., surely qualified them as hobbyists, don't you think?

Some hobbies are of long duration, others just a flash in the pan. A few in this latter category that I remember in Quimper, or at least in the years prior to 1958: 1) making crepe paper flowers, (hundreds of them went on the trellis Frank made for a garden scene dance performance); 2) hats made of crepe paper — long thin tightly twisted strips of crepe paper serving as thread; 3) punch-work cushion tops; 4) men's neckties made from scratch and painted; 5) chokers made of sequin-covered little balls hung on a velvet rope; 6) corsages made by forming leaf and petal shapes with thin copper wire, then stretching bleached and dyed pieces of nylon hose over them. I wonder if any of these specialties have been saved.

I don't know of any boys who had an autograph book, but I think every teen Quimper girl had one — and sometimes even more. These mini-books with their different colored sections were continually being handed to others with, "Please put *something* in my autograph book", but this didn't mean just your name. Philosophy, good advice on life's goals, mottoes, poetry in both lofty style or in poor taste, etc., all turned up. Some who loved to draw or paint did a page with just this. Ethel, Alma and I come to mind. Olive lent me her old autograph book and I have two of my own. It certainly is a nostalgic trip to go through these, seeing those old familiar handwritings and matching what they wrote with our recollections of each one. As we now see again someone's advice to us, we feel good where we've perhaps come somewhat near to their expectations, but feeling equally bad where we have

Ethel put this in her sister Olive's autograph book.

Handmade Easter card.

Christmas card made on birch bark.

fallen so much short.

Some verses, mottoes, etc., got pretty repetitious from book to book — or even within the book, as not everyone took time and effort to read what others before them had written. Particularly welcome therefore were new ones published in the Free Press or Western Producer. Another outlet for some of us with an artistic bent, was in making valentines and cards for birthdays, anniversaries, etc., each one different. Some pictures we painted, framed and gave as gifts. Alma and I and maybe some others too, did some painting on glass — often silhouettes.

One winter when Frank worked down in eastern Saskatchewan, he got some birch bark for me. It could be peeled in layers, each having a unique shade or tint of brown or tan. You could paint on it in as fine a detail as on paper. One Christmas I made all my cards and a few calendars with it.

Frank was always coming up with some very

(Continued on page 234)

Come to Glenvern Hall

Friday, Nov. 10th, 1933 8.30 p.m.

THE QUIMPER PLAYERS will present

"Among the Breakers"

A Drama of Fairpoint Lighthouse

IN TWO ACTS

TIME OF PLAY: TWO HOURS

CAST OF CHARACTERS:

DAVID MURRAY, Keeper of Fairpoint Lighthouse	Walter McConville
LARRY DIVINE, His Assistant	Alex. Kelman
HON. BRUCE HUNTER	Bert Cross
CLARENCE HUNTER, His Ward	Kenneth Miller
MINNIE DAZE, Hunter's Niece	Kathleen McCullough
PETER PARAGRAPH, A Newspaper Reporter	Charlie McCoy
BEN STARLIGHT, cast up by the waves	Ernistine Lallier
MOTHER CAREY, A Reputed Fortune Teller	Mrs. P. Claydon
SCUD, Hunter's Coloured Servant	John Kelman
BIDDY BEAN, An Irish Girl	Dorothy Claydon

Stage and Storm Effects by FRANK ADSHEAD — Director, MRS. PERCY CLAYDON

DON'T MISS THIS, ELSE YOU WILL REGRET IT!

Bring Your Own Lunch — We Supply Coffee

DANCE AFTER THE LUNCH

Admission — Adults 15c — Children 10c

GLENVERN HALL COMMITTEE

Frank, our teacher, **Miss Armstrong's** younger teen aged brother, had come to spend a few days with us one winter — to get a taste of country life, I guess. Their home was in **Regina**. Going to Glenvern one winter night in a closed-in jumper, Frank was terrified — no street lights and bouncing along over drifts of snow for endless miles (6 miles). There are many jokes about country hicks in the big city for the first time, but we country kids were having the opposite experience. I must admit we had the same sort of reaction, not a very kind one to be sure. We were amused by his terror.

A REAL HOLIDAY CELEBRATION AND DANCE

FOR PETE'S SAKE

THE GREATEST FARCE OF A LIFETIME

Presented by

QUIMPER PLAYERS

in ANEROID THEATRE

Easter Monday

(April 14th)

Proceeds in aid of Canadian Legion Funds

DANCE

MUSIC BY THE

Young Orchestra

Cast of Characters:

(In the order of their first appearance)

Miss Sarah Pepperdine .... ALMA BJORE
Peter's Aunt

Jasmine Jackson .... HELEN GAMMIE
Aunt Sarah's Darky Cook

Cicero Murglethorpe .... WILLIAM BUSCH
The Dean of Elwood College

Peter Pepperdine .... ALLAN CLAYDON
Always in Hot Water

Bill Bradshaw .... DENNIS SHADDOCK
Pete's College Pal

Thorndyke Murglethorpe .... ROBT. McCONVILLE
(Mugsy) A College Grind

Mrs. Georgina Clarkston .... ISABELLE McCONVILLE
A Social Climber

Nadine Clarkston .... OLIVE McCONVILLE
Peter's Sweetheart

Peggy Clarkston .... NELLIE McCONVILLE
Bill's Sweetheart

Malvina Potts .... MADELEINE DUMONT
Mugsy's Goddess (Society Reporter)

John Boliver .... GORDON DONALD
A Wealthy Banker

Dupont Darby .... WALTER CROSS
The Poet of Elwood College

Curtain rises at 8 o'clock

Admission: Adults 35c. Children under 12 years, 15c.

Erinlea being quite far east of Glenvern Hall had more of their own events at the home school. Sometimes for a dance they hired Quimper's musicians. Kit on piano, Alex on violin.

This three-act play was put on by the Quimper Players in 1941, first at Glenvern Hall and then repeated in the Aneroid Theatre. The Young Orchestra played at both events. I don't remember any program or play being repeated in the same spot which seems a bit odd — so much work for *one* performance. Probably it was because there had been 100 percent turnout the first time around and a second might have to be too far away to get a different audience.

ATTENTION PLEASE!

THERE WILL BE A

DANCE

AND

An Hour of Vaudeville

AT GLENVERN HALL

Friday, Nov. 2nd at 8.30 p.m.

We will dance till 10.30, then have lunch. After lunch, an hour of vaudeville by the Quimper Young People; Cowboy Jack and his Serenaders, Singing and a Stringed Instrument Orchestra. After that, the Pinto River Homemakers' Club

HOPE CHEST

on which they sold tickets, will be drawn for. Don't miss it.

MUSIC BY THE YOUNG ORCHESTRA

BRING YOUR OWN LUNCH — WE SUPPLY COFFEE

Admission: Adults 15c. Children 10c.

GLENVERN HALL COMMITTEE

This flyer gives us a little different flavour of programming at the hall — part put on by the Quimper Young People and part by others (it doesn't say where Cowboy Jack and His Serenaders were from), The Pinto River Homemaker's Club was at the end. Also, some money was being raised by a raffle on a Hope Chest — so we know these women had been busy with needle and craft materials. A Hope Chest, for young folks of today who don't know what this is, was a collection of linens set aside for a girl's hoped-for wedding day. Sharing its contents was a pleasant pastime for teen girls.

AT LAKE PELLETIER

Quimperites having fun at Lake Pelletier.

Alex and Frank in foreground canoe, other Quimperites in distance. Row boats and canoes were much more common in the early thirties than motor boats.

Earl, June, Mildred, Alex, Mary K. and Frank at the Lake.

Lake Pelletier was a long narrow lake about 50 miles away with a resort at either end. Quimper folks always went to the north end, while folks near Simmie (my husband's home town) always went to the south end.

The dance pavillion at Lake Pelletier.

Early days at the lake. Did they drive the buggy into the lake to tighten up the spokes?

Rob with a cute puppy.

Alma, Wilma and Mrs. McCoy.

unusual things for us, especially if he had worked elsewhere, maybe in a city and had taken a few lessons. Once this was tap dancing, another time, clog dancing. And it was thanks to him, as a beautiful, graceful dancer, that many of us learned the *correct* way to do an old fashioned waltz. And everyone in Quimper, I guess, credited him with us enjoying The French Minuet. It was fortunate for him and his hobby of making scenery for the many plays put on at Glenvern, that we had a basement where he could get enough working space. As for other props for plays, Mom used to laugh saying it looked like we'd been robbed as so many things were carted off for these performances.

Dad Saved This

One day in going through some old things I ran across Dad's copy of "Be Careful How You Say It." These, he said, were extracts from genuine letters received by a pensions office. What laughs!

1) I am writing these lines for Mrs. J. who cannot write herself. She expects to be confined next week and can do with it.
2) I am sending my marriage certificate and six children. I had seven and one died, which was baptized on a half sheet of paper by the Rev. Thomas.
3) In answer to your letter, I have given birth to a boy weighing 10 lbs. I hope this is satisfactory.
4) In answer to your instructions, I have given birth in the enclosed envelope for twins.
5) You have changed my little boy to a little girl. Will this make any difference?

Just Getting There

Mom, Grandma, Rob and I with Old Honey. He is looking his age here, too. He had been a Mountie's horse. He lived to near 30.

Its concert night! All is ready at last to set off in horse and buggy. Debate. Which horse — Dad's choice, Barney — Mom's, Old Honey. She was scared of flighty Barney and Old Honey wouldn't let them down or do something to cause an accident, she argued. After some time they are on their way with poor Old Honey who can't be persuaded to even trot, and it took a lot of persuasion to convince him that at Uncle Tom's there was still a little ways to go. Robert and Mary were impatient and Nellie was tired of her abundant wrappings. Dad was unhitching Honey and Mom was trying to get kids and a cake (none of those neat cake carriers we have now) out of the buggy and into the school house. Mary, in her haste to beat Robert inside, trips and drops it. Mom can't get the baby carriage unfolded for her by now pretty cranky baby. All is chaos. But finally, after quite a few "drat its" said with plenty of fervour by Mom, all are welcomed as the concert gets underway. Chairman **Mr. Donald** rushes Dad on stage for his singing number. For all her frustration and ill temper of only a few moments before, Mom has a hard time suppressing her giggles as Dad is singing "Home Sweet Home".

Another Mishap

Counter and storage space for freshly baked pies and cakes was always at a premium, especially in shacks. Mom thought one time that the *safest* place for her freshly baked lemon pies for the picnic was the floor in the bedroom. But she'd gone on to other jobs and had forgotten momentarily about the pies and didn't catch in time those wild kids, Robert and Mary, chasing each other. A scream told it all. Feet had landed in the pies!

Yellow and Black

Madge is Quimper's teacher. It's in the 30's. I don't remember who suggested our colors, but no doubt our yell was a joint effort — and I suppose it was only natural to choose the name "Oriole", a yellow (though I think their *yellow* is more *orange*) and black bird. Maybe Quimper had a **Baltimore Oriole** fan!

When one thinks of it, perhaps **Meadowlark** would have been a better name seeing as these birds were so common in our area. But this thinking is what we call 20/20 hindsight, isn't it? Anyway, here's our yell:

Yellow and black, yellow and black
We're as quick as a cracker jack
Lots of pep and lots of glee
In the kids of the Q.S.D.
Zip bang whee, zip bang hah
Quimper, Quimper, rah, rah rah

This idea of school colors and a matching yell were ideas brought by Madge to our district, if I remember rightly. But one other innovative idea I'm certain came with her. This was a school newspaper. Only one copy was made up and it was read aloud to us all on a Friday afternoon as part of the regular Junior Red Cross meeting. I wonder how many other Quimper kids who later became teachers themselves, did as I did — introduced this idea of a school newspaper at their schools. At my last school there were only five families, counting me, the teacher, as one of them, so we just divided up all the copies on the last day. One of my treasures from teaching days are these old newspapers. I wonder if anyone saved any of Quimper's.

A Male Teacher

This would be a new experience. Ever since our house had been built in 1924-25 and the teacher had boarded with us from then on, Quimper had had only *female* teachers. Now a rather shy young man, **Ken Miller**, had come to teach. Quimper's teen aged girls could hardly wait to see him. In desperation they had finally gathered outside our door after a ball practice, with the flimsy excuse of each wanting a drink of water. Mom was enjoying the whole scene. Finally she just came out with it. "I know you're all here to meet the new teacher, so come on in." The other half of this story is somehow missing — did Ken come out to meet them or not and what did he think of all these girls, many of whom would be in his classroom on Monday morning?

It wasn't too long before Ken had set those heart flutters to rest, for one weekend he had asked if he might have his girl friend and a friend of hers come for a visit. Of course, the answer was yes. Mom said, one of the nicest things about having boarders (they had them again when they retired — at least partially — in Vancouver) was all the nice people they met, many of whom joined a list of lifelong friends.

(Ken was the teacher Rob credits with saving his life when he was burned so badly in 1935.)

Ken and I were both somewhat uncomfortable with each other so I usually was *doing something* as he left for school — a two and a half mile walk. This way it relieved both of us of trying to carry on some sort of a conversation if we'd been walking together. Also, we would have had trouble with *who* would be *in front* on the single pathway.

Not long after Ken had broken the ice, Quimper got another male teacher, **Bill Busch**. So, now let's have a glimpse or two at Bill's first days in the Quimper District as he had just walked over to the school to get set up for school Monday morning. The dismal scene that greeted him both outside and inside made him so depressed he hardly knew what to do. But do *something* he must, to the layers of dust everywhere.

He'd hardly begun his task when he heard a car drive up. Now this story can go into first person as a tall man offered Bill his outstretched hand and in his Scottish brogue said, "I'm Jack McKenzie, chairman of the board. What in the world are you doing here today, lad?"

"Well, school starts Monday, I thought I'd better —"

"Oh lad, you'd better clear out of here fast before the ladies show up. Oh, oh. Too late. Here they are now."

"Sure enough, two cars turned into the gate and about ten women obviously dressed for work spilled out with pails, brooms, mops, etc. Jack and I were shooed out. I learned later that it was **Mrs. Bjore** who commanded her small army like a benevolent general. At about four, when the last car had left, I couldn't resist heading the two and a half miles back to school. The yard was its same dreary self, but I was truly unprepared for what greeted me inside. It was cleaned and polished throughout, and bright clean curtains hung at the shining windows. Even the clock was wound and set at the right time! I rushed downstairs. Yes, it had had the same treatment.

What a wonderful surprise this was to me! But I soon found out that this spirit pervaded Quimper district to such an extent that I count my two years there among the happiest of my life."

Stage Anecdotes

When an actor does such a good job that a member of the audience comes to believe they *are* who they *are playing,* that's a feather in their cap. Dad, playing the part of an Irishman who had just come into some money, had little **Allan** asking his mother if Mr. McConville really did have $40,000!

Clean shaven **John Kelman** needed a beard. Getting the hair was no problem — just snip some off a horse's tail — but how would it be stuck on? Solution. Roger's golden syrup. In the cold barn it was fairly stiff, but in the indoor temperature, it got sort of runny. Need more be said?

Frank had the urge sometimes to turn a serious, solemn moment into a lighter one. **Mr. Browning** was singing "The Hunting Song" in his booming bass voice when Frank found a background prop — a broomstick. It turned into a "horse" as Frank rode back and forth across the back of the stage. The singer was at a loss to see why his serious song was making the audience practically roll in the aisles with laughter. It is to be hoped he had a sense of humor.

Little **Dorothy** was half way through her recitation. Her seamstress mother had made her doll an elegant dress for the occasion, but in her excitement Dorothy had forgotten it and dashed off stage to get it —

coming back to finish as if there had been no break in continuity.

It's hard being the youngest of four sisters, especially at Christmas concert time. When the teacher asked if there were any problems — a teacher was expected to solve any and all of them — **Olive** piped up "Please, Teacher, how am I going to get my hair curled? Minnie, Ethel and Isabelle have used up all the curlers and bobby pins."

It was concert time and a nervous, rather thin **Robert** had a recitation that didn't quite fit, for it started out, "See the width across my back, for I am growing strong."

Sometimes little ones such as myself, who had not yet started school, but wanted to take part in the Christmas concert, were given a little recitation to learn at home. Our hired man, **Fred Shaddock**, was my coach. We were still living in the shack so it didn't take much volume to be heard at the *far* end of a room. The English have a rather odd way of saying "Talk loud", it's "Shout up." When I stood on the stage to say my piece, I remembered I was to *shout* so people at the back could hear me. I did, literally, and in short order the laughter drowned me out. Besides, with such tremendous effort, *breathlessness* took over so I suffered a double defeat.

Little **Billy** was nervous and sometimes this makes it difficult to know what to do with one's hands. Solution: give them something to do — roll them up in your shirt. Poor little guy, almost chokes himself to death.

Earl Cross was playing the part of an absent-minded professor and doing his part a little too realistically — forgetting to fasten the fly of the pajamas he was wearing. His wife, **Mildred**, in the audience, was trying desperately to get his eye, but to no avail. He wasn't *really* absent minded, for he was fully dressed underneath the pj's.

Glenvern Hall was built with a modern sophisticated stage curtain — one that looked as if it *lifted* up — none of this simple, pull to the side type. However, the roller was heavy and it took a strong man to turn the handle for the lifting — but he, **Mr. Vandergrift**, can't see the stage from his working station. A table with a cloth on it is set too close. The cloth is getting wound up also which gums up the mechanism and the rolling up is stalled. **Margaret Symington** is on a sofa weeping. In all the commotion over the curtain problem, her weeping turns into convulsive laughter. But in true fashion of "the show must go on," she gets back into her role when the curtain finally rises.

One of the most beautiful of all the scenery for plays turned out by Frank was the garden scene trellis bedecked with hundreds of homemade crepe paper flowers. Even the more sophisticated town crowd of Aneroid gasped at its beauty when they saw it. And what went on in front of it was one of the real highlights of all Quimper's productions in the 30's — a bevy of girls dancing and singing in their pink and white bustle style crepe paper dresses. (I wonder if some little girl has found her mother's or grandma's dress.)

Two Mini-Mini Dramas

Number One:

Setting: Inside Quimper School (specifics, such as money amounts, are fictitious).

Time: Early 30's. The Depression is here.

Characters: Complainer, Problem Solver, Doer.

Complainer: This floor is in terrible shape. It's simply worn out after nearly twenty years.

Problem Solver: So what we need is a new floor. That takes money for materials, but we can do the work ourselves. We men somehow rounded up 15¢ each to come to the dance tonight and the women have provided our late supper. Starting with tonight, let's raffle off one of the uncut cakes and put our admission money into a Floor Fund. When we have enough, we'll cash-bargain with the lumber company.

Doer: I just counted the money. We have $2.25. I just caught them downstairs before they cut the last cake. I've ripped up and numbered little pieces of paper. Thirty are in the hat here at 10¢ each. I have duplicates in this box. As soon as all the tickets are sold, we will have the drawing.

This is done and Doer announces: Here's $3.00. That makes $5.25 towards our fund. With similar takes every Friday night, it won't be long till we have a brand new floor. Right?

All clap their enthusiastic approval and the job gets done.

Number Two:

Setting: Inside Quimper School

Time: Late 30's — Depression still here.

Characters: Complainer, Problem Solver, Doer

Complainer: These walls look terrible. They haven't seen paint since the late 20's sometime.

Problem Solver: So we need some paint then. Almost ten years ago they were as hard up for money as we are now, but they saw the need of a new floor, followed a simple plan to get it and just did it. Their plan involved Friday night dances so why don't we do something similar to get some paint? Flooring was more expensive, much more than paint, too, but they did it all the same. Theirs was more of a *community* effort, but let's make ours a *school class project.* (Teacher Bill Busch volunteers to do the painting.)

All clap their enthusiastic approval and it gets done.

The Gift of Play

Some have the gift of song and some possess the gift of silver speech,
Some have the gift of leadership and some the ways of life can teach.
And fame and wealth reward their friends; in jewels are their splendors told,
But in good time their favorites grow very faint and gray and old.
But there are men who laugh at time and hold the cruel years at bay;
They romp through life forever young because they have the gift of play.

They walk with children, hand in hand, through daisy fields and orchards fair,
Nor all the dignity of age and power and pomp can follow there;
They've kept the magic charm of youth beneath the wrinkled robe of Time.
And there's no friendly apple tree that they have grown too old to climb.
They have not let their boyhood die; they can be children for the day;
They have not bartered for success and all its praise, the gift of play.

They think and talk in terms of youth; with love of life their eyes are bright;
No rheumatism of the soul has robbed them of the world's delight;
They laugh and sing their way along and join in pleasures when they can,
And in their glad philosophy they hold that mirth becomes a man.
They spend no strength in growing old. What if their brows be crowned with gray?
The spirits in their breasts are young. They still possess the gift of play.

The richest men of life are not the ones who rise to wealth and fame —
Not the great sages, old and wise, and grave of face and bent of frame,
But the glad spirits, tall and straight, who 'spite of time and all its care,
Have kept the power to laugh and sing and in youth's fellowship to share.
They can walk with boys and be a boy among, blithe and gay,
Defy the withering blasts of Age because they have the gift of play.

From **The Path to Home,** Edgar Guest, ©1919

Bibliography

The Folk Dance Book, by C. Ward Crampton, ©1909
Folk Dances of the British Isles, by Duggan Schlottman and Rutledge, ©1948
Sing Children Sing, by Leonard Bernstein, edited by Carol Miller for Unicef, ©1972
Jewish Folk and Holiday Songs, by Schaum Publications, ©1964
Aesop's Fables
Once Upon a Childhood, by Mac Donald Coleman, ©1978
Once Upon a Little Town, by Mac Donald Coleman, ©1979
Once Upon the World and Me, by Mac Donald Coleman, ©1984
Once Upon Toronto, by Mac Donald Coleman, ©1985
Fun with Brain Puzzlers, by L.H. Longley-Cook, ©1965
Crazy English, by Richard Lederer, ©1989
Card Tricks Anyone Can Do, by Temple C. Patton, ©1968
We Dare You to Solve This, by John Paul Adams, ©1955

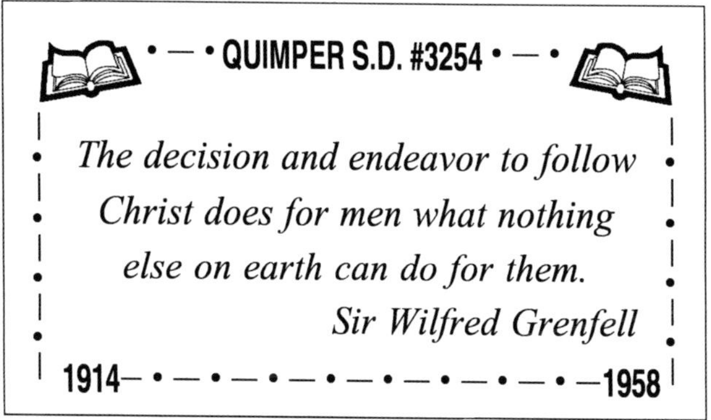

QUIMPER S.D. #3254
The decision and endeavor to follow Christ does for men what nothing else on earth can do for them.
Sir Wilfred Grenfell
1914—1958

In all your ways acknowledge Him and He will direct your paths. — Prov. 3:6

8 — We Worship

Just supposing it's a lovely June 20, 1926. The Klein family has gone by that morning in their democrat heading for Ponteix and morning mass — three miles down and nine to go. In the afternoon, Protestant kids are headed for Sunday School on the same paths they walk on to regular weekday school, but today they will be in their Sunday best with some pennies tied securely in a corner of their handkerchief. There are no adult Sunday School classes so parents will arrive by car an hour later. The only adults there as they arrive will be the superintendent, **Mrs. McCoy,** and some adult teachers, **Bert Cross, Mary Kelman**, and **Nellie McCoy.** (Later on in the 30's, **Ed McCullough** would be the superintendent, along with other teachers — **Mildred Cross** and some older teen recruits, **Mary Donald** and **Rob** for two.)

We always sat double for Sunday School — a sort of best friend pairing up. Three or four of us were encouraged, as we got far enough along with our piano playing, to take turns playing the hymns for both Sunday School and Church. Only the pianist had music, but having a words-only edition was no handicap to the singers. Rarely have I heard in any years since, any more enthusiastic singing.

The **United Church** did not come into being until 1925, but the copyright of our hymn book was 1916. However, the preface stated the **Canadian Hymnal** had been in use in several denominations for twenty-five years prior to this and had been "generally recognized as the best book of its kind in existence." In the revised edition about a half were replaced with "newer and better ones likely to appeal to the young people." Seeing as many were copyrighted, stern warning was given against reproducing for the stereopticon any such without special permission. For violations there would be heavy penalties. I wonder how many Quimperites read this preface!

A Wider Perspective

When we lived in **Farragut, Idaho** from 1947 to 1949, there were not enough of any one Protestant denomination for a church, so it was a bit like Quimper — they *had* to merge if they wanted to have a church. We, therefore, were founding members of the Community Church there. When we came to Yakima, we happened to rent a basement apartment across from Presbyterians whose kids and ours became immediate playmates. We visited one or two other churches, but seeing as there was neither *my* church nor a Lutheran one Bud felt any real tie to, we were soon Presbyterians and have remained so since then.

A worldwide movement, but known by different names in some countries, is **Church Women United.** It "brings women together into a community of prayer, advocacy and service, unified by a common faith in Christ, seeking the elimination of poverty of women and children and concerns itself with issues of peace and justice." In June of 1980 I attended a world conference of C.W.U. in **Los Angeles**. What a wonderful experience! I met women from so many different countries including **Canada**, **Russia** and a number of countries in **Africa**. It was so good to meet the lady who began "The Fellowship of the Least Coin", **Shanti Solomon** of India. (I wonder how many of you have this prayer fellowship in your church.) We seldom think of how political affairs and wars affect so profoundly what faith we were brought up in, or our permission to travel to any country in the world we may wish to visit. This Least Coin Fellowship is an example. Shanti was with a group of six women on an international peace-seeking trip, but because of political differences between two countries involved she and a Japanese woman were not permitted to go on one leg; so remained in Manilla. While waiting to rejoin the group, she worked out this simple plan inspired by the story in the BIble of the widow's mite (Luke 21:1-4): because women are seldom *in control* of family money, often they cannot give what they would like, but most *can contribute* once a month the *smallest coin* of their realm — for Americans and Canadians, therefore, a penny. This puts all women on level footing. With the coins go prayers for missionaries. It is surprising how much money comes in and in what wonderful ways it has helped so many. The money is distributed by a special committee of the East Asia Christian Conference, headquartered in Bangkok. The fascinating story of this fellowship is found in the book by **Grace Nies Fletcher**, © 1968, *The Quest of the Least Coin.*

Back to Quimper! After a number of hymns, the offering and a prayer, we were off to our classes — anywhere the teacher could find a spot to be out of earshot of other classes — a corner of the schoolroom, the cloak rooms, or in the basement. Bert Cross's boy's class met in the furnace room. On a nice day many would be outdoors. After class time all would be back in the main room for more singing, and a closing prayer. Memory work would be heard, tickets and story cards turned in, wall mottoes chosen, and our Sunday School papers handed to us. My favorite was one for the younger ones called "The Jewel". I wish I had saved at least one of these. Did any of you?

We had a short free time prior to time for church.

After the service folks often stayed another hour just to visit. Then families frequently went to each other's homes for supper and a musical evening.

Sunday School Favourites

1) All Things Bright and Beautiful; 2) When Mothers of Salem; 3) Jesus Loves Me; 4) When He Cometh; 5) I am So Glad; 6) There's a Friend for Little Children; 7) Father We Thank Thee; 8) God Sees the Little Sparrow Fall; 9) Can a Little Child Like Me?; 10) Hear the Pennies Dropping; 11) I Love to Tell the Story; 12) Jesus Bids Us Shine; 13) Jesus Wants Me For a Sunbeam. I'll bet many Quimperites could still sing these and maybe *all* the verses.

Three little-tot songs I learned in our Presbyterian Sunday School here in Yakima are 1) The Magic Penny; 2) Oh Be Careful Little Eyes What You See; 3) Jesus Loves the Little Children. That second one, if translated into *adult* behavior, could perhaps transform the world! Other verses say: 1) Oh be careful little ears what you hear; 2) Tongue what you say; 3) Hands what you do; 4) Feet where you go; 5) Head what you think. The third one makes the point that God loves *all children* — red, yellow, black and white — but of course, no one could miss the implica-

Rob and Mary ready for Sunday School.

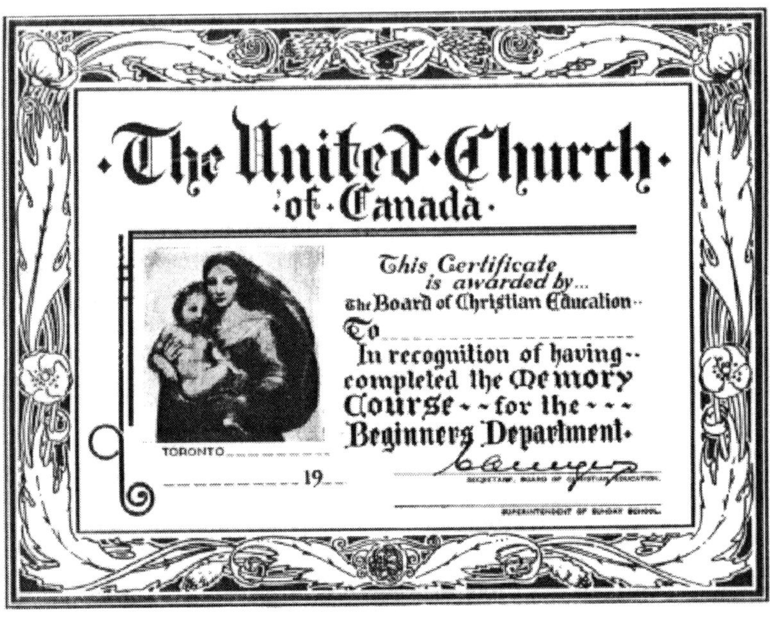

·The United·Church·
·of·Canada·

This Certificate is awarded by...
the Board of Christian Education..

To

In recognition of having completed the Memory Course for the Beginners Department.

TORONTO .... 19....

SECRETARY, BOARD OF CHRISTIAN EDUCATION.

SUPERINTENDENT OF SUNDAY SCHOOL.

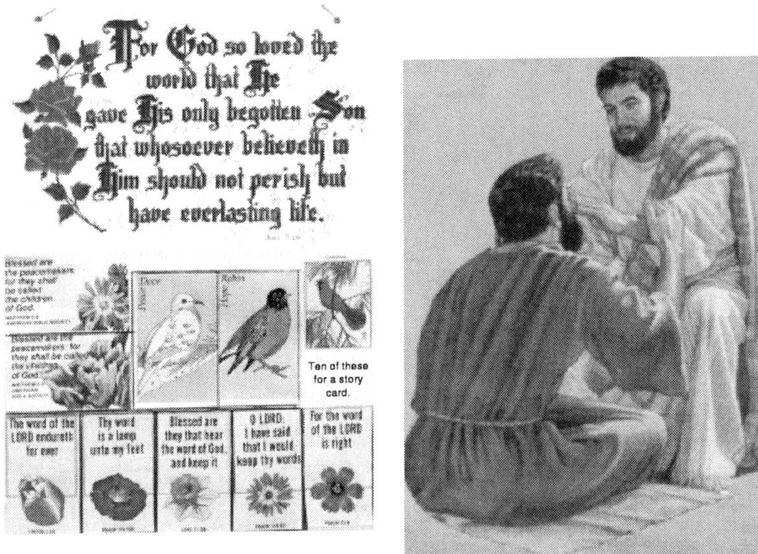

The church had a definite set of scripture verses and passages for each Sunday School Department. For attendance there was a three-step program — a ticket each Sunday; a story card for a 10 ticket turn in, and a wall motto to keep for a three story card turn-in.

tion that grown-ups are also included. Probably Quimper Sunday School kids in the 50's were also singing both those old ones plus these and other new ones.

Church Favourites

I am only going to list some which are *seldom* sung nowadays — at least not in our Presbyterian church here in Yakima. These are from our well-worn, old green, "New Canadian Hymnal": 1) Abide With Me; 2) Come Ye Disconsolate; 3) Encamped Along the Hills; 4) Face to Face; 5) Father Again in Jesus' Name We Meet; 6) From Greenland's Icy Mountains; 7) God Be With You Till We Meet Again; 8) He Leadeth Me; 9) I Am a Stranger Here; 10) I Am Trusting Thee; 11) I Must Needs Go Home; 12) I Need Thee Every Hour; 13) In the Hour of Trial; 14) I Think When I Read that Sweet Story of Old; 15) Jesus Calls Us O'er the Tumult; 16) Jesus is Tenderly Calling; 17) Jesus, Keep Me Near the Cross; 18) Jesus Savior Pilot Me; 19) Lord, Jesus, I Long to Be Perfectly Whole; 20) Must Jesus Bear the Cross Alone?; 21) My Hope is Built on Nothing Less; 22) Oh Happy Day; 23) Oh Jesus I Have Promised; 24) O Jesus, Thou Art Standing; 25) Out of My Bondage; 26) Pass Me Not, O Gentle Savior; 27) Rescue the Perishing; 28) Safe in the Arms of Jesus; 29) Softly and Tenderly; 30) Sowing in the Morning; 31) Take the Name of Jesus With You; 32) Take Time to Be Holy; 33) The Great Physician Now is Near; 34) 'Tis the Blessed Hour of Prayer; 35) What a Fellowship; 36) When Peace Like a River; 37) Who is On the Lord's Side?; 38) Whosoever Heareth; 39) Why Do You Wait Dear Brother?; 40) Work for the Night is Coming; 41) Yield Not to Temptation; 42) You May Have the Joy Bells Ringing in Your Heart. Again I say I'll bet many of you can sing most of these old hymns and *all* the verses.

I have quite a collection of hymn books, but a couple of things are hard to understand — why so *many* hymns can be found in practically *every* one, while others you can't find at all. Sometimes it is possible to detect the doctrinal stand; the style of worship or the racial/national background of the church which put out the hymnal — by either what *is in* or what is *left out*. For example, there was not a single Negro spiritual in our Canadian hymnal! The only place we found these were in secular song books. Some examples: 1) Go Down Moses; 2) I Ain't Goin' Study War No More; 3) Swing Low, Sweet Chariot.

On the other hand, whenever and wherever there was community singing, or as we used to call it, a sing-song, part of the time would be devoted to hymns everyone knew, no matter what church they belonged to. Thus, in *secular* song books there was quite a variety of *sacred* songs. I just checked one, "The Golden Book of Favorite Songs", ©1915, 1923, 1946 and found no less than 23 in this category.

A Couple of Anecdotes

Bill Busch gave me an interesting description of one church service, but for now I will just excerpt an anecdote — as grown-ups were squeezed into desks meant for children. He and Dad were sitting together — both singing in fine voice with mouths wide open when — a fly flew in Bill's. His gasp of horror made him swallow the fly! He left in hasty retreat in his state of shock, with Dad having a hard time to squelch his urge to laugh out loud.

Here is another anecdote — this one involving another pair in one desk — Wilma and I. In the Dust Bowl years it was the duty of whoever got there first to dust *everything*. But this time somehow, the teacher's chair (that is the minister's for a church service) had been missed. When he got up to write the hymn numbers on the blackboard, there was a big "heart" of dust on the seat of his pants. It struck Wilma and I funny. What agony trying *not* to burst out laughing!

But humor aside now, a service in those days was similar in most mainline Protestant churches — a solemn reverent time. Ministers in training were even *discouraged* from putting personal stories in their sermon and there was *no clapping* at *any time*. Ministers were always addressed as Rev.________. We wouldn't even *know* their first names! How different it is now with everyone on a first name basis! Other changes too would never have been dreamed of back then. No woman would be in church *without hat* and *gloves* nor any man *not* in a *suit,* and the minister *always* wore his *clerical* collar.

An Easter Service

In the 30's Quimper had a Young People's Group which often was involved with the service. Madge made notes on a service in 1932. She will tell of it here:

"The Special Easter Service held in the Quimper school house last Sunday was a splendid success. The beautiful flowers created a happy Easter atmosphere and the many people present were delighted with the service which was carried out by willing Sunday School pupils and members of the community.

First on the program came Mrs. C.B. McCoy's class of girls with Easter exercises and flowers; then the little tots of Miss Roger's class (note the formal names) each holding an Easter lily (crepe paper ones, no doubt), brought a glad message. Mr. Bert Cross's class of boys after singing 'At Easter Time' received hearty approval from Rev. Martin with these words 'It was good to hear you boys singing.' Then Miss Mary Donald's class, first the girls, then the boys, brought tidings of joy in their Easter recitations. The young ladies of Miss Mary Kelman's class very ably rendered 'I Know That My Redeemer Lives' followed by a recital of the 28th Chapter of Matthew by Bessie Donald and Wilma McCoy. Rev. Martin spoke on 'The Message of Easter' and his words gave inspiration to all. A duet entitled 'In the Garden' was sung by Mrs. E. Robins and Mr. J. H. McConville. Then came the quartet — Miss Mary McConville, Mrs. E. Robins, Mr. B. Cross and Mr. E. Robins, singing 'Calvary.'

The whole program was very effectively arranged and those taking part are to be complimented. Much credit is also due to the superintendent, Mr. Ed McCullough, the accompanists, Mary and Robert McConville, and the teachers whose cooperation and supervision played a great part in the success of the event."

What Church Do You Belong To?

Most of us would like to believe that we are of a certain faith — in Quimper either R.C. or Protestant, and, if Protestant, of a particular denomination — prior to 1925 that is, through *conscious choice*. But more likely it is actually because of *who* had won *certain wars* on the continent of *Europe*, or whether a certain monarch was Protestant or Catholic. This was especially true in England. Upon ascension to the throne each monarch would send out a decree that everyone would *have* to adhere to *their* belief — Protestant or Catholic. What *confusion* for everyone in their realm! Because of this, *they* pretty much determined whether *you*, today are Protestant or Catholic. The persecution that took place with these switch-overs often led to migrations of peoples, first *within* Europe and later to the New World. But this didn't always settle the problems of those who refused to conform, because their strong beliefs often led to a repeat of persecutions in their new location. Thus, in countries that over many years became almost totally Protestant or Catholic, there would remain pockets of committed believers of the other faith. So we had the Huguenots in France, and Catholics in Holland and Scotland. Is this perhaps too simplified an explanation of why Quimper had a Dutch and a Scotch R.C family? Those from down East or the States came from places where there were enough of their denomination to have their own church — thus arriving in Quimper as Baptists, Presbyterians, Methodists, or Congregationalists. Still others didn't have a strong background in any denomination and were open to most any church affiliation. There were no Pentecostals, Eastern Orthodox or Jews in Quimper.

Births and Baptisms

Because customs and practices for births, are so much a part of religious beliefs, it seems appropriate to give some details about these events in Quimper, but sometimes from an outsider's point of view.

In the homesteading days almost all babies were born at home, with the aid of a midwife probably, but it is likely that many took place without even this much assistance. Young fathers sometimes had to put their veterinary experience to work. But, alone, or with help and comfort from another, women would go through childbirth without the aid of anesthetic.

In "Learning from the Indians" written in 1908 by **Wharton James**, an Englishman, who came to America in hopes of recovering his health and who spent many years living with Indians of various tribes, he tells us of birthing by Indian women. Most of them, he said, had a much easier time of it than white women. He attributed this to a number of things — their comfortable non-restrictive clothing, their outdoor life style and a general, healthy, knowledgeable attitude towards sex, as given them by their mothers. As one who had studied medicine (he didn't say he was a doctor), he said he was privileged as few white men were, to attend Indian women in labour and in giving birth. They could, if on a march, give birth and rejoin the group in a short time. They would even give themselves and their new baby a bath in a cold clear stream. He came to believe that white people, by wearing too much clothing and living in closed up overheated houses, inhibited the body's natural ability to regulate itself. He soundly condemned their usual diet also, with so much refined, overcooked foods. Nevertheless, as I read what seemed to me some rather extreme positions on achieving and maintaining good health, I couldn't help but agree with many of his conclusions. For births of those of us now in our 70's and 80's, pioneer women seldom had the "luxury" of a few days bed rest. Then came the era of medical authorities believing a woman needed a *lengthy* stay in bed after childbirth, and along with this, freedom from the pain of actual birth with as much anesthetic as was needed to accomplish this! Added to this was the belief that a *formula* was just as good, if not better for the baby than *mother's milk*. And at this time, a father had *no* part to play at all except to rush his wife to the hospital. What a contrast to *our children's* experience, with classes for parents-to-be and even other siblings; fathers going through the whole experience *with* their wives and a new mother being *expected to nurse* her baby — even if she goes back to work shortly afterwards — all of these dramatic changes in *one* lifetime!

As I read this book written before I was born and the hygiene text book we had in school, plus, any number of modern articles, I was struck with a *common thread* throughout. In spite of all the twists and turns over the years, health is promoted for the most part, by wearing sensible, comfortable clothing, getting lots of fresh air and exercise, eating a simple varied diet, and avoiding those things plain common sense tells us are not good for us. Perhaps it can be summed up by saying we all have trouble balancing what we *like* to do with what we *ought* to do. Nevertheless, we must be doing *something* right. Is it proof of the pudding that the life span has increased tremendously in so short a time, and that some so called alternative medicines are coming into their own? We have been pretty arrogant in believing we knew best and that native peoples were simply ignorant and superstitious. *Finally*, we are learning that we *can learn* from each other if only we have an open mind.

Because so many babies were born at home, many Protestant baptisms took place in homes also when a young minister would be travelling about. However, he was not apt to call in the winter, so many little ones would be six months old or more when baptized.

As there has been such radical changes in medicine, so has their been in child raising, and again, it seems we go from one extreme to the other — *severe authority*, and *harsh punishment* when rules were broken, to the opposite of *too much leniency* and *lack of behavioral* standards. Now, however, the old pendulum swing theory seems to be operating, as most people are coming to realize the value of a *two parent home*, *wanted* children, *time together in the family*, a *healthful diet*, *outdoor exercise*, and most important, *having spiritual roots*. Though in the absence of some or even all of these advantages, some will achieve what most would call a successful life, having them gives a higher chance of it happening.

Children Learn Through Experience

(Many of these mottoes are not original, while others are)

If children live with criticism, they learn to condemn.
If children live with hostility, they learn to fight.
If children live with ridicule, they learn to be shy.
If children live with shame, they learn to feel guilty.
If children live with tolerance, they learn to be patient.
If children live with encouragement, they learn to be confident.
If children live with praise, they learn to appreciate.
If children live with quarrelling, they learn to quarrel.
If children live with security, they learn to have faith.
If children live with approval, they learn to like themselves.
If children live with acceptance, they learn to love.
If children live with friends, they learn to be friendly.

If children live with fairness, they learn to be fair.
If children live with two parents, they learn to parent.
If children live with laughter, they learn to laugh.
If children live with gratitude, they learn to say thanks.
If children live with gentleness, they learn to be gentle.
If children live with loyalty, they learn to be loyal.
If children live with listeners, they learn to listen.
If children live with kindness, they learn to be kind.
If children live with trustworthiness, they learn to trust.
If children live with foul language, they learn to use profanity.

If children have Christian parents, they will probably become Christians, too. Remember — "How the twig is bent so grows the tree."

But children do grow up. When Jesus said we were to become like little children in order to enter the kingdom of God, was He not thinking of just the above *positive childlike* characteristics we hope they are acquiring by our *example?* And where we fail as parents in any area, we hope and pray that others will supply the better input.

Now let us turn our thoughts back to Quimper. Most of our generation was parented by those with high standards, which was reflected in a high percentage of we, their children, who respected their elders and people in authority; who did well in school and later at work, and who kept their marriages together rather than give in to divorce.

The Quimper Fellowship Club

As an important part in the life of Quimper's young people in the 30's, more should be said about this lively, happy group, in spite of it being the decade of the Great Depression. I don't know if there were national headquarters and guidelines for such organizations, but in going through some old boxes back on the farm, I came across the book "Freedom in the Modern World", by **John MacMurray** with the subtitle "Broadcast Talks on Modern Problems". As I glanced through it, I saw there the background for many of the things we did in our regular meetings — the Bible studies, program ideas, topics chosen for speeches and debates, and so on. In the final chapter, the author sums up his view that *"true freedom* is based on a capacity for *friendship* which in turn can only operate if we are free to *do* and *feel* what is worthwhile."

To those who were misinterpreting his talks, he asked that they read the New Testament carefully for "what Jesus or even St. Paul was teaching on Christianity."

Regular meetings were generally in serious vein, as evidenced by more of Madge's notes:

"One formal debate was 'Resolved that Foreign Missions are more important than Home Missions.' The negative side was upheld by

Mary Donald and Ken Robins, while Robert McConville and Dorothy Claydon took the affirmative side. Judges were Miss Rogers, Stanley Taylor and Frank Adshead. They decided for the affirmative by a narrow margin."

On another evening the topic was *Citizenship* and again we are looking at notes Madge kept:

"The singing of 'O Canada' opened the program. After the business, Walter McConville gave a talk on Public Speaking and a discussion followed. Topics for fifteen three-minute speeches were then handed out. Each speaker was to be judged *secretly* by all the others and then *confidentially* told later their strong or weak points. It worked out fine, most being quite pleasantly surprised by their own ability to speak well. After the speeches, Miss Rogers conducted a character test as suggested by 'The Pathfinder', their official magazine. A hymn closed the meeting."

Here are a few tidbits from minutes of the Quimper Fellowship Club, 1935-1937. Names of those participating in these meetings were: (not in any order — just as they showed up in the minutes) Bessie, Andy, Frank, Elmer, Alice Mc., Ethel, Lawrence, Mary K., Louis, Alice B., Mary Mc., Alma, Minnie, Mr. Foss, Ed, Wilma, Julienne, Gordon, Ken M., Stuart, Nelson, Alex, Camille, Madge, John, Arnold, Vernon, Jim Mc., Walter, Kit, Mrs. E. Cross, Roland, Charlie, Jim McC.

Much of the business at the meetings was in regard to ball tournaments, trips to Lake Pelletier and refreshment booths. There was discussion on who to invite as participating teams, who would be chaperones for camp at the Lake, which orchestras would play for the dances and so on. It was interesting to note that even though it was a *Quimper* club, names indicate that quite a few from nearby districts were on the roll and taking an active part. All meetings began and ended with some patriotic song.

A big sports day at McCoys.

It was customary, then as now, to give better financial support to male athletics than female, apparently with no questioning back then. Winners in boy's games were: $5.00 first, and $3.00 second, and for the girls — $3.00 for first and $1.00 second.

Ones who liked art were the appointees for making posters — Alma, Ethel and I.

There must have been an organizational meeting sometime prior to June 1, 1935, but minutes, if taken are, apparently lost. It was puzzling, too, why there was very little mention of Glenvern Hall. Apparently there was no official meeting for dissolution of the club. The last minutes were for June 7, 1938.

They didn't seem to have any *regular* meetings either, nor terms of office. There was no mention of *who* called for a meeting and they just appointed a secretary on the spot. But it would appear that in spite of such a loose organization, it served its purpose for the short time it existed and as quickly faded into history, perhaps because farewells were too frequent and sad. A small collection would be made for a little gift and in a circle with hands crossed and pumping up and down in traditional manner, everyone would sing, "For She's (I don't remember a similar send-off for a boy going away) a Jolly Good Fellow" and "Auld Lang Syne."

Most of us girls were off to Normal School, business college or nurse's training. As this trend accelerated, it wasn't long before *more had left* than *remained* and I'm sure the heart of community life had gone with them, never to be again. After the war, followed by the closing of rural schools, all social life went into the towns. Even families discontinued visits to each other's homes for the most part, so that now rural folks may not even know one another — almost like city folks who live next door or on the same street, and don't even know one another even by sight. I often wonder if this aspect of life today will ever change. Once in a while I catch a glimmer of hope when I read of city folks going to live *on* farms (but not to farm), and of some cities abandoning the large consolidated schools in favor of smaller ones in self-contained neighborhoods. Even though cars and good roads enable people to live their lives in a very large area for work, church, education, and recreation, there are a number of things working against this — traffic jams, huge use of gas, and the loss of neighbors helping to raise children.

Secret or Exclusive Groups

We would like to think that something as out of line and bigoted as the Klu Klux Klan never stretched its ugly tentacles into Quimper, but, though no meetings were ever held in the school house, there were some in Aneroid. **Aylmer Boulter** and **Earl Cross** were singled out for credit in exposing this organization for what it was. It is very troubling to see how misunderstandings and feelings of injustice can so quickly be fanned into flames of hatred. We must all be very grateful it was defused before violence broke out. The would-be instigator from the U.S., a **Mr. Hawkins**, was deported as soon as his true colours were brought to light.

Personally, I have never believed in any *secret* organizations as by their very nature, they are often looked upon with suspicion by those on the outside. Added to this, women are relegated to a *secondary* status in an auxiliary, and in lodges, they can only come in on a man's coat tails — a very demeaning aspect, in my opinion.

Again there were religiously oriented divisions — the **Catholics** having their **Knights of Columbus** and **Protestants** their **Masons**.

Quimper's Ladies Aid. Though not secret, there has been trouble in more recent years over traditional *all men* or *all women, all boys,* or *all girls* organizations. Integration may have some good points, but there are negatives too, especially for social clubs. At least this problem hadn't raised its head in Quimper when the women had their **Ladies Aid**. Nevertheless, some men did show up at the beginning and end of the meeting simply because many women at this time did not drive a car. It took one more generation down the line for as many women to drive as men.

Oh, I must tell you of a **Ladies Aid** at our place. Custom was that the hostess would provide the tea and coffee and two other ladies the cake or cookies. To Mom's consternation *nothing* to eat showed up. Luckily, she had her own fruit cake, so she cut it up and served it as if nothing were amiss. There were some embarrassed apologies as soon as it came out just who had forgotten the goodies — and high praise for the delicious fruit cake.

Ladies Aid about 1925.

Special Days

As in many rural charges — the minister resided in town and had, as a rule, three schoolhouse churches to serve. We only had summer-time services and then only every other week. But the Sunday School operated every week, spring to fall. Once a year we had what was called **Rally Day** when the rural Sunday School classes would prepare special singing for the "big" church in Aneroid.

One such day in the Aneroid church when I was about eleven, I was playing the piano for Quimper kids to sing — "Onward Ever Upward to the Promised Land" and "You May Have the Joy Bells Ringing in Your Heart." Afterwards a big tall man, **Mr. Baker**, complimented me on my playing. To a little girl who sometimes *didn't make it* because of horrible nervousness, his words were wonderful and long remembered.

Everett Baker, the man with the fabulous memory, and his wife, Ruth.

This man also had a phenomenal memory for names and faces. As head of the Wheat Pool, he travelled all over Saskatchewan's wheat growing area and was in the **Medstead** area when I was teaching at Cater School some ten years later. To put his ability to an almost impossible test, **Mrs. Orr** said "I will have you both over to supper. I bet he will still remember you." He not only *did,* but *apologized* for *not recognizing* me *sooner* — as I was walking down the road still a little distance from the house! You read more of the Bakers elsewhere in this book.

Religious Trouble. You have read of the ill feelings in our district over the moving of the school, but I must now tell you of another time when there was disagreement, this time over religion.

In the nearby town of **Pambrun** a Bible School had been started. Those in training would scatter to hold meetings in rural schools like ours. In the early days, Baptists such as the Crosses, and probably some others too, had come to believe that dancing and card playing were *not* the evils they had been brought up to condemn. On the other hand, the Bible Students were now teaching that if you went forward at the invitation to be a follower of Christ, part of your commitment was *never* to *dance* or *play cards* again. Some of my girl friends — I don't remember any boys — made this promise at the beginning of the week's meetings. I thought then as now, that neither dancing nor card playing were sinful in themselves. It was the things that sometimes were *associated* with them that were wrong — fighting, drunkenness, gambling, and moral misbehaviour.

But these were *not* taking place at Quimper's whist drives and dance socials. The community was being polarized over these issues. However, it wasn't very long after the meetings were over, that ones who had gone forward apparently came to the conclusion that they were *not going back* on their commitment by taking part in these community events as before.

But at that time I did take a new and more positive viewpoint on a type of singing that is so popular in our contemporary church services today — that is choruses. I still sing one I learned from the Bible Students, "Wonderful, Wonderful Jesus is to Me." They brought some traditional type of hymns also that were new to us. One in particular I became very fond of and recall singing it often as I walked down the road to or from school — "I Walked One Day Along a Country Road" — how appropriate the title you will notice! I have never seen *this* hymn in any hymn book and I have a whole shelf full! (If any of you find it, will you please let me know, as I can't remember *all* the words.)

Most R.C. parents would have been pleased, I think, to have a son go into the priesthood or a daughter become a nun, but I do not know of any Quimper young ones who did, though some of the Lallier girls did take initial probationary training. The restrictions on family contact and strict rules of quietness were too much, perhaps, for fun loving Geraldine for one. I was permitted to visit her once at this time and suspected she was not going to go on much longer. I believe their trial commitment was for a year.

Protestants in Quimper did little more, it seems to me, than mention Lent, while our Catholic neighbors followed their church's very strict observances — no entertainments, no meat, and probably other rules in their homes. And they were *required* to *go to church* every Sunday and to make *regular confessions.* But I was surprised one day (I was boarding with this Catholic family for a short while right after Bud's mother died) when my landlady mentioned that she would like to go to so and so's wedding, but would have to *ask* Father_______ if she could.

Mrs. Koch gave me another surprise one day too. She was feeling sorry for Bud having just lost his mother, and his dad in the hospital, and said to me, "Why don't you persuade Buddy (his folks, and therefore the

Quimper Sunday School, 1924.

neighbors, called him 'Buddy') to smoke — it would at least be *some* company for him." You can be sure this was *not* advice I took!

Illustrating and Translating

Of all the types of illustrations in different Bibles, I've always been most fascinated by those of a Swiss lady, **Annie Valloton**, in the **Good News Bible**. In the New Testament alone there are nearly 400 of her drawings. They transcend nationality, language, and race in such a simple, yet meaningful way.

Though we learned our memory work from the old King James Version with its Elizabethan English, it is wonderful to have modern English translations. Most of our generation are comfortable with "thee, thou, thy" and the "eth" ending on words, and if leading corporate prayer, will use this kind of English, but this is not so with most younger ones.

Another problem for many our age is in *writing*. We were taught that not only *nouns*, but *pronouns* referring to deity were to be capitalized. But, if this rule were followed even in the Bible itself in *any* translation, it would look odd and would hinder the flow of the reading, would it not? So, once again, we are in trouble — where to capitalize and where not to. Again, some go to extremes — *deliberately* using small letters, even for proper names — as a way to catch our eye, we assume, or mixing up capital and small letters within words in hodge-podge fashion, on purpose at first, but now done quite unconsciously by many people.

English is lacking in some respects, also, though on the whole, willingness to *adopt into* the language words from many others makes it a rich and growing tongue. For example, how many times has a minister felt the need to explain which *kind* of *love* he is referring to — storge — affection; philia — friendship; eros — romantic love; or agape — divine love. One of my favorite tape albums is **C.S. Lewis**' "The Four Loves". I like these tapes, not only for content, but because they are the only preservation, it is believed, of this Englishman's voice. One of the best films of recent years, in my opinion, is "Shadowlands", which is fairly close in most respects to his real life. I don't think any theologian is more quoted from the pulpit than this man.

The United Church of Canada patterned its intern training after that of the Presbyterian Church and, as far as I know, this basic plan is still in operation. Two books widely spaced in time — "The Galloping Gospel", by **Angus MacLean** with setting 1910 to 1916 and "The Sinbuster of Smokey Burn" by **Hugh W. McKervill** with setting in the mid-fifties — tell fascinating first-hand experiences of these young men in training for the ministry, and both working in **Saskatchewan** for the most part. A mixture of high humor, pathos, adventures, despair and a cast of many unforgettable people fill their pages. The early ones were called "gospellers" and their circuits, of course, were covered on horseback. Therefore, the descriptions of the many horses they rode is one of the most intriguing facets of this book. The second takes place in the car era when these young men were called student ministers. They were a little older and had had some seminary training. The gospellers in the first story were: the narrator, **Angus MacLean** aged 17, and his beloved cousin, **Duncan**, aged 15. They had been recruited in the Maritimes by a **Dr. Carmichael** who "was from the prairie provinces where he superintended the services rendered by the most uncertain flock of fledgling preachers any church ever sponsored." It is nigh impossible to picture, even as we read their *first hand* experiences, of two *boys* doing this sort of thing. There are drawings by the artist-author, but of course, no photos as you see in the Sinbuster book. Do try to find these books for yourself. They will bring to life for you the spiritual aspects of our parents' homesteading days and its counterpart in our own generation.

Double Standards

Can there be a *double standard* — a higher one for leaders such as

Notre Dame church in Ponteix.

The United Church at Ponteix.

Aneroid's United Church. The manse on the right was the scene of Hilda and Jim's wedding.

ministers and teachers and a lower one for those they are ministering to or teaching? Some believe so, but I do not. There were, I observed, three examples of this in Quimper. Most older men in the district smoked, but if the *minister* did, that would have shocked everyone. And if *women* had smoked, that too, would have got the same, or even a worse, reaction. A third evidence was over dancing. I remember a young student minister one night came to a dance at Quimper and *danced*! Mouths fell open and eyebrows raised! Afterwards, when this breach of propriety was being discussed, I spoke my mind. "If it is wrong for *him* to dance, it's wrong for *us* too, and if there's *nothing* wrong in it, why are you condemning him?" At the same time I wonder about Catholics. I have seen priests smoke in a social setting, but I never saw a nun smoke and, though French-Canadians (and therefore usually Catholics) love to dance, I suspect they would not approve of their priests or nuns participating. Somehow, these examples point to double standards, yet most of us seem to accept them nonetheless. Other ways it shows up are in sexual mores. How often did we hear "Oh he was just sowing his wild oats", but a girl who stepped out of bounds was looked upon with different, more condemning eyes.

When we read in Gal. 3:28 in the Bible, where it states "there is neither Jew nor Greek, slave nor free, male nor female for you are all one in Christ Jesus", doesn't this mean we are all on one moral code? And when the woman caught in adultery was brought before Jesus, didn't the man, though not brought also, get the same condemnation? But she was *there* to receive Jesus' forgiveness and told *not to repeat* this sin while the man, we are left in doubt about. Reading between the lines, when word came to him about what had happened, did he realize Jesus' words on this issue were meant for him also? And though there *should* be no double standard, James 3:11 cautions that those who become teachers will be more harshly judged if their life and words don't match up. It was, in fact, this very issue which prompted my first letter to the editor many years ago. On the front page of the local Sunday paper was a *large* picture of a male high school teacher being "honored" for his pipe-smoking "ability". I could hardly believe my eyes. This sort of thing when we're trying so hard to have young people *not* take up smoking? The bad influence is so much greater when one who is looked up to falls off the straight and narrow.

Sunday School here in First Presbyterian Church, Yakima, in the 50's and 60's was in many ways, I'm sure, very similar to Sunday Schools most anywhere. It was strong on memory work, especially with the younger ones. How delighted I was when we were supplied with an award book with pictures throughout of Jesus *smiling*. As one reads certain portions of scripture, it seems almost incongruous to try to match up an *unsmiling* Jesus to the story. Would children have flocked to such a man or would he have been a solemn person at a wedding? Translating the Bible into any language from the originals is very difficult. Word for word, even where possible, would be hopeless to the flow of reading, and yet how far can translators deviate and still be faithful to the meaning? And where can *sign language* give an added and beautiful expression to an oral reading? How many of you have seen Indians, as does our Yakama tribe, present the Lord's prayer in this fashion, and all dressed in their beautiful native dress? (Just recently the tribe changed the "i", as in this city's name, to an "a".)

I remember many years ago hearing that some African tribe considers the *liver* the seat of the emotions as we, erroneously of course, attribute feelings to the *heart*. Should one therefore for this tribe say "I love you with all my 'liver'"?

A number of years ago in a Bible study class the teacher illustrated the order of priorities in the Christian faith by drawing three concentric circles. The *inner circle* represented what most would say constitute the *basics* — Jesus, God's son, came into the world to be our Savior; He died on the cross and was resurrected on the third day; He ascended into heaven and will someday return to earth; He showed people how to live and promised believers eternal life in heaven. The *next circle* showed things churches have their differences over, but which are religious questions — the time or mode of baptism; forms of worship and mode and frequency of communion (generally set out in a statement of doctrine by each church). The *third or outer circle* represents what most people consider trivial differences, but which have sometimes caused church splits — how to furnish the church; what is correct in dress or food; what kinds of singing or what musical instruments are right or wrong, etc.

When I was in my teens, the theme of one radio program I liked so well was this:

You go to your church and I'll go to mine
But let's walk along together.
Our Father is rich in houses and lands
So let's walk along together.

Speaking of radio programs, two of my present favourites, "Haven of Rest" and "Morning Chapel Hour", have been on the air over 50 years.

Marriages

For most pioneers there was often no such thing as a formal time of engagement with a ring to seal the promise. Courtship was often by letter — sometimes exclusively so, as with Mom and Dad. Frequently the young man came alone to claim a homestead and his girl came a year or so later. Winnepeg was the scene of many weddings. Finding a minister nearer to their future home was not a certain thing and few would settle for a ceremony by a justice of the peace. In looking at old wedding pictures, brides and grooms of this era often wore dark clothes. In fact, wedding attire *had* to be *practical* for wear *after* that day! Then in the 20's, special distinctive dresses came into vogue, though a man just wore a good suit. Most of Quimper's homestead couples were married prior to the 20's, which explains why there were so many of us of school age at the same time, and in the 30's, few of our generation were yet old enough to get married. Coupled with the fact that economic disaster of the 30's usually prevented the establishment of a home and children, it wasn't until the 40's that Quimper again had many weddings. And again, wedding dresses had to revert to the kind which would be worn afterwards. Also, because of the war, many marriages took place down East as young people were going into war work there or entering the service. Many others postponed their wedding until after the war. For those who chose to get married just prior to or during the war, one economic fact was often a big consideration. A wife's allowance could be saved up to provide some ready money for their new home when he was a civilian again.

The kind of wedding so common today was coming into being in the latter 40's — a church wedding with the bride in a long white dress. The groom however, would still be in just his best suit — no

My home was the scene of two weddings — my cousin's' and my own.

A garden wedding, 1939.

A home wedding in December, 1945 — outside pictures in the cold and snow.

tuxedos yet. Some of us were in what we might call a transition period — able to choose a long white dress, but not being married in a church. Homes, the church manse, or a garden were often the setting.

Most of you will have heard of chivarees. These were a certainty in homestead days, but had almost petered out by the 30's. Mom, a new bride from England in 1916, did not know of this custom as for some reason, Dad had neglected to tell her. When all that noise burst forth right outside the door — banging, yelling and what not, Mom thought they were being attacked by Indians. A horrible experience at the start of her new life on the prairies, but fuel for many laughs later on.

During the Depression it was hard to come up with money for the simplest of weddings for those brave enough to launch out, and those having a shower for the bride-to-be had next to nothing to spend on gifts, so most were hand-made and involved very little outlay. Quimper women and teen girls got together on a gift for bride-to-be **Madge**. A scribbler was purchased for a dime or 15 cents. Alma's artistic talent was enlisted — she turned a black cover inside out and printed with gold oil paint "Quimper's Favourite Recipes" and across the top "The secret way to a man's heart is through his stomach." All the hand-written, signed recipes were then put into their right categories. It's really nostalgic to see so many familiar names and handwritings. At this time a favourite little artistic pastime was making monograms, so

In the 30's mock weddings were a common form of entertainment — probably tinged with sadness as most longed for the *real* thing.

A wedding in just one's best clothes.

A church wedding, but the reception and dance in the home.

beside their contributions, Alice and Alma Bjore made theirs.

Yes, Madge Rogers and Ed McCullough were married in 1934 on the proverbial shoestring. She had the $2.00 for the license and he got a new tie, but by the 90's, there were ten pumping oil wells on their place, with the mineral rights to go with them! They just missed their 60th anniversary when Ed died from cancer.

This may seem hard for young folks to believe, but I never attended a church wedding for any relatives or friends until after we came to live in **Yakima**. Therefore, I was in the dark on some customs at a big church wedding. This led to a very embarrassing moment. I was in **Regina** with Nellie for a few months prior to Bud being out of the service. A friend of hers was getting married, so I asked if she thought it would be OK if I went to the service. I was simply curious to see one. I was on my own as I entered the church because she was elsewhere with some task for the event. One of the ushers offered his arm and asked which side I wanted to sit on, the bride's or the groom's. I hadn't the foggiest idea of what was going on. I thought the guy was being, as we termed it then, "fresh", so I ignored him and went on my own to sit down. Later when I learned what a goof I'd made, my face was red, to say the least, and I imagined that usher telling about *that* "strange" (or worse) woman who had come to the wedding and didn't even know either bride or groom and had so rudely brushed off the arm he had offered her.

Births

During the 40's and 50's it was customary to send out birth announcements. They could be bought in packages at the store, but we who were fond of art liked to make our own. And for thank you's, they too were often hand done. Here are samples:

To let you know that I've
arrived,
And then to tell you, too,
I'm looking forward to
the day
I'm introduced to you.

Name: Carl David Stennard
Date: Jan. 28, 1958
Weight: 8 lbs. 15½ oz.
Parents: George & Mary Stennard

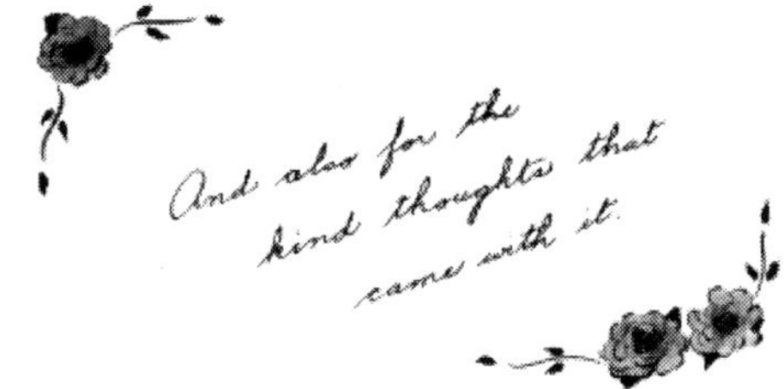

Deaths, Funerals and Cemeteries

Roman Catholics and Protestants would, when a death occurred, set aside their differences that applied in practically all other religious practices. Aneroid had no Catholic church or cemetery, but they would attend a funeral in the United Church. Ponteix had their *big* Catholic church and a small Protestant one, and there were side by side R.C. and Protestant cemeteries. I don't know just when it began to take place, but when there was to be a big Protestant funeral in Ponteix, the service might be held in the Catholic church. The funeral for **Dennis** was such a one. One more example of better ecumenical relations is a funeral service conducted jointly by both clergy. At one of these, such as that for **Doris**, there were some very interesting elements of this kind of cooperation, especially in regard to the instrumental music and the singing. How beautiful and appropriate it was when her granddaughter sang Doris' favourite hymn "My God and I."

Some people attach great importance to *where* one is buried — not only in *what* cemetery, but *with* whom. To Grandma this was of such concern that she went home to England to live her last years with her sister so she could be buried beside her husband.

In recent years there is much more leniency on what is done with the body after death. Physical considerations such as *how* the person died sometimes have to be taken into account also. For instance, when **Alma** died with polio, the great fear of it spreading determined what kind of a funeral would be held. Cremation is becoming more common now, as well as what will be done with the ashes.

In the early days there were no funeral homes or directors, so everything had to be taken care of by family, neighbors and friends. A service might be held in a home as was the case for Aunt Phoebe in 1942. Often there would only be the graveside service. Nowadays most funeral services for Quimper people would be almost identical to that in any little town or city. I do not know when the custom of memorials came into being, but it is, I think, a most appropriate way to both honour the one who has died and to show to the still-living, love and support in their loss. In early days, news of the death of a loved one, especially if from a great distance, perhaps overseas, usually came via telegram or a letter edged in black. (There was a song by this name.) It's hard for us to visualize today the great delay between a death and notice of it to far-away relatives. Often it might be years in the days of sailing vessels. A significant speed-up was made possible when in 1866 the first transantlantic submarine telegraph cable was laid from **Heart's Content in N.F.L.** to **Valentia, Ireland**. But it was still weeks, if not longer, when we were young.

Perhaps those who can comfort best are those *at hand* who themselves have lost close loved ones. No matter all the details of death itself, the funeral, and what is done with the body — surely all are of small importance to the hope of every Christian that we will someday be with our Savior and our loved ones where there will be no more weeping or pain.

Recently I attended the funeral of a friend who lived to 101°. Here was her pattern for a long life:

Campfire Law

Worship God, Seek beauty,
Give service, Pursue knowledge,
Be trustworthy, Hold onto health,
Glorify work, Be happy
— The law of my life

Irene Jenkins

Ponteix Cemetery Entrance

People should make out a will — but it isn't wise to leave it to the last minute, as did this man, and find one's self doing it in a tragic setting: **George Harris**, a Saskatchewan farmer, had had his tractor roll backwards over him. He was pinned and bleeding to death. As he died, with his penknife, he scratched on the tractor fender, "In case I don't get out of this mess, I leave all to the wife." This will stood up in court and, fender and all, is on file in the District of Kerrobert Surrogate Court.

Words of Comfort for the Bereaved

It's all right to limp a little
Just keep walking and stand tall
All improvement comes with practice
Never be afraid to fall

No one says, "You must be perfect."
Be yourself what'er you do
And enjoy each step you journey
Live the life you travel through

Love the people that you meet there
Let them love you back again
Share your sunshine, warmth
and laughter —
Lighten up their private pain.

Give your best — but as you give it
Take some pride in what you do
Love yourself and share with others
And their best will come to you.

Hold your faith, as you go, gently
Faith in God, in yourself too —
And He'll shed light on your pathway
He'll take your hand and walk with you.

Jeanie

Jeanie Zink is a Yakima resident. Her recovery from very serious mental illness is truly a miracle. Her prayer poems are loved by many, as is she herself. At present she is caring for her 97 year old mother. Reprinted with permission.

Crossing the Bar

Sunset and evening star
And one clear call for me,
And may there be no moaning
of the bar,
When I put out to sea.

But such a tide as moving
seems asleep,
Too full for sound and foam,
When that which drew from out
the boundless deep
Turns again home.

Twilight and evening bell,
And after that the dark!
And may there be no sadness
of farewell,
When I embark;

For tho' from out our bourne of
time and place
The flood may bear me far,
I hope to see my Pilot face to face
When I have crossed the bar.

This lovely poem by Alfred Lord Tennyson has been a comfort to many at the death of a loved one, and very often it is sung. Ref. Isa. 43:2.

In Loving Memory

We watched you fade away
You suffered much in silence
You fought so hard to stay
You faced your task with courage
But still you kept on fighting
Until the very end.
God saw you were getting tired
When a cure was not to be
So He closed His arms around you,
And whispered: "Come with Me."

In Loving Memory of Doris McConville

The Twenty-Third Psalm

The Lord is my Shepherd: I shall not want.
He maketh me to lie down in green pastures
He leadeth me beside the still waters
He restoreth my soul: He leadeth me in the
paths of righteousness for his name's sake.
Yea, though I walk through the valley of the
shadow of death, I will fear no evil:
for thou art with me: thy rod and
thy staff they comfort me.
Thou preparest a table before me in the
presence of mine enemies:
thou anointest my head with oil
my cup runneth over.
Surely goodness and mercy shall follow
me all the days of my life: and I will
dwell in the house of the Lord for ever.

These words have been set to many different tunes, *crimond* probably being the best known.

Did you know that it was in **Prince Albert** in our own province that a worldwide outreach of the gospel was begun in 1946 by **Jack McCallister**? It began as "World Literature Crusade", but is now called "Every Home for Christ" with **Jack Eastman** as its president. Their stated aim and prayer is that by the turn of the century, country by country, every home will have handed to it in person at least one piece of Christian literature in their own language and which they may reproduce at will.

I think most of us get a very special thrill when we have the privilege of meeting famous people in person. In this category I am able to name the astronaut, **Bonnie Dunbar;** the "Each One Reach One" literary program founder, **Frank Laubach**; the Olympic gold and silver medalists, the **Mahre twins, Phil and Steve**; **Rochunga Pudaite**, who began the program "Bibles for the World"; **Rosalyn Carter**, who is working at having all children immunized by age two, **Bill Pearce**, who hosts one of my favourite radio programs "Nightsounds", and **Shanti Solomon**, who began the "Fellowship of the Least Coin".

Science and Faith

With argument we spent the night,
He for his science and its fact,
I for the faith which sheds a light
The least among us to attract.

He must be sure beyond the doubt,
Must hold the test tube in his hand,
And from his reckonings cast out
All that he fails to understand.

By reason only would he move,
By judgment cold and fact severe,
Discarding all he cannot prove,
Accepting naught that isn't clear.

Said I: "We never can agree,
And vainly here we now dispute;
Your science tells you 'tis the tree
Which bears the blossom and the fruit.

From **The Light of Faith,** Edgar Guest, ©1926

Bibliography

The Sinbuster of Smokey Burn, Hugh W. McKirvill, ©1993
The Christ of Every Road, E. Stanley Jones, ©1930
The Winds of God are Blowing, Bernard & Marjorie Palmer, ©1973
Points with Punch, by Dennis Fakes, ©1982
Surprised by Joy, C.S. Lewis, ©1955
The Power of Positive Thinking, Dr. Peale, ©1952
I Married You, Walter Trobisch, ©1971
Against the Night, Charles Colson, ©1989
Come Before Winter, Charles Swindoll, ©1985
A Shepherd Looks at Psalm 23, Phillip Keller, ©1970
Cameos, Women Fashioned by God, Helen Kooiman, ©1968

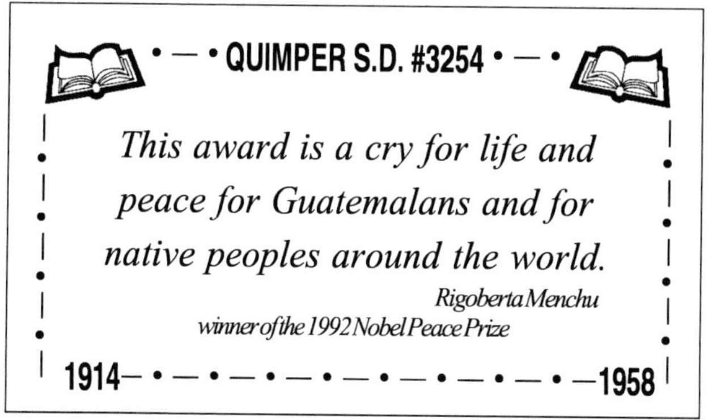

Justice is the harvest when peacemakers plant seeds of peace. — James 3:18

9 — War, Peace and Politics

Why Wars and Who Serves

All life is governed by thoughts, some good and some evil. We are born with *both* soon tugging at us. On the losing side are jealousy, anger, pride, covetousness, lying and a host of other negative thoughts; on the winning side are love, joy, peace, patience, kindness, humility, self-control, etc. Most of you will know these come from the New Testament. There are fuller lists in more than one place.

Thoughts become *words* and *words* lead to *actions* which *involve others.* Our genes, our upbringing, our culture, and our religious convictions are the main influences on our thoughts. Christians acknowledge their need of the Holy Spirit to control their thoughts, their tongues and their actions, and in this way, they may attain a certain degree of inner peace and the ability to live in peace and harmony with others. However, no matter how well we may do, it is often *others* who have *control* over *us,* for in Rom. 12:18 we read, "As much as is in our control we are to live at peace with others," implying this very problem. This brings into focus not only the personal aspects of peace, but what takes place on a national level. After all, nations are governed by those who are ruled by *their* own thoughts. Therefore *everything* regarding how, why, when and where *wars* are fought; the items in *peace treaties* and the regulations *after* the war; all stem from the *thoughts* of those in *political* power. Common people are led, manipulated or forced into the military or they are excused on certain grounds. Age, home responsibilities, certain occupations, health, citizenship, etc., are factors used in determining whether one enters the service or not. The number of soldiers required for the objective may sometimes lead to bending the rules. Volunteers in sufficient numbers, or even a professional army, may negate the necessity of conscription and, though I do not know how it is in other countries, Canada and the U.S. do have provisions for those whose conscience or religious beliefs preclude them having to serve. Some religious groups left the old country and settled in their new land specifically to get away from a military draft. In war time especially, such people are often shamed and ridiculed for their stand. They frequently serve in the medical corps. Some escape their homeland as individuals — probably changing their name and acquiring a new identity. As fugitives they would thus give up hopes of ever being reunited with their families. Still others, whether going into the service or not, anglicized their German names during both World Wars.

Issues of war and peace are so complex and emotionally laden that it is easy to see why the Bible says there will be wars and rumors of war till the end of time. However, in spite of this, people long *so* for peace, they set up organizations such as the League of Nations after WWI and the United Nations after WWII; they try to make just, workable

Mary showing off her granny square shawl — a gift from her boyfriend, Bud, over in Sicily.

Mary and Bud have a get -together in Vancouver, B.C. shortly before he gets out of the service. Cousins Roy and Evelyn are the other two.

peace treaties; they try to eradicate the root causes of war and so on. They even put on their rose colored glasses! The Great War (WWI) was even billed as "the war to end all wars," as it was believed that it was so horrible, the weaponry so terrible, and people so sick of war, that no nation in the future would dare to start another. In light of what has happened since, how hollow those words sound!

Right, Grandma, who came to live with us in 1922. In only six months she had lost two sons in the war and her grief-stricken husband.

Many attempts have been made to classify wars: defensive or offensive; just or unjust; secular or religious, and so on. In trying to clarify my own thinking, I have read many books — some of them: "A Preacher Looks at War", "Hanford and the Bomb", "The Underside of History", "Women in the Wake of War", etc., and I've read many personal stories of those who have endured the horrors of war. Even trying to understand Biblical teachings on war, sadly, I'm left with few firm convictions. If a country is *not* armed, they are easy prey for an aggressor; if they have *super* armed power, they may be tempted to use it. The sale of arms from one country to another is usually more of an economic issue than a moral one — sometimes armaments being sold to *both* sides by *one* supplier! Should a strong nation

My Uncle Henry and his girlfriend. He came to Canada in 1913, but decided to go back to England. His Dad greeted him with prophetic words "I'm so glad to see you, my boy, but I wish you hadn't come." He was killed in France in 1918, as was his younger brother, Bob, the same year.

come to the aid of a weaker one which is attacked? When should other nations intervene in civil wars? How far should the military go in ruining habitat and environment, directly or indirectly in waging war? What punishments should be meted out to individuals or nations when they are the aggressors? What help should be given the defeated so they won't start a rebellion because of an unjust treaty? On and on go the questions that seldom have clear answers.

The Peace Corp

One of the things I greatly admired **President Kennedy** for was the establishment of the Peace Corp. We usually think of these ambassadors as young people, but all ages can and do participate. A Yakima retired couple served in **Fiji**. What an interesting story they told us, especially **Nadine's**. Figians didn't quite know how to accept a woman being treated as her husband's equal. One of Bud's nephews, **Craig**, served in **Afghanistan** where he became very close friends with a young Muslim who eventually became like a foster son to his folks. **Yahyah** came from a large upper class family and most of them managed to get to the States. He had had to go back and serve in the military for two years and, as is a Muslim custom, his wife was chosen for him. They have two charming children. Bud and I were invited to their home in **Everett**. They showed us wonderful hospitality and the cuisine was different and delicious.

1995 was the peak year for this government sponsored organization — 1200 volunteers in 94 countries. Now budget cuts are requiring cut-backs in their numbers. How sad when, as their spokesman **Brendan Daly** said, "we are *wanted* by so many countries and there is so *much to do* yet."

From an Almanac

In a chapter titled "War" *some subheadings* in a 1975 issue were: **1)** Famous Battles in History — Land, Sea ad Air (490 B.C. to 1954); **2)** Weird Weapons of the American Military from the U.S. Camel Corps to the U.S.S. Dolphin (these are two of the most unique and fascinating accounts, but at times sad and poignant, of animals being used in the military); **3)** Roll Call: A Who's Who of Military Brass (one of whom was **T.E. Lawrence** of Arabia — the ones featured here were chosen for their *uniqueness* rather than *overall importance* in the military picture); **4)** Court Martials around the World; **5)** Small Incidents that Started Big Wars (I'll give a few details from this part at the end of this paragraph); **6)** An International Array of Spies (beginning with the Biblical account of eleven spies going to the land of Canaan), and last, **7)** An Aesop's fable — "The Wolf and the Lamb" illustrating "Any excuse will serve a tyrant."

In the "Small Incidents that Started Big Wars" I will note but six. As I read these accounts, I wondered what common soldiers *were told* to persuade them to *fight* in these wars! **1)** In 1152 **France** and **England** began a war that raged 301 years — all begun over a king who refused to regrow his *whiskers* to please his wife, so she divorced him, married an English king and the war was over his refusal to return her dowry of two provinces so she could give them to her new husband! **2)** Two states in **Italy** fought over the stealing of an *oaken bucket* and with its recovery, the restoration of honor. Thousands of lives were lost in the 12 year war. **3)** In 1704 an **English** woman's *spilling of a glass of water (?)* intentionally or accidentally on a **French** marquis was the excuse to fan the flame of deeper antagonisms and power plays. The five year struggle ended when the French king put his grandson on the **Spanish** throne. **4)** England and Spain in 1739 began an eight year war over a Spanish coast guardsman *cutting the ear off* English **Captain Robert Jenkins**. The insult served as an excuse for England to take over the **West Indies**. **5)** England was able to conquer **India** using as an excuse to put down a mutiny, their insistence that troops use a new rifle which needed pig fat (offensive to Moslems) and cow fat (offensive to Brahmans) to operate. **6)** At **Zanzibar** in 1896 an English admiral let his sailors disembark to watch a soccer game. The concentration of warships in the harbor angered the sultan, who declared war and sent his one battleship into action; the British leveled the palace and killed or injured 500 of his soldiers. The battleship opened fire. The British' big guns sank it. Zanzibar sued for peace. The war lasted 37 minutes, 23 seconds, the shortest war in world history.

I wonder how English servicemen felt about fighting in the *Opium War* in 1840 in **China**. England was attempting to make up financial losses in its balance of trade with China by pouring illegal opium into the country. The Chinese ordered all this opium destroyed and England declared war. Because of Britain's superior military power, China surrendered and was forced to give up Hong Kong and pay 21 million indemnity. After over 50 years of opium going in, the Chinese tried to get revenge in the *Boxer Rebellion*. (Boxers were a society whose name means *Righteousness and Harmony.*) Secretly 40,000 of them organized to throw foreigners out of their country, but **England**, the **U.S., Germany, Russia, France** and **Japan** sent in troops and defeated them. The indemnity they had to pay was in the millions, and China had to allow foreign legations and troops in Peking. Six decades later Premier Chou Ein-Lai was boasting of *finally getting even* by promoting opium use by American soldiers in Viet Nam.

The Opium War illustrates just how unfair issues of trade and profit-making coupled with military might can lead to terrible international relations and wars that last for many, many years, even a number of generations. And yet the principle of *profit* is what keeps economic wheels turning. Nations try to protect their own industries with tariffs, boycotts, sanctions, etc., while free trade is held up as an ideal. Workers try to assert their rights with unions and owners may have to go out of business if they can't make a profit. One turn of

Quimper's William McKenzie, killed in WWI. Percy Claydon wore his uniform for Armistice Day church services and I can remember seeing him winding those putees around his legs.

Canada mobilized so quickly when WWII was declared that old WWI uniforms were used for first recruits. Jim McConville.

events that seems to me so refreshing is when a manufacturing plant is run by its workers. In such cases, *cooperation* has to rule instead of the frequent tug-of-war between *sides*. Nevertheless, we read of company owners and *managers* that *do try* to be *fair,* and *workers* who do *honest* work for their *pay,* and as a result, this system can work well. How wonderful to read stories now and again (remember those in this book?) that are good illustrations of such goodwill and sense of fair play even in very large businesses.

Quimper and the Military

All of this about the military, politics and trade — how did they affect our little corner of the world — *Quimper* — and her neighboring districts? Three ways, among many, are most obvious. First, *everyone* was involved either directly or indirectly in both World Wars. Some gave their lives for their country (**William McKenzie, James Kelman, Jim McConville** and **Terance McCoy** from Quimper), and some suffered serious wounds in France (**Percy Claydon** and **Frank Morin**). **Joe Cyr** lost his hearing in the war. Ones who served but mustered out safely were **Earl Cross, Charlie Heaman, Maurice** and **Roland Dumont**, **Rob, Louis Bjore, Gordon Donald, Tom Symington,** and four **Bender brothers, Bill, Albert, Manuel** and **Fred.** Maurice won the Victory Medal for having given a warning that saved many lives.

This little boy, Terance, grew up to serve in Germany where he lost his life in 1962.

Roland Dumont, born 1920, served in the Canadian Air Force in Africa. He suffered a severe car accident in 1953 from which he took four years to recover, but at the hospital in Moose Jaw his nurse was his wife-to-be.

Ethel and Bill.

Alma and Rob.

Gertrude and Emile.

Alice and Micky.

Quimper brides with the grooms in uniform.

Ole Johnson (it was not known whether he became a Canadian citizen) served in the U.S. army and was in the Philippine War. There he contracted a fever which left him very vulnerable to the cold, so he wore woolen underwear even in the summer.

In the Legion Hall in Aneroid there are photos of all those who served in WWI and WWII from this area and outside at Ponteix is a plaque with such names, also.

Though I never read of any confirmation, I've often wondered if the 1918 or Spanish Flu was spread so far and wide in part by returning servicemen being carriers.

Even in peace time, our area had a military presence. Just outside of Quimper's borders lived homesteaders **Cleve Jacob** and **Gordon Howard.** Both had enlisted and fought in France and Belgium and both returned home safely to farm. In 1925 Capt. Howard organized a militia unit in Aneroid. At this time all units took summer training at **Camp Hughes** in Manitoba.

Even then there was truly a *horse artillery* and all officers, as well as senior NCO's, and some gunners were mounted. The 60th Battery was organized in 1927 and members came from a radius of up to 30 miles. A unit member got a day's pay for two drills of two hours each. When the Great Depression hit in 1929, this pay was often the only money these men saw. In 1931, because money was not available for training camps at the usual places, one was organized at **Lake Pelletier**. It was the only artillery unit in all of Canada to have a summer camp that year.

When war was declared in 1939, quick full mobilization took place. In a short time, three units were in a regiment and on their way to **Petawawa Camp** in Ontario. This was where Jim McConville was killed while in training. This **17th Field regiment** saw service in **England, Wales, Italy** and **Northwest Europe**.

Gordon Donald, when serving in England, was welcomed for many pleasant musical evenings into the home of Dad's sister, **Evelyn**, her friend **May** and May's two sons.

The unit was disbanded at the end of the War.

The Red Cross

Though it was invaded by many enemies throughout its history, since 1800, when its perpetual neutrality was guaranteed by its warring neighbors, **Switzerland** has been a small island of peace in the centre of Europe. Many important top level leaders have met in **Geneva** to work on peace treaties and it was here the **League of Nations** had its offices. Later, though it did not join the **United Nations**, believing such membership inconsistent with its status of permanent neutrality, Switzerland has remained prosperous and has for many years served as a haven for refugees from war and persecution. Its people have led many humanitarian and peace movements — the most notable being the Red Cross, founded by **Henri Dunant**. As a young man travelling in Italy in 1850, he had just witnessed the appalling aftermath of the battle of **Solferino** — dead and dying everywhere. He called for a world conference to form societies of volunteers to care for the wounded in war time and to prepare medical supplies and train nurses in peace time. But the military feared these nurses would be spies in war time. **Florence Nightingale** encountered just this in the **Crimean War** and the Germans executed **Edith Cavell** (this story is in the Canadian Reader Book Four) during WWI because she insisted on nursing the wounded of *both* sides. In Alberta, there is a mountain named in her honour. In 1949 the International Red Cross set up new rules to give protection to civilians in occupied nations, and certain rights to prisoners of wars.

We could clearly see the Red Cross in operation at the local level in Quimper as we had our Junior Red Cross in school and the Senior Red Cross for grown-ups, mainly for women, it seemed.

August, 1931, was the date chosen to mark the day the rest of Canada came to realize what was happening in the **Palliser Triangle**, for on this date the Canadian Red Cross launched an appeal for "food and clothing for 125,000 destitute farm families who had just suffered their third consecutive crop failure." Up till then, this gradually building disaster had gone mostly unreported — even in next door provinces of **Alberta** and **Manitoba**. However, this appeal and the tremendous response, especially in **Ontario**, "did more to remove West-East antagonism than anything that happened before or since." (Quotes from "Men Against the Desert" by **James Gray**.)

Nowadays both in war and peace time, one of the most successful services of the Red Cross is in finding missing persons or in transferring all sorts of personal information from hospital patients to their families, even across enemy lines. Prisoners of wars may also get messages to their families, and sometimes they even get food or other supplies in return. After a war, loans and free training are given to the disabled, and communities are helped in reconstruction. When any kind of disaster strikes — fire, flood, hurricane, volcanic eruption, etc. — a permanent emergency staff goes into immediate action. When not involved in some disaster, they can be found training others in all sorts of ways — nutrition classes; teaching swimming and rescue; first aid; blood donor assistance, and even recreation and entertainment services.

Junior Red Cross societies in school promote friendship and understanding on an international basis by exchanges of gift boxes, school art, music and correspondence. Sometimes they send supplies to other children who are victims of disaster, famine, political unrest and war.

I always thought it interesting that the Red Cross flag is the reverse coloring of the flag of Switzerland where this wonderful organization actually began. In our Junior Red Cross we always looked forward each year to new, different-colored buttons. Did any of you Quimperites save these?

Graphic War Scenes

On the radio just now, I'm listening to a dramatic presentation chapter by chapter of the life story of **Florence Nightingale**. The story in our reader called her "The Lady With the Lamp." It was due to her efforts, and those who joined her, that men, wounded and dying on a battlefield (**Crimea** at this time), were taken to field hospitals. For the most part, up until then, military heads and governments tried to ignore their misery, and its true nature was kept hidden, as nearly as possible, from the general public.

The first photos of actual warfare were taken in **Saskatchewan** during the Rebellion of 1885. There is an album of these pictures in a small museum at **Batouche**. They brought the horrors of war into common view, but not in nearly as graphic a way as the soon-to-be silent films, and then the talkies. In our youth, we saw war scenes at the theatre, and, though *real* and *recent*, unless we had some personal connections, they often failed to hit home.

Finally came T.V. and video, which has so saturated our minds and emotions of the here and now with the horrors, injustices and suffering caused by wars and crimes that we have lost normal reactions to them. We can find ourselves casually eating or doing ordinary work while people are being blown up, shot at or tortured on that screen. The latest news is of teens, or even children barely in school, committing crimes such as murder, and, seemingly feeling no remorse whatsoever for what they've done. How tragic and frightening for our society that this can be! Are we beyond making a turnaround? Surely not, because without hope, all is lost. Is it too simple to say that we must get back to valuing a traditional family and having technologies *under* control instead of *in* control? As I look around, I can see some wonderful things — more *traditional* families coming into being with fathers taking part in the raising of children, establishing essentials of honesty, financial soundness, commitments to partners and offspring, and, perhaps as important as anything, simply having fun together, *all participating,* that is, not just *spectating.*

Hopes of Peace

Though all too rare, how refreshing it is to hear or read of such *gestures of peace* as these: **1)** I heard it first from Mom — of that incident in WWI where soldiers from both sides climbed out of their trenches and, in No-Man's-Land, sang Christmas carols together. One wonders what might have taken place if their officers had *not* been able to "persuade" them to resume fighting. **2)** Though we are much more apt to read of how the League of Nations and then the United Nations have *failed* to keep peace, it's wonderful to get it somewhat in perspective by reading some of their *success* stories. The World Health Organization

Christ of the Andes

(WHO) and United Nations International Children's Fund (Unicef) have done some excellent work — e.g. the ending of smallpox and making great strides on other communicable diseases thus saving many children's lives. (It is so good to be able to support Unicef by buying such a variety of products from different countries.) **3)** Though some dreams have since been dashed, still many people are deliriously happy, I'm sure, over the **Berlin Wall** having come down. And what admiration we had for those brave students in **Tiananmen Square! 4) Argentina** and **Chile** were at war for many years until finally they both decided they'd had enough of it and erected that beacon of peace high up where it could be seen for great distances, "The Christ of the Andes". **5)** But we don't have to go *that* far to see another beautiful evidence of two countries, **Canada** and the **United States** after their 1812 war, promising never to go to war with each other again. Later, **Canada** and the U.S. built the **Peace Arch** at **Blaine**, Washington, right on the border. How we cherish the words on it "Children of a Common Mother" and "May these Gates Never Be Closed!" **6)** I'm sure there are a number of bridges over border rivers which people from either country may cross over freely, but I wonder if any have a more appropriate name than the **Ambassador Bridge** between **Detroit, Michigan** and **Windsor, Ontario**. **7)** Early this year (1996) the United Nations announced an unprecedented multibillion aid package for **Africa** "to improve education, health, government sanitation and peace building there." **8)** How delightful it is to

Peace Arch.

see and read nowadays in our papers of *international* crews on space ships! And not only these from different countries, but also of men and women working harmoniously together way up there. **9)** And what could be better to promote peace than student exchanges between countries?

Just as individuals can be taken to court, so can nations. Cases go to the *World Court* at the **Hague** in **Holland** which, under the United Nations, combined two previous international courts, one on *Arbitration* and the other on *International Justice.* Even *prior* to WWI there had been two world peace conferences which met at the Hague — in 1899 and 1907 — both called by the czar of **Russia**. Not *all* nations could agree on the two main objectives of these conferences — **1)** to formulate a plan for settling international disputes by arbitration instead of war; **2)** to get an agreement to reduce or limit national armaments. *None* of the great powers except the United States and Great Britain were willing to limit their armaments, and the German delegation refused to consider "any such scheme". Among the 13 "conventions" or agreements proposed were: **1)** defining the rights of neutral nations; **2)** outlawing such military tactics as naval bombardment of undefended towns and **3)** outlawing the use of poison gas and aerial bombs.

As we know from subsequent wars — WWI, WWII and all other wars after these — countries at war have not only *disregarded* these rules, but have added even more *horrible* weapons. It makes us wonder if *all* of the *26* countries at the first conference and almost *52* at the second, *had come* to a *unanimous agreement* at that time, could *both world wars* have been prevented?

And if the borders set up in the southern half of Africa and in central Europe, first by the colonial powers and then the victors of WWI and WWII, had been negotiated at the Hague, could the ghastly wars going on now in these areas have been averted?

As the 30's End

People at the local level were enjoying leisure time activities even during Dust Bowl years — probably even more than when farming was normal, strange as this seems. But also at the provincial levels, some things were happening in the realms of music and art. Reading was coming into its own both as cheap individual enjoyment, and as a source for people to try and figure out what had gone wrong with the world. **Edna Jacques'** and **Edgar Guest's** poems were being enjoyed and books by **Wallace Stegner, W.O. Mitchell, Paul Hiebert** and **E. A. McCourt** were being widely read. In 1928 **Barbara Barber** had organized a **Saskatchewan Women's Art Association**. Schools of art and galleries were opening up and artists from outside of Canada were coming on the scene. The **Regina Conservatory of Music** was begun as was the **Saskatchewan Drama League**.

But toward the end of the decade, storm warnings from aborad were coming into Saskatchewan consciousness as **Germany, Italy** and **Spain**, and, in fact, all of Europe was becoming militarily involved. **Hitler** was rearming the Rhineland; Italy had conquered **Ethiopia**; **Japan** had invaded **China**; some Jewish refugees had already come to Saskatchewan and Canada was debating the sale of scrap metal to **Japan**. Democracies seemed paralyzed and impotent. The visit of British Royalty in May of 1939 gave some relief from the long Depression and the ominous news from abroad. They symbolized stability and the ideals of freedom and justice. People didn't realize just how soon they would be at war — only four months later on September 10th.

The Right to Vote

A whole history book could be written on this one topic: where wars have been fought to get such a right; on what grounds it has been denied to people; how those in power have construed to try and make it swing their way — gerrymandering (named for the Massachusetts politician in 1812 who so blatantly reapportioned his district in this way); and all the *methods* of actual voting, from voice, to raised hands to standing up — all the way to secret balloting — without which the *right* to vote would be of little real value.

It was interesting to note that February, 1916 ushered in that *special* day for Saskatchewan women. Here I must put in a personal note: Mom got the right to vote the same year she was married, but at election time, even if she didn't *really agree* with how Dad was going to vote, she would vote *his* way anyway, believing it was showing some sort of disloyalty to Dad to do otherwise! She would say, "Oh no, I can't kill his vote." So in reality, Mom chose *not* to exercise *her* vote while Dad actually had *two*! How sad after the hard won battle by the suffragettes! There are some interesting stories of this struggle in the books "Women of Achievement" and "...and Mighty Women, too."

Money

Because *money* plays such a tremendous part in all military and political dealings, I thought it would be interesting to look this word up in the encyclopedia. Here are a few tidbits from this source: **1) Moneta** was the name of a Roman Temple where in 269 B.C. silver coins were first made, and to distinguish them from copper coins, they were called *monetas*. Later of course, the name became *money* and took in all metal coins; while still later it meant all money, metal or paper; **2)** Early Spanish dollar coins were broken into 8 pieces — thus it took "2 bits" to make a quarter. **3)** In **Siberia,** up until the end of the 19th century, a solid block of tea was used as money; **4)** The saying "It's not worth a continental" originated at the time of the American Revolution when the **Continental Congress** issued so much paper money it "was not worth a continental"; **5)** In olden days, first aid for an injury was to apply a piece of paper soaked in some liquid such as vinegar or tobacco juice thinking them to have medicinal value. Remember the second verse of **Jack and Jill** — "Up Jack got and home did trot as fast as he could caper and went to bed to mend his head with vinegar and brown paper?" **6)** Shinplasters were paper money of so little value as to be worn in rough games to protect shins. (Did any of you save the *shinplaster* worth a quarter that was used a short time during the Depression?) **7)** Pin money was originally just the very small amount needed to buy pins. Later it was enlarged enough to buy many small personal necessities. Now the term can mean a small allowance by a husband for his wife.

Satisfying Our Curiosity

As you have no doubt noticed, I like to ferret out curious bits of knowledge not often found in general reading. So here are some related to war that I've run across recently in reference books, and have put in more or less chronological order: **1)** *Carrier pigeons* were used during the **Gallic Wars** to send messages from the front lines back to **Rome**; **2)** The *longest siege* in history is believed to be from 1648 to 1669 when **Candia** in **Greece** was besieged by the **Turks**; **3) France** in 1793 was the first modern country to revive the ancient Greek and Roman system of universal military *conscription*; **4) Gustavius Adolphus** of **Sweden** was the first military leader to supply his troops from *fixed bases,* thus eliminating the need to get such by pillaging and foraging; **5)** Wars are sometimes named for *how long* they lasted. The Hundred Years War is the longest so designated; **6)** During the American Revolution 40,000 to 60,000 **United Empire Loyalists** moved to Canada, forming the main population base of Ontario; **7) Acadians** deported from **Nova Scotia** in 1755 to **Louisiana** later came to be called **Cajuns**; **8) Russia** survived at terrible cost in both lives and property, two attempts to conquer it, first under **Napoleon** in 1912 and under **Hitler** in 1942-43. Both attempts so weakened the aggressors that they never recovered former military strength and they themselves were defeated not long afterwards; **9)** Up until WWI *guns would be silenced* at the end of a day of battle so both sides could get their dead and wounded off the battlefield. Later, *dogs*, with their keen senses, were used to locate such soldiers. They carried first aid kits which, if a soldier was not too badly wounded, he could use for himself; **10)** War dogs also stayed in the trenches with the men, serving as both *companions* and *rat destroyers*; **11)** The beginning of *summer fallowing* had an odd connection with war. In 1885 all farm horses had been conscripted to haul supplies for the army during the Riel Rebellion, and by the time they were released, it was too late to put in a crop. But they worked the land anyway and the next year, in spite of almost total crop failure on other land, the summer-fallowed fields produced a bountiful crop. Later tests by **Angus McKay**, the first superintendent of the Dominion Experimental Station in **Indian Head**, confirmed the value of this method for dry land farming and it was adopted all across the prairies. The downside, however, was that it was one of the decisive factors in the forming of the Dust Bowl; **12)** War is devastating to the environment, not only *directly* in war zones, but *indirectly* on huge areas far, far away. Because of the enormous demand for *lumber* during both World Wars, forests in both Canada and the U.S. were cut down far above their level of sustainability. Similarly the demand for *wheat* led to intense cropping on all agricultural land, including much marginal land which never should have come under cultivation; **13)** Most people believed the reason for *gas rationing* was to conserve gas for the war effort, but in reality it was to *prevent mileage on rubber tires*. **Japan** had cut off raw rubber supply lines and synthetic rubber was not yet into high enough production to meet Allied needs; **14)** The **Navajo tongue** is very, very difficult, so in WWII it was used for secret messages. The *code* was never broken by the Japanese. **15)** The Nazis had set up a heavy-water plant in **Norway** and there was great fear by the Allies that **Germany** was going to succeed in making and using the first atomic bomb. The task of destroying this plant in a very rugged, isolated, snow-bound area was assigned to a very select few of the **Norwegian Resistance Fighers**. The first attempt failed. The second succeeded, but the plant was back in operation in six months. The third succeeded also, but at the cost of sinking a ferry with many civilians aboard. After the defeat of Germany, it was learned that they were not nearly as close to having the bomb as had been believed; **16)** *Kamakazi* (suicide Japanese pilots) were considered very honorable when they volunteered to dive their bomb-laden planes onto the decks of enemy ships; **17) Eisenhower** said it was impossible to overestimate the aid to the Allied cause of the invention of the *"humvee"*, the vehicle that could travel on both land and water; **18)** Britain developed the modern battle tank using farm tractors as their prototype; **19)** The armistice *ending* WWI was signed in a railroad car; **20)** German zeppelin balloons were used in WWI for both observation and bombing; **21) Lawrence of Arabia**, an Allied hero of WWI but of mixed character qualities, refused all honors and decorations, changed his name twice and died in obscurity as an enlisted man; **22)** *Uranium* for the first atomic bomb came from **Great Bear Lake** in the **Northwest Territories**; **23)** Canada is the only United Nations member that has regular troops designated for peacekeeping and observation duties; **24)** Rain arrived at a crucial time once during WWII, when it put out some coastal forest fires which had been set with incendiary balloons by the Japanese; **25)** German prisoners of war were set to work as loggers and sawmill workers to help keep pace with the demand for lumber; **26)** When tractors were replacing horses on prairie farms, a huge problem was what to do with all the horses. Under the plan and operation of **L.B. Thompson** — a man who was said to be "the greatest one-man faith restorative that ever hit Western Canada" after the long, long despairing 30's — set up *horse meat canning factories*, which supplied thousands of tons of tinned meat to troops in **Europe**. (I wonder how many servicemen knew they were eating horse meat!) **27)** The **Maritimes** and **Newfoundland,** being closest to **Europe,** took on added importance in WWII. Ports became staging and supply centres for both Canada and the States. **Gander Field**, which opened in 1938, became a strategic command and refueling base, and for some time after the war, was a hub for commercial air service. However, when jets could fly longer distances, it would be bypassed; **28)** On the very northern tip of land on **Ungava Bay**, the Germans landed an automatic weather station in 1943. It transmitted data about 3 months and then lay silent and unidentified until 1981; **29)** A soft cover book by **Bruce Barton** titled "The Book Nobody Knows" (the Bible) was given to U.S. servicemen in WWII; (I do not know if Canadian servicemen got a similar book); **30)** An International Military Tribunal in 1945-46 sat at **Nuremberg** to try Nazi leaders for their crimes against humanity after 1939. Of the 22 tried for torture, deportation, persecution, murder, and mass extermination (such as the killing of 6 million Jews), 19 were found guilty, three were acquitted, 12 got the death sentence, three got life imprisonment, and four received lesser prison terms; **31)** On June 25, 1945, 46 nations with 300 delegates, after nine weeks of intensive work in **San Francisco**, completed the Charter of the United Nations. Its aim was "to save succeeding generations from the scourge of war"; **32) Gavrilo Princip**, the young assassin who killed the **Archduke Ferdinand** in **Sarajevo**, precipitated the first shots of WWI. He is "honoured" with a bridge named after him! What a choice!

Political Facts and Figures

In spite of more than 120,000 *Japanese-Americans* being stripped of their civil rights, reclassified as "enemy aliens" and placed in internment camps, their sons, went on to fight in both **Europe** and the **Pacific**. In Europe their units became the most decorated in U.S. history and their stories there have been well recognized. However, their Pacific service received little recognition, even though, according to **James Zumwalt**, they were ultimately credited with shortening the war by at least two years. They were especially valuable in decoding Japanese communications. At the end of the war, many stayed on in Japan to help make the transition to peace. Prejudice against orientals and blacks was so strong, they both had to serve in their own units — until **President Truman** ended this type of segregation.

In both WWI and WWII Canadians lost heavily in proportion to their population, but their prestige and power in the world had risen tremendously. Steel production had doubled, aluminum had increased sixfold, and new factories of every kind were in operation. The U.S. became respectful of Canada as an independent nation — not one tied to Britain's apron strings. Canada won the right to have Canadian regiments (WWI) under Canadian command — thanks to **Sir Sam Hughes,** who refused to follow **Lord Kitchener's** orders to split them up and incorporate them into British regiments. In hauty ignorance, his words, "they are, of course, without training and of very litle use to us as they are." Hughes replied that unless they could be under their own separate Canadian command, he doubted they would enlist, and he walked out.

In encyclopedias, history books, and many T.V. documentaries, there are many opportunities to learn details of all the many battles, leaders, political aspects, etc., of both WWI and WWII. For example, in my 50's set of Compton's, there are nearly nine full, three-column pages with just such information.

Trade

One of the most interesting games our children had was "The Seven Seas". Players had little cargo boats which travelled the oceans picking up and delivering products. Money values were given for each product, also, so many aspects of trade were being learned with the roll of the dice.

I loved the salt and flour maps we used to make in school. While still in wet relief form, we stuck on real products — coal, wood, grain, etc., and when dry we would water paint the political divisions, so if this was a world map, we had a working knowledge of the water routes for world trade and what was cargo.

The most primitive form of trade is no doubt bartering and though, of course, only practiced nowadays probably on a local one-to-one basis, it is still, in *actual* principle, one of the biggest factors in international trade today under the term "the balance of trade". Commodities for trade are called *bargaining chips*. Now add to the simple basic, the *needs* of would-be *consumers* and the *suppliers* of those needs, a multitude of fingers-in-the-pie others and factors — trade unions, co-ops, private and corporate ownerships, politics, nationalism, language and cultural differences, and on and on. So perhaps, instead of despair over what *isn't* working and *why,* perhaps we should be surprised that it works at all. Nevertheless, when needs and supplies get too far out of balance, one of the most potent causes of war is at hand.

One of my favourite types of literature is *biography — autobiography*, and for this chapter I want to wet your appetite to read some of these books. All of them are set in modern times and *all* tie together widely different locales — **South Africa, China, Holland, Sweden, Honduras, Russia, England** and the **British Columbia** coast and **Viet Nam**— *all* taking us into the intimate lives of but seven caught in the throes of *war* — and *all* giving us evidence of *miracles* that can take place when one has an unshakable *faith* in Christ.

1) The Little Woman

Gladys Aylward was a little English girl working as a domestic. When still a teenager, she made up her mind to become a missionary in **China**. Because she didn't "qualify" she got no help from mission boards. Her train trip across Eurasia; her adoption of Chinese dress and culture; prison reform; the Japanese attack; her escape over the mountains with a

Gladys Aylward.

hundred orphans; her work with mandarins in getting the custom of bound feet outlawed; the discontinuance of infanticide and concubinage, and many, many other details will keep your eyes glued to the printed page. Her story was put on film by 20th Century-Fox in 1958 under the title "The Inn of the Sixth Happiness." I hope I can see it someday.

2) The Hiding Place

No doubt many of you saw the film by the same name. **Corrie Ten Boom** tells the story of her life in **Holland**; the German occupation; her family sheltering Jews; being discovered; living in the concentration camp; deaths of her father and sister; her liberation and later missionary work all over the world. She also authored many books and died only a few years ago.

Mark Mathabane with Stan Smith at his graduation from Dowling College in 1983.

3) Kaffir Boy

Tennis champion **Mark Mathabane** of **South Africa** tells of his life under the horrors of apartheid; how he came to be helped by a few white South Africans; of his coming to the United States and of his dream of freedom for his fellow blacks to live in dignity in the land of their birth. Since this book was written, his dream has materialized, at least politically.

4) The Persecutor

Sergei Kourdakov's life span, 1951 to 1973, was similar to our Jim's 1955 to 1977, but oh how different were their lives — except for one all important similarity — they both died as truly committed Christians. Sergei was orphaned at 6; lived "a brutal existence in **Russia's** infamous state-run children's homes"; had outstanding leadership abilities and steadily climbed the ladder in communism, until in the naval academy, he was chosen to "terrorize and arrest Russian Christians". After more than 150 such raids, he gradually became sickened by the brutality and chose sea duty to get away from it. His ship was given permission to ride out a vicious storm inside western Canada's coastal waters. He jumped ship and fought a desperate battle for survival in the raging, freezing waters. Next morning he was found half naked, battered and unconscious, and rushed to a hospital. He spoke of his new-found faith as he enlisted aid for those he had once persecuted, and thanked them for "their unknowing contributions to his own changed life." His instant death from a gun shot was carried interna-

Sergei Kourdakov, who led attack raids for Russia's secret police, points to the place off British Columbia, Canada, where he escaped from a Russian naval ship to begin his search for the faith of those he once persecuted.

tionally as a *suicide*. An inquest called it an accident, but, because he had frequently said his life was in danger at all times, it is believed his death was an assassination.

5) For Those Tears

Though I have not seen it, a friend told me that **Nora Lam's** story is on film under the title "China Cry" and follows this autobiography very well. Nora was adopted by one of China's oldest and richest families; was educated in Christian schools and became a lawyer. She finally escaped from Red China to Hong Kong. She was in an unbelievably abusive marriage for many years. She came to California and then to Denver, where she was befriended by a family who gave her and her three children a home. As an evangelist, both in the United States and back in Taiwan, there were some incidents of the working of the Holy Spirit that made you think of many similar happenings in Acts. I heard her speak one time in Yakima and have an autographed copy of her book.

Nora and her mother.

6) Majken

In 1945 **Majken Broby**, a Swedish nurse, knelt and asked, "Lord Jesus, show me my calling." In a vision she saw "wringing hands, hollow eyes and cries for help." In answering her call, she brought hope to refugees from Communist terror all over Europe; then in the 60's, help to thirsty Muslims in North Africa, and in the 70's, to devastated flood victims in Honduras. One of my favourite radio programs, "The Haven of Rest", has raised money to help with her work.

7) There are a number of books written about or by those who suffered through long years as prisoners of war. One of the best I've read is "In the Presence of Mine Enemies." **Howard Rutledge** was shot down over **Vietnam** and was in a Hanoi prison for seven years. For five of those years his wife and four children did not know if he was alive or dead. Only his deep Christian faith enabled him to survive.

Seven hundred people, three hundred of them children, lived in this windowless bunker in **Braunschweig, Germany**, during the 1950s.

What Can We Do?

Are we really surprised at what our world is like today when we tie it to study of secular history and the Bible? Do we have any means to prevent it getting ever more worse as everything and everyone seems to be speeding up? We read and see on T.V. every day graphic pictures of war, poverty, starvation, disease, terrorism and abuse. The ever-increasing world population determines the exploitation of our natural resources along with the horrendous problem of what to do with the waste we generate each day.

Add to this awesome set of problems the hate and desire for revenge continually being passed on from one generation to the next and with these goes more injustice, fear and despair. What a gloomy picture!

But think of some bright spots — the ever-growing trend of recycling, the groups and individuals who are making real changes happen, either locally or on a higher level. Sometimes wise people of the past or present are being heeded, and few would deny that, as **Mahatma Ghandi** said, "To make war on war we must begin with the children."

At Expo '86 in the United Nations Pavilion, I had about five minutes to state my answer to "What one thing could be done to promote world peace?" My answer, "Have children's folk dance groups go to other countries to join hands with similar groups in line and circle dances. Language would be no barrier and the physical touching in love and friendship would make them less likely to shoot at each other as grown ups."

At the Peace Table

Who shall sit at the table, then, when the terms of peace are made —
The wisest men of the troubled lands in their silver and gold brocade?
Yes, they shall gather in solemn state to speak for each living race,
But who shall speak for the unseen dead that shall come to the council place?

Though you see them not and you hear them not, they shall sit at the table, too;
They shall throng to the room where the peace is made and know what it is you do;
The innocent dead from the sea shall rise to stand at the wise man's side,
And over his shoulder a boy shall look — a boy that was crucified.

You may guard the doors of the council hall with barriers strong and stout,
But the dead unbidden shall enter there and never you'll shut them out.
And the man that died in the open boat, and the babes that suffered worse,
Shall sit at the table when peace is made by the side of a martyred nurse.

You may see them not, but they'll all be there; when they speak you may fail to hear;
You may think that you're making your pacts alone, but their spirits will hover near;
And whatever the terms of the peace you make with the tyrant whose hands are red,
You must please not only the living here, but must satisfy your dead.

From **The Path to Home,** Edgar Guest, ©1919

Bibliography

For Those Tears, Nora Lam and Cliff Dudley, ©1972
Kaffir Boy, Mark Mathabane, ©1986
Majken, Carl Lawrence, ©1981
The Persecutor, Sergei Kourdakov, ©1973
A Preacher Looks at War, Daniel A. Polingr, ©1939-1943
Christian Attitudes Toward War and Peace, Roland Bainton, ©1960
Hanford and the Bomb, S.L. Sanger, ©1989
From Sea to Sea, Canada 1850 to 1910, W.G. Hardy, ©1959
Answers to Life's Problems, Billy Graham, ©1960
The Little Woman, Christine Hunter, ©1970
The Book of Women's Achievements, Joan & Kenneth Macksey, ©1975
. . . And Mighty Women Too, Grant MacEwan, ©1975
Tramp for the Lord, Jamie Burkingham, ©1974
In the Presence of Mine Enemies, Howard and Phyllis Rutledge, ©1973
Who Speaks for God, Charles Colson, ©1985

A number of hese authors have written other books, which I may have, so just ask if you are looking for a certain one. In fact, I have oodles of books on my shelves — so many in fact, that one day Bud said so seriously, "I think we're going to have to move out." I fell for his words with a worried "Why?", and he replied "Well, the books are taking over!" Even if I've borrowed a book from the library, I may go out and buy one of my own if I like it well enough, and that way I can star, underline, and make margin notes to my heart's content — and have copies to lend.

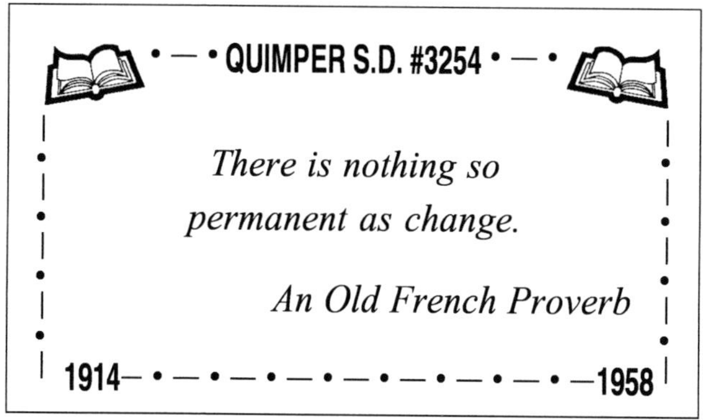

QUIMPER S.D. #3254
There is nothing so
permanent as change.
An Old French Proverb
1914
1958

May God, the source of hope, fill you with all joy and peace. — Rom. 15:13

10 — Making Connections — Then and Now

As with my ash book, things which reached me too late to get into the *right* chapter are here along with many other items which I simply couldn't make up my mind as I went along, just where to put them. There are also a number of other similarities in these two books — the name, the format, even the number of chapters and, I realize more and more, my style of writing. It makes me happy when I'm told that one can pick up my ash book — and I hope that will be true of my Quimper book, also — and read *any part* without having to make definite connections to what is *before* or *after*. When I was doing that first book, my hired help (none of us had written a book before nor had taken any special training to do so) and I usually conferred on *what would go in* or what would end up in the *waste paper basket.* This worked very well most of the time, in spite of the great amount of material we had to work with. But I must tell you of a couple of instances when things fell through the cracks. The first was in *not* getting in the story of how I chose that odd name for my book.

The second was about the **Galapagos Islands**. One night, while watching a T.V. program on volcanoes, I admit I was sitting there with a real smug feeling — thinking I'd covered *that* on these volcanic islands quite well. However, when I went to check out *just what* was *really* in my book, I was quickly deflated — there was *nothing* there! But now, *when,* not *if,* similar types of omissions occur in my Quimper book, I will have only myself to blame, as this is more of a solo effort.

Perhaps some of you may not know till you read it here that last year, the fifteenth anniversary of the giant eruption of **Mt. St. Helens,** I had a reprint done of my book. In the back I put a supplement and also had it made separately with a different picture and story on the back cover. This supplement gave me a second chance to tell why I had the word "Potpourri" in the title. By the way, have you ever looked up that word in a dictionary? It's a sort of *fancy* French word for the lowly English word *stew.* Well, with a stew, it usually doesn't matter in what order you add ingredients — so with a literary potpourri (by definition it needs only one tying ingredient — *ash* in my first book) it matters little in what order things go in. This time, I guess, the tying ingredient is the *era of rural schools* in Saskatchewan, Quimper in particular.

I had thought *that* word lent a *unique* quality to the titles of my books. Wrong again! Just the other day when I was reading about wonderful accomplishments of some Saskatchewan women, what should I read but this, "In 1895 **Kate Simpson Hayes** of Regina published her book, "Prairie Pot Pourri"! The only difference was in her using it as *two* words and mine is only *one* — this being the advice of a college professor here in Yakima way back in 1984. Now, at almost the last minute, I found out that still another book, "Passion and Pot-Pourri", was written by **Richard King** back in the 20's!

Language Differences

Until **Canada** became a dual language country, French-Canadians in **Quebec**, and often elsewhere too, chose *not* to learn English and the English chose *not* to learn French. It has been said that to learn another's language is one way to show love and concern for them. If this were also so as one *people* to *another*, perhaps French-Canadians and English, and all nationalities, in fact, in proximity to those of other tongues, might bridge their differences better if they were able to *talk* to each other more understandably.

Canadians, coast to coast, speak remarkably alike in English, all putting that "eh" on the end of many a sentence and giving the "ou" sound its own peculiar inflection. Americans, on the other hand, still speak a dialect of a certain *part* of their country — the South or New England for instance, or even of a certain *part* of a city such as Brooklyn.

If Canadians have *no* accent as some insist, how can they *lose* it? When I was first living in the States, people *knew* I'd come from

Canada, but nowadays my background is seldom spotted. But the English of both Canadians and Americans certainly isn't the English of England! And that small country even has its matching dialects for different parts — *Lancashire,* for intance. (That's what those folks are talking on "All Creatures Great and Small" or on the T.V.program we can't get in the States, but which is so popular in Canada, "Coronation Street" — How Mom and Dad enjoyed this program!) And Londoners talk Cockney and Devonshire folks have their own talk. **Mrs. Shaddock** was from **Devon** and we used to laugh at her peculiar way of using the objective for the subjective — for instance, "Her was a good girl." Though brought up by a Dad and Mom right from England, I truly believed that *they* had *no accent* — until I heard them with *ears* that had been at a distance awhile when I was away teaching. Isn't it peculiar how this can be? Here's a funny incidence to prove it. I called my Mother "Mom" — I thought — when a friend one day said "No you don't Mary, you call her 'Mum'." I denied it, but a few minutes later when "caught" in the act, so-to-speak, she made her point. Yes, I did say "Mum".

Canadians *and* Americans have a very strange utterance for confirmation, "huh huh", and an equally odd one for denial "uh uh", both of which are probably accompanied by the appropriate head movement. I guess the English don't do this, for when Mom first came to Canada she said, "If we have any kids they certainly aren't going to go round using those silly expressions!" Well, she lost *that* battle before it was fought! (These words *aren't* in Websters either!)

More than likely, "Our Mother" in place of "Grandmother" would fit most Quimper families:

PIONEER WOMAN

Grandmother, on a winter's day
Milked the cows and fed them hay,
Slopped the hogs, saddled the mule
And got the children off to school;
Did the washing, mopped the floors,
Washed the windows, and did some chores;
Cooked a dish of home dried fruit,
Pressed her husband's Sunday suit,
Swept the parlor, and made a bed,
Baked a dozen loaves of bread;
Split some firewood, and lugged in
Enough to fill the kitchen bin;
Cleaned the lamps and put in oil,
Stewed some apples she thought would spoil;
Cooked a supper that was delicious,
And afterwards washed up all the dishes;
Fed the cat and sprinkled the clothes,
Mended a basketful of hose;
Then opened the organ and began to play,
"When You Come to The End Of a Perfect Day."

— Anonymous

One of the most interesting studies, I believe, is the study of language. If *connections* between Latin and English had been made more clear (maybe they *were* clear, but *this* student had closed eyes and mind, I'm afraid), I'm sure I would have had a different attitude towards it. I hated Latin — nothing but stories about war, it seemed to me. My very good grade in it on Grade Nine finals I credited to learning its connections to English grammar and my making jingles out of those declensions, some of which I can still rhyme off! Because so many of our words are of Greek origin, why wasn't this also a subject we studied in school, I wonder?

Recently at church, I attended a class giving the basics of Greek — just to satisfy my curiosity. But though I hate to admit it, I never succeeded in getting even the alphabet to slip easily off my tongue! It's a good job I wasn't going to have a test on it!

Reunions

There are opportune times for reunions, whether it be for family, school classes, town or whatever, and sometimes if such opportunities *are not* acted upon, there is no repeat chance. I don't know how many of Quimper's families have had reunions, but I know the Claydon's did and, because of Doris' efforts, the Jim McConvilles did also, but ours wasn't strictly for family, as it included many others. Doris said, "Nowadays family stories are not being passed on to children as they should be, so *you three have* to write up your story. We did and how

RECENT GET-TOGETHERS

A few of the out-of-town guests.

The Claydon reunion in Ponteix.

Three Jim McConvilles and their spouses at the 50th of a McConville cousin, Ethel and her spouse, Bill.

Old friends meet in Yakima: Betty (Sutherland) Teeter of Guelph, Ontario, and Finis (Hulbert) Lepper of Vancouver, B.C., 1985.

Four McConville cousins enjoy being at a 50th in 1972 in Lethbridge.

Old Quimperites meet at Mildred Cross's apartment in Coburg, Ont. in 1987.

grateful we are to this wonderful lady who set all the wheels in motion for this job and all other parts of our wonderful celebration — the food, a hayride, singing, a quilt, and perhaps best of all, the continuous reminiscing — with lots of laughs, and we must admit, a few tears too, as we all sensed it was truly the end of an era, and we missed those who couldn't be there.

In 1980, when **Saskatchewan** was celebrating its Diamond Jubilee as a province, almost every little town got in touch with everyone far and wide inviting them to *come home* and, because at that time, many of the first generation of the original settlers were still in good enough health to travel and could come with their offspring, there was a wonderful response. Quite a few of these towns had, in the years following WWII, built huge quonsets that could be used in many ways — for hockey, curling or figure skating in winter and big entertainments and eating events the rest of the year. And there were some wonderful parades — many floats depicting either present life, or what it was like back then — sewing clubs, an orchestra, a square dance group, a wildlife exhibit, legion veterans, old fashioned dresses, replicas of schoolhouses, churches, hospitals (in Aneroid — the old Indianola sod school) the Mounted police, medical personnel, cars old and new (one old-looking-one was made from a kit), field implements — ancient and modern, horses and riders decked out in their finery, and so on. There were also events reminiscent of those old picnics and ball tournaments. All in all, a wonderful way to link the past and the present. If the celebration took place at just the right time, there might be a demonstration of what threshing was all about before the days of the combine.

Threshing

I didn't happen to get in on the threshing scene, but the more I thought about it, the more I began to believe that I'd sooner just keep my *memories* of how it *really* was rather than see a sort of small version, which could be more to teach younger ones a bit of history than to revive our own recollections. After all, there is no way a re-creation could recapture the excitement of the arrival of the threshers. In fact, I think *that* day rivaled what most thought of as the Biggest Day of the Year — (the title of one of John Charyk's books) the day of the Christmas concert.

Threshing Back Then

. . . meant long days of very hard work for the grown-ups, but Rob and I were just the right age to enjoy it. We still lived in the shack at ages 5 and 6 — younger — we would not be able to remember it, and older — we might have been given some work to do!

Let me now be 5 years old once again! It is nearing supper time. The threshers have just finished at a neighbor's and the first empty racks come thundering and rattling down the road with horses at the gallop. Somehow I think they must have had some sort of a bet on as to who would get there first, or maybe the first arrivals got the best accommodations for their horses, or themselves. Anyway, to this excited little girl, it only meant they'd *arrived* and would soon be in for supper. Just in case she hadn't heard the racket for herself, we had run like mad to the house with the exciting news "Mommy, Mommy, they'd coming down the road." Of course, preparations for their coming had been going on for days. A long table with benches (planks on logs) was set up in the dining room, the room lit, but not too brightly, by our pretty hanging coal oil lamp (it had gold chains to raise and lower it; and the shade had beautiful roses and crystal dangles all around.) Though I don't remember exactly where Rob and I were while the men ate, I'm sure we were following stern repeated instructions "Keep from underfoot." After eating, the men all went out to bed down for the night — on top of a few bundles on the ground or in the rack, in a granary or wherever. (Dumont's outfit didn't have a bunk or cook car.) Just outside the back door, the wash-up spot was reset for morning with clean pails of water, fresh towels and making sure there was enough soap. No wash cloths were used and certainly no provisions were ever made for bathing. Maybe they dumped pails of cold water on themselves at the pump — I don't know. The question never entered my head! Perhaps they just went the season with only hands, arms, face and neck getting washed and just wore their same clothes all the time. If so, the air indoors must have been a little "high", but again, though I then had a keen sense of smell (not like now when I've almost lost it), all I remember is the *smell* of all the *good food* heaped on big platters for those hungry men. Mom, of course, had help — usually a neighbor woman who had experience feeding such gangs. Her first time at it — in 1916, found her busy preparing bread for the table, cutting it in nice thin slices and buttering each piece and placing it neatly on a plate — until caught in the act, with quick instructions on a *different* way for threshers — just *thick* slices in *huge* quantities! In fact, for any food, the women had plates and bowls piled high *before* the men were called in to eat. Mom often spoke about once when she put a plate of pancakes on the table and the first guy slid the *whole lot* onto his plate! I think the crews at our house were all tea drinkers — at least I don't remember any coffee being made.

Threshing time was the only time we kids got tea to drink and, though I drink tea sometimes now, it has never had that *special* taste at any occasion since.

Mom's biggest concern after supper was over (my how "big" we felt sitting on the threshers' benches!) was to get us off to bed so they could set the table for breakfast and do whatever else they could for next day preparations. Also, the regular everyday jobs, both the *outside* chores — milking cows, feeding pigs and chickens, etc., and the *inside* ones, washing, ironing, churning, etc., couldn't be set aside while one had the threshers. As we think of the small houses of those days, one wonders how they ever managed. And if not tripping over each other, or kids underfoot, there was that ever lurking danger, the *trap door* to the dirt cellar. Somehow it always seemed to be placed in what appeared to be the worst spot possible — right in a traffic lane. In our shack (maybe in most all early houses — I don't remember) the lean-tos — kitchen and bedrooms usually — were one step down from the dining room and the trap door was in the kitchen right at the foot of this stair. Somehow I doubt that any family in such a house ever escaped having *someone* at *some time* fall down these cellar steps! In vignettes, you read of Mary Donald and a scar she was left with from just such a fall. But humor enters into all sorts of situations, it seems. I recall someone saying of a talkative person "All of a sudden there was a lull in the conversation." The talker had fallen down the cellar when someone had left the trap door open! In our big house we again had such an entrance to the cellar — now called the *basement*. However, it was in the shed and was only used as a secondary entrance, for taking potatoes, boxes of apples or other bulky things downstairs. The main entrance was via a regular door off the hallway by the kitchen, much safer, of course, being fairly well lighted and with a railing.

Back to the threshers! For both regular field workers and the threshers, many women provided a morning lunch at around 10:00, but we never did. The men no doubt just filled their water jugs when they took to the fields in the morning and there was always a pail of water and a dipper near the separator. But come afternoon, there was another happy time for us kids — loading the buggy with the sandwiches, cakes and big container of tea — sugar and cream (the *real* stuff for both — none of this dairy creamer or artificial sweeteners!) already in it — hitching up old Honey and heading to whatever field they were in. Again, when the men were all done, we got to drink as much of that sumptuous tea as we wanted, and eat any sandwiches or cake left over.

This routine went on until field threshing was done. Then the tractor pulled the separator into the yard to thresh some oats which would be made into chop. Our dog, Bess, loved this stuff and always got a handful or two when we were dipping some out to put in the mangers each morning.

Stacking

Part of the stooked oat field was left unthreshed so that a week or so later came the stacking job. For this the McConville brothers worked together, but at Uncle Sam's the bundles were put in the loft of his big barn instead. Stacks were built in a small fenced-in area behind the barn, the number depending on how much stock had to be fed. A stack was begun with a circle of sheaves laid side by side, heads pointed inward, the middle being filled in as you went, keeping the centre higher, building the outer rim perhaps seven or eight feet high and then making each additional layer smaller, until you capped the cone with a few sheaves that would hopefully shed rain. Finally, to keep the wind from lifting sheaves off the top, some two-by-fours were tied together to drape down the sides of the cone. To use these stacks, sheaves were pulled out here and there all around the bottom until weakness led to collapse. This was feast time for the cats as mice were running everywhere. On the farm, cats were outdoor animals. After all, they were very necessary to keep mice in check. In summer they would catch the odd gopher and drag it up to the barn to feed their kittens.

Fall Sights

Before the Dust Bowl years, a sure sign that winter would soon arrive was the night sky lit with burning straw stacks. One or two might be saved for bedding for the livestock, but most went up in flames — a very bad farming practice, it was learned later. The same with manure

Jim McConville with his dog team. Notice the stack in the background.

It was 1928. A road over the Canadian Rockies was more a trail than a highway. Here you see Dad and Uncle Frank just before heading back to the prairies from Vancouver, B.C. Frank's newly widowed sister told him he could have her Model T (this one in a parade, an exact replica) if he came to get it. An overheated, hissing motor called for frequent stops on the steep, narrow, gravelled curvy road. While the car cooled enough to dare taking off the radiator cap, hind wheels were blocked and Dad or Uncle Frank scrambled down the mountain side to the stream far below for more water. To further emphasize the need for slow careful driving, at especially dangerous spots, signs were posted, "Prepare to meet thy Maker.

Left, there is now a colony on the old Paterson place about six miles south of Ponteix. This is a Hutterite family in their distinctive style of dress.

No parade would be complete without a grain elevator float. Ponteix, Aug. 5, 1989, just passing Kouri's store

piles. If these sources of humus had been plowed or disced back in, perhaps the soil blowing of the 30's would not have been so severe. A *good* field, you see, was a *bare* one, kept free from weeds by cultivating. The *trashy* look was not yet the *"in"* way. Newly broken up land, had had the thick tough roots of prairie grass to hold it for a few years, but farmers from central Europe or other agricultural areas, or those with a non-farming background, would, by the 30's, have a lot to learn, much of it the hard way, about dry-land farming. If they and the many men who were college professors or heads of the Experimental farms had not worked so wonderfully together and used all the ingenuity they could muster among them, some believe that it was possible the whole Palliser Triangle may have turned into a permanent desert. Though we were *living through* it, Bud and I never made the *connections* between all the radical changes being made in farming methods until reading only a few years ago, a book that tied it all together — "Men Against the Desert". In fact, I had never even heard the term "Palliser Triangle" until I read it here. Also, it was good to read of due recognition being given to others who were also struggling with the horrendous problem of soil erosion in similar agricultural areas. However, lessons learned are not always incorporated in *permanent* fashion *after* problems seem to have been solved. Thus, with huge implements and no stock to provide manure (and therefore the need for high use of chemical fertilizers) there is the tendency to want to again have *big* fields, unhindered by rows of trees (mostly caraganas in our area) and narrow-strip fields. The potential lurks for a repeat of the horrors of the 30's. In fact, we could hardly believe what we saw not many miles from Yakima in dry land area — a field *cleared* of *all trash* cover and no less than *two miles* without a break of any kind to prevent the wind blowing away that precious topsoil.

New Attitudes and New Things

One of the biggest changes in daily living from our youth to the present has been the conversion from the *save it, use it up, make it do, don't waste* mentality, to the *throw away* pervasion of today. There are numerous reasons for this about-turn — the high wages which makes it uneconomical to repair something, the ease with which we can buy a replacement, health laws which prevent use of leftover food (I could never stand to work in a restaurant), and the stigma of wearing second-hand clothes. (We garage and yard sale addicts have decided there is *no such negative* today and we brag to each other about our bargains). To illustrate why we seldom get anything repaired nowadays: I got these comfortable just-right sandals one day for 50 cents, but decided to get new heel lifts on at a shoe repair — $5.50! Then, there's the element of saving time — ready-made clothes making sewing a hobby rather than a necessity; prepared foods and eating out replacing cooking from scratch at home; the use of plastic in place of the old, usually repairable wood, metal and leather and transportation so speedy and accessible that people just dash into town for parts, especially at harvest time, rather than even attempt a home repair. Besides, today many things are far too complicated for amateurs to repair and often the "works" are *sealed* in. It was a common saying way back then that a farmer could repair anything with haywire and a pair of pliers. Now cars have to go through a computerized diagnostic clinic to even *find out what's* wrong, never mind how to fix it!

Here are but a few more ways this radical change has affected us — perhaps younger ones will get laughs out of some of these: **1)** Toilet paper and indoor plumbing replaced the outdoor toilet and Eaton's catalogues. **2)** Kleenex has done away with handkerchiefs — more sanitary, of course, but we miss those beautiful three-some boxes, which were a most common and appreciated gift. And how little ones "drooled" over those bright all-over print ones! And those initialed, white-on-white ones for men were always "safe" for those on our male gift list. Besides, one *can't* put embroidery, tatting or crocheting on a kleenex! **3)** Good clothes, or "Sunday" clothes, as we called them, are now wash-and-wear, so why have kids change them as soon as they come home from school or after church. **4)** Plastic has replaced leather for shoes, so one no longer has to polish them, and velcro fastenings make obsolete the washing of shoelaces for our "good" shoes. It used to be that on Saturday afternoon, somebody would have the job of polishing their own shoes plus those of others, too, very likely. Every household had its box of shoe care materials — black, brown and tan wax polishes for sure, and maybe navy blue and red also — liquid white and black applied with a Q-tipped bottle lid — a shoe brush and buffer, or rags. **5)** Melmac, Corelle or other unbreakable dishes and storage containers have made metal plates and cups for baby and toddlers obsolete. **6)** Stainless steel flatware has taken the place of Roger's silverware, which had to have regular polishing with good old Bon Ami — remember the trademark — a fluffy, yellow chicken and the words "It never scratches"? **7)** Refrigerators and freezers made big changes in the housewife's way of safe and easy food preservation, not only on the short term basis for every day, but the long term methods for season to season. Many women have given up canning alto-

(Continued on page 310)

gether. Others, like me, still can fruit as it is so much better tasting than commercially canned. Freezing vegetables is so much easier, faster and sometimes healthier, too — no hours and hours of cooking and no worry over botulism.

Electric lights eliminated those time consuming daily jobs of filling coal oil lamps, trimming the wicks, and polishing the chimneys. Electric and gas stoves gave women another chunk of time to call their own — no longer having to shake the grates, empty the ashes, clean out and empty the soot from around the oven or to get kindling and bigger pieces of wood, and coal on hand. (Remember our "quickie" fires from cow chips? It was the kids' job to round those up.) Paper towels or hot-air dryers in public rest rooms have done away with those roller cloth ones. Sanitary napkins weren't yet on the market in our mother's day and in fact, not until in the 30's. (I could find *no* information on *feminine hygiene* in *any* of my almanacs, big dictionaries, or encyclopedias!) Young ones will find this unbelievable, but our hygiene texts made *no* mention of the *differences* between *male* and *female* bodies — only in the photographs with fully clothed people did you get an inkling that human beings came in two sexes! Now, just to give one more illustration of how things have changed on this subject, I recently received a letter from my niece in which she told me that at a sex education class at school (Grade 10), they were teaching the proper use of a condom! Surely from one extreme to the other, eh?

Female Circumcision

It was good to read that **Canada** and **France** are leading the way in passing laws forbidding the ritual practice of female circumcision (more correctly known as mutilation) within their borders. The picture of a little four-year-old African girl named **Mary** who had just undergone this operation, haunts me. And to think of the millions who are suffering the pain, humiliation and injustice of this abuse even as I write this, is most difficult for we Westerners to comprehend. Even more incomprehensible is how, only now, are we hearing about this age-old barbaric custom.

It's a Small World

We've all said this when an unexpected meeting takes place but I must tell you of one in which the odds were absolutely astronomical. I was "part" of just such a meeting, though thousands of miles away. A Yakima friend, **Joan Palm,** and her husband were on a trip to **Hawaii** — as was a former pupil of mine from my Saskatchewan teaching days, and her husband. They were on the same elevator and though complete strangers, decided to chat. Between floors (I don't know how many), they made *connections*! They *both* knew **Mary Stensrud** from **Yakima** — that she was a folk dancer and that she had written a book about Mt. St. Helens. And of course, they shared enough of their own lives that led up to the connections — that **Leonora** was originally from **Saskatchewan** and the Grand View School District where I had taught, and that Joan and I knew one another from mutual membership in Yakima's Ladies Musical Club — I wish some mathematician would come up with the right amount of zeroes on a number to show the chance of such an encounter. To say the least, I was flabbergasted when they both told me about it. And all in the short time it took to go a few floors on an elevator!

Aprons

The first mention of them is in the Bible and they were used to cover Adam and Eve's nakedness using what was at hand — fig leaves. From this account therefore, they were also the first item of clothing. Later, aprons were made of many different materials, leather, cloth, fabrics, etc., and instead of being *the clothing* they would be worn on top of that clothing. They were sometimes just ornamental, other times they were to protect and keep one's clothes clean or dry. Farm men only wore an apron, it seems to me, when they were cutting up and wrapping meat, but women were seldom without one except when they went out. Yes, their *main* use was to protect a dress, but they had many other uses you may not have thought of: **1)** as a pot holder; **2)** to wipe a little one's face; **3)** to whip off and use as a fly swatter; **4)** if the reversible kind, to switch to the clean side if unexpected company was arriving; **5)** to carry eggs in if you decided to collect them on the spur of the moment or had forgotten to bring the usual small pail for the job; **6)** and I read of one mother who would throw it up over her face so her little ones wouldn't see her crying, or to prevent herself saying something she would regret later.

The Union Jack and Other Flags

Our civics text book began this way: "This course aims particularly to teach children loyalty to our King and to our country. It aims also to 'cultivate a deep regard for democracy and an intelligent appreciation of democratic institutions, to develop those qualities of character and methods of action which are of special significance in a democracy, to develop the willingness and the ability to co-operate effectively in a demo-

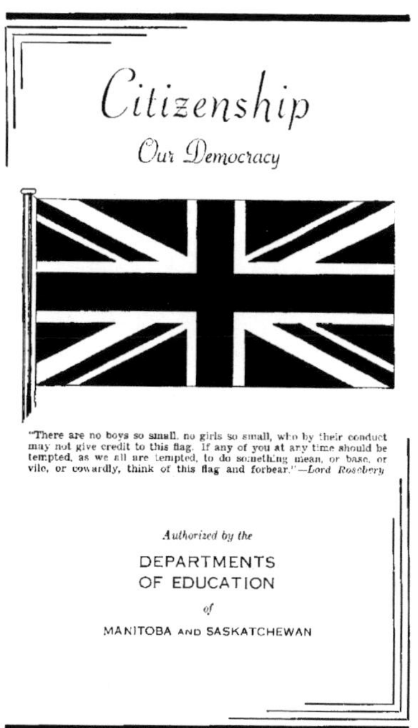

Citizenship

Our Democracy

"There are no boys so small, no girls so small, who by their conduct may not give credit to this flag. If any of you at any time should be tempted, as we all are tempted, to do something mean, or base, or vile, or cowardly, think of this flag and forbear."—*Lord Rosebery*

Authorized by the

DEPARTMENTS
OF EDUCATION
of
MANITOBA AND SASKATCHEWAN

PRINTED IN 1944

St. George's Banner

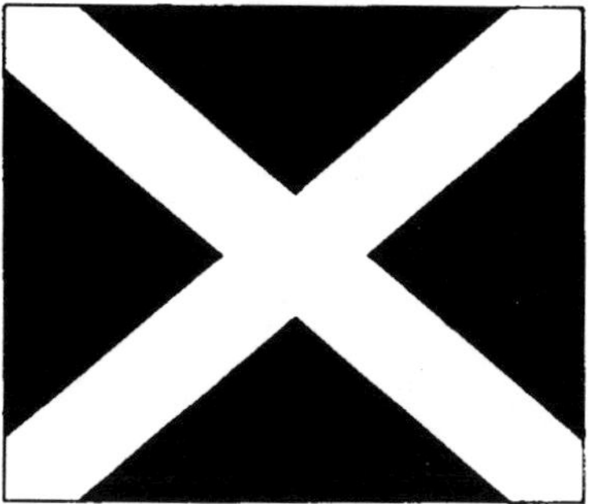

St. Andrew's Banner

The Union Jack of Queen Anne, 1707

St. Patrick's Cross

Clever super-imposing finally made The Union Jack. Canada at this time (1944) had special flags for the Royal Navy, the Navy Reserve, Canadian Government vessels, the British Mercantile Marine, and the Canadian Mercantile Marine. Each of these flags used the Union Jack in the corner with the main part of the flag being red, white or blue. Some had the coat of arms of the first four provinces on the right main field. Later flags — **Canada's Maple Leaf** flag, formally adopted on Feb. 15, 1965, may legally share side by side flying with the **Union Jack**.

THE ARMORIAL BEARINGS OF THE DOMINION OF CANADA

(Assigned by Royal Proclamation, 21 November, 1921)

"Canada was founded by the men of four different races: French, English, Scottish and Irish—and Canadians inherit the language, laws, literature and glory—and the arms—of all four mother countries. Upon these considerations has been based the achievements of arms which the King has authorized Canada to bear.

"The Arms are those of England, Scotland, Ireland and France, with a 'difference' to mark them as Canadian, namely, on the lower third of the shield a sprig of maple on a silver field.

"The crest is a lion holding in its paw a red maple leaf, a symbol of sacrifice. The supporters are, with some slight distinctions, the lion and unicorn of the Royal Arms. The lion upholds the Union Jack, and the unicorn the ancient banner of France.

"The motto is new—'A mari usque ad mare'—('From sea to sea.') * * * It is an extract from the Latin version of Ps. lxxii, 8—* * * 'He shall have dominion also from sea to sea, and from the river unto the ends of the earth.' ('Et dominabitur a mari usque ad mare, et a flumine usque ad terminos orbis terrarum.') There is a tradition that the Fathers of Confederation derived the designation 'Dominion' from this verse.

"Above the whole 'achievement' depends the Imperial Crown."

—"*The Arms of Canada.*"

Provincial and territorial coats of arms.

I would like to have seen blue side panels instead of the red, to represent the **Pacific** and **Atlantic** Oceans. This would have matched the motto on the coat of arms "From sea to sea".

Left, the emblem of the **Canadian Legion**. The flowers at the bottom represent the poppies that "blow in Flander's fields" — from the famous poem by **John McCrae**.

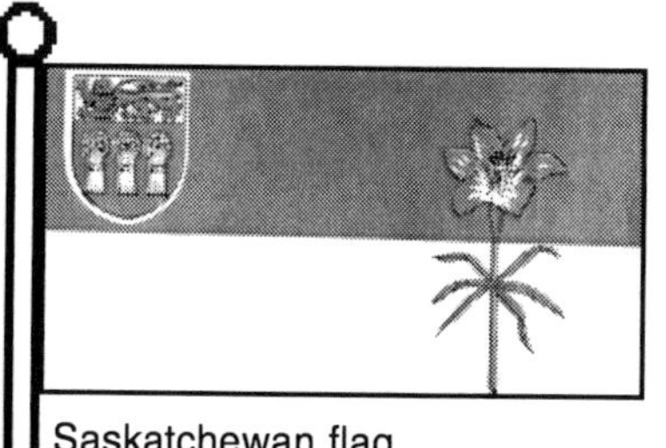

Saskatchewan flag.

Anthony Drake, an immigrant from England in 1962, submitted the winner among 4025 entries in 1969 for a prize of $1,000 for this design. The lower yellow half represents wheatfields and the upper green half, the parkland and far northern areas of the province. The red lily is the provincial flower. The Saskatchewan coat of arms is upper left.

Fransaskois flag.

The Fransaskois flag was the result of a contest throughout Saskatchewan communities with a francophone representation, so Ponteix qualified. "Fransaskois" is a contraction of "Francais" and "Saskatchewan" with the suffix "ois" to indicate belonging. The lily is stylized. The cross is a reminder of the Catholic heritage. Background colors are the same as the Sas–katchewan flag.

cratic society and to develop an active interest in, and concern for, the progressive development of the democratic ideal.'" (Printed in 1944.)

Besides learning the symbolism of the colors: Red — Be Brave; White — Be Pure; Blue — Be True, we had to learn to draw the Union Jack, noting carefully the diagonal, narrow and wide stripes — a bit tricky.

Because the British Empire encompassed large self-governing nations, it was called "The British Commonwealth of Nations."

By 1928 every man and woman over the age of 21 (except Indians) had the right to vote. When George VI was crowned in 1937, his title included "King of Canada". The Royal visit in May-June, 1939 was a real highlight for Canadians.

A Special Dress

If a dress could talk, Madge's beautiful, long, frilly, organdy one would tell you an interesting story. It might go like this: "I began as fluffy white balls in a cotton field — eventually becoming a dream come true. I was carefully packed as my proud owner headed from the bush country of eastern **Saskatchewan** to **Quimper** district in the prairie west. I had no idea that between my many washings and ironings I would become almost community property. It was Depression years and a lovely latest-fashion dress was almost impossible to come by no matter how important the occasion. So, Madge lent me out. I was used in a play and at special dances. I was even a bridesmaid's dress for a city wedding. And — best of all — I became my owner's wedding dress! Her groom was in his Sunday best suit — it too from pre-Depression days, but they wanted *something new*. A tie? That would be it. Surely they could find a quarter for one that would look just right with me.

Madge in her special dress.

And the vows sealed that day so long ago lasted for very nearly 60 years. I'm still Madge's, but I will be passed on one of these days to a younger family member. I hope they will treasure me many years into the next century and pass me on to their children eventually."

Quimper has been quite shy of weddings for a number of years now. In fact the celebration of Golden Weddings is now more

Ed and Madge reach their 50th and — almost a 60th.

Raymond and Agnes on their wedding day, April 10, 1995.

common than "originals". But **Raymond Bjore** saw in **Agnes Hapke** the one he wanted to spend the rest of his life with and she saw the same in him.

One day I thought it would be interesting to pretend I was reading headlines for newspapers during the years Quimper was open — so this is what I came up with as I worked on my list from time to time. Why don't you make *your* list?

1914 War is Declared
1915 First Canadian Contingent in France
1916 Women of Manitoba and Saskatchewan Get Vote
1917 Ship Collision Halifax — 1400 Dead
1918 Guns are Silenced — Armistice Signed
1919 Allies Form League of Nations
1920 Bubonic Plague in India — 2 Million Die
1921 Radio Goes Commercial
1922 Britain Admits First Woman to Veterinary College
1923 Canada's Banting and Best Share Nobel Prize for Medicine
1924 Cholera Hits India — 500,000 Dead
1925 The United Church of Canada Inaugurated
1926 Woman Swims the English Channel
1927 Canada and U.S. Establish Diplomatic Relations
1928 Lindberg Solos the Atlantic
1929 Stock Market Crashes
1930 Saskatchewan Government Claims Natural Resources
1931 Canada Restricts Gold Exports
1932 Welland Ship Canal Opens
1933 Turkish Women Get Vote
1934 Fire Destroys City of Hokodata, Japan
1935 Italians Use Suez to Transport Troops and Arms to Ethiopia

1936 Sonja Henie Third Time Olympic Winner
1937 King Edward VIII to Abdicate?
1938 U.S. Promises Aid if Canada Invaded
1939 Poland Invaded — A Television First
1940 Quebec Women Get Vote
1941 U.S. Enters the War
1942 U.S. Organizes Planned Parenthood
1943 Allies Hold Quebec Conference
1944 (1) The C.C.F. Wins (2) Larger School Unit Act Passes
1945 The War is Over
1946 The Philippines Gain Independence
1947 Apartheid Established in South Africa
1948 Japanese Earthquake Kills 5000
1949 Canada Replaces Privy Council with Own Supreme Court
1950 Canada Drops Dominion from Name
1951 Princess Elizabeth Tours Canada
1952 Vincent Massey — First Canadian-born Governor General
1953 Stalin is Dead
1954 U.S. Declares Racial Segregation Unconstitutional
1955 Atomic Power Propels a Ship
1956 Canada Admits 37,566 Hungarian Refugees
1957 Russia's Sputnik in Orbit
1958 (1) Canada and U.S. Establish Joint Defense
(2) Canada's Population Reaches 17 Million
(3) Major Work on St. Lawrence Seaway Completed
(4) Ripple Rock Blown Up — 1370 Tons of Explosive
(5) World's Largest Gas Well Opens — 150 miles N.W. Edmonton
(6) World's Longest Pipeline — 1930 miles — Redwater, Alberta, to Port Credit, Ontario
(7) Diefenbaker Leaves on World Tour

In 1958, the year Quimper closed, I couldn't seem to choose *one* or even *two* possible headlines, so just listed all seven.

This book is giving minimum space to more recent history of Canada, or Saskatchewan in particular, but I want to mention a few events with a more personal aspect. Though we did not get to attend it, my sister, Nellie, and her family, did go to the World's Fair in **Montreal** in 1967. What a wonderful way for French-Canadians and English speaking Canadians and others around the world to enjoy each other! And, then there was **Expo '86** at the other end of Canada in **Vancouver, B.C.** We did attend this fair — not once, but a number of times. Not only did **Canada** do itself proud, but **Saskatchewan** had what many considered one of the best pavillions there. And just prior to the fair itself, one of the most unusual reunions took place. Though our family didn't qualify by the "letter of the law" — seeing as it was for former Saskatchewan folks then *living in B.C.,* they said in a letter that we were welcome simply as former Saskatchewanians. At the fair, many Americans,\ and of course, numerous others, both fellow Canadians and those from other countries, got to see the famous **Mounties Musical Ride**. I had wanted to see it ever since hearing Mom talk about it so enthusiastically after the Regina fair in 1928. (Upon returning home they faced a great distaster — a predicted bountiful crop frozen into nothing.)

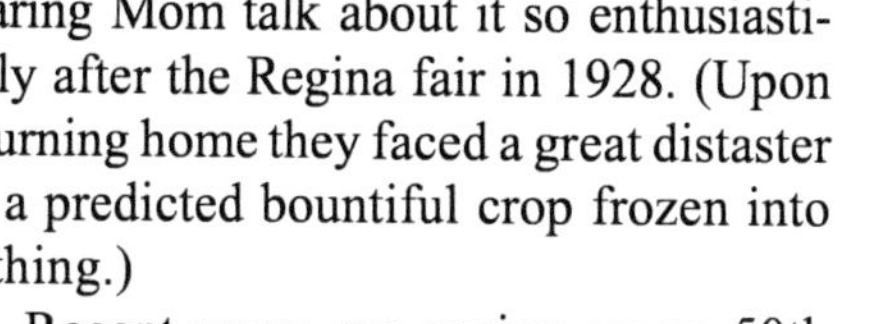

Recent years are seeing many 50th

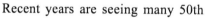

This ten story tower contained the workings of a potash mine, illustrations of how a grain elevator worked, and a panoramic view from near the top.

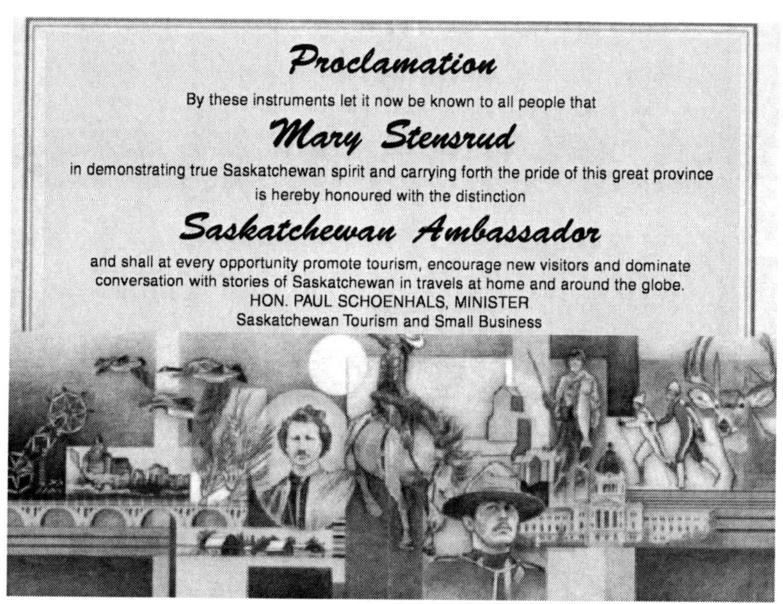

Proclamation

By these instruments let it now be known to all people that

Mary Stensrud

in demonstrating true Saskatchewan spirit and carrying forth the pride of this great province is hereby honoured with the distinction

Saskatchewan Ambassador

and shall at every opportunity promote tourism, encourage new visitors and dominate conversation with stories of Saskatchewan in travels at home and around the globe.
HON. PAUL SCHOENHALS, MINISTER
Saskatchewan Tourism and Small Business

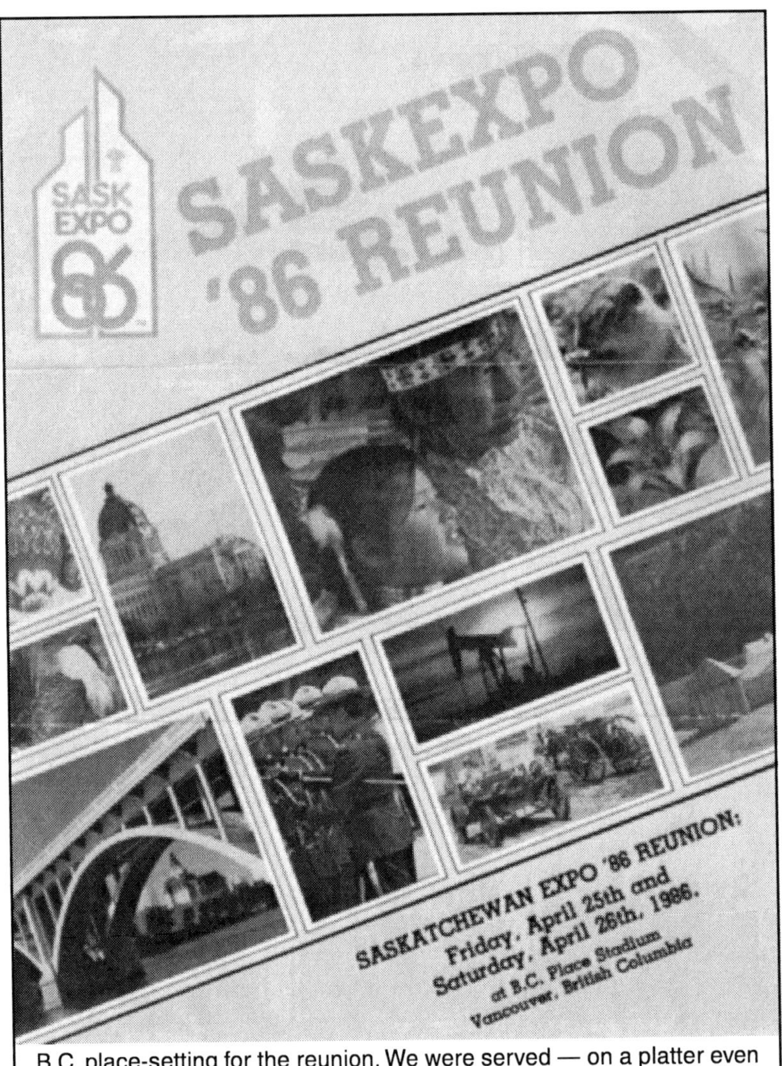

B.C. place-setting for the reunion. We were served — on a platter even — a most delicious meal.

Here's a wee vignette I missed in chapter five: Red nail polish had just come on the fashion scene, and my cousin **Alice** was right in style one day when at our house for a visit. You know how one can catch something out of the corner of the eye. Well, Mom did, and thought she saw blood, and let out a near scream. "Alice, what in the world have you done to your fingers?" Alice's hands quickly went behind her back as she muttered, "Nothing, Aunt Martha." Soon both saw the funny side of it.

Anniversary gatherings, family reunions and celebrations for the founding of their town. And for Saskatchewan's 75th anniversary of becoming a province, perhaps it was a rare town that *didn't* have a celebration. How wonderful these were for those who had stayed in these places and made all the arrangements, and for those who came from afar to visit old friends and to see what appear at their old stomping grounds — beautiful parks, golf courses, swimming pools, huge quonsets, etc.

How can we get young folks to be curious about the period in history we older folks have lived through? There are many ways, of course, but here are just a few suggestions:

(1) Get out the old *photo albums* and stacks of post cards. Perhaps they could help choose ones for a video.

(2) Have them *interview* us for a school project, linking their heritage to the present.

(3) For entertainment, have them *produce* (in our days this fancy word was just to "put on") an old time Christmas concert. Have all things *not* present then taken out of sight or disguised. TV's, computers, overhead projectors, etc. Green or white blackboards would be covered with black paper and light switches masked over.

(4) Help a local museum set up *one* room as an old time one-room rural school.

(5) A *big* project for the community — find an old schoolhouse, haul it into town, restore it and have it *operate* as a tourist attraction. (This has been done at the **Ohmstead Museum** near **Ellensburg**. Someone is hired to be the "teacher" and on-the-spot *tourists* become the *pupils*.) This was fun!

45's, 33-1/3's, and 78's

Kids may know what a 45 or a 33-1/3 is, but what is a 78? Yes, another record speed. Just this last week, when searching for a book and casually waiting to talk to a lady who might help me, I began thumbing through a box of 33-1/3 long plays. Imagine my delight to find one by **John McCormack**! Though we had him on 78's on our old gramaphone back at the farm, I just supposed *he* had died *with* those 78's, if not before. Now I learn he lived until 1945 (born 1884). You can be sure I wasted no time in borrowing it to play on our modern "gramaphone" — now called a turn-table. It was all I dreamed it would be — the jacket cover calling him "the Irish Minstrel" and this record "a centennial tribute". How marvelous is modern technology that has made it possible to bring forward into today this man's beautiful tenor voice! Audio cassettes are far more portable, but a long-play jacket can give a lot more information in both words and pictures and print is big enough for aging eyes to see.

Though most of us think of McCormack as a singer of ballads, he also sang in many operas. It is rare, even among well trained singers, then or now, to find one who enunciates words so well. His decision to acquire this ability followed a charity concert when he was but 16. Next morning the cook said, "Oh, Mr. John, you sang just grand last night, but why did you sing in all them foreign languages?" He was flabbergasted and swore that from that moment on he would "sing in such a way that *every word* could be understood by *everyone* in the audience."

Though born in Ireland, he became an American citizen and sang all over the world, but died back in his beloved homeland. In 1937 he retired from professional singing, but emerged for a brief time during the war to sing for Red Cross benefits and for the servicemen.

As I listened with pure nostalgic joy to this man's singing, I, at times, could also hear again Dad singing "Kathleen Mavorneen", for instance, and "The Rose of Tralee". Dad, too, had a lovely tenor voice.

On another personal note — though it may lack the technological excellence of a professional recording — one of our family treasures is Dad and Nellie on a record they had made at a studio in Vancouver.

I have a collection of 33-1/3rds. In it is one with a painting of a chivaree on the jacket.

Religious Music of the 60's

France with its almost total R.C. faith, according to one almanac, began to lose its domination of Catholics in Canada at the time of the French Revolution. The carnage terrified them and yet they felt the loss of the tie. However, their independence made them even closer to each other and more free to pursue religious matters in keeping with their Canadian interests and traditions. Since the 60's, church leadership has been more enlightened and has supported government moves to raise educational standards. Some find trouble in the dualism of clerical austerity and French-Canadian joviality. Also, as all over the world, tremendous changes in the R.C. church came with John Paul the 23rd — the mass in English and nuns not being required to wear a habit, for but two.

Because they did not have the background of what is termed *main-*

line hymnology, some credit the tremendous revolution of recent years in church music to R.C. openness and creativity. Who of us can forget, though still in their habits, those Mission Sisters who came on the scene in the 60's and had us all singing "with" them (I wonder what happened — they vanished from the scene along with their music about as quickly as they appeared). I treasure my four books of their gospel songs "Knock Knock", "Seasons", "Joy is Like the Rain", and "I Know the Secret" along with long-play records to match. And most of you know the hymn "They'll Know We Are Christians By Our Love" — I first saw it in a **Lutheran** quarterly, sang it first in a **Church Women United** special service and learned it was composed by a **R.C. Priest**! And one titled "Let There Be Peace on Earth" I first heard in an elementary public school by a 6th grade choir, this too, back in the 60's.

Moral Teaching

I don't know about in Canada, but seeing as both countries seem to follow pretty much the same thinking and therefore make corresponding laws on what it means to keep *politics* and *religion* separate, there is disaster in public schools. *No* religion has, in the final analysis, led to *no* morals. But recently there is coming into being some togetherness, even between such disparate religious faiths as that of Jews, Christians, Buddhists, Muslims, etc., as they try to agree on *some basics* — mostly on the order of the Ten Commandments. Perhaps they will be able to come to some consensus on what *principles have to operate* if people are to learn to live together on this planet. Could this list include the Golden Rule, be kind to one another, honour parents, don't covet things that belong to others, treat one another justly, be honest and so on? Children playing together ignore differences of skin color for instance, unless trained by grown-ups to do otherwise. Nevertheless, on individual differences — too fat, too thin, big ears or nose or whatever — children can be very cruel on their own. A wise teacher will curb such behavior as quickly as possible, certainly without any conflict over religious differences.

Just recently I was sent four late but outdated copies of "The Observer", The United Church magazine. This was in answer to my request for articles which would be of special interest to Saskatchewan

(Continued on page 316)

Did you know there was a song about our province? "This was made famous by the Princess Patricia Band under the Auspices of the Robert Simpson Western Ltd., Regina, Sask."

I wish the cover had some information about the ones who composed it, seeing as it came from England. I wonder if some one from there visited Saskatchewan and went home and wrote it.

Saskatchewan

Arrangement for "Banjulele" Banjo and Ukulele by ALVIN D. KEECH

There were two verses, but I decided to just copy the chorus. Notice also it has the tune in sol-fa.

folks. I will summarize two of these:

It was reminiscent of Depression days when the United Church in Ontario sent carloads of food and clothing to the desperate people in our area, but on a smaller scale. It was, however, significant in kind and concern. One Ontario family, the **Barkers** were joined by a **Dutch Reformed** couple and a **R.C.** nun in helping to build a new church for the Saulteaux (Indian) community at **Cote**, Saskatchewan. They got to know one another as they took special joy in singing gospel songs together and in square dancing. After being back home, these folks have sent to their new friends some warm winter clothing and some knitted baby clothes. (I'm sure their friendship continues.)

In another Observer under the title "Determined to Survive", I learned of what has been going on at **Cutarm**, Saskatchewan — another example of ecunemism at work. Still under the old way of a charge centred in a town, but with rural meeting places in the surrounding area, **Lutherans**, **Anglicans** and **United Church** folks have regular 5th Sunday services together, as well as special ones on Christmas Eve. At a musical in which 50 from all parts participated, they showed concern for those in need at a distance by giving the $1,100 they raised to the **World Development and Relief Fund**. Though small in numbers and scattered, these Saskatchewan believers don't say "Why doesn't *somebody* do *something*, they just *do it.*

Reprint of a clipping from the Manchester Guardian:

They made a farm on the prairie

Success came the hard way in Canada to Altrincham-born Jim McConville, who, with his wife Martha and sister Mrs. Ellen Kirkpatrick, has just paid his first visit to England for more than 40 years. They stayed with relatives in Hale.

Jim, now 72, emigrated in 1904 and for six years worked on a farm in Manitoba. Then he and his brother, who had gone to Canada a year previously, were granted a piece of land — virgin prairie — in Saskatchewan.

Pioneering job

"The Government," Jim told a "Guardian" reporter, "gave us three years to bring 30 acres under cultivation. We built a shack, and made outhouses from sods, because timber had to be hauled 64 miles to us. We also dug a 40-foot well."

During each of the three years, they had to find work elsewhere to make ends meet. Afterwards they bought a pair of oxen and equipment.

When Mr. McConville retired in 1946 to let his son take over, there were 480 acres of flourishing wheatland under cultivation.

A Few Tid-bits About Canadian Inventors

1) The snowmobile and

Ski-Doo were invented by **J. Armond Bombardier.** His machines were mainly for fun, but were adapted for tanks and troop carriers in war, and for travel in difficult terrains, such as muskeg, the Sahara, sugar cane fields and logging trails. **Valcourt**, **Quebec**, was his hometown.

2) William Stephenson discovered how to send wire photos and contributed a lot of the know-how for radar, lasers, jet engines, T.V. and sound recordings. He had the first plastics company. **Britain** was the first to use his pressed steel for car bodies. Real close to home, he made improvements in our can openers.

3) Reginal Fessenden had so many inventions, it was very hard to choose a few for this tid-bit. However, I list these: wireless telephones; insulating compound to get the electricity industry past a major problem; the addition of Ganzibar gums into varnish; which gave a beautiful shiny finish; and made it cheaper and longer-lasting; revolutionized the light bulb industry with brighter, cheaper, longer-lasing bulbs; used silicon steel in electric motors to prevent them overheating; discovered wireless Morse code transmission, micro-photography, the pocket pager, much T.V. technology, the secrets of the atom, etc., etc.

4) Thomas Willson has patents for over 60 of his inventions, among them — many improvements in aluminum, the arc light, the acetylene gas light, nitrogen fertilizer and the party-line phone system.

5) Mabel Bell, wife of the inventor of the phone, was one of five who did much work on the earliest of airplanes. Discovery of the tetrahedron made possible the method of building the first practical, strong, lightweight wings.

6) Georges Desbarats discovered how to send photos on a grid — invaluable to the newspaper business for many years.

7) William Leggo figured out how to print many copies of one photograph.

8) Abraham Gesner discovered much of the knowledge which led to the petroleum industry of today — much of it relating to greases, paints and varnishes.

9) Sanford Fleming devised our system of Standard Time. He was put in charge of the survey work for both transcontinental railways, the Canadian Pacific and the Canadian National.

Elsewhere in Canada

Big things are happening in northern Quebec. I haven't seen anything about it lately, so what I have here is approximately three years old.

The more population grows and the more industrialized the world becomes, the more *trouble* over *water* escalates. Ecology, environment, jobs for people, trade, the rights of native peoples and many other factors add to the troubled mix.

But one example is the huge **James Bay Project** in **Quebec**. In November of 1993 the **National Geographic** put out a special edition titled "Water — the Power, Promise and Turmoil of North America's fresh water." Eight pages in this case study is on Canada's mind boggling-sized plans to supply energy not only to Quebec, but even part of the north-eastern States. **John Mitchell** wrote the article and **Stuart Franklin** was the photographer. The sub heading is "Where Two Worlds Collide", as this is **Cree** country and they are fighting it every way they can. According to this article, it was to be completed in 1995, so as in all the power struggles between natives and white men, which began almost as soon as Europeans landed in the New World, probably **Cree** and **Inuit** protests have fallen on deaf ears.

The initial project began in 1971, and by 1993 had flooded more than 6000 square miles. The Cree call electricity *numischiluskataau,* "the fire that shakes the land", and indeed most, whether proponents or opponents, agree it shakes the tundra of an area greater than the size of Montana. The French of Quebec or Francophones, as they are now called (just "French-speaking" in our school days), look upon this astronomical amount of water power as a bargaining financial windfall in dealing with English speaking Canada. The Cree say it threatens their livelihood and the environmentalists call it a "disaster on a par with the devastation of the Amazon rain forest". In 1975 the Cree signed an agreement to accept $225 million for compensation, but most say no amount of money can make up for possible losses — a way of life, even the caribou. Their burial grounds will be covered and fish will become tainted by toxins from decaying flooded vegetation, they contend.

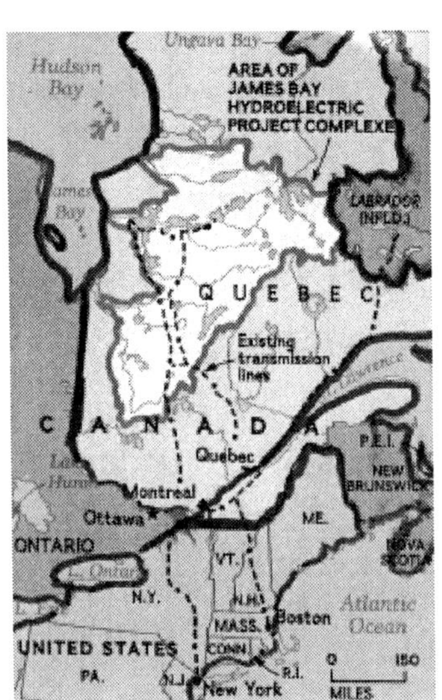

The James Bay hydro-electric project.

Big changes have come to Quebecers with the advent of electricity. I suppose it's much higher now, but by 1993 all-electric homes had doubled in only a decade. Smelters for aluminum and magnesium, along the St. Lawrence, which use huge amounts of water, were not only welcomed, but were, in fact, induced to come by cheap power rates. The old chemical process in pulp and paper mills was changing over to the electromechanical.

Ontario and **Manitoba**, too, are developing power projects on their rivers that flow into Hudson and James Bays and, though impacts of even national and possibly global concerns are still impossible to assess, these aspects are on many minds.

By the way, did you know that **Saskatchewan** had Canada's first licensed airport and pilot?

Medicine

Though all fields of science have been advancing at lightning speed in recent years, that of *medicine* is the one, I believe, that comes closest to home. Most of us know one or maybe a number of people who have had heart, liver, lung, kidney, bone or some other transplant or joint replacement. We have even read of whole limbs being re-attached! The blind and deaf have had these senses either brought back or even *given* to them initially when *born* with these disabilities.

We didn't know her personally, but how wonderful it was to see on T.V. a little girl *hearing* for the *first* time in her life. And in Yakima just recently, a young woman who had lost her seeing eye dog to cancer not long before, has had an operation giving her enough sight to read again and, with glasses, is hoping for near 20/20 sight before too long. And a man in our church, **George Martin**, who had worn very strong thick glasses from a child, was able to throw them away on his 80th birthday! And what of laser surgery — gallstones and kidney stones being blasted apart and removed with suction through a tiny hole? Even knocked out teeth can sometimes be re-implanted, or single artificial ones set in to work like originals. And just think of how plastic surgery and fabulous — even life-like-looking — prostheses, can enable people to do things never thought possible only a few years ago. Now even those bound to a wheel chair from spinal cord injury have a realistic hope of someday walking again. Amazing as are all of these, add the very latest — gene therapy, the preservation of sperm and eggs for future use, surrogate mothering and on and on. Our minds are simply boggled not only with what we *see now,* but what *may be in the future.*

Nevertheless, we must surely look at the down side of this whole picture, for in the end, *people are the same* as they've always been. Some invention may be the answer to one person's prayers, while another will turn it to some evil purpose. Or the same is true for whole groups of people — the classic example being a labor saving device that leads to unemployment. There are mind altering drugs which sometimes can do *good* things for the mentally or emotionally ill, but how many use them as dope to *ruin* what was a *good* mind? Then too people's *bodies* might be operating *and not* the *mind*, opening up Pandora's box on what is termed the *ethics* of living and dying.

Then there is the whole wide field of alternative medicine, especially that of herbs and good nutrition. It's hard to pinpoint any *timeline,* but I remember when modern doctors first began to really acknowledge the power of *mind* over *body* and the part *prayer, meditation* and *fasting* might play when *their* ways had failed completely. Folk medicine is now being investigated and valued as never before. Even witch doctors are sometimes viewed with "different" eyes, for, without tacking the "right" scientific facts together, as we might say, they *knew* that simply *believing whatever* was being done could *help* or even fully *cure* a person's ills. Faith was half the battle.

And how can we talk of the field of medicine without speaking of the changes in all aspects of sexuality? When we were in our teens, the beginning of our menstrual period was termed "coming sick". What a distorted way to refer to a natural function! Now for a backwards peek at childbirth. In the 40's and 50's we were *in bed* for *days,* and nursing was considered more of a bother than anything, because with bottle feeding you could *know* just how much your baby was getting. Formula was not yet common either. We were using canned milk with some sugar added, and vitamins were given separately in cod liver oil (A-B-D-E-C drops). A pacifier was a *no-no* for sure, and disposable diapers were a long way down the line. And now there's the wonderful innovative change of *fathers* taking part in the whole birth process instead of just sitting it out in the waiting room! And who could miss the high costs of having a baby nowadays? Our second one in 1949 was $35.00 for delivery and $90.00 for the hospital for 9 days whether you stayed the full time or not.

Many people, especially with cancer, get caught in the middle — going the route of surgery and chemo or radiation treatment *or* opting for good nutrition, prayer, or other hoped-for cures. Most perhaps, choose to *combine* or *take in tandem* what they believe will be best for them but, as *varied* as treatments may be, so are the *outcomes*. Some go into complete remission, or are permanently cured, while others are taken in death no matter what modern medicines, confident faith or any alternative methods are tried.

On an upbeat note, I want to tell you of **June**, not a Quimper girl, but a visiting niece of the Earl Crosses when we were kids. Her **Aunt Mildred** had invited me to spend a few days with them as company for June. However, we did not keep in touch, so it was only last year that I "found" her again. June believes she would have died from her cancer if she had not switched from chemo therapy to the alternative of a very strict diet and other measures which are generally accepted as ways to maintain or recover good health — in other words, a healthy lifestyle, but under the care of a Natureopathic doctor.

Let me tell you a couple of experiences in my own life which are a mix of *modern*, *folk* and *alternative* medicines.

I was badly burned when a pressure cooker exploded (I did not have the gauge on it as that gadget had always made me nervous.) I learned, after the fact, that you should never cook anything such as beans or pieces of something, that has a tough skin, as a little piece can cover the vent hole so the steam cannot escape. I was cooking cubed apple with skins on. After cooling the cooker, explosive steam was released when I turned the lid. Applesauce was plastered everywhere. I employed every method of dealing with a burn that I'd heard of, using anything I had on hand, and adding my own ideas besides. I first applied cold water, an ice cube (my own idea), vanilla, and vitamin E oil. I never had any pain, never went to the doctor, and healed beautifully.

Then there is my leg cramps story. How I wish I'd known of this when Dad was still here and subject to such terrible ones! It sounds absolutely ridiculous, but it works. As you feel a cramp just starting, or even if it has become full-blown before you catch it, just pinch and keep holding your upper lip as hard as you can. It will prevent it developing, or if too late for this, the cramp will simply fade away. What wonderful relief!

A True Old Wive's Tale

We've all heard the saying "Oh, that's just an old wive's tale" meaning it can't be believed. But let me give you the synopsis of a *true* old wive's tale that happened in our area of Saskatchewan before the days of settlement. A great prairie fire had swept the **Qu' Appelle Valley** and the buffalo had gone west into **Blackfoot** country to get to grass. The **Cree** were desperate for food and in order to get buffalo, they too, were in the area. The Blackfoot attacked, but because of fierce resistance, disappeared into the hills to prepare for a stronger try the next morning. Some old Cree women thought up a trick that let all the rest of their members get safely home, but in which they would lose their lives. They kept fires going all night with buffalo chips so the Blackfoot would think *everyone* was still in camp. Finding themselves tricked the next morning, the Blackfoot angrily massacred these brave old mothers. The lake nearby came to be called **Old Wives Lake**. Then, at the turn of the century, its name was changed to **Johnson Lake** to honor a titled Englishman who had hunted in the area. However, during the following 50 years, there was much negative talk about this name, and in 1953 its old name was restored.

Saskatchewan people are still advancing in many fields, economically, spiritually, athletically, and socially.

Some things that have taken place locally in this last few years: care for the aging and the sick in the Manor and the Foyer in Ponteix; the building of a big, more efficient elevator in Ponteix; more ecumenical church events (we hadn't yet *heard* in our younger days this now common word), and many local celebration days, with their sports activities, parades, re-enactments of early days, either indoors, such as in Aneroid's wonderfully, huge quonset, or outdoors in their natural setting.

Saskatchewan has established its own Hall of Fame for its national and internationally famous athletes. One name on it is **Roger Eddy** of the Erinlea District. He was on the Canadian luge team — near winners at **Grenoble**, **France**, in 1968, barely missing a medal. He also coached the luge team in Germany at the 1976 Olympics.

Saskatchewan has some of the best artists and handcraft artisans found anywhere — some now receiving international acclaim — among the usual paintings, pottery, weavings, beadwork, embroidery, leathercraft, sculptor and woodwork, etc., you will find some unusual ones (some new, some old) such as biting designs into folded sections of birch bark, pysanky (decorating Ukrainian Easter eggs), and wheat weaving (a continual demonstration at Expo '86). Watch for these signs along the highways which will direct you to where handcrafts are for sale and where you might see these craft persons at work. Genuine Saskatchewan-made crafts may have this tag on them.

The Saskatchewan Craft Council number is 306-653-3616.

There are five major entry points into Saskatchewan and year round information centres in its 12 cities. Tourism Saskatchewan may be reached toll free at 1-800-667-7191 or fax 306-787-5744.

Did you know that Saskatchewan's very popular restaurant at Expo '86 is still in operation and serving the delicious saskatoon pie and ice cream?

SEEN RECENTLY

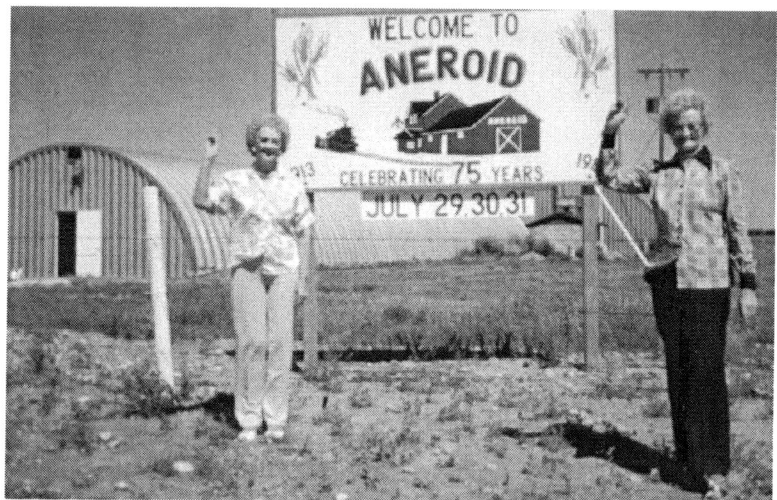

One of our greatest thrills was returning to Aneroid for its 75th Reunion. What a wonderful time we had! That's Isabelle and Olive.

Nellie and Sig on the Ponteix golf course. The "putting green" is dirt.

Elevators hold things other than grain. Highway trash bins.

Main building and left wing — Royer Cultural Centre. Right wing, Henri Liboiron's Notukeu Heritage Museum. Ponteix.

Above, Henri when his museum was still in his rural home.

Henri's model of a buffalo pound. Hanging up against the window is an Indian chair. It becomes a bed when put on the floor.

Above, Henri mixes paints just the way the Indians did. Notice his dinosaur chart on the left.

Left, model of the plesiosaur dug up in 1992 not far from Ponteix on the banks of the Notukeu Creek.

Some modern kids learn an old-fashioned game — crokinole.

Mr. and Mrs. Bender celebrate their 65th wedding anniversary.

Imagine being able to move such a top heavy building!

Saskatchewan produces over 60 percent of all wheat grown in Canada.

Built in 1982. Capacity 160,000 bushels. Two 5000 bu. per hour legs. Office has fully modern computer. Three fertilizer bins and quonset to store chemicals and twine are nearby.

Right! That's *not snow*. It's potash, one of Saskatchewan's major products, it having over half of the world's known recoverable reserves.

80's Motels Ltd.
PHONE 625-3553
BOX 294
DAN GERVAIS PONTEIX, SASK. SON 12D

A very nice place to stay. A mini-gym on left.

Looking west from our Motel 80 room in Ponteix in June, 1995. We saw many trains like this in Saskatchewan, but not a single passenger one.

A Quimper house moved into Aneroid and remodeled. (It was Uncle Tom's.)

The kind of big implement needing huge quonsets for winter storage. The sides fold up enabling it to go down the road.

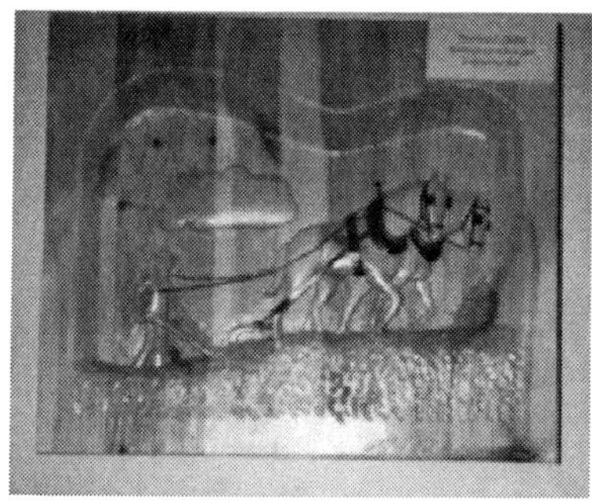

The wood carvings of **Raymond A. Chabot** of **Shaunavon** — both permanent, as this one, and in a traveling exhibit — are excellent. Perhaps someday you'll see them in your museum. Here he is honoring his "beau-pére" as he guides his walking plow to break sod.

Then or now a picnic is still a lot of fun. *Then* we sat on the grass and it was just a day's outing. Here the **Athertons** have been on a tenting trip and we joined them at **Oliver**. This tent is quite different than ones we stayed in in the 30's at Lake Pelletier, but the string clothes line is just the same.

Left, the vehicle we saw in Montreal called a humvee, which can travel on land or in water. **Eisenhower** gave the military version of it credit for winning the war. **Andrew Higgins** was its inventor. Servicemen called it a Duck.

Below, **Annie Pain** in 1996 will have her 100th birthday. You see us here when she was 97 and living in the Ponteix Manor. Annie gave me first-hand information about the Indianola sod school.

Left, **Eldon** and **Wilma** *looking* old-fashioned, but engaged in today's hobbies. He restores old tractors and she is carrying her butter making bowl and paddle.

Our three, Milla, Roy, and Carl, had a wonderful 50th celebration for us. Doris had a beautiful, unique quilt made for us by her friend **Alfhild Foss.** She incorporated photos of all the Stensrud family, a wheat motif, horse-shoe shape stitching and a border of applique "S"'s.

Doris by one of the many oil wells on the McCullough farm at **Manor**, Saskatchewan.

Joseph Lallier's restaurant in **Black Lake**, Quebec.

Nowadays, fresh fruit and vege–tables are trucked direct from the **B.C. Okanagan Valley** to **Swift Current.**

At the door of **Holy Trinity Anglican Church** in **Winnipeg** — the very one Mom and Dad and Ed and Emily went in and out of on April 7, 1916.

Visiting museums is a favorite thing to do for some of us when on vacation. We all remember when a gas pump looked like this — much more interesting to watch working than ones nowadays.

Above, a train depot moved into the country for a house. Left, it's fun to get into some really old fashioned clothes — sisters, Nellie and Mary.

JUST SOME FAMILY FAVOURITES

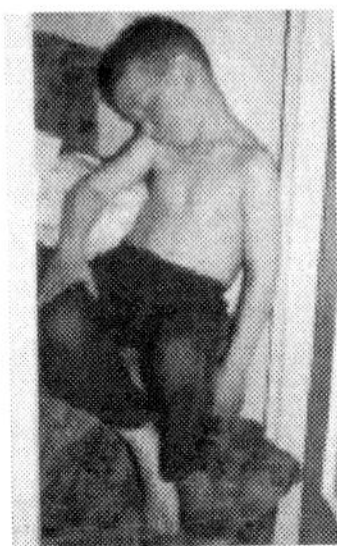

Left, poor Carl, just couldn't make it up those stairs! 1962.

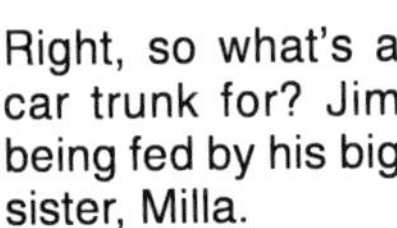

Right, so what's a car trunk for? Jim being fed by his big sister, Milla.

Wow! My boxes and boxes of "ash" books on pallets in our basement, Feb. 1985.

Our little Andy!

I'm a folk dancer on the Gruzia for a trip down the St. Lawrence, 1994.

What grandparent can resist? These are four of ours. Jake, Eric, Angie and Andy.

Milla's trying — so is Roy! Goals are just opposite.

Much used transportation for our first-born, Milla. 1947.

Angie and Suzette — same size, same interest.

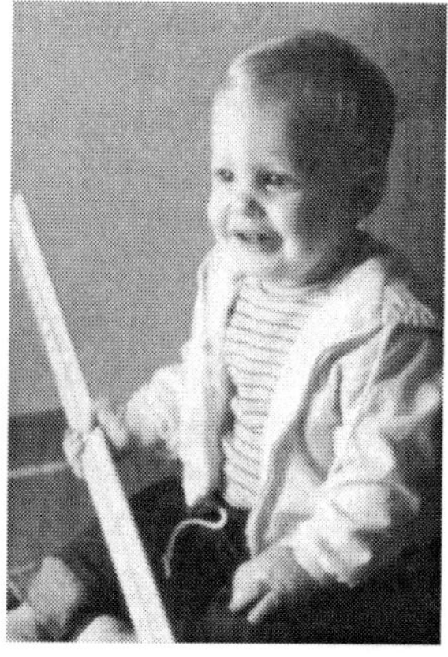
Our first grandson. His favourite toy — a yardstick.

Angie calls her Mom from Grandma's house.

Mutual love! Dad and Suzette — both old — Dad 93 and Suzette 13.

100 YEARS OF GRAIN FARMING

1) A sulky plow — the kind Quimper's homesteaders used. At first seed was broadcast and wheat harvested by flailing — but all three soon gave way to 2 and 3 bottom plows, a seeder pulled by four horses and regular threshing. **2)** The bagging of grain to take to market was no longer being done by the teen years. **3)** By the 20's most farmers had a tank like this for grain hauling. **4)**A few farmers in the 20's got these huge steam engines that could pull 10-12 bottom plows, but they never became real popular. Fletcher Walls changed back to horses, but this, too, on a grand scale — about 50 of them. **5)** Plowing was replaced by soil-working methods such as *listing*, as seen here, others left a trash cover in the field. **6)** Some threshing outfits arrived at a farm complete with cook and bunk cars in tow. Mary K. worked on a cook car many years. **7)** Some farmers use giant sized trucks for hauling grain. **8)** Now we're up to the 90's! Combines have long since replaced threshing machines. This is how grain is now loaded into the truck for the trip to town.

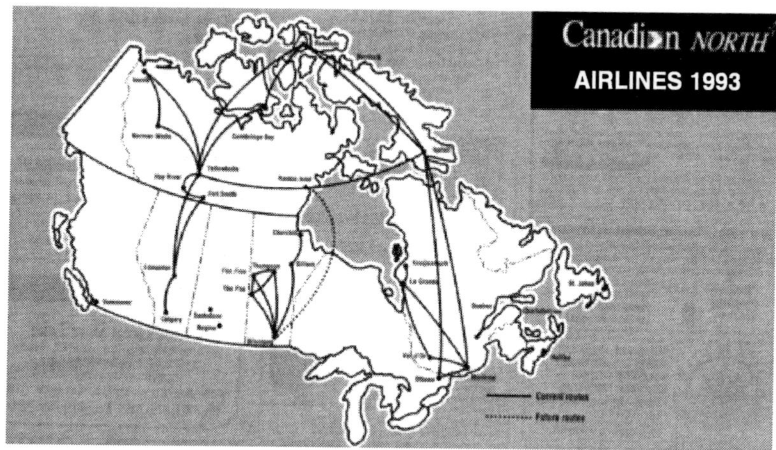

Canada's Far North. This map tells you a lot about Canada's *true* North. (To Quimperites I was going to the *far north* to teach when heading for **Medstead**! How ludicrous! I was still in the lower third of Saskatchewan.) Looking carefully you will see, though, that Saskatchewan gets short shift, for not a *single* air route of this airline serves our province — unless the last three years has changed things. However, Saskatoon is a very busy hub for some other airlines.

From tourist promotional material for the North West Territories and the Yukon, their pavilions at Expo '86, etc., I have been updated on very surprising modern ways and productions up there — skyscrapers, accommodations, transportation, industries, even diamonds, etc. In 1996 **Yukon** is celebrating the 100th Anniversary of the Klondike Gold Rush. I was fascinated by the contrasting lists of supplies for 1898 and 1995.

It was gratifying to read of the part native peoples, called **First Nations**, are playing in this part of the world, especially in their crafts, sports, entertainment and pride in their heritage — language, songs and culture.

Populations: **Whitehorse**, 22,911 (1994); **Yellowknife**, 15,179 (1991); **Inuvik**, 6,206 (1991); **Dawson City**, 2,019 (1994).

1898 Chilkoot Trail Supplies

McDougall and Secord
Klondike Outfit List
(clothing & food):
2 suits heavy knit underwear
6 pair wool socks
1 pair heavy moccasins
2 pairs german stockings
2 heavy flannel overshirts
1 heavy woollen sweater
1 pair overalls
2 pair 12-lb. blankets
1 waterproof blanket
1 dozen bandana handerchiefs
1 stiff brim cowboy hat

1 pair hip rubber boots
1 pair prospectors' high land boots
1 mackinaw, coat, pants, shirt
1 pair heavy buck mitts, lined
1 pair unlined leather gloves
1 duck coat, pants, vest
6 towels
1 pocket matchbox, buttons, needles and thread, comb, mirror, toothbrush, etc., mosquito netting/ 1 dunnage bag
1 sleeping bag/medicine chest
pack saddles, complete horses
flat sleighs
100 lbs. navy beans
150 lbs. bacon
400 lbs. flour
40 lbs. rolled oats
20 lbs. corn meal
10 lbs. rice
25 lbs. sugar
10 lbs. tea
20 lbs. coffee
10 lbs. baking powder
20 lbs. salt
1 lb. pepper
2 lbs. baking soda
1/2 lb. mustard
1/4 lb. vinegar
2 doz. condensed milk
20 lbs. evaporated potatoes
5 lbs. evaporated onions
6 tins/4 oz. extract beef
75 lbs. evaporated fruits
4 pkgs. yeast cakes
20 lbs. candles
1 pkg. tin matches
6 cakes borax
6 lbs. laundry soap
1/2 lb. ground ginger
25 lbs. hard tack
1 lb. citric acid
2 bottles jamaica ginger

1995 Chilkoot Trail Supplies

To fit in one backpack:
tent
sleeping bag
sleeping pad
warm layered clothing
broken-in hiking boots
rain/snow gear
quick-cooking nutritious food
energy bars/chocolate
coffee/tea & powdered milk
camp stove
pots & pans
cutlery
binoculars
camera & film
journal or novel
trail book
personal toiletries
first aid kit
bug repellent

Martha Louise Black, abandoned by her first husband en route to the Klondick in 1898, hiked over the Chilkoot Pass, sailed pregnant down the Yukon River in a homemade boat to Dawson, bore her child in a log cabin, raised money, bought a sawmill, bossed 16 men on a mining claim, married George Black who became Yukon's Member of Parliament and upon his illness ran for, and won, his seat. Martha Black became Yukon's first, and Canada's second, woman Member of Parliament. What a woman! (From **Canada's Yukon**, 1996)

Come to **Glenvern Hall**

—ON—

FRIDAY EVG., MAR. 31

CONCERT

PRESENTED BY:

The Quimper Young People's Fellowship Club

THE PROGRAM WILL INCLUDE:

Scenes from Shakespeare's **"MACBETH"** and **"JULIUS CAESAR"**
by MADGE ROGERS and WALT. McCONNVILLE.

ORIGINAL SKIT :: Complete with Orchestra :: **All Local Comedians**

Extra! SEVERAL LIVELY DANCE NUMBERS BY NINE BUDDING QUIMPER CHORINES **Extra!**

PLAY: "The Area Belle"

CAST:

PITCHER, Policeman .... WALT. McCONVILLE
TOSSER, Grenadier .... ALEX. KELMAN
PENELOPE, The Area Belle .... MADGE ROGERS
CHALKS, Milkman .... JOHN KELMAN
MRS. CROAKER, "The Missus" .... MARY KELMAN

The Whole Program Will Be Interspersed With Musical Numbers. All Local Talent.

DANCE AFTER LUNCH

Admission: Adults 15c Children 10c

Bring Your Own Lunch :: The Hall Furnishes Coffee

These three Glenvern programs arrived in the nick of time. Because I couldn't seem to choose but one I just decided to include all three.

It was not customary to put the year with the production date so it has taken some time to make a match with a table of calendars — an interesting bit of sleuthing. Only one of six flyers reprinted in this book had the year listed.

AT GLENVERN HALL AGAIN!

WHERE ALL THE GOOD THINGS ARE

MONDAY, DECEMBER 31ST, AT 8.30 P.M.

A "NEW YEAR'S IN" PLAY, in four acts, by the 1934
QUIMPER PLAYERS (They're Always Good)
who will present

"An Arizona Cowboy"

Playing Time, 2¼ Hours.

DIRECTED BY FRANK ADSHEAD

CAST OF CHARACTERS:

Louis Bjore.......Farley Gault, The Cowboy Sheriff
Andy McConville.......Paul Quillian, His Partner
Kenneth Miller, Duke Blackshear, a Stranger from Frisco
Bert Cross.......Hezekiah Bugg, a Glorious Liar
Alex. Kelman.......Yow Kee. a Heathen Chinese
John Kelman.......Big Elk, a Navajo Chief
Charlie McCoy.......Grizzley Grimm, a Cattle Thief
Ernestine Lallier...Marguerite Moore, the Pretty Ranch Owner
Wilma McCoy.......Coralie Blackshear, Duke's Sister
Margaret Simpson.......Mrs. Petunia Bugg, from Old Indiana
Mary Donald.......Fawn Afraid, an Indian Maid
Dorothy Claydon.....Young 'Un, Not Much of Anybody

A LUNCH ——and after the lunch—— A DANCE

The year just passing has not been anything "to write home about." You can't change it now, but you can, if you will, profit by experience when election time comes again. In the meantime, you may as well dance and enjoy yourself. ¶Too much idle thinking is useless.

BRING YOUR OWN LUNCH WE SUPPLY COFFEE

MUSIC BY THE YOUNG ORCHESTRA

Admission: Adults 15c. Children 10c.

GLENVERN HALL COMMITTEE

As I carefully looked over and compared all these Glenvern posters, I was struck with the fact that these Quimper folks were not in a rut — not on the age range of players, the director, the type of program and so on. They didn't give special honors to the director it seemed — for "For Pete's Sake" they never even gave the director's name!

At GLENVERN HALL

Friday Evening, March 16th

A Play will be presented by 1934

THE QUIMPER PLAYERS

ENTITLED

"The Clay's the Thing"

UNDER THE DIRECTION OF BERT CROSS

CAST OF CHARACTERS:

Jack Norman, a college student	Louis Bjore
Luke Galloway, his friend	Andy McConville
Jerry Taylor, Jack's room-mate	Alex. Kelman
Dudley Brigg's, Jack's uncle	Bert Cross
Millie, the Brigg's maid	Kit McCullough
Mary Norman, Jack's sister	Dolly Claydon
Jessie Stewart, her friend	Ernestine Lallier
Sarah Briggs, Dudley's wife	Mary Donald
Clayton Parmer, a poetic capitalist	Frank Adshead
Julia Parmer, his wife	Mary Kelman
Thomas Deems, a theatrical magnate	Charlie McCoy

Playing Time, Two and One-Half Hours.

A CLOG DANCE NUMBER by THREE YOUNG LADIES

You May Be Sure This Is Good

A LUNCH and A DANCE WILL FOLLOW!

ADMISSION: ADULTS 15c; CHILDREN 10c.

GLENVERN HALL COMMITTEE

In the back of the minutes book for the Quimper Fellowship Club, was the bookkeeping. Here are a few notes I found interesting: **1)** alabastine for painting the school $3.06; **2)** balls, bats and caps $7.54; **3)** girls won $1.00 at Erinlea — gate fee 80 cents; **4)** gas for McCoy's truck, 50 cents; **5)** to Ellen for General Ring, 50 cents; **6)** given for S.S. (Sunday School) papers, $5.00; **7)** whist drive prizes, 60 cents.

Memories

by Aileen (McCoy) MacDonald — *Reprinted with permission*

The years roll by, they spin they fly
like clouds across a prairie sky.
Look back, reflect and memories share
Old days, old friends, for we were there.
Look back to a child's summer, gay and bright
Simmering hot days, dark cool night.
A thousand stars in that vast sky
Like a brilliant blanket there on high.
Look back, look back to a winter's fun
Sparkling snow, like diamonds in the sun.
Smoke curling crisply from a snow topped roof
Northern lights dancing cold and aloof.
We remember Christmas, always white
And the school concert, a thrilling night.
Excitement ran high as on with the show
The gasoline lamp casting its yellow glow.
Look back, look back to the days of toil
As spears of green pierce the stubborn soil.
Nourished, cherished, guarded as it grows.
For this is life as the farmer knows.
And only he can know the crushing pain
That desperate cry "O give us rain".
When the winds wail a restless tune
And the sky is dark as night at noon.
The thistle leans and bounds through the air
And your heart is heavy with despair.
Through drought and grief you strive for life
Each day, each year mounts the strife.
Then comes the awesome news, it's war they
say
A sobering thought on this ominous day.
The roll of drums and bugle call
They leave us, so straight and tall
And march away while our hearts must yearn
Bravely they go, some never to return.
The years roll by, and take their toll
The weathered face searches the grassy knoll.
A prairie crocus peeks forth amid the green,
Violet petals, a mirror of nature's sheen.
Overhead flies the strident crow
And soft spring winds over prairies blow.
We thank God for these precious years
Guide us now and banish our fears.
Look back, to days of joy and sorrow
Look ahead to a bright tomorrow
With friends and family whose love we share
For in their hearts we are always there.

Memories

by Karen (McConville) Atherton — *Reprinted with permission*

In the moments
When I reflect
Upon the things
In life that bring
Me happiness,
You come to mind.
And I remember . . .
Raisin biscuits, dill pickles,
Turkey bunwiches and Jam-jams,
Little cotton print dresses, doilies,
Tiger lilies, baby breath,
and bachelor buttons.
And climbing over the fence
to the flower garden, where I
was safe from the turkeys.
Canasta games and Christmas decorations,
Long ago — a toy box full
with old lids, spools, dishes
and other goodies
Mickey mouses —
Quilts where everyone picked out
and smiled when they saw
a piece from their dress, skirt or apron.
A warm cozy house,
Turkey dinners with people buzzing around.
These and oodles more.
When I reflect — a color movie speeds up.
Fond memories go back
to stories of Uncle Mickey rocking to sleep
a fussy baby Karen
to life on the Collins farm
my second home
with its tree-walled playhouses
and its crusty clay soil
so good for constructing small roads
with tin can culverts
and walking in
with bare feet
after a rain,
to a place at the table
by my Uncle's left hand
and the buttered bottom half
of a slice of bread
he always gave me,
to winter sleigh trips
snuggled under a cow robe
to good food and canasta games
at happy family gatherings
each Easter, Thanksgiving and Christmas
But treasured most of all
is the recall
of that secure, warm hug
Uncle Mickey always had for me
and his greeting
How are you doing, Suzie Q?
He made me feel special.

Gratitude

Be grateful for the kindly friends that walk along your way;
Be grateful for the skies of blue that smile from day to day;
Be grateful for the health you own, the work you find to do,
For round about you there are men less fortunate than you.

Be grateful for the growing trees, the roses soon to bloom,
The tenderness of kindly hearts that shared your days of gloom;
Be grateful for the morning dew, the grass beneath your feet,
The soft caresses of your babes and all their laughter sweet.

Acquire the grateful habit, learn to see how blest you are,
How much there is to gladden life, how little life to mar!
And what if rain shall fall today and you with grief are sad;
Be grateful that you can recall the joys that you have had.

From **A Heap O'Livin' Along Life's Highway**, by Edgar A. Guest, ©1916

Bibliography

Saskatchewan, the Color of a Province, ©1987, by Gene Hatton
What's in a Name, , ©1973, by E. T. Russel
#3 People's Almanac, ©1981, by David Wallechinsky and Irving Wallace
Canada's Incredible Coasts, ©1991, National Geographic
A Heart for the Prairie, ©1993, by Janette Oke
Prairie Smoke, ©1987, by Melvin Gilmore
No Tadpoles, Please, ©1975, by Marguerite Robinson
Canada, the Land, the People, the Spirit, ©1967, by Brian Moore
Inventors, Profiles in Canadian Genius, ©1990, by Thomas Carpenter
Men Against the Desert, ©1979, James H. Gray
Amy Vanderbilt's Everyday Etiquette, ©1952, 1954, 1956
Today's Music, ©1990, Al Menconi with Dave Hart
Fit to Be Tied, ©1991, BIll and Lynne Hybels
Men and Women, ©1991, Dr. Larry Crabb
The Best Half of Life, ©1976, Ray and Ann Ortlund
Drummers and Dreamers, ©1986, Click Relander

All books listed in the Bibliography at the end of each chapter are my own books that I would like to lend out to any of my readers who can't find a certain book I have listed. Many of these authors have written a number of other books I might have.

If you borrow a book from me, I like it if you sign your name in it and add any marks or comments as you read. I enjoy reading these when I get the book back again.

The **National Geographic** has carried some excellent articles on Canada — the best for our own province being "The People Who Made Saskatchewan" in the May 1979 issue.

Many original old Geographics are available from the Society. They range in price from a 1914 one at $36.00 to a 1979 one at $2.65. At these prices maybe some of you have a little "gold mine" on your bookshelf!

Appendix

Edgar Guest was described by a friend as "simple as a child, common as an old shoe, friendly as a puppy, and foolish like a fox." He describes his own poetry this way, "I just take simple everyday things that happen to me and figure that they probably happen to a lot of other people and I make simple rhymes out of 'em and people seem to like 'em."

His life matched his words in all respects. His mother didn't approve of him exposing the private family life, exclaiming "Eddie have you no shame?" Yet it is this very quality that endears his poems to us. He married his **Nellie,** and their **Bud** and **Janet** were often integral to his works.

He experienced extreme poverty — his family having left England in 1891 in a "financial panic", according to a biography in a 1941 encyclopedia. He wouldn't buy stock in *any* company including his good friend **Henry Ford's** cars. At age 13 he began work at $1.50 a week as office boy for the **Detroit Free Press**, gradually climbing the ladder until he became a well-off man through his poetry — one a day for a column — therefore by age 60, around 10,000. Also, he sold some 3,000,000 copies of his books. He had a half hour radio broadcast for about ten years, but on his three day trips to Chicago for them, he was always very homesick. Fame and money never changed him a bit. He remained a genuinely friendly person to all he rubbed shoulders with including waiters, bellhops and porters — he wanted the same ones all the time.

I hope you've enjoyed this thumbnail sketch of a man, I say, did for poetry what Norman Rockwell did for art.

The poems I chose for the end of each chapter are from second-hand books I've been lucky enough to find. Our paternal grandmother's maiden name was Guest, so we like to think that maybe he was a relative!

Relationships of kin in book

Dad .... James McConville
Mom .... Martha McConville
Rob .... Older Brother
Nellie .... Younger Sister
Aunt Phoebe .... Wife of Sam McConville
Aunt Ella .... Wife of Tom McConville
Unlce Frank .... Frank Adshead — Mom's Youngest Brother
Aunt Mag .... Mom's Older Sister
Grandma — maternal .... Mary Adshead

Note : Elders were always addressed by Mr., Mrs., Miss, or by title, Rev. or Dr.

Married names of Quimper school girls

Alice Bjore .... Collins
Freda Bender .... Sutton
Marion Cross .... Simpson
Alison Cross .... Seale
Connie Claydon .... Wilks
Dorothy Claydon .... Scharer
Lorraine Cyrenne .... ?
Nora Cross .... Will
Millicent Cross .... Wright
Betty Claydon .... Claydon
Theo Claydon .... Jones
Audrey Claydon .... Watson
Mary Donald .... Atherton
Madeleine Dumont .. McColder
Mildred Dumonceaux ....
.... Palaschak
Helene Dumonceaux ...... Tinant
Agnes Dumonceaux ..... Walters
Marie Dumonceaux .... Cherpin
Edna Dumonceaux .... Steanik
Eva Gorrill .... ?
Minnie Gammie .... Logan
Helen Gammie .... Jacobsen
Gladys Gammie .... Barager
Dorothy Gammie .... Finlay
Elvina Gammie .... Finlay
Andrea Gammie .... McBlain
Marguerite Goffinet .... Bleau
Rose Goffinet ...... Dumonceaux
Mary Kelman .... Broley
Nellie Klein .... Peters
Mina Klein .... Tobin
Gertrude Klein .... Tinant
Anna Klein .... Pemble
Ernestine Lallier .... Bellaire
Julienne Lallier .... Harton
Geraldine Lallier .... Gagnon
Therese Lallier .... Bergeron
Cecile Lallier .... Ferland
Lena McCullough .... Gunter
Kate McCullough .... Sutherland
Pheobe McConville .. Baughman
Evelyn McConville .... Fox
Hilda McConville .. Hardement
Minnie McConville .... Walls
Ethel McConville .... Busch
Isabelle McConville .... Cadel
Oliver McConville .... Hannah
Mary McConville ...... Stensrud
Nellie McConville .... Schmidt
Karen McConville ...... Atherton
Wilma McCoy .... Adams
Aileen McCoy .... MacDonald
Maggie McKenzie .... Malasky
Mary McKenzie .... Dodds
Suzanne Morin .... McKinnon
Jean Robins .... Thurlow
Margaret Symington ... Simpson
Dorothy Symington .... Aspen
Winnefred Taylor .... ?

<u>NOTE</u>: Not listed here if deceased, or if they attended Quimper for a very brief time. I regret not being able to learn the married names of a few in this list.

Acknowledgements

When so many people should be given an acknowledgement, it is dangerous to attempt to list names in case one slips up and misses some which have a rightful place there. However, by setting up special categories and boundaries, I hope that few will slip through the cracks.

First there are those I know personally, from my pre-marriage life in Saskatchewan who took time to: answer my questionaire; send me their stories or pictures; phoned information to me; did research for me in family records, recollections or Canadian reference books; or simply but most importantly, urged and encouraged me for a long time now to get this book written. Names here are in no special order and are under their present names. Relatives are not separately designated. (Names of those who have died while my book has been in progress will be found only in the text or captions.) Mary Atherton, Alice Achter, Ruby Cross, Bill and Karen Atherton, Jim Cross, Arnold Bjore, Alice Collins, Hilda Hardiment, Freda Sutton, Dorothy Scharer, Laura Claydon, Theo Wollgar, Mary Broley, Aileen MacDonald, Eva Peale, Suzanne McKinnon, Madge McCullough, Marilyn McCoy, Gertrude Tinant, Geraldine Gagnon, Phoebe Baughman, Jean Thurlow, Rita Dolan, Ormond and Dorothy Young, Ambrose and Finis Lepper, Betty Teeter, Bill and Ethel Busch, Minnie and Kelso Walls, Walter McConville, Annie Pain, Henri Liboiron, Gary Shaddock, Alex Kelman, Isabelle Cadel, Jim and Olive Hannah, Leonora Unruh, Fred and Ann Brown, Robert McConville, Sig and Ellen Schmidt, Allan and Gerry Oliver, Betty Fennel, June Burman, Don Symington, Raymond and Agnes Bjore, Pauline Bovair and lastly, my husband, who could recall many relevant facts and incidents from his own life in the same area and era in Saskatchewan as myself.

Then there is that group of people I have met only by phone or through correspondence — librarians, archivists and public relations officers for businesses and organizations, etc.: LaVale Smith — Shaunavon School Division #7; Larry Weiler, Patrick Wilson and Bob Krauczyk — the T. Eaton Company; James McArthur, Joanne Denton and Leanne Kiddie — the B.C. Sugar Company; Debbie Miller — Rit Dyes; Anna Esser and Anna Messenger — Watkins; Steve MacRae, Rose __________ and Marie Lauro for Neilson-Cadbury Companies; Anne Morton — Hudson's Bay Company; Fran Oliver, Ruth Wilson and Diane Haglund — the United Church of Canada; Morley Seis —

Saskatchewan Chief Surveyor; Joe Bergeron; Rebecca Landau and Mary Lynn Gagne of the Saskatchewan University Library; Margaret Lipp for her research of Saskatchewan school curriculums; Elizabeth Kalmakoff of the Prairie History Room in the Regina Public Library; Diane Giroux for her research on N.W.T.'s cities and Betty Phouts of the Port Townsend Historical Museum for her research on the name Quimper. I must also acknowledge all the help given to me by Cynthia Garrick and her staff in the research section of our local library and Walter Toop, a bookstore owner here in Yakima.

Other local people I must give gratitude to are three who helped me so much with suggestions of all kinds, editing, and proofreading — Rose Andreotti and her daughter, Jill, and Ethel Siegele.

And how can I forget so many of my Yakima friends who have read and complimented me on my "ash" book, have kept on inquiring how my book is progressing and keep telling me they're anxiously awaiting the completion of my Quimper book.

In conclusion, I know I will have missed names that should be here, so to you I offer my apologies.

Epilogue or Epilog?

Even for a heading, you see I have a problem. For my ash book I tried to be consistently *American* and for my Quimper book I've been aiming at a hundred percent *Canadian* — only to find, as I come to write these concluding words, that I've wasted considerable time and effort. A recent article in our Yakima Herald-Republic sums it up by saying Canadian spelling is a "split personality — sometimes sticking with its British (or should we say English?) roots, and at other times adopting American usage." Then to top it all off, all *three* of my large comprehensive dictionaries — two Websters, 1944 and 1984, and my Canadian Winston — do not claim *exclusiveness* for their spelling of almost all the troublesome words. So it seems that whether my spelling is American or Canadian makes little difference!

Nevertheless, in spite of this truth, certain words will give the game away — either in pronunciation or in a common name for something. Canadians are fond of their "eh?" on the end of a sentence and the letter "z" is "zed" with Canadians; "zee" in the States. And if you ask for a serviette in an American restaurant or a toque in a clothing store, be prepared for a "funny" look.

But on the whole, differences over spelling, grammar, pronunciation and word usage are of small consequence compared to trying to be accurate on history — all the way from casual family writings to what goes into its history texts and reference books. All of us, no doubt, are influenced by a tendency to put a good light on some accounts and to avoid putting into writing some things we would just as soon keep hidden. In other words, looking through our "rose colored glasses" gives a different picture than what another might see from the "other side of the fence." Even so, most of us writers strive hard for accuracy.

Remember that C.S. Lewis said that mistakes spotted by readers should be pointed out to prevent them being passed along. Please take his advice when you read this book.

So now, with all my foibles over English usage or historical data, it is my hope that you have read this book mainly for simple enjoyment.